D1557537

The Genius of Parody

The Genius of Parody

Imitation and Originality in Seventeenth- and Eighteenth-Century English Literature

Robert L. Mack

First published 2007 by
PALGRAVE MACMILLAN
Houndmills, Basingstoke, Hampshire RG21 6XS and
175 Fifth Avenue, New York, N.Y. 10010
Companies and representatives throughout the world

PALGRAVE MACMILLAN is the global academic imprint of the Palgrave Macmillan division of St. Martin's Press, LLC and of Palgrave Macmillan Ltd. Macmillan® is a registered trademark in the United States, United Kingdom and other countries. Palgrave is a registered trademark in the European Union and other countries.

ISBN-13: 978–0–230–00856–4 hardback
ISBN-10: 0–230–00856–9 hardback

This book is printed on paper suitable for recycling and made from fully managed and sustained forest sources.

A catalogue record for this book is available from the British Library.

Library of Congress Cataloging-in-Publication Data
Mack, Robert L.
    The genius of parody:imitation and originality in seventeenth and eighteenth-century English literature/by Robert L. Mack.
        p.   cm.
    Includes bibliographical references and index.
    ISBN-13: 978–0–230–00856–4
    ISBN-10: 0–230–00856–9
    1. Parody in literature.   2. English literature—Early modern, 1500–1700—History and criticism.   3. English literature—18th century—History and criticism.   4. Parody.   5. Originality in literature.   6. Imitation in literature.   I. Title.
    PR438.P37M33 2007
    827'.4—dc22   2006052031

10   9   8   7   6   5   4   3   2   1
16   15   14   13   12   11   10   09   08   07

Printed and bound in Great Britain by
Antony Rowe Ltd, Chippenham and Eastbourne

Contents

Acknowledgements

A great many students, colleagues, and other scholars have listened to conference papers and to other academic presentations of much of the material presented here as part of a work in progress; my writing has invariably benefited from their criticisms. More particularly, I would like to thank my colleagues in the School of English at the University of Exeter, many of whom have read and commented on specific versions of the material included in the present volume. I wish also to take this opportunity to express my sincere gratitude for the continued advice and support – over the years – of a group of friends and regular readers, including Margaret Anne Doody, Regenia Gagnier, Allan Hepburn, Adeline Johns-Putra, Ivo Kamps, Alvin Kernan, Bob Lawson-Peebles, Jane Spencer, and Ashley Tauchert.

1
Introduction

Born Originals, how comes it to pass that we die Copies?
                                        – Edward Young (1759)[1]

In a sense, we write nothing original and everything we
compose is a re-ordering of events, scenes and ideas that other
storytellers put together long before we were born. If someone
composed an entirely new story, perhaps we wouldn't recognise
it as a story at all.
                                        – Phillip Pullman (2005)[2]

Ours, it appears, is destined – for better or for worse – to be an age
of parody. Or is it? In the past few decades, prominent critics such as
Roland Barthes, Jean Baudrillard, Homi Bhabha, Judith Butler, Jacques
Derrida, Gérard Genette, Fredric Jameson, Julia Kristeva, Michael Riffa-
terre, and Edward Said (to name only a few) who are otherwise irreconcilable in their wider interpretive strategies could all be counted on,
at the very least, to have agreed that the creation of any truly *original*
work of art was not only a theoretical but also a practical impossibility. As recently as 1979, Malcolm Bowie, investigating Jacques Lacan's
indebtedness to Freud, had yet felt it necessary to preface his account
by reminding readers that a 'lingering Romantic conception of genius
leads us to expect of an original thinker that his ideas will spring in
fully formed splendour from within himself, or from nature, or from
nowhere'.[3] As Bowie justly observed at the time, most of his readers
would only naturally have assumed that 'where lesser minds may find
proper employment in reading and elaborating texts from the past, the
true innovator is expected to do everything for himself'.[4]

All such assumptions with regard to this 'Romantic conception of genius', however, seem to have disappeared – if not exactly overnight, then at least with a remarkable suddenness. To whatever extent today's authors might still aspire to position their works as in some way unique or 'monumental', it would be no less axiomatic now to assert that quite the opposite is true; rather, all individual utterances or 'speech acts' simply imply the momentary coalescence of an infinite number of possible textual relations.[5] Within a matter of just a few years, long-standing but increasingly old-fashioned notions of meaning were completely overturned. Modern debates on interpretation focused instead on the technological processes of reproduction whereby already-existing cultural codes and practices (codes and practices that manifestly bore increasingly less relation to the supposed 'realities' of any external world than to the very media through which they were expressed) were reduced to such a degree that writers themselves seemed compelled to recognize – often in the face of their own lingering, cherished pretensions to originality – that their products were in actual fact mere fragmented 're-presentations' that had been opportunistically harvested from a vast field of 'already-existing language'. The work of criticism, certainly, no longer entailed any precisely detailed attempt to recover authorial intentions or explicitly literary contexts. 'The deconstructionists', as David Boucher observed in a summary of the era, 'further undermined contextualism by announcing the death of the author, the vanishing text, the disappearing knowing subject, the illusion of the historical agent . . . and finally the dissolution of the interconnected network of intellectual discourse'.[6] Those poems, novels, and dramas that might in the past have been regarded only common-sensically as the ideologically neutral insights of a single author's unique consciousness or (dare one even venture to suggest it) genius were now conceded to be merely the hitherto-unarticulated manifestations of texts that had fortuitously been snatched from far wider, culturally encoded contexts of signification. If thinkers such as Roland Barthes and Michael Foucault had indeed together publicly announced the death of the author in the heady days of the late 1960s, then many of the theorists who followed them were content to spend the better part of their own time hammering a tremendous number of critical nails not merely into the coffin, but – in their often angry crusade against the long-standing deceptions perpetrated by the phantom agency of such fantastic scriptors – into the very 'tissue' of the corpse itself.[7] If, that is, they could ever manage actually to locate one in the first place.

That having been said, one of the more positive results of the late-twentieth-century's fascination with the interdependence of all forms of literary creation was to pave the way for a thorough revaluation of a literary mode, the defining essence of which was *precisely* its orient-ation of formal reference: parody. Parodies, after all, are the textual products of a myriad of sophisticated literary processes that seek not to obscure but rather to highlight – and, not infrequently, ostenta-tiously to flaunt – their status as in some way marked or derivative. The originality of any given parody (if one could even suggest that a parody can be said to possess any originality in the first place) would appear paradoxically to lie precisely in the simple fact of its *un*originality. The mode's boastful acknowledgement of formal dependency – the same characteristic that had for so long served only to render it a disreputable referential practice, and to banish it beyond the bounds of respectab-ility – was spectacularly rehabilitated in a self-consciously post-modern era. Parody was guilty of nothing more than parading its own refresh-ingly roguish charm. In fact, it possessed a rare and disarming *honesty* in its gestures towards multiplicity and plurality – a 'celebration' (one encounters the word again and again) of all that resisted stabilization or confinement. Other genres might, in their pretence to a seamless mimesis, seek anxiously to bury their pasts; they might look to draw their readers' attention *away* from the determining precedents of generic boundaries and source-texts, or to perpetuate a deceptively naïve game of pseudo-Aristotelian realism. Parody alone, or so the theoretical inter-vention of the past several decades would have us concede, fearlessly embraced its task of disruption with an often giddy abandon – with an affirmation of textual indebtedness that was both playful and inviting. The rehabilitation in contemporary cultural theory of all that was fashionably imitative, trans-textual, and poly-semic arguably allowed parody for the first time to stake a credible claim to being a legit-imate and even a defining feature of the most consequential products of English literature and culture. Recent modern and post-modern parodies, in particular (it was often specifically argued), were said to be distinguished by a positive 'ethos' that widened their possibilities to embrace not only the mocking and ridicule so often associated with the kind, but extended the pragmatic range of its facilities for combinat-orial play to include highly self-aware, meta-ironic acts and gestures of reference and 'homage'.[8]

It comes as something of a shock therefore – particularly given its writer's close to uncontested status as the primary champion of parody as a nearly unavoidable literary practice – to discover Mikhail Bakhtin, of all people, asserting (in his tremendously if belatedly influential collection of essays translated in 1981 as *The Dialogic Imagination*) that 'in modern times the functions of parody [have become] narrow and unproductive'. 'Parody', Bakhtin contended of its contemporary manifestations, '[had] grown sickly, its place in modern literature [was] insignificant'.[9] Almost equally unsettling – although certainly less unexpected, considering his own underlying conjectures with regard to the post-modern dislocation of the governing, oppositional structures of Western thought – was Fredric Jameson's suggestion that the radical eclecticism of contemporary culture had led to a situation in which parody had been left 'without a vocation'.[10] In the absence of any strictly 'normal' or dominant culture against which to define itself, Jameson claimed, parody would be compelled to yield to a different *kind* of inter-textual practice, one that he distinguished as mere pastiche. 'Pastiche', as Jameson qualified,

> is, like parody, the imitation of peculiar masks, speech in a dead language: but it is a neutral practice of such mimicry, without any of parody's ulterior motives, amputated of the satiric impulse, devoid of laughter, and of any conviction that, alongside the abnormal tongue you have momentarily borrowed, some healthy linguistic normality still exists.[11]

'Pastiche', the Marxist Jameson concluded, 'is thus blank parody'. Jameson's assumption that 'ulterior motives' prompt all attempts to speak in the 'abnormal tongue' of parody (to say nothing of his implicit and wrong-headed equation of the functions of parody with those of satire) is open to serious question. However, his more comprehensive point that the dialogic kinetics of parody *per se* could not even be set in motion when those very same stylistic, generic, and cultural norms that those parodies would logically have been intent on disrupting no longer even existed is considerably more problematic. With no dominant cultural ideology or targeted logonomic system to dislodge, in other words, parody was left without any real purpose.

Jameson's bleak view for the prospects of any 'healthy' literary activity in an era in which parody is perceived to function less as an 'alternative practice' than as a standardized process of empty signification in a cultural state of 'ironic supersaturation' has, to some extent, been addressed by subsequent commentators when discussing the role of the parodic in modern discourse.[12] Even more significantly, and in the face of what emerges as Jameson's pessimism, we appear for some considerable time now – both as readers and as critics – to have begun acknowledging that we are gradually passing through what might be described as a distinctly 'post-theoretical' moment. This particular moment could well turn out to be one of considerably extended weight and duration. Without question, a great many academic (to say nothing of non-academic) readers have begun to confess to a deeply felt need – a need that amounts for many to a form of aesthetic imperative or even existential *obligation* – for a return to some sort of consensus or standard, collective habit (the vocabulary here is still vague and volatile) of cultural *meaning* and *value*. There has been an increased demand for criteria and standards of interpretation and merit. Many of my own recent students, and not a few of my professional colleagues, certainly, express a desire for a reformulation of philosophical or discriminatory aesthetics – if not an acceptance of any single, coherent metaphysical 'system' – that is still in some way reconcilable with the most recent advances and depredations of so-called cultural theory. As Colin Falck presciently insisted some time ago,

> The anti-spiritual language of much post-Saussurian theory has gone to incoherent lengths to avoid acknowledging the necessary role of insight – of insight into a reality which is revealed or disclosed, *by* someone in a cultural and historical situation – in the literary-critical process. The arguments of post-structuralists against the systematic theory of, for example, [Ferdinand de] Saussure himself – *inter alia* (in effect) its classifications presuppose an Olympian classifier – are in fact valid against the entire apparatus of rhetorical theory in general; but the post-structuralist can go no further than this, because his conceptual framework prevents him from giving any account at all of what it is for us to recognize literary (or any other artistic) *success* or *failure*.[13]

This insistence that we return to a tacit acceptance of the relationships that connect literature and the arts to our own experiences as embodied human subjects who exist *materially* outside the structures of human language and sign systems is increasingly incontrovertible. Falck's own patiently argued analysis exposing the embarrassingly sophomoric, decontextualized misreadings of so many of Saussure's structuralist and post-structuralist followers, and his insistence on the essentially physical or *gestural* aspect of language, is itself masterful. The demand that we somehow manage to incorporate in a redefined notion of artistic achievement and expression both the few advantages and the many and often catastrophic fallacies of the culture of theory that so casually jettisoned the truly material and anthropocentric nature of all practices of reading and interpretation is too strong to be ignored. 'It will continue to be the case that the essential function of the literary text', as Falck defiantly asserted 'is one of revelation or disclosure [and] the essential requirement of a piece of writing if it is to have any significance to us as a piece of literature is that there should be a sufficient degree of reality or truth in it to be revealed or disclosed'.[14]

So what, specifically, do such assertions regarding the need for revitalized forms of cultural discrimination have to do with parody? The answer seems to me to be a simple but a mighty one. Most significantly, a deeper understanding of our yet-prevalent and now firmly institutionalized culture of repudiation – particularly with reference to the demand for a comprehensive redirection in our understanding of aesthetics – will only necessarily advance the fact that parodies (and, indeed, most other forms of literary reference, imitation, echo, and response) can and should be looked upon as activities that have long constituted an inherent and positive facet of almost all artistic (and specifically literary) endeavour. A proper reorientation of our theoretical conceptualizations of creative contiguity, that is to say, entails an acceptance of the fact that parody, so often trumpeted as a literary mode that is anti-canonical, critical, destructive, and even anarchic, has played a far more complex role in – and has contributed in a far more creative manner to – the greatest achievements of our literary traditions.[15] We will be compelled to admit that parody is not – as critics such as Jameson, Baudrillard, John Barth, and others would have had us concede – a quasi-mechanical routine of 'pointless resurrections of past styles and past voices', but, rather, plays an astoundingly dynamic role in the dialectical processes of creation. Moreover, unlike those who have for so long insisted on 'celebrating' the supposedly disruptive and subversive power of parodic 'ambiguity' and 'play', we will need to focus our concerted attention just a little bit more closely on the intrinsic role of formal parodic imitation and echo in traditional acts and gestures of *meaning* and *significance*.

To be sure, this meaningful aspect of parodic reference has always been acknowledged by many aestheticians of the first class. Following in the footsteps of Immanuel Kant, Arthur Schopenhauer, Friedrich Schiller, Benedetto Croce, F. H. Bradley, and George Steiner, for example, R. G. Collingwood observed in his mid-twentieth-century study *The Principles of Art* that

All artists have modelled their style upon that of others, used subjects that others have used, and treated them as others have treated them already. A work of art so constructed is a work of collaboration. It is partly by the man whose name it bears, partly by those from whom he has borrowed. . . . [I]f we look candidly at the history of art, or even at the little of it we happen to know, we shall see that collaboration between artists has always been the rule.[16]

Assertions such as Collingwood's remind us that the imitative gestures of parody can be restored to their proper status within the various taxonomies of creative endeavour and exemplary expression without being undervalued as mere forms of whimsical literary playfulness. For all the apparent progress that has been made in recent years, the critical resistance to a *real* understanding of parody may yet be more deeply rooted than we would ever care openly to acknowledge. To whatever extent post-modern parodies have been allowed more explicitly to enact their role in the referential dialectics of creation – to whatever extent parodic reference has been redeemed and celebrated by the advocates of post-modernism itself – there still hovers about the mode and its practices a toxic cloud of textual disrepute. It seems as if post-modern parody – like some wayward juvenile delinquent – has finally been let out to play, but has never seriously been permitted to *work*. To return once again to the insights of Colin Falck, an accepted valuation of the 'play' of parody, like the imaginative play inherent in the mythical dimensions of religion and poetry itself, 'will not be a merely fanciful or truth-free sporting with images, but a play of the imagination which never wholly loses awareness of its dimension in which the play of our imagination makes possible the disclosure of reality or truth (ἀλήθεια)'.[17] Perhaps it is about time that we began to take parody just a little bit more seriously.

The range of works examined in the pages that follow inevitably entails being highly selective – on occasion perhaps even arbitrarily so. My own primary aim is merely to begin the task suggested above – to lay some of the more practical and often admittedly anecdotal groundwork for its possibilities, perhaps by drawing attention to the sheer versatility of the possibilities with regard to parody available to writers throughout the extended period examined here. Consequently, I shift my attention variously and in turn from drama, to poetry, and even to modes of prose fiction and narrative autobiography. Indeed, I have deliberately taken the risk of looking to demonstrate the omnipresent and unavoidable pleasure (and, no less frequently, the perceived threat) of parody in the seventeenth and eighteenth centuries precisely by seeking out the pervasiveness of techniques of parodic provocation and response where we might *least* expect to find them. Although the chapters that follow might be read as a series of separate 'case studies', so to speak, they are united in their more ambitious aim of resituating the strategies of literary parody within a new ethical and conceptual philosophy of art.

The traditional animus against parody, again, has been unusually deep-rooted and long-standing. Chapter 2 looks simply and broadly to survey the critical history of the *idea* of parody in English. Parody, far from being a maliciously derivative critical activity, is in actual fact a literary mode essential to the work of some of the most widely read and influential English writers. We must aim to restructure the historiography of parody by examining the figurative language typically used to describe parodic poetic activity in English; we need to achieve some understanding of the manner in which the critical trends of the late-twentieth and early-twenty-first centuries have necessarily tended towards a reassessment of the long-standing, anti-parodic critical vocabulary that had dominated the traditions of interpretation and literary value for hundreds of years. One of the first times the word 'parody' is mentioned in English, as we will see, it is used to designate the products of a dangerous literary disease. The 'parody' that is recognized in the drama of Ben Jonson is thought of as a literary plague that manifests its potential to infect and to destroy all forms of legitimate literature – a literature that somehow partakes of the 'right language' of stable linguistic authority typically sanctioned by Jonson at the end of his satiric plays. Jonson himself is in some respects the harbinger of an entire literary-critical tradition that comes in time consistently to posit 'parody' as little more than 'para-literature'.

The early appearance of the word parody in one of Jonson's comedies leads me, in Chapter 3, to trace more thoroughly the sources of such a designation of parody-as-plague in Jonson's own work, and further links the parodic mode to the new cluster of authorial anxieties that began to emerge among writers in the early seventeenth century. A close reading of the final scene of the dramatist's *Every Man in His Humour* (1601; 1616) reveals Jonson drawing an elaborately coded connection between parody, on the one hand, and threats of treason, sedition, and the visitation of a deadly plague, on the other. Jonson is highly suspicious of those tactics of textual appropriation and abuse that – to his mind – seem so suddenly to have insinuated themselves as dominating features of the literary ethic of the period. Chapter 3 traces throughout some of the playwright's work, generally, and examines within the resonant language of his early tragedy *Sejanus* (1603), in particular, the fears that I describe as having constituted Jonson's nascent 'anxiety of parody'. The idea that his own words might be used against him – the possibility that his own language could be transformed, manipulated, and somehow reshaped by another author in a manner hostile to his own intentions and inimical to his own, avowedly classical, literary standards – was a particularly unsettling prospect for the playwright to contemplate. (Jonson had himself, as some readers will recall, gone so far in his later years as to wrangle with the printer he seems to have deemed incompetent – John Beale – in his various attempts to maintain authorial control over his writings even as they went to press.)[18] For a writer of Jonson's temperament, the usurpations of parody constituted a form of surrender – a surrender of material that was ostensibly more often perceived to be subject to the poet's own inalienable prerogative of interpretation and meaning – into the hands of an indiscriminate mass of readers and (even worse) a growing body of self-appointed, professional critics. Parody was not merely a disease; it was a disease that robbed the hard-working, literary craftsman of the inherent value of his labour.

The chapter also emphasizes the fact that the rapid-fire, text-specific dialogues that flair up in Jonson's era (encounters that included the so-called *Poetomachia* or 'War of the Theatres' from 1599 to 1602) were perceived as phenomena that constituted something decidedly *new* to English authors.[19] The inter-textual relationships that from time to time connected earlier literary documents, by contrast, might more accurately be described as typically respectful or ancestral. Such relationships constituted not so much a challenge, but a form of inheritance – a bond that was less a burden than a positive bequest. These earlier textual relationships tended to involve both temporal and geographical distance (extending often to the practical necessities of translation and patient cross-cultural assimilation). The comparatively primitive mechanics of textual reproduction and dissemination prior to the early modern era likewise entailed, at the very least, the necessity of a patient and *considered* response. Textual 'dialogues' prior to the seventeenth century, that is to say, were by sheer force of circumstance much less frequently matters of precise stylistic or formal indebtedness and specific, rhetorically targeted parodic reference than they were a general and often quite genial inter-textual debate structured on a leisurely pattern of formal, thematic, and stylistic exchange. The parodic redactions that began appearing in the early seventeenth century, by contrast – those heralded by Jonson's precise articulation of the word 'parody' – were soon to establish a very different kind of textual dynamic indeed.

In Chapter 4, I pause very briefly to consider the manner in which even those works that were not explicitly responding to the fierce and competitive standards of the new poetic age – even, that is, those literary and dramatic efforts that were not engaged in an explicitly text-specific dialogue involving recognizable hallmarks of parodic manipulation and appropriation – can arguably be elucidated by a hermeneutic practice that acknowledges the pervasiveness of parodic activity and reference as the final years of the sixteenth century gave way to the dawn of a new political and literary era. Given the probable date of its composition and earliest production (1599), Shakespeare's *Henry V* suggests itself as an ideal piece to examine in this light. Indeed, one might argue that Shakespeare's popular historical drama provides a model well worth exploring, if only because the Chorus in Shakespeare's play has continued to develop into a very specific *kind* of overtly parodic figure in many recent productions of *Henry V*. I merely suggest in this chapter that the figure of Shakespeare's Chorus is likely to have originally conjured an unusually specific kind of parodic resonance and meaning. Shakespeare's stage figure is himself the descendant of a long line of choral commentators who had only recently, in the final decades of the sixteenth century, begun to lose the theological authority and the homiletic voice that had characterized their immediate predecessors in the indigenous traditions of the sacred drama. One of the more obvious effects of the gradual secularization of theatrical material in England throughout the sixteenth century was the tendency of the newer dramas to shatter the authoritative and sometimes even apodictic monotone of such choral commentaries – commentaries that lent a legitimacy to the speeches of (for example) the Vexillators in *The Castle of Perseverance* (*c*.1405–25), or of the messenger who serves as the Chorus-Prologue to the anonymous *Everyman* (*c*.1495). It is entirely fitting, therefore, that a work such as *Henry V* – a play that points at every possible moment to the elements of role-playing and of exploitable, manipulative dramatic ritual inherent in the activity of kingship itself – should itself in turn be guided and, in effect, masterminded by a cipher recently emptied of significance, and opened in a similar manner to the possibilities of parodic play. The parodic fate of the Chorus-as-Dramatic-Ritual, that is to say, re-enacts within the analogy of the play's dramatic, onstage action the destiny of the king himself. Just as Shakespeare's cynical young monarch appears already to have recognized that positive value adhere to the activity of kingship only insofar as that same activity is situated and defined (and constantly redefined) by its relationship to the several other, warring elements that constitute the social and political structures of his authority, so too the Chorus in Shakespeare's play stands, as the language of one once-fashionable school of criticism would have put it, as a signifier effectively cut off from its signified. Not at first recognizable as a parodic construction, the *Henry V* Chorus reveals only within the meaning-constitutive contexts of its original theatrical situation its inherent potential for genuine parodic resonance – a resonance that would nevertheless still appear to exert its native or latent influence even within the most vigorously contemporary productions of Shakespeare's history play.

Chapter 5, on John Dryden, explores at greater length the manner in which the post-Restoration author confronted the vehement threat of parody. I argue that Dryden chose eventually to adopt preventative, defensive, and self-parodic techniques – techniques the vigorous aggression of which was rooted in the perceived efficacy, in the instance of any literary dispute, of a textually debilitating 'first strike', as it were, against one's literary or ideological enemies. The language of plague, disease, and contagion that had by the early-eighteenth century come to characterize almost all references to parody (Dryden's near-contemporary Andrew Marvell refers with undisguised contempt to the appropriative poets of the era as 'paper rats' and 'book scorpions') suggests, in the first instance, a possible designation of Dryden's self-parodic activity as purposefully preventative or 'homeopathic'. Dryden was among the first authors to recognize that the parodic mode, when employed aggressively in the textually dangerous morass that some twentieth-century critics accurately dubbed the 'early Augustan battleground', could not only deflect, but even, on occasion, destroy his critical antagonists.

Chapter 6, on Alexander Pope, turns much more specifically to examine an early parody of that poet's 1717 heroic epistle, *Eloisa to Abelard*. Pope himself, of course, employed obvious techniques of parody and burlesque in almost all his poetry and translations. *The Rape of the Lock* (1712; 1714; 1717) and the *Dunciad* (1728; 1742; 1743) are only the best known of his many works that reveal the vast referential potential of Pope's parodic technique at work. My own discussion of Pope, however, turns to focus our attention on the most significant of his popular works that is *not* generally considered as having anything much to do with parody; I consequently explore a fascinating example of the complex way in which the parodic mode could influence an author in the eighteenth century, in the shape of *Eloisa*. The character of Eloisa, as she is presented within the lines of Pope's fictional epistle and in her arguments with reference to her difficult position in the paraclete, echoes and effectively parodies the actual language of the historical Peter Abelard. Although such conscious echoes of the earlier, published versions of the couple's original medieval correspondence have rarely received the attention they deserve, there is, admittedly, nothing startlingly new in merely pointing them out to readers. The Eloisa of Pope's poem is herself a parodist, and the individual whose language she chooses to parody is no one other than her own correspondent and former lover, Abelard. What I find to be particularly intriguing about Pope's *Eloisa to Abelard*, however, is the opportunity the poem seems to have offered at least one other mid-eighteenth-century parodist to advance an *apologia* for his own appropriative poetic practice. This 'secondary' parody of *Eloisa* to which I subsequently turn my attention in the chapter – Richard Owen Cambridge's *Elegy Written in an Empty Assembly Room* (1756) – picks up on this very dialectic between past and present potential, and explicitly calls attention to the fact that Pope's is a poem that asks its readers to bring the specifics of its target text – to bring the language and intention of Pope's own *Eloisa* – along in their memories, in such a manner that the 'original' work pointedly forms the basis for the imaginative vagaries of the subsequent redaction. I would even venture to suggest that Cambridge's parody itself 'understands' the greater resonance of the personal crisis that Pope sought to depict in his poem, but chooses finally (on at least one level) to diminish that crisis. While acknowledging in the parodic *form* of his own work the dialectic between memory and imagination that creates meaning in Pope's poem in the first place, arguably all that remains in Cambridge's lines of the actual substantial drama of Pope's work is an obsessive, myopic egomania and materialism. Lady Townshend, who replaces the original's Eloisa as the speaker of the piece in Cambridge's satiric parody, laments the fact that she has not been invited to a large evening assembly at the home of the Duchess of Norfolk. In his own poem, Pope himself had presented to his readers a sympathetic female figure; he then explored that same figure's possible ostracism from society, and delineated the existential crisis contingent upon such exclusion as a subject worthy of serious poetry. For Cambridge, however, the subject of female subjectivity and identity provides the basis for a mere *jeu d'esprit*. The chapter concerns itself finally with the various ways in which a parodist can transform his or her target text – it explores the manner in which the truly perceptive parodist can respond not only to the formal and linguistic cues of his or her original, but can no less certainly tap into the deepest meanings that rest beneath and behind those cues.

Chapter 7, my final chapter, deliberately takes us in an altogether different direction, and rather more ambitiously makes use of the opportunity offered here to widen our notions of parodic reference by reacquainting the reader with the work and personality of the celebrated eighteenth-century actress and writer, Charlotte Charke. Charke is of course best known to most modern readers of eighteenth-century literature for her autobiography, *A Narrative of the Life of Mrs Charlotte Charke* (1755). I turn our attention instead to an examination of the rather less celebrated achievement of her 1756 novel, *The History of Henry Dumont, Esq., and Miss Charlotte Evelyn*, and the referential relationship that the novel establishes with the author's earlier *Narrative*. Charke's novel implicitly rejects and refutes her earlier work, which had itself been an extended justification and portrait of the failed artist as an outcast. Although a few critics, subsequent to the early feminist reassessment of Charke's significance in the 1980s and 1990s, drew attention to the seemingly out-of-character, penitential reinforcement of patriarchal values in the later fiction of the otherwise chronically transgressive Charke, the frequently subtle self-parodic reference of that same novel's narrative has been left largely unexplored. Charke's early and deliberately parodic experimentations with the yet-emerging tropes of genres such as the romantic novel and the personal, confessional autobiography reflect her own particular obsessions, but they also significantly anticipate the treatment of sexuality and its representation in subsequent eighteenth- and early-nineteenth-century fictions. In so doing, the work offers a vision of some of those ways in which the potential of the genre of the novel itself related to the era's definitions of power and representation. Charke's self-parodic *History* arguably establishes a particularly formative and hitherto unacknowledged (though possibly quite influential) inter-textual, parodic dialogue of its own with later novelists, including – most significantly – not only Frances Sheridan, but also Elizabeth Inchbald, 'Fanny' Burney, and Emily Brontë. What we finally see in the affected persiflage of Charke's novel is an innovative attempt at a novel form of parodic autobiography. Having already presented her own story in a more straightforward manner to her (original) intended audience, and having seen her textual experiences rejected by that same audience, Charke turned instead to the yet-emerging forms of romantic, narrative fiction, and put those forms to work as a means of distancing her experiences in the guise of parody. Having experienced brutal rejection when she presented the 'truths' of her life to her father (and to a larger, only slightly less patriarchal readership that did not wish to listen to them – much less to understand them), Charke looked to articulate her meaning and so give voice to her own sense of self by means of an acutely self-conscious parody.

2
'We Cannot Think of What Hath Not Been Thought': Or, How Critics Learned to Stop Worrying and Love Literary Parody

> Let's not theorize about humour; . . . it's utterly fruitless and makes the very dullest kind of conversation.
>
> – Robertson Davies, *World of Wonders*[1]

The stigmatization of literary parody as an essentially *parasitic* activity, and the concomitant denigration of parodic reference as an authorial technique manifestly unworthy of serious critical scrutiny, exerted the force of profoundly influential stereotypes within our literary culture for an extraordinarily long time. An indignant F. R. Leavis, endeavouring in the last century to express his personal contempt for the mode in the kind of language that even he reserved only for his most vitriolic criticism, not only insisted that parody 'demeaned the integrity of [its] subject', but went so far as to characterize parody as nothing less than 'the worst enemy of creative genius and vital originality'.[2] Parody was an act of lacerating discursive rebellion – an enemy to literature worse (or so Leavis would have had his readers concede) than the frustrating impotence consequent upon the arbitrary stasis of writer's block; worse than the casual or (for that matter) intentional misconstructions of one's audience; worse than the rhetorical arrows drawn from the quiver of a hostile rival; worse than the ill-intentioned carpings of unsympathetic critics; and worse, Leavis would have compelled his readers finally to admit, than those constraints that are typically brought to bear upon an author forced to produce his or her work within the ever-vigilant shadows of an inflexible ideology. To whatever extent the demands of a compulsory political orthodoxy might well prove intolerable to any writer intent on maintaining the integrity of his or her own voice, the passive submission of the perversely wilful parodist would yet appear to entail a treacherous resignation of creative authority far more disrespectful (and ultimately, in its promiscuous complicity, far more damaging) to the very activity of writing itself. Voluntary participation in the parodic mode constituted an unseemly form of betrayal – an act of aesthetic treason – far too slavish ever to be countenanced by any readers (and certainly by any critics) chary of their own carefully cultivated reputations. Whilst most readers would already have sympathized with William Hazlitt's observation that aesthetic 'rules and models' work generally not to foster but rather to destroy 'genius and art', more destructive still was the literally con-forming ethic of composition at work within those traitorous collaborations that would so forget themselves – and so forsake the dignity of their vocation – as to submit to the restrictive dictates of those same 'rules and models' of their own volition.[3] What could be more contemptible than the work of those authors who – even when left to pursue their craft precisely as they saw fit, and when guided only by the their own creative impulses – would nevertheless persist in submitting to such formal 'rules' and perversely remain within such structural 'models' as necessarily determine the gestures of extrinsic reference inherent in any act of parodic imitation? Having surrendered any prior claims to those qualities of inspiration traditionally recognized as the hallmarks of the truly independent 'genius', parodists consciously (and, by implication, suicidally) divorced themselves from whatever modicum of real talent they, too, might once have possessed.

The derision held in store for the destructive practitioners of parody by commentators such as Leavis, however, constituted only the uppermost tip of a deceptively extensive critical iceberg. The implications of such a stance (insofar as 'parody' was itself at the time conceptualized as constituting not so much a distinct *type* or *genre* as embodying, rather, a more nebulous though still recognizable *approach* or *mode*) rested on a number of contemporary critical assumptions regarding notions of authorship, genre, imitation, tradition, and authority in English criticism. The implications of such a devaluation of parody, in fact, proved on closer examination to be extraordinarily far-reaching and aesthetically consequential. (And it must be emphasized that the Cambridge critic appears on this occasion to have been speaking not merely for himself, but rather succinctly to have been voicing the cumulative, inflexible contempt of a long-standing tradition of dismissal.) The corrosive potential of parody, Leavis's judgement looked waspishly to remind those wayward readers who might otherwise be seduced into extending the mode some small degree of tolerance or (far worse) appreciation, was *in esse* to be positioned as existing *exclusively* in adversarial relation to the constructive powers of 'creative' literature. According to the necessary terms of such a definition, parody was inimical to the very potential of literature *per se*. (The latter designation in Leavis's writings referred, the reader was left to suppose, to some exalted body of writing that managed somehow – and in the face of such an insidious enemy – always to retain its privileged status as real, aware, or, should we choose to retain the organically charged subtlety of Leavis's own suggestive terms, 'creative' and 'vital'.) The critic's very recognition of parody as a literary mode proved a double-edged sword. To be sure, in acknowledging parody even to exist, Leavis and the many critics who in this instance followed in his angry footsteps may admittedly (if only in a strategically qualified manner) have conceded the terminological necessity of acknowledging parody as having long constituted a distinct method of textual reference. Yet the wider, inflexible paradigms of literary creation within which those same critics at once situated the parodic mode (paradigms themselves structured, by no means incidentally, upon the priorities embedded within a post-Romantic cult of awareness and originality) consigned the inter-textual activities of parody to the seediest underworlds of modern print culture.

Any practising parodists, it should once again be stressed, would themselves be assumed to maintain the posture of demonstrably inferior subalterns within the posited hierarchies of 'genuine' literary endeavour. The simple articulation of such a predetermined, formal subservience on the part of parody within the culturally transcendent taxonomies of literary creation, entailing as it did a harshly judgemental subsumption of the mode to almost every other genre and method of composition, seemed, nevertheless, often to strike readers as having constituted only a necessarily formal statement – an emphatically public acknowledgement – of the existence of a particular kind of textual indiscretion that was extended considerably less mercy (and treated with considerably less toleration) when actually encountered in print. The hectoring resonance of Leavis's own pronouncement, it must be admitted, possessed a raw, rhetorical power that is capable even today of bullying its more intuitively tolerant readers into a position approaching that of abject submission. Previous observations on the general sustainability of his judgement regarding literary appreciation notwithstanding, Leavis's attitude towards parody appeared at the very least successfully to have filtered the sheer force of his deeply rooted and strangely personal contempt for the mode through the screen of a critical vocabulary that recollects, in its tone of dogmatic inflexibility, the familiar voice of paternal and punitive authority. He thus appeared capable of prompting within many readers what to his mind must have seemed a cowed and suitably flaccid response of tractable acquiescence. The only perceptibly lively impulse generated by such a docile passivity (with regard to critical matters) was to pursue the implications of such a dismissal even further in the direction of its possible sources. If nothing else, readers were compelled by the straightforward urgency of Leavis's judgement to trace his desire for a containment of parodic literary activity – a confinement that amounted, in its assertions of total restraint if not absolute annihilation – to what can only be interpreted as a form of literary quarantine.

(I)

The discredited, pseudo-Arnoldian notions of the older generation of liberal humanist critics of which Leavis stood representative might appear at first to be of very little relevance to today's readers. Yet it is nearly impossible to overstate the extent to which such a simultaneously impassioned and contemptuous vilification of the parodic mode and (more particularly) such a perception of a non-negotiable dichotomy inherent within the terms of the sort of judgement that posited parody as a conceivable textual entity only to the extent that it cringed in futile opposition to the 'vital originality' of true 'creative genius' seem for a remarkably long period of time not only to have been recognized but also to have been enthusiastically seconded by a great many literary critics on both sides of the Atlantic. 'A true parodist', as J. B. Price could reiterate in the mid-twentieth century, 'does not really create anything'.[4] And therein – when taken together with parody's already enervated participation within the extended history of what was not so very long ago designated as genre theory in English – lies at once the significance, the continued relevance, and the sustained power and consequent influence of its judgement.

It should be stressed that until the advent of the analytic criticism of the late 1960s, little if any serious attention had been paid to the status of parody as an identifiable mode or genre at work (or even at play) within the valued traditions of English literature. Little toleration was ever willingly extended to the transformative operations of parodic technique within the work of our so-called 'original' or truly 'creative' authors. 'Real' authors got on with their business and *wrote*. Parodists, on the other hand, having perhaps first failed in their own attempts to dethrone the present idols of the literary marketplace, devoted their energies to belittling the culturally significant achievements of those geniuses whose works they were assumed, more often than not, incapable of ever truly appreciating, much less emulating.

The role of parody in the work of English authors of the seventeenth and eighteenth centuries seems to have been particularly neglected. The editor of one of the most popular anthologies of English parody to remain in print throughout the later decades of the twentieth century, for example, included only a handful of eighteenth-century parodies in an otherwise admirably representative volume, noting that although the era *'should* have been a great age of parody', there was 'surprisingly little' definite or identifiable parody in the period; 'the century', he apologized, 'seems to have been too self-confident to feel the need for parody'.[5] Such an attitude was unfortunately not limited to cursory surveys of the seventeenth or eighteenth centuries alone, but found its way into the most ambitiously comprehensive anthologies of parody available to the modern student; it managed also to creep into some of the most influential histories of English literature in general.[6] A generously inclusive and well-informed history of parody as a distinctive technique in the sixteenth, seventeenth, and eighteenth centuries has yet to be attempted. The dismissive attitude towards parody as a literary mode more generally, of course, long remained unchallenged. Guides to literary terminology and self-designated handbooks to literature and poetics invariably ignored the actual range of parodic activity in English so as to focus their definitions exclusively on the perceived destructive capacity of the mode. 'Parody, in verse as in prose', ran one such representative definition, 'is a comic or satirical imitation of another piece of writing that exaggerates its style and subject matter in a sort of *reductio ad absurdum*, playing especially upon any weakness in structure or content of the original'. Moreover, the definition went on to add, 'parody is best understood when the original is known, and some of the most hilarious effects can only be fully grasped by one conversant with the solemnities of the work being parodied'.[7]

This condescending stance regarding parody – a stance that comprehends the view that parody itself is typically 'low' or useless, as well as the received perception that the seventeenth and eighteenth centuries produced few, if any, parodies worthy of our attention, anyway – became for a long time an entrenched part of the English literary tradition. George Kitchin's influential 1931 survey *Parody and Burlesque in English*, which remained for many years the *only* full-length critical study of the parodic tradition in English, was content to define parody as a mode the essential aims of which were inevitably critical and conservative.[8] Parody was a 'polite art' – the 'watchdog of national interests', social respectability, and 'established' literary forms. 'Parody', Kitchin's volume observed, 'since the Seventeenth Century represents the reaction of custom to attempted change, of complacency to adventure of the mind and senses, and of established political and social forces to subversive ideas'.[9] By imposing this brand of Whig historiography on the parodic legacy in English, Kitchin unapologetically privileged those parodies that acted as acts of literary *criticism* (the works of 'our great age of parody' – the often fastidious productions of mid-Victorians such as C. S. Calvary, Algernon Swinburne, and J. K. Stephen), and backed away from the fact that parody is far more often a very messy (and a *very* adventurous and iconoclastic) business indeed. Kitchin's narrow definition of parody, and his broad exclusion from the mode of any formally imitative productions that did *not* serve the purposes of stylistic critique, worked only to limit the scope of literary parody. Any parodies that did not measure up to the standard of the new order were stigmatized as somehow 'rude' or 'childish'. The entire parodic tradition prior to the newly conceived Golden Age of English parody was soon dismissed altogether as an undesirable if necessary step in the development of the mature genre, as it was to manifest itself in the work of the late-nineteenth-century parodists such as Beerbohm and Calvary. Those twentieth-century critics and anthologists who followed Kitchin's lead (Gilbert Highet, for example, and, to some extent, Richmond P. Bond) continued to transform the remarkable variety and resourcefulness of parody to its own disadvantage. Such attempts to revitalize the popular perception of the mode have unfortunately felt it continually necessary to sacrifice large portions of parody's legitimate heritage in the quest for aesthetic respectability.[10]

As already noted in my Introduction (Chapter 1), one of the primary purposes throughout these pages is once again to question and hopefully to contribute to what began to emerge only in the late 1980s and 1990s and in the earliest decade of the new century as a clearly discernible effort on the part of an increasingly diverse group of scholars and critics to overturn this still widely accepted characterization of parody as an authorial strategy that is necessarily parasitic in its methods, base in its intentions, and vulgar in its effects. Far from being a literary mode that exists only on the scarred and tattered margins of our literary culture – and far from being one that can ever confidently or for very long be confined *to* those margins – parody ought clearly to be included within the legitimate taxonomies of culturally valued literary endeavour. The practical analyses entailed by such a study further insist that we are today in a position not only to confront the long-standing demand on the part of parody to be recognized as a respectable literary activity, but that we ourselves – in our various capacities as scholars, critics, educators, and informed readers – finally begin to redress that same demand; parody has played a significant and very often determining role in a wide range of works by both canonical and non-canonical English authors.

The participation of parody in the work of such authors, it should once again be stressed, remains a facet of literary creation that traditional critics have rarely shown themselves eager to champion or even, for that matter, openly to acknowledge. Although the element of parody has always, to some extent, played a necessary role in the history of aesthetics, one of the several notions that I hope to advance is that a particular *dynamic* of text-specific parodic dialogue and (consequently) correspondingly particular and specific techniques of practical parodic redaction and response arguably made their first appearance in English from the earliest decades of the seventeenth century. Within the span of a single author's lifetime (a period that I posit as extending *roughly* from the succession of James I to the English throne in 1603, and continuing through the era of the Civil Wars and into the reign of the restored Charles II), the simple possibility of being parodied in print was to establish itself as one of the unavoidable *conditions* of the writing life in England. The manifest possibilities of parodic replication very soon, in those early and increasingly turbulent decades of the seventeenth century, developed into an inescapable *reality*. The troubling, recombinative force of parodic imitation necessarily confronted any writer bold or foolish enough even to contemplate setting pen to paper.

Different authors, of course, would only naturally develop different strategies in response to the reflective and transgressive potential of literary parody. The parodic mode constituted an activity that was instantly perceived to pose a new threat to (or, depending on one's point of view, a serviceable weapon *against*) the privileged status and the seemingly autonomous authority of the printed word. Many such responsive or reactionary strategies, as one might expect, were themselves pre-emptively and often defensively *self*-parodic in nature. Those professional authors who necessarily participated in the aggressively appropriative ethic of the new literary era, not surprisingly, more often than not desired themselves to make use of parody and self-parody as a means of diverting potential detractors away from their own 'original' writings – writings that those same authors typically, though long before the days of copyright law, regarded only naturally and with a common sense typical of the era as constituting a portion of their own private literary 'property'. An authorial technique that looked strategically to incorporate a carefully measured element of self-parody in its design might conceivably lead adverse imitators astray in their own reading, and might thus practically render the work of such malicious enemies the contemptuous products of (in the language of the period) mere 'Mouths' and 'Shake-bags'. Parody, as any perceptive student of the period begins very soon to realize, exercised a determining if often unacknowledged influence within that same cluster of modern, authorial anxieties that – as critics such as Walter Jackson Bate and Harold Bloom argued quite some time ago – began to make themselves felt with increasing force in England in the years immediately following the Restoration.[11] Through an examination of the precise historical circumstances surrounding the initial moment of socialization – that is, the first, public appearance of a text and its relinquishment, on the part of its author, to public scrutiny and (mis)interpretation of the works of several of the most influential authors of the seventeenth and eighteenth centuries – we can see the extent to which the calculated disruptions of parodic play constituted an inextricable part of (and exercised an inescapable pressure on) the very development of the professedly and on occasion ostentatiously 'original' texts of the era's most popular and influential writers.

(II)

Parody, as all writers on the subject have been compelled to admit, has never been an easy term to define. On the contrary, the permeable, formal parameters of parodic literary imitation as well as the *modus operandi* that might conceivably constitute the techniques of any representative parodic methodology are by their very nature notoriously elusive concepts. The author of one eponymous book on the subject typically if tautologically declared very early in his volume that 'when he [spoke] of parody', he meant precisely 'that which we conventionally mean when we speak of parody'.[12] Other modern critics have appeared eager to mask their own (apparently unresolved) anxieties regarding the imprecision that has historically haunted the term by – rather than referring with any regularity to parody or to parodists by any such traditional designations – self-consciously directing their readers' attention instead to the supposedly more identifiable dynamics of techniques such as 'inter-textual dialogism', 'bitextual synthesis', 'paratextuality', or 'diachronic duplication'.[13] Such baldly apologetic euphemisms can unfortunately very soon assume the status of seemingly invaluable (if yet verbally Jesuitical) tools in the analysis of parody itself. One professional colleague cautioned me early on in my own interest in the subject that most attempts to expand the meaning of the term 'parody' to include any form of imitative literary activity beyond a genially inconsequential brand of humorous and derogatory textual imitation – the implied intention of which was to criticize or playfully to poke fun at the formal and stylistic peculiarities of a specific work or a specific author – risked creating, in its grander aspirations, a term similar in its idiosyncratic and arguable inutility to the 'translation' of George Steiner's otherwise brilliant 1975 study, *After Babel*.[14] In attempting to expand or even legitimately to retrieve the etymological, diachronic range of meaning implied by the designation 'parody', one might very easily push the resonance of the term so far beyond the bounds of its more conventional meanings so as to render it nearly unrecognizable and, consequently – at least as a helpful, functional signifier of literary form and/or intention – very close to useless.

Be that as it may, the specific kinds of parody that we begin to see emerging in the work of the poets, the dramatists, and finally the writers of prose fiction throughout the seventeenth and eighteenth centuries – the forms of parody that I recognize and write about in these pages – *do* seem insistently to constitute a mode that is very often far more integral to the processes of literary creation, as most professional scholars would today define those processes, than the simple-minded echo – the lightly humorous recollection – that so often announces the fleeting presence of the purposefully ephemeral stylistic critique more typically conjured by the designation 'parody'. All pretence to definition, as the novelist Samuel Butler conceded in the nineteenth century, may ultimately amount to nothing more than a vain attempt to enclose 'a wilderness of ideas within a wall of words'.[15] Even so – or at least as long as the inherent profusion and indigenous diversity of any such artificially enclosed 'wilderness' remain acknowledged and plainly in evidence – the prudent circumscription of a useful definition will generally construct only those walls that are capable of withstanding both the pressures of its internal contradictions and the ever-expanding volume of its intramural growth. The artificial constraints imposed by any definition, however repugnant they may be to our sense of scrupulous and thoroughgoing rigour, remain, in the face of all such protestations, constraints that are nevertheless indispensable to the progress of all practical analyses. And, as such, despite the awkwardly pseudo-scientific formulations proposed by some critics, the parameters of their restraints must be tolerated. Such a practical definition must also, from time to time and even from generation to generation, be reformulated even as it is handed down within the inextricable legacies of human experience and tradition.

Strictly speaking then, and at its most basic level, literary parody – insofar as such parody can ever be said to constitute a specific 'mode' or method of deliberate literary recollection or allusion – typically involves the formal and/or substantive invocation or alteration of an *already existing text* within the creation of a *novel and yet in some way purposefully derivative* work. Such parody generally depends for its meaning (and some readers might find it useful here to conceptualize this essential element of *dependence* or textual reliance as quite literally and precisely 'dependent', in the sense of 'suspended from', or 'resting' and 'hanging upon') on the explicit invocation of *a pattern of pre-formed literary language* (i.e., on poems, plays, novels, newspapers, magazines, and 'texts' and media of all varieties already 'written' and generally known or available to a wide audience). The element of paratactic contingency, in the most basic sense of 'close connexion or affinity of nature' or 'close relationship' is essential to the parodic method. The extrinsic or extramural verbal, linguistic, and stylistic references of parody – the patterns by means of which parody structures and positions itself, in other words – are quite often readily, necessarily, and purposefully identifiable. The very playfulness and innovation of much (if not *all*) parodic imitation is frequently the intentional product of the experience and complicity of an active (or, more accurately, an interactive) reader. All parodies are to some extent, by their very nature, what critics such as Roland Barthes would once have designated *scriptible* or 'writable' texts (although, of course, according to some readings of Barthes's criticism, *all* texts are necessarily the exotic and erotically charged products of a complicitous engagement between the *écrivain* and the reader).[16] Parodies are texts that are conjunctive; they are quite literally 'articulated' – connected by nature – and their coherence relies on the vitally connective participation of their readers. However, in the absence of any such reference to precise and identifiable textual models or authors, parody can just as easily ground either its form or its meaning (or, indeed, both) in a similar recollection of, for example, pre-existing and familiar literary conventions, traditional literary themes, subjects, characters, and *tropes*, or even, on occasion, the very sorts of imagery and textual situations that any reasonably experienced reader might in almost any another context justifiably dismiss as clichéd, hackneyed, stereotyped, or openly recognizable. Literary parody differs from almost all other methods of explicit textual imitation in that the fundamental emphasis of the purposefully inclusive and kinetic textual dynamic of the parodic mode invariably relies for much of its force at least as much on the substantive *distance* that separates any derivative (or alternately 'secondary', dependent', or 'subsidiary') work from its formal progenitor, as it does on the simultaneous structural or linguistic *proximity* that nevertheless and inevitably immediately links and will forever connect those same two works as conceptually inseparable and generically dependent literary cousins. The determining textual orientation of parodic imitation, to put it rather more simply, situates itself as a simultaneous (if at the same time paradoxical) affirmation of both distance *and* proximity.

Parodies characteristically underscore their indebtedness to the past. Indeed, they often 'celebrate' that debt and, not infrequently, highlight the precise historical, literary, and situational moment to which they owe their own textual nascence or genesis, while at the same time brashly trumpeting the incontrovertible self-assertion of their own independence. However deeply rooted in precise circumstances of cultural and literary history, parodies nevertheless routinely insist on signalling their inherent potential for – and arguably their inalienable 'right' to – still further innovations of meaning. The *possibilities* of parodic resonance – as so many of those texts that participate in the mode intimate with an excitement that is often effervescent, yet no less characteristically subdued and wary in the realization of its dangerous power – are theoretically endless. Like the poetic form of the rhymed heroic couplet (a metrical form so often used by eighteenth-century parodists and satirists), parodies are themselves theoretically endless. Parody can in fact lay some substantial claims to recognition as the mode of the infinite; it is the literary gesture closest both in theory and in actual practice to the eternal, cosmic principles of change, flux, and metamorphosis. Parody is the literary method closest in its impulses and in its transmutations of existing reality even to the ancient and primordial chaos that informs the patterns of the universe itself – it is the logical literary heir to the hustling and dynamic metaphysics of Heraclitus and other pre-Socratic philosophers. Far from delimiting or debasing the potentials of real 'literature' or creative genius and originality, in other words, parody is just as easily conceived rather as constituting the formal and liberating *mis-en-abîme* that would appear candidly to reflect, in the dizzying, eternal mirror of its transformations, the inherent instability and the inescapable mutability of any and *all* textual activity.

While the terms of the wide-ranging definition I have just been rehearsing are, of course, by no means intended to stand as in any way definitive, the calculated depth and flexibility of such a

conceptualization of parody can at the very least allow the word itself
to be of some functionally playful use to the practising critic and reader.
Included within the parameters of such a notion of parody, we might at
once observe, are those works that structure themselves just beyond the
parameters of a precise and formal mimeticism, yet nevertheless recognizably remain, for most if not all readers, in the literally reactionary or
complimentary positions of 'beside songs' – of etymologically precise *para
odoi*, from the Greek παρα, meaning 'by the side of' or 'along side of',
and ἀείδω, signifying the transitive verb 'to sing'.[17] (Strikingly, the first
recorded usage of the actual Greek word παρωδία or 'parody' occurs, as
one might expect, in Aristotle's *Poetics*, wherein Hegemon of Thasos [fifth
century BC], author of the *Gigantomachia*, is referred to as 'the inventor
of parodies', a metrical verse *form* that Aristotle describes as a variation
on the general project of μιμησις or imitation, insofar as it represented
people as 'worse than they are'; the related word παροδος – of a different
derivation – was a technical term employed in the theatre to designate
'the first entrance of a chorus into the orchestra, which was made *from the
side*'.)[18] The latitude inherent in any such etymologically precise definition at the very least allows us quite reasonably, for example, to recognize
a work such as Jonathan Swift's *Gulliver's Travels* (1726) as constituting,
on at least one, admittedly primary level, a loose and extended parody of
Daniel Defoe's *Robinson Crusoe* (1719). Such an expansive understanding
of parodic redaction permits us likewise to acknowledge within the framework of a suitable and comprehensive terminology the position of Henry
Fielding's *Joseph Andrews* (1742) as it stands in relation to one of that same
novel's ultimate source-texts, Samuel Richardson's *Pamela* (1740). We
can similarly acknowledge Richardson's epistolary romance as obviously
participating, seminally, in the wider traditions of English parody as they
have just been defined, despite the fact that Fielding's picaresque derivation of Richardson's material (markedly unlike his earlier and more obviously dependent *Shamela* [1741], or related works such as Eliza Haywood's
Anti-Pamela [1741]) only infrequently positions itself as a *formally* explicit
or linguistically precise imitation of its original or so-called target text.

(III)

In rueful retrospect, one of the few incontestable virtues of the often
calculatedly transient structuralist and post-structuralist criticism of the
latter decades of the twentieth century was the simple fact that it
persistently drew its readers' attention to literature's seemingly limitless

capacity for self-reference. Edward Said once commented with unwonted accuracy that the modern obsession with 'textuality' had effected a corresponding transformation in what critics actually meant when they took it upon themselves to speak of 'originality' in literature. The latter term seemed suddenly, incontestably, no longer to refer to that which was fresh, underivative, spontaneous, or independent of existing styles and forms.[19] In light of the view that literary creation was merely the redeployment and 'refunctioning' of already existing writing, originality had less to do with the uniqueness of individual expression than with a particular ability in the reflection and trans-contextualization of previous 'texts'.[20] The modern and post-modern imagination revelled not in the Romantic ideal of the poet who created (as Coleridge had put it) something 'perfectly unborrowed and his own', but rather privileged a literary impulse that was comprehensive and (one could only hope) constructively dependent.[21] The vital originality of the truly representative twentieth-century artist (at least) was, as Said noted, best described as a 'facility for combinatorial play' – a penchant for pastiche.[22] Art itself was primarily to be thought of as a 'field of play' for alternative possibilities. If *sprezzatura* – that quality which Northrop Frye once so precisely described as that near ecstatic 'sense of buoyancy or release that accompanies perfect discipline' – had once stood as the much sought-after and audacious characteristic of that 'art which hides its own art', then analytic theory insisted to some extent on advancing the very antithesis of such a classically based (one thinks, for example, of the life-like achievements of a Pheidias or an Apelles) ideal. Baldesar Castiglione, of course, had in his *Book of the Courtier* (1528) memorably been compelled 'to speake [the] new word' *sprezzatura* to describe the nonchalance peculiar to that grace that nevertheless effected 'a certaine disgracing to cover arte withal', and allowed an individual 'whatsoever he doth and saith, to do without paine, and (as it were) not minding it'.[23] (Continental writers had long boasted of their participation in a Horatian tradition that valued the qualities of self-conscious poetic craftsmanship and artifice over originality and vatic inspiration; as Pierre de Ronsard conceded in the sixteenth century: 'Ils ont un art caché qui ne semble pas art'.)[24] The creation of any corresponding neologism to designate the antonym of such creative nonchalance, it need hardly be said, would have worked almost comically to negate the very principles it sought to define. True art, in any case, was now paradoxically the very antithesis of all that was once embodied in such a liberating and exuberant aesthetic. The best way for the critic to appreciate the (non)innovative creativity of the truly 'original' artist was to look not for first instances, Said had argued in 1984, 'but rather to seek parallelism, symmetry, repetition . . . [and] parody'.[25] Acts and gestures of authorial power, control, and initiation – whether creative or interpretive – were ultimately illusory, invariably despotic, and destined to be frustrated. The originality of the individual artist or author was itself exposed as a tyrannical myth. Originality, in the post-structuralist era, was typically recognized to be the skulking obsession – the shameful bourgeois fetish even – of the petulant or ill-informed novitiate.

Of course, as a few of the examples noted even in the very brief discussion above intimate, this was not the first time that the related issues of imagination, originality, imitation, allusion, parody, and even plagiarism had been the subject of debate among literary artists and their critics in the Western tradition.[26] The writers of the seventeenth century had similarly, themselves, only naturally engaged in what were typically far more lively and informed discussions regarding the amount of imitation necessary or proper for what Sir Philip Sidney, in his *Defence of Poetry* (1585), described as the '*right* poet' – not neglecting to note that however much English writers such as Gower and Chaucer may have been 'encouraged and delighted with [the] excellent fore-going' of their continental counterparts such as Dante, Boccaccio, and Petrarch, the 'priority' of those same writers did not *per se* guarantee their superiority.[27] Edmund Spenser, who in his posthumously published fragment on 'Mutabilitie' (1609) reminded his readers of the manner in which that same descendant of the Titans had

> the face of earthly things so changed,
> That all which Nature had established first
> In good estate and in meet order ranged,
> She did pervert, and all their statutes burst . . . [28]

throughout his poetry betrayed an unparalleled awareness of the protean instability of the post-lapsarian world that seemed to inform all his work, and would probably have intimidated even the Pythagoras of Ovid's *Meta-morphoses*. Spenser's most transparent layering of secondary narratives in his *Faerie Queene* (1590; 1596) alone – the fabric of which work would only on the most obvious levels be woven from the skein of textual reference that included the Book of Revelation, the legends of St. George, the *Aeneid*, Boiardo's *Orlando Innamorato* (*c.*1480), Ariosto's *Orlando Furioso* (1532), and *Gerusalemme Liberata* (1581) – demonstrates that he would have had nothing to learn from post-modern theory's musings on the discourses of authority and exclusion, or from supposedly radical perceptions of phenomenon such as *différance, sillage,* and the *supplément.*

In much the same manner as their sixteenth- and seventeenth-century predecessors, the writers and critics of the eighteenth century – Jonathan Swift, Alexander Pope, Richard Hurd, Edward Young, and Thomas Warton most prominently among them – throughout that period all vigorously debated the necessary status of the poet's relationship to a body of past tradition (both classical and foreign, as well as indigenous). The question of the complex dynamics that always exist as a form of creative tension between 'tradition and the individual talent', to use T. S. Eliot's phrase, as such writers were well aware, had in any event been with us at least as far back as classical antiquity.[29] The Alexander Pope who so thoroughly disassembled and undermined notions of authorship and authority in works such as the *Dunciad Variorum* of 1729, or the Jonathan Swift who initiated the often bizarre inter-textual crises precipitated by the Bickerstaff Papers of 1708–9 are unlikely to have benefited in any significant respect from the work of their twentieth-century descendants.

The work of Swift, in particular, provides perhaps the best example of the manner in which parody and the often unpredictable give-and-take of inter-textual parodic exchange were features that played important and intractable roles in nearly every essay, poem, and polemic that could be written in the period. Although Swift's own authentic or, strictly speaking, 'proper' voice could be extraordinarily persuasive in its own right (an ability he ably demonstrated in works like his early *Conduct of the Allies* and *Some Remarks on the Barrier Treaty* [1711], as well as in such earlier productions as the more formally and rhetorical conservative odes of 1694), the satirist seemed always to thrive most when writing in or through the voice of a fictional persona; he thrived most, that is, when given the opportunity to display his incomparable genius for literary ventriloquism. On the simplest of levels, Swift possessed an unerring ability to mimic the diction, the cadences, and the idiolects of his designated political and ideological targets or 'enemies'. Whether this talent was being exercised with an eye towards a particular and overtly comic purpose (as it is, for example, in comparatively light-hearted pieces such as the 'Humble Petition of Frances Harris' [1701]), or being employed to more serious ends (as in works such as his *Examiner* essays of 1710, or 1711's *An Argument Against Abolishing Christianity*), Swift's was a transformative skill that appeared to come to him almost effortlessly.

Yet however natural or unforced a feature of his idiolectic poetic expression, Swift's tendency for parodic irony in his most mature and sophisticated works, his proclivity for echoing other voices, for mimicking other forms, and for reflectively ridiculing the perceived cant of ideological positions anathema to his own were nevertheless abilities that were (paradoxically) all too likely to lead the author to build indescribably complex literary-referential constructions, the most memorable of which is perhaps the stunning achievement of *A Tale of a Tub* (1704). As one of Swift's most perceptive twentieth-century biographers, David Nokes, commented: 'One of Swift's favourite satiric techniques throughout his career was to mimic and parody the voices of his enemies. In the guise of an astrologer he undermined the astrologer Partridge; as a political economist, he subverted the modest proposals of political economists.'[30] In the *tour de force* of his *A Tale of a Tub*, Swift engaged in a veritable kaleidoscope of literary forms and voices, each of which sought to make itself heard while yet buried under or encased within the clamour of the author's more comprehensive parody of modern learning, generally. The precise aims of Swift's satires, and the legitimate, un-ironic perspective of positive truth such satires necessarily (and again paradoxically) both announced and concealed, can very often be difficult to discern clearly, if only because the work in question will, in almost every instance, so effectively have accomplished its author's rather more ambitious intention of mirroring the chaos of a world in which classical standards have been forsaken, and in which they were consequently in danger of being altogether abandoned.

Such parodic complexity, not surprisingly, has frequently worked both *against* Swift himself and against his literary reputation. Critics have on occasion appeared too eager to diminish Swift's satire into something far less complicated (and something far more direct and, it so often seems, far less consequential) than it really was, and pertinently remains. The breath-taxingly inappropriate transformation that has been wrought upon *Gulliver's Travels* so as to render it a volume as suitable to the nursery as it would be to the library of the statesman or the philosopher is only the most obvious example of this impulse to render Swift's stylistic and ideological caviar palatable to the general. The deceptively cartoonish or caricatured simplicity of *Gulliver* (or at least of its earlier books) fostered responses that have led the book to be deliberately degraded and simplified for its perceived audiences. It is remarkable that some critics, for example (to say nothing of far too many students and general readers), yet insist on reading the Houyhnhnms encountered by Gulliver on his fourth voyage as representing – both for Swift and for his audience – a political and societal ideal. On closer examination, of course, the community of the coldly rational Houyhnhnms is on one level itself a parody of the ideal that seventeenth-century thinkers had themselves set up such a utopia – it is a parody, in fact, of the increasingly widely accepted Enlightenment belief in the melioration and even perfectibility of human nature. Other critics have attempted, in much the same manner, to simplify the manifold significance of Gulliver himself as a satiric figure. Swift's unlucky voyager may to some extent be presented as a 'Modern' in the novel. Gulliver, as readers so often note, has little if any difficulty in learning other languages; he betrays a distinctly 'modern' interest in science and scientific experiments; he protests a belief in political and social hierarchies that are not merely humane but human constructions; and he is reported to be a near relation of the historical William Dampier, an explorer who was even at the time of the volume's publication engaged in the progressive mapping of the hydrographic state as were some of the most prominent philosophers of the surveys off the coast of Australia. It is important to remember, at the same time, that however forward-looking Swift's hero may be, he is also an allegorical figure whose precise signification seems to flutter into new meanings with every turn of the page. If *Gulliver's Travels* begins as a text that seems to advance the cause of the 'Moderns', in fact, it soon transforms itself into an altogether different (if yet political and provocative) text, emerging finally as a work that parodically attacks those very same 'Moderns' whose work it superficially and at first appeared to champion. The character of Gulliver is also parodied in the figure of 'the foreigner abroad' (readers will no doubt recall the psychological realism that motivates the hero's defence of English polity in Book II). Generically, the novel further parodies several diverse forms and interests, among them the conventions of contemporary travel literature, the pamphlets and optimistic pronouncements of England's many 'projectors', and – as noted earlier – novels such as Defoe's own *Robinson Crusoe*.

Swift's parodies, in the final analysis, are notoriously complicated largely because the author recognized himself to have been placed in an extraordinarily complicated historical and cultural situation. If Frances Bacon's reformation of the sciences and his advancement of an inductive method of learning led in time to the epistemological impulse that would shatter Swift's world (or at least shatter the world-vision that rendered life and living for Swift only just bearable), the same movement seems paradoxically to have liberated a schizophrenic impulse in Swift as an author. This second impulse made possible his most creative works, facilitating his instinctive impulse to mask his own proper voice beneath the constructed cacophony of others. By means of parody, Swift could effectively distance himself from both the ideological resonance and the practical, political consequences of his own utterances.

In works such as his *Verses on the Death of Dr. Swift* (1739) and the *Life and Genuine Character of Dr. Swift* (1733), the author even accomplishes the rhetorically defensive *tour de force* of writing 'proleptic' parodies; he produces his own anticipatory parodies, in other words, of such formally complimentary and antagonistic 'texts' as have not even yet been written. Swift speaks in these works not in one voice, but rather in a multitude of voices that in turn find their immediate sources among a bewildering array of poetic personae. They highlight their author's characteristically complex and consequential response to the challenges posed by parody as a defensive literary mode, and to the dangers posed by the emerging and pervasively parodic environment; they allow him, at the same time, to respond to such challenges in what was to become the archetypal manner of the discourse of the eighteenth-century literary marketplace.

(IV)

Some of the debates regarding the nature and necessity of originality in the late twentieth century were admittedly wide-ranging – insofar as they had ridden the crest of an intellectual movement that nevertheless presented itself, at least at the time, as having seriously qualified the possibilities of any future metaphysics in the Western philosophical tradition. The phenomena of structuralist and post-structuralist criticism and the ensuing legacy of post-modernism were movements that collectively presented themselves as confronting the traditional, conservative literary world with an unprecedented degree of terminological sophistication and strategies of seemingly unassailable stylistic and self-conscious rhetoric. Overall ideological coherence aside, the post-structuralist debate was at least, in its earliest stages, successful in drawing the interest of critics away from the simple, vexed questions of literary filiation and direct indebtedness (and, one might also argue, away from the reductive Oedipal terminology of Bloom's neo-Longinian *agon*) to the greater historical, cultural, and psychological issues at stake in the politics of literary 'production'. The fragmentation of the text and the exposure of the manipulations of the cultural praxis of discourse and the virtues of 'outsideness' rendered any pretensions to such qualities as insight or inspiration, if not suspiciously disingenuous, then at best positively quaint. More than ever before, it seemed, originality *was* incontestably and indisputably merely part of an endless process of reinvention, repetition, distortion, iterability, alteration, and rewriting.

Given such a thoroughgoing redefinition, it was hardly surprising that we should at the same time have been witnessing a rehabilitation of the idea of literary parody. Parody remains, after all, the product of a literary technique that, however one chooses to define it, seeks not to hide but rather to flaunt its status as marked and dependent, or even as fragmented or deliberately decentred. Earlier in the twentieth century, theorists had already begun to foreground parodic texts in their attempts to draw attention to larger questions of literary form. European genre theory – in particular, the work of critics such as Roman Jakobson, Yuri Lotman, Vladimir Propp, Pavel Medvedev, and Tzvetan Todorov – seemed invariably to draw attention to the 'double-voiced word', to the discourse of the other.[31] Parodic stylings or 'metalinguistics' were perceived to be a crucial forum for contending discourses – 'an arena of battle between two voices'.[32] Victor Shklovsky's formalist analysis of *Tristram Shandy*, Boris Tomashevsky's reading of *Gulliver's Travels*, Jurii Tynyanov's discussion of Dostoevsky, to say nothing of the work of Mikhail Bakhtin and Valentin N. Voloshinov (see below) all assumed that parody and parodic play were to some extent fundamental to the development of literary systems.[33] Similarly, the interest of Anglo-American New Critics in the rhetorical strategies of 'irony', 'paradox', and 'ambiguity' inherent in poetry led (despite the fundamental humanism of the New-Critical movement, at least in America) to oddly similar, formal analyses of essentially parodic works as not merely typical but representative of all literary strategies, and parody again became the focus of detailed critical attention. Cleanth Brooks teased out the paradoxical resonances of Alexander Pope's mock-heroic *The Rape of the Lock*; William Empson touched on the role of parody in such wide-ranging areas of the double plots of Elizabethan drama, John Gay's *The Beggar's Opera*, and Lewis Carroll's *Alice* books.[34] R. P. Blackmur focused on parody as a 'form of transition' in his analysis of Thomas Mann's *Doctor Faustus*.[35] Even later, critics such as Wolfgang Iser and Hans Robert Jauss returned to some of the same examples used by formalist critics earlier in the century to elucidate the interconnectedness between text and reader. The capacity of parody to imitate and even to quote texts already familiar to the reader can raise certain generic expectations – expectations that can then be modified and redirected.[36] The status of parody as a marked mode or genre draws explicit attention to the paradigms that structure and control a reader's 'horizon of expectations'.

Such recourse to some of the recognized, canonical texts of parody in the Western tradition did much to revitalize the popular perception of parody and more simply to encourage readers to identify parodies *as* parodies when they encountered them. Other critics were more interested not so much in using parodic texts as subsidiary examples of larger linguistic phenomena, but rather in reviving the aesthetic respectability of parody as a creative-critical act in its own right. Many such critics accordingly stressed the importance of parody as an essential and unavoidable component – one of the fundamental building blocks, even – of all literary form. Mikhail Bakhtin, most prominently, along with his associate V. N. Voloshinov, located an important role for parody in the historical poetics of the novel. Bakhtin's general interest in the festive mockery of authority in the subversive relativity of the 'carnivalesque', in the 'multi-accentuality' of literary signs, and in the plurality of textual voices in prose fiction, in particular, all made significant contributions to late-twentieth-century's aesthetic redemption of parody. In his essay that famously examined the 'prehistory of novelistic discourse', Bakhtin addressed the question of parody directly, and in attempting to define the stylistic *specificum* of the novel, found himself tracing the *specificum* of parody as well. Although Bakhtin still saw parody as often ridiculing 'straightforward' genres and assigned to early parodic activity a goal that was essentially parasitic ('a parodic poem', he stated at one point, 'is not a poem at all'), he nevertheless acknowledged the productive *heteroglossia* of parody, and stressed the unique ability of the parodic mode to act as an aesthetic and ideological challenge to the 'monotonic' language of authority.[37]

Michel Foucault was of course another deeply influential theorist who, in the midst of far larger concerns, found a crucial role for the parodic mode in his history of representation and discourse. An essentially parodic work such as *Don Quixote* became one of the more significant texts in Western culture ('the first modern work of literature', Foucault contended) because it signalled the emergence of the positivities – the discursive practices – of a new *episteme*.[38] Cervantes's parodic masterpiece was the heraldic text in which 'language [broke] off its old kinship with things'. Hence it was a work that anticipated those later texts in which the privileged discourse and 'rationalist epistemologies' of the Enlightenment began to break down.[39] 'The parody', as Vladimir

Nabokov was to put it in his lecture on *Don Quixote*, '[had] become a paragon'.[40]

Other late-twentieth-century literary methodologies – however otherwise unrelated – tended to make similar gestures of inclusion regarding the pervasive and hitherto unacknowledged role played by parody in a wide variety of discourse. Pioneering feminist critics, such as Elaine Showalter, Sandra Gilbert, and Susan Gubar, examined the role of parody in the formation of female discourse of the novel. Such critics indicated that women writers – both individually and as a self-conscious group of authors ultimately working against the aesthetic assumptions of a dominant male culture – often moved through a phase or period of parody *towards* that dominant, male, aesthetic style. The palimpsestic nature of women's literary endeavour – its continued attempts to rewrite a male culture – only naturally employed parody as one of the central tools in the redefinition of female writing. The strategies of parody could on occasion seem self-defeating. Showalter, for example, found 'parody' and 'whimsy' in Virginia Woolf's *A Room of One's Own* (1929) evasive and 'dishonest'.[41] Elsewhere, however (and one might point here to innumerable reappropriations of patriarchal forms by nineteenth- and twentieth-century women writers) parody can be an enabling step on the way to the development of a truly female literary voice. A great many subsequent critics working in the traditions of feminism have frequently had reason to note the parodic techniques employed by a wide range of women writers in English from at least the seventeenth century onwards.[42] Nor was this attention to parody limited to the Anglo-American school of socio-historical feminists's criticism. Luce Irigaray, for instance, in a similar fashion seems to have found a place for imitative parody and mimicry not only in the quest for feminine language (for Irigaray the distinguishing feature of women's language was, like the distinguishing feature of parody, one of contiguity), but in her own writing style as well. Irigaray's original doctoral thesis, as Toril Moi pointed out, was essentially a 'parody of patriarchal modes of argument'.[43] Women under patriarchy, feminists such as Irigaray argued, had no choice but to imitate – 'to play with mimesis' – and to parody male discourse.

And it is worth underscoring the extent to which not only the feminist school of criticism, but other traditions formerly perceived as having been marginalized or otherwise liminal have had positive recourse to the concepts and definitions of parody when formulating their own responses to the supposedly dominant (variously patriarchal,

Eurocentric, homophobic, etc.) modes of discourse. As the film critic Ella Shohat so aptly observed of parody and parodic discourse,

> Parody is especially appropriate for the discussion of "centre" and "margins" since – due to its historical marginalisation, as well as its capacity for appropriating and critically transforming existing discourses – parody becomes a means of renewal and demystification, a way of laughing away outmoded forms of thinking.[44]

It came as no surprise, therefore, that Henry Louis Gates, Jr's persuasive arguments regarding the rhetorical strategy of 'signifying' in the Afro-American literary traditions found their origin in a college seminar on parody, or that Gates's later studies took pains to situate the concept of signifying in the African tradition in an explicit relation to Western concepts of parody and pastiche. 'The texts of the Afro-American canon', Gates observed, 'can be said to configure into relationships based on the sorts of repetition and revision inherent in parody and pastiche'.[45] Critical attention was also directed in the comparatively recent past to the manner in which parody functioned as a mode that defied the boundaries of genre and – like its problematic and similarly disruptive sibling, satire – worked its transformations from *within* any existing forms. Parody is not bound by generic distinctions; rather, it (casually and typically) invades, reappropriates, and overtakes others genres. Geoffrey Galt Harpham was among the first to explicitly characterize another form closely related to the parodic – the grotesque – as a mode that resists precise conceptualization because it is 'capable of assuming a number of forms'.[46] The formally dependent or derivative nature of parody implies a similar mode that 'inhabits' a number of forms, rather than one that constitutes a unique literary type itself. Tuvia Shlonsky suggested that the protean impulse of parody in itself renders it 'generically neutral' or even 'anti-generic'. 'Insofar as it is not a simple imitation but a distortion of the original', Shlonsky observed, 'the method of parody is to disrealize [sic] the norms which the original tries to realize, that is to say to reduce what is of normative status in the original to a convention or a mere device'.[47] This 'destructive' or at least corrective role of parody thus highlights its anti-generic status.

The rich relationship between parody and satire, in particular, has also been examined by an extraordinarily wide range of writers, Shlonsky and Leon Guilhamet among them. Commenting on the complicated literary partnership between the two modes, Shlonsky again emphasized the connection between parody and the Russian formalist focus on literature as a distortion of 'practical' language: parody – a kind of enlarged version of literature in general – is structured in such a way that it lays bare its own devices. The famous defamiliarization (*ostrananie*) accomplished by the parodic text typically and obtrusively foregrounds the technical skill that distinguishes 'literary' from 'non-literary' language. Since the moral, ethical, or religious standards that are essential to satiric correction and castigation are extra-literary, they are foreign to the 'purely literary mode' of parody.[48] Other critics have reiterated a more traditional subordination of parody to satire. Guilhamet, for instance, noted that the generic mingling that characterizes the tradition of satire places satire in a close relationship with parody. While parody of itself 'does not constitute satire', Guilhamet observed, it is one of the most powerful *agents* of satire.[49] An earlier school of traditional textual critics including Edward and Lillian Bloom similarly characterized parody as a 'strand' of satire.[50]

The critical redemption of parody was far from limited to theorists or to those seeking the most comprehensive possible awareness of parody as a literary mode. An increasing number of more traditional academics commented extensively on the role of parody in individual genres, and in the work of individual authors. Such studies have done much to question and, eventually, constructively to revise some of the most prevalent, derogatory critical commonplaces regarding parody. The notion that parody is an essentially debilitating, early stage of a writer's development (a preconception that will be examined in greater detail in the next chapter) came under some heavy fire both by critics who argue that parody is in most cases a more pervasive and enduring element of literary technique and by those who suggest simply that there is, in any event, little that is elementary or 'basic' in such instances of parodic imitation in the first place. Paula Backscheider, for instance, noted that Daniel Defoe's essentially parodic manipulations and amalgamations of supposedly 'mono-referential literary forms' (e.g., domestic conduct books, travel literature, spiritual biographies) work *throughout* his literary career to produce more complex fictional structures, and more fully integrated and emotionally engaging narrative forms.[51] Claudia Johnson likewise observed that Jane Austen's parodies are 'never so essentially prescriptive nor so unitary', as they may at first seem. The parody of gothic conventions in *Northanger Abbey* (1817), for instance, may poke fun at the outward trappings of novels such as Radcliffe's *The Mysteries of Udolpho* (1794), but, according to Johnson, ultimately undertook a form of social criticism that was significantly more volatile and political than strictly literary.[52] Johnson also noted that parody remains an important part of Austen's literary technique throughout her career, operating not only in the earliest fiction but also in later novels such as *Sense and Sensibility* (1811) and *Mansfield Park* (1814).

Having thus effectively begun to disarm the Romantic aesthetic that looked upon parody as base and parasitic, many theorists were free to explore some of the more wide-ranging questions raised by the acceptance of parody as a recognizable and significant literary phenomenon. A few early critics had been content to follow carefully in the footsteps of scholars such as Paul Lehmann, and begin once again by addressing the central problem of definition.[53] What, it had first to be determined, *is* parody? What are the distinguishing characteristics of the mode? How can it be described – indeed, *can* it be described – in formal terms? A small number of critics writing in the later decades of the twentieth century, including Ulrich Weisstein, Henry Markiewicz, and G. D. Kiremidjian, were among the first to formulate various definitions of parody. Not uncharacteristically, each critic located the distinguishing feature of parody in a different place. Weisstein, for instance, rather aggressively but by no means inappropriately characterized parody as 'imitation with a vengeance', and concentrated on the 'humorous and/or critical-satirical intention' of most parodies.[54] Kiremidjian, conversely, focused not on the desired effects of parody on the response of the reader, but rather on the element of formal imitation; he accordingly stressed a more neutral effect of 'jarring incongruity' at the expense of any particularly humorous intent.[55]

Given the wide range of incompatible definitions formulated by modern critics of parody, one can easily sympathize with Joseph Dane's evasive decision at one point to define parody, in his late 1980s study of the subject, as 'that which we conventionally consider parody'.[56] Dane in fact offered an admittedly 'preliminary' definition of parody earlier in his study: 'the imitative reference of one literary text to another, often with an implied critique of the object text'. Yet the acknowledged discomfort regarding traditional definitions of parody (and the concomitant unwillingness to describe the characteristic of a genre so 'formally parasitic') was eminently understandable in a critical undertaking that professed to be 'a study . . . of our own discourse of parody'.[57] Claiming that his work on the subject has made him 'very sceptical of claims for the universality of a parodic genre', Dane attempted to demonstrate that it is only after the codification of a language of parody in the seventeenth and eighteenth centuries and the inclusion of parody in an 'official linguistic system' that one can begin accurately to talk of a 'canon' or even a 'tradition' of parody. Dane argued that the types of literature that we usually call parodic – the plays of Aristophanes, for instance, or the travel tales of Lucian and Rabelais – have been misrepresented and distorted through the imposition of a literary language that has been anachronistically imposed upon them. Dane noted, for example, that the neo-classical language of textual parody does not adequately describe the larger, non-literary references to dramatic performance and to Old Comedy dramatic conventions referred to in plays such as Aristophanes' *Acharnians* and *Thesmophoriazusae*.

Several other critics moved well beyond the problems of definition, and began to embrace the possibilities of recognizing the parodic as an essential and even defining feature of most if not all literary creation. At the very least, the work of these critics possessed the virtue of taking parody 'seriously'. Gérard Genette's 1982 study *Palimpsestes: la littérature au second degré*, for example, focused on what some subsequent commentators would describe as the attitude (or 'stance' or 'ethos') of parody, proper, towards the text from which it derived.[58] Genette's approach had the benefit of drawing precise distinctions between parody and its related literary modes – burlesque, imitation, pastiche, satire, travesty, etc. (parody was in most instances apparently less critically satirical or mocking than such related forms) – but initiated the rather less felicitous if increasingly necessary resort to decidedly unlovely terminological distinctions. *Palimpsestes* contrasted the derivative, parodic 'hypertext', on the one hand, from the originating 'hypotext', which it sought to transform in some playfully comic fashion, on the other. (The first of Genette's terms at least had the etymological virtue of taking its prefix from the logical Greek preposition υπερ, in its sense of 'against' or 'contrary to'; unfortunately, the majority of modern English *hypo-* formations – from the same root – belong to the vocabulary of modern science, and have no actual Greek prototypes, and are less in accordance with Greek principles of word formation. Genette ultimately suggested a distinction between at least five different 'types' of 'transtextuality': inter-textuality, paratextuality, metatextuality, architextuality, and hypertextuality.)[59] The clinical precision of Genette's distinctions similarly situated those works that were not formal, linguistic, or stylistically *precise* imitations of any designated 'hypotext' beyond the bounds of the strictly parodic. Consequently, such 'obviously' parodic works as, say, Alexander Pope's *the Rape of the Lock* cannot be described as a parody on at least two counts: its qualified satire (or travesty?) both of its subject and of its originating text, and, secondly, the multiplicity of texts and authors – Homer, Virgil, Milton – on which it based its mimicry. Moreover, as has often been pointed out, what interested Genette most about parody – and what distinguished its operations from those of other inter-textual 'counter genres' – are not the similarities *to*, but rather the transformations it undertakes *on* other texts.[60] As Genette himself wrote (and I here quote from the original French):

> Il est impossible d'imiter *directement* un texte, on ne peut l'imiter qu'indirectement, en pratiquant son style dans un autre texte.... Voilà pour quoi imiter une oeuvre singulière, un auteur particulier, une école, une époque, un genre, sont des opérations structurale-ment identiques – et pour quoi la parodie et le travestissement... ne peuvent en aucun cas être définis comme des imitations...'.[61]

> [It is impossible *directly* to imitate any one text – one can only imitate *indirectly*, in practice imitating the style of another text. This is why imitating a particular work or a particular author (or a school of writing, a period, or a genre) are by their nature structurally identical processes, and why parody and travesty... cannot ever, strictly speaking, be defined as modes of imitation *per se*.]

Another important critic, Margaret Rose, produced influential studies of the subject that attempted to define parody as a specific literary mode distinct from related forms such as burlesque, satire, persiflage, irony, cento, and pastiche, and that – more significantly – examined parody in its more general form as 'the metafictional mirror to the process of composing and receiving literary texts'.[62] Rose's important 1979 *Parody/Metafiction: An Analysis of Parody as a Critical Mirror to the Writing and Reception of Fiction* was followed in 1993 by *Parody: Ancient, Modern, and Post-Modern*. Rather than formulate a comprehensive theory of parody, however, Rose's wide-ranging studies emphasized the manner in that parody, as a self-reflexive and self-critical form of discourse, is a literary mode that by calling attention to its own formal artificiality, 'problematizes mimesis', and continually works against naïve or simplistic concepts of literary representation. At her most insightful, Rose drew positive attention to the constructive potential of parodic resonance and replication, and offered her readers a particularly acute sense of the complex multiplicity of both generic and specific 'readerly' expectations that the successful parodist confronts and often delightfully confounds in his or her work. Most significantly, and standing as a distinction that separates Rose's theorization from competing definitions of the mode, the emphasis placed in her work on the notion that parody is most often 'the critical quotation of preformed literary language with comic effect' logically extends itself to acknowledge the 'comic rather than paradigmatically ironic effect achieved by parodic texts'.[63]

Yet another critic, Robert Phiddian, although in his most significant work specifically addressing the parodic techniques of Jonathan Swift in his *Swift's Parody* (1995) – and even more specifically focusing his examination on the monumentally comic, referential masterpiece of *A Tale of a Tub* (1704) – nevertheless brought to his historically precise study of one writer's use of the mode a deep and sophisticated under-standing of the work of structuralist and post-structuralist theorists, most notably Roland Barthes and Jacques Derrida. From the latter, in partic-ular, he adopted some of the notions first explored at length in the 1967 *L'Écriture et la différance* (translated into English as *Writing and Differ-ence* only in 1978), and soon expanded in *De la grammatology* (1967) and *Positions* (1972). In these texts, Derrida suggested that the determ-ining structures of linguistic meaning – inscribed and made possible by preceding structures of signification and dependent always on the alternations of 'différance' or prior sequences of differentiation – can never truly find their 'original' point of origin or meaning. An irresolv-able perspective of dialectical play – the elusive opposition of presence and absence – arises between any one speech act and the preceding signifying event that supposedly grants it a condition of signification or (tenuous and ultimately illusory) presence. The situation in which the writer finds his or her self – often translated as the condition of 'writing under erasure' – suggests that one is perforce compelled to make use of the very language one recognizes *even as one uses it* to be inadequate. As famously expressed by Derrida himself in the standard English transla-tion of one passage from his *Of Grammatology* (1977):

> The writer writes *in* a language and *in* a logic whose proper systems, laws, and life his discourse by definition cannot dominate absolutely. He uses them by only letting himself, after a fashion and up to a point, be governed by the system. And the reading must always aim at a certain relationship, unperceived by the writer, between what he commands and what he does not command of the patterns of the language that he uses. This relationship is not a certain quantitative distribution between shadow and light, of weakness or of force, but a signifying structure that critical reading should *produce*.[64]

Phiddian, in turn, made use of Derrida's notion of 'erasure' and of the necessarily random and allusively referential dissemination of language to highlight the status of parody as a mode uniquely positioned to examine what Genette, above, would have referred to as the 'hypotext':

> A necessary modification of [Derrida's] original idea is that we must allow the act of erasure to operate critically rather than as merely neutral cancellation of its object. Parodic erasure disfigures its pre-texts in various ways that seek to guide our re-evaluation or refiguration of them. It is dialogical and suggestive as well as negatively deconstructive, for it (at least potentially) can achieve controlled and metaphysical commentary as well as purely arbitrary problemitisation.[65]

Phiddian's application of such an understanding to a text as wildly complicated, as historically embedded, and as self-aware as Swift's *A Tale of a Tub* may not make for the easiest reading, but his subsequent exploration of the subject in extended essays such as 'Are Parody and Deconstruction Secretly the Same Thing?' pursued some of the most insightful possibilities of his specific inquiry to real purpose. Phiddian argued that Derridean deconstruction 'is not just a (serious) theory couched in a parodic mode (i.e., a parodic theory of language) but . . . treats language and questions of truth and reference as if they were already in a play of parody (i.e., a theory of parodic language)'.[66] Parody and deconstruction, Phiddian finally conceded, 'are the same thing'.[67]

Perhaps the most widely available study of parody in the late twentieth century, however, was Linda Hutcheon's slim but ambitious *A Theory of Parody: The Teachings of Twentieth-Century Art Forms* (1985).[68] Hutcheon, who further explored the topic in *A Poetics of Postmodernism: History, Theory, Fiction* (1988) and *The Politics of Postmodernism* (1989; 2nd edn 2002), emphasized the manner in which modern and post-modern art establishes a dialogue with the past – revising, inverting, and re-creating what Barthes had characterized as the 'always already written'.[69] Hutcheon, like Rose, stressed the fact that those texts that we label 'parodic' need not necessarily involve any denigrating comparison between the derivative work and its 'target' text. Hutcheon stressed the fact that the prefix *para* meant not only 'counter' or 'against' but also 'close to' or even 'beside' – it could suggest accord and intimacy no less confidently than it could imply contrast.[70] Ridicule, in other words, is by no means a *necessary* feature of parodic play. Hutcheon herself initially defined parody simply as self-conscious 'repetition with a difference'. Her notion of parody could be described as a variation on the Renaissance notion of *imitatio* with an added dash of irony. What *was* peculiar about the ironic imitation of parodic works in the twentieth century, Hutcheon argued – and there remains much to be gained by paying close attention to her study in this respect – is the 'critical dimension of distanciation' that such irony takes towards the literature and artwork of the past.[71] In modern art, the irony that signals the critical distance between a backgrounded work and an incorporating text – although it most frequently politicized representation, and contributed to the larger project of deconstruction in its potential to resist and unmask ideological positions that made claims of truth or transcendence – could theoretically be employed to any number of ends or purposes. The pragmatic range of literary parody in the twentieth and twenty-first centuries, Hutcheon argued, was widened to include not only the mocking and ridicule traditionally associated with the kind, but comprehended those works that might likewise invite admiration and imitative respect as well. Joyce's *Portrait of the Artist as a Young Man* (1916), the poetry of T. S. Eliot, Thomas Mann's *Doctor Faustus* (1947), the plays of Tom Stoppard – all were examples of this extended form of parody. Parodies routinely 'cite' earlier texts and conventions only to make fun of them. 'The prevailing interpretation of postmodernism', Hutcheon observed with an eye towards the work of theorists such as Fredric Jameson, is that it 'offers a value-free, decorative, de-historicized quotation of past forms and that this is a most apt mode for a culture like our own that is oversaturated with images'.[72] Hutcheon contended instead that parody 'through a double process of installing and ironizing... signals how present representations come from past ones and what ideological consequences derive from both continuity and difference'.[73] Indeed, rather than emptying the text or the work of art of ideological meaning or significance, parody performs the work of 'de-doxification' (the term, though obviously gesturing towards Barthes's *doxa*, in the sense of the prevailing or accepted view of things, is her own) and, in so disturbing the illusions perpetuated by the practitioners of the *écriture bourgeoise*, acts as an effective counterbalance to the truth claims of any and all ideologies. The typically transmutative operations of parody, in other words, both value and legitimize the liberating possibilities of alterity; 'it both legitimises and subverts that which it parodies'.[74] Her emphasis on 'serious' irony as the defining mark of the parodic ('ironic inversion', she insisted, 'is a characteristic of *all* parody') remains open to some question, but further links her to critics such as Robert Burden, and also (and rather less predictably) to the Anglo-American school of New Critics, mentioned earlier.[75]

Writers on parody such as Rose and Hutcheon and those who refer to them, such as Clive Thomson (thought not, it must be said, Genette) seem on occasion to oversimplify the significance and complexity of parodic imitation prior to the twentieth century.[76] The supposedly distinctive, 'positive ethos' of modern parody – the ruling intended response achieved by the parodic literary text – that these critics saw as the exclusive characteristic and provenance of twentieth-century parodies had in fact always existed in the kind. Classical usage of the word 'parody' makes it clear that while the term was often used to describe those imitations that had a humorous connotation (the element of humour is included in the definitions of Aristotle, Athenaeus, and Diogenes Laertius), 'parody' appears likewise from its very inception to have designated a wide range of linguistic repetition in works that might otherwise be classified as instances of simple imitation, verbatim quotation, and what we would now call pastiche.[77] The synthetic term 'parody' could refer to the redactions of Euripides and the *centos* of Ausonius as well as the more obvious – or at least more obviously comic – transmutations of an Aristophanes or a Lucian.[78] In any case the typical 'ethos' of most classical parodies towards their target texts was a positive one; a line or passage of Homeric verse might be included by Lucian or Diogenes Laertius in order to display the wit and technical virtuosity of the authors, or, alternatively, to highlight the verbal ingenuity of one of their characters. 'The humour of the parody', as Lelièvre asserted with reference to these classical texts, 'is not at the expense of the original author; in fact it would not be true of most ancient parody to claim that it is usual'.[79]

Much the same observation could be made regarding many English parodies. Although some definitions in the eighteenth century, for example, did indeed specifically qualify parody as a 'burlesque change of another's words', critical commentaries in the period were likely more often to hedge their bets by defining the verb 'parody' simply as 'to copy'; many willingly recognized that literary parody 'does not always carry with it any Sneer at the Author parodied'.[80] The mock epic is an excellent example of a parodic form in which the ethos is one of light-hearted respect towards the backgrounded or target text, rather than scorn. Usage of the word 'parody' in the eighteenth century would like-wise seem to indicate the status of parody as a poetic activity that was more accurately to be categorized as complementary or supplementary, rather than deprecatory.[81] Alexander Pope several times refers unself-consciously to his own imitations of Horace as 'parodies', and Bishop Warburton, writing in 1751, noted that those same Horatian imitations were the sort of 'parodies' that 'add reflected grace and splendour on original wit'.[82] Later in the century Thomas Warton would note in a similar fashion that Joseph Hall's imitations of Juvenal and Persius were 'parodies of these poets'.[83]

Certain popular parodies of the late eighteenth and early nineteenth centuries – the parodies by George Canning, George Ellis, and John Hookham Frere of the Wordsworthian ethos at work in poems such as 'Simon Lee' (1798) and 'The Old Hunstman' (1800) included in the pages of the *Anti-Jacobin Journal* (1790–1810), for example, or Byron's brilliant evisceration of Southey's *A Vision of Judgement* (1821) in his own 'The Vision of Judgement' (1822) – admittedly united the modes of parody and satire to splendidly destructive effect. Nevertheless, Samuel Johnson's 1755 seminal definition of parody as 'a kind of writing in which the words of an author are taken, and by a slight change adopted to some new purpose' – a definition in which, it may be noted, any hint of a scornful or satiric ethos in the derivative text is carefully avoided – is implicitly treated by critics such as Rose and Hutcheon, at least, as though it were completely anomalous to the *prevalent* parodic practice of Johnson's day, and of the entire eighteenth century, more generally. The period's valorizing of wit and irony, we are told, led to 'an almost paradigmatic mixing of parody and satire' in the era – so much so that parody degenerated into the vehicle for malicious attacks on literary mannerism. The attitude towards the target text 'had to' be derogatory, and parody was at worst the result of personal animosity and spite. Parodies prior to the twentieth century were thus rejected or at least overlooked in favour of more recent examples, in which the positive ethos is seen to dominate. 'Parody' – as another important, early critic of the mode, Robert Burden, observed with a dismissive eye to ironic imitation *prior* to the twentieth century – 'is a serious mode, unlike some types of playful imitation that are also identified in the same category'.[84]

Easily the most lucid and accessible modern discussion of the fundamental nature of parody as an inescapable component of all discursive interaction and, indeed, as an essential feature of all language, generally, to emerge in the earliest years of the twenty-first century has been Simon Dentith's brief but comprehensive *Parody*, a volume that first appeared as part of Routledge's 'New Literary Idiom' series in 2000. (Strikingly, Dentith makes a point of prefacing his discussion with the observation that when John Jump prepared the volume on *Burlesque* for the original 'Critical Idiom' series in 1972 – no such title on parody was even contemplated for inclusion at the time – parody itself 'played a minor, not to say disreputable, part in critical discourse', and was subsumed under the aegis of burlesque, which was then taken to be 'the generic word for the parodic form'.)[85] In his own study, Dentith approached the issue of definition with commendable caution. He first discussed parody in terms of its seemingly straightforward connection to the notion of inter-textuality, which he succinctly described as 'the interrelatedness of writing, the fact that all written utterances – texts – situate themselves in relation to those that precede them, and are in turn alluded to or repudiated by texts that follow'.[86] 'At the most obvious level', Dentith conceded, parody 'denotes the myriad *conscious* ways in which texts are alluded to or cited in other texts: the dense network of quotation, glancing reference, imitation, polemical refutation, and so on in which all texts have their being'. 'In this sense', he continued, 'parody forms part of a range of cultural practices, which allude, with deliberate evaluative intonation, to precursor texts'.[87] To this extent, Dentith's initial attempts at definition recall the observations of critics of Bakhtin, such as Gary Saul Morson, who noted that 'literary parody is, in short, a special form of a more general communicative possibility, and many aspects of its nature and function are revealed when we begin to ask certain questions suggested by its more general communicative status'.[88] Faced still with the need to delimit the legitimate resonance of the term to refer more precisely to those sorts of works that most readers would nevertheless specifically and more immediately recognize as *parodic*, however, Dentith opted to distinguish the typical scope of parody from merely constituting 'one form of the more general inter-textual constitution of all writing', and chose specifically to focus on what he described as 'the inter-textual *stance* that writing adopts'. He concluded with a definition of parody as including 'any cultural practice which provides a *relatively polemical allusive imitation* of another cultural production or practice'.[89] The references to 'cultural practice' quite logic-ally allow Dentith to include within his discussion the increasingly wide range of 'textual' activities – for example, novels, films, videos, music, advertisements, multimedia presentations – in which parody can be said to play a part.

The carefully qualified notion of polemics, however, constitutes perhaps the most useful and innovative aspect of Dentith's definition. As he noted,

> In order to capture the evaluative aspect of parody I included the word "polemical" in the definition; this word is used to allude to the contentious or "attacking" mode in which parody can be written,

though it is "relatively" polemical, because the ferocity of the attack can vary widely between different forms of parody.... [S]o the polemical direction of parody can draw on the allusive imitation to attack, not the precursor text, but some new situation to which it can be made to allude. Such parodies, indeed, are the stock in trade of innumerable compilations of light and comic verse and of literary competitions, and their "polemical" content is often very slight indeed.[90]

In such a manner, Dentith cleverly included within his definition the contentious nature – the element of strife or verbal controversy, as it were – that can so often figure in the mode, yet managed at the same time to leave the precise if variable nature or direction of this parodic *animus* open. The further negotiations undertaken by Dentith in a glossary that charts a careful course between the frequently treacherous terminological nuances that can distinguish 'parody' from (for instance) 'burlesque', 'carnivalesque', 'heteroglossia', 'hudibrastic verse', 'hyoptext/hypertext', 'imitation', 'inter-textuality', 'metafiction', 'mock-heroic', 'novelization', 'pastiche', 'spoof', and 'travesty' are close to magisterial.[91]

One last writer whose relatively recent work on parody will no doubt prove to be worthy of serious attention is film theorist Dan Harries. Harries's *Film Parody* (2000) may have gained much of its popular currency because of its legitimate claim to being the first full-length study to offer 'a rigorous theoretical account of how parody operates on textual, pragmatic, and socio-cultural levels', but its long-term value may rest on its easy and unembarrassed acknowledgement of the fact that certain popular films served as 'cogent markers of a culture steeped in an ever-increasing level of irony; an era where post-modern activity has become more the norm than any sort of alternative practice'; we exist, Harries asserts with confidence, in a cultural state of 'ironic supersaturation'.[92] Parody, in other words, seems not only to have been thoroughly absorbed within a specific culture industry – film-making – but to have attained a newly acknowledged status as *the* dominant discursive mode of the culture at large. Almost paradoxically, parody, as Harries correctly observes, has become 'a process more akin to canonization than any type of radical critique'.[93]

All this comparatively recent interest in parody (and its newfound respectability) is to be greeted no doubt with a profound sigh of relief. Any acknowledgement of the ubiquity of literary parody is for the better. The early, influential work of critics such as Hutcheon and Rose has the advantage of being firmly rooted in the widest possible range of twentieth-century art, while at the same time pursuing the theoretical implications of modern parodic practice and – perhaps more importantly – attempting to account for its prevalence and popularity. Moreover, such studies (despite a lingering shame that at times attempts to disguise parody by calling it 'bitextual synthesis' or 'inter-textual dialogism') at least avoid the shortcomings of those limited histories of parody published earlier this century, almost all of which managed to assign a normative role to parody before degenerating into quasi-anthologies of little or no theoretical value.

It must again be stressed, however, that the complexity of the parodic mode and the extreme variety of parodic methods of inter-textuality have by no means been limited to the modern or post-modern imagin- ation. While some of the critics noted in the preceding pages devote their attention to eighteenth- and nineteenth-century works, one soon notices that the same few, obvious examples (e.g., *Gulliver's Travels*, *Joseph Andrews*, *Tristram Shandy*, *Northanger Abbey*) are being invoked again and again.[94] There has, in any event, been surprisingly little attempt to coordinate these observations on the historical role of parody in literary creation. Parody seems able to pop in and out of literary works and literary periods almost at random; it is *still* seen to be unpredictable, unreliable, chaotic, or even flighty. Thus parody, in spite of any serious critical revaluation, tends once again to emerge as an unstructured and un-structuring and in some ways an historical literary mode. As I hope at least to begin demonstrating in the pages that follow, parody in fact emerged throughout the seventeenth and eighteenth centuries at once as one of the most versatile, idiosyncratic, and potentially *creative* tools available to literary artists in the period. What they made of its possib- ilities was nothing if not original.

3
Parody as Plague: Ben Jonson and the Early Anxieties of Parodic Destabilization

> Can we believe that one man's breath
> Infected, and being blown from him,
> His poyson should to others swim:
> For then who breath'd upon the first?
> Where did th'imbulked venom burst?
>   – Thomas Dekker, *Newes from Graves-end: Sent to Nobody*[1]

The earliest appearance of the word 'parody' in English – at least to the extent that it has since been immortalized as an entry in the *Oxford English Dictionary* (*OED*) as the first recorded usage of the word – is found in the final lines of Ben Jonson's early comedy, *Every Man in His Humour*.[2] The passage in which the word is used constitutes one of those scenes that critics would, in time, tend to read as typical of Jonson's ambivalent and often disturbingly punitive comic endings. Having allowed the play's various wits and fools to pursue their idiosyncratic humours for nearly five acts, Jonson draws his characters together in the closing moments of the drama (in a manner he had to some extent learned from the conclusions of the *fabula palliata* of the enormously popular New Comedies of Terence and Plautus) before finally placing them at the mercy of a nominal figure of authority. In this instance, that figure – introduced as an 'old merry Magistrat[e]' – passes by the somewhat disingenuous name of Justice Clement.[3] As any reader or theatregoer familiar with Jonson's later *Volpone* (1606) or his *Alchemist* (1610) will already have anticipated, the characters in this earlier play, too, have been gathered together so as pointedly to receive not only their (for some very few) anticipated rewards, but also (for a rather more significant number of others) their seemingly well-deserved punishments. Jonson, as has often been noted, would throughout his career as a writer for

49

the popular stage experience a customary difficulty when it came to the manner in which he intended to reform or possibly to redeem his comic malefactors. The gentle leniency with which we have become rather more accustomed by virtue of our familiarity with the endings of so many of his rival William Shakespeare's earliest comedies – to say nothing of the spectacular scenes of reconciliation that figure so prominently in the later romances – is conspicuously absent from Jonson's work. For Jonson, at least, the quality of mercy – as will so frequently prove to be the case in his oddly vindictive yet still (ostensibly) generically 'comic' dramas – is not merely strained; it is drawn taut to such a degree that it would for many viewers appear to have been stretched well beyond the most punitive extent of any of its conceivable Old Testament extremes. To put it another way, had Jonson rather than Shakespeare been the playwright destined to dramatize what now stands as the famous courtroom scene in Act IV of *The Merchant of Venice* (1600), it is far from certain that Portia's pointedly deferred insistence on the finer distinctions implied by some of the less obvious niceties of the laws of Venice would yet have carried the day. Not only might Jonson have allowed the justice of Shylock's claim to the bloody forfeit of his bond – he may very well have assisted him in sharpening the knife.

Among those hauled before the bench of justice in *Every Man in His Humour* is one Matthew – a character described succinctly in the play's *Dramatis Personae* as 'the town gull' (F *EMI Dramatis Personae*: 19–20). Matthew is in actual fact a fine early example of those typically inefficient social climbers who have a tendency to make their presence felt in almost all of Jonson's stage comedies – a character of the type that Jonson could clearly not refrain from mocking, since they also manage to make their appearances in his dramatic tragedies (as well as in many of his shorter poems indebted to Martial). Matthew, however, is no simple 'gull' or impressionable fool; he has been more particularly identified in the course of the play as an outspoken gallant who has misguidedly cultivated a passionate ambition to achieve a reputation as a fashionable poet. Yet far from having demonstrated himself to be a 'true Artificer' in the carefully sanctioned tradition to which Jonson had himself aspired since his earliest days as a student under William Camden at the Westminster Church school, and equally as far removed from the standards that the dramatist took pains always to cultivate throughout what he once referred to as his own 'barren and infected era', Matthew has instead throughout the comedy voiced a preference for the over-familiar and – even by that date – decidedly *un*fashionable rhetoric of works such as Thomas Kyd's *The Spanish Tragedy* (1592).[4]

Jonson's references make it clear that Matthew's particular enthusiasms would have been perceived by nearly everyone in his audience to be ridiculously hackneyed; they are quite simply out of date. (Although, admittedly, only the most hard-hearted of modern readers could not help but sympathize to some extent with Matthew's wildly impassioned veneration for some of his most idolized poetic models; referring to one passage from Kyd's tragedy, for example, he gushes early in the play with the oddly familiar enthusiasm that is recognizable even today in the overwrought language typical of any besotted, adolescent admirer for some otherwise undistinguished, contemporary lyric: 'Is't not simply the best that ever you heard?' [F *EMI* I.v.62–3]).

Unfortunately, an over-zealous admiration for the work of others has not been Matthew's only weakness. He has demonstrated throughout the play a more alarming tendency to 'imitate', to 'borrow', and, apparently, brazenly to plagiarize from rather more popular and still well-respected works such as Samuel Daniel's *Delia* (1592) and Christopher Marlowe's *Hero and Leander* (1598). Wishing passionately to be recognized as a genuine poet, Matthew has instead demonstrated himself to be something more akin to a grossly inept literary con artist – one whose very kleptomaniacal imitations, though only just barely recognizable as such, would have been deemed both by the characters in the drama and by the increasingly knowledgeable members of his Shoreditch audience to be catastrophically inadequate imitations of 'the real thing'. Matthew, throughout the play, demonstrates his penchant for that which not only has been condemned as tasteless and out of date, but further remains the identifiable property of another.

In the play's final scene, Matthew is accordingly dragged before Justice Clement while still in the company of his most prominent accomplice – one of Jonson's most outstanding dramatic characters – the braggart soldier Captain Bobadil (the same *Miles Gloriosus* role in later years so admired by amateur actors such as Charles Dickens). When the Justice discovers that Matthew prides himself on the distinction of being a poet, Clement challenges him *extempore*, and asks him to recite some of his verses in his own defence. Clement's oral examination of the would-be poet is unfortunately interrupted by one of the play's protagonists, who with a sneer informs the judge that Matthew's inclinations as a versifier are rather, as he phrases it, 'all for the pocket-*muse*' (F *EMI* V.v.15–6). Sure enough, when Matthew is physically searched by Clement's officers, entire bundles of inept 'translations', poorly contrived burlesques, and barely disguised 'imitations' tumble from the capacious depths of his pockets onto the stage. 'What! all this verse?', Clement cries with disbelief upon being confronted with such a tremendous quantity of scribbling. 'Body o' me', he exclaims of Matthew,

> he carries a whole realm,
> a common-wealth of paper, in's hose! Let's
> see some of his subjects!
> > '*Unto the boundless Ocean of thy face,*
> > *Runs this poor river charged with streams of eyes.*'

(F EMI V.v.19–21)

'How?', a puzzled Clement immediately exclaims: 'This is stolen!' Upon which observation yet another character, the elder Kno'well, father to the play's romantic hero, identifies it in a fit of terminological ecstasy as 'A *parody*! A *parody*! With a kind of miraculous gift, to make it absurder than it was' (F *EMI* V.v.26–7).

Clement's response to Matthew's work is unequivocal: 'Is all the rest, of this batch?', he asks, of the remaining material. When informed that, indeed, it is, he promptly demands of one his officers, 'Bring me a torch'. 'Lay it together', he then commands his men, 'and give fire. Cleanse the air'. 'Here was enough', he observes of the parodies – as if to himself, and with a genuine sense of concern – 'to have infected the whole city, if it had not been taken in time!' (F *EMI* V.v.27–8).

Matthew's pages are immediately reduced to ashes. As the flames mount ever higher, Clement observes with an oddly irreconcilable combination of hygienic satisfaction and worldly regret,

> See, see, how our poet's
> glory shines! Brighter and brighter! Still it increases! Oh, now
> it's at the highest: and, now, it declines as fast. You may see. *Sic
> transit gloria mundi.*

(F EMI V.v.28–31)

The character of the elder Kno'well – again, the father of the play's otherwise undistinguished romantic lead – cannot help but smirk with wide paternal satisfaction, directed as much at his own son as it is at Matthew: 'There's an emblem for you, son, and your studies!' (F *EMI* V.v.35–6). Kno'well is, of course, referring here specifically to the well-known motto voiced by Clement ('*Sic transit gloria mundi*'), although, as we shall see, there is something peculiarly absurd in the fact that, in so doing, he should inadvertently remind everyone concerned of those relatively recent forms of literature that combined individual morals or short poems with engraved illustrations of some sort; emblem literature, that is to say, had become popular primarily by virtue of the new printing technology – the newly developed art of engraving – that had helped to render the possibilities of its conceits particularly 'modern' and successful. Ironically, in attempting to include his son in the humiliation of the moment by ostentatiously mocking some of the relatively popular literary forms that appealed to a new and youthful audience of readers, the misguided father cannot help but refer to those same conventions (or at least to the technology that facilitated their increasing production) himself. In attempting to ridicule those sorts of writing that are popular, modern, or new – in this case, both emblem books and parodies of several different kinds – Kno'well manages only to display his own affinity with all that is itself swiftly becoming old-fashioned and out of date.

Matthew, having been thus publicly exposed as a criminal parodist, stands as a precursor of what was soon to become a peculiar and recognizably Jonsonian breed of linguistic malefactor; he is the sort of character who exists only so long as he has access to a particular brand of borrowed speech. The moment Justice Clement has set the torch to his verses (and has thus incinerated his fantastic, private language of both conscious and perhaps unintentional parody), Matthew, too, likewise goes up in a puff of smoke, and effectively disappears from the text. No more poetry – this subsequent silence on his part seems to imply – no more Matthew. If Shakespeare's Iago, in his *Othello* (*c*.1611), departs from the scene of Desdemona's murder in the closing moments of that play veiled within a famously enigmatic silence that has often been interpreted as the strangely speechless testament to his own capacity for 'motiveless malignity', the total absence of Matthew's language from the concluding comic dialogue of *Every Man in His Humour* represents a no less powerfully satirical comment on the vocal impotence of a character who has been deprived his voice. He leaves the stage a mere cipher of what he must have thought himself actually to have been, and departs as a symbol, rather, of a textually supplied authority that has proved ultimately to be extrinsic to himself. Matthew's fall from grace is in many ways – for all of Jonson's attempts elsewhere in the passage to instil in his characters a language of proper poetic decorum – rendered a rather dispiriting moment. It is with some small degree of regret that we must watch as the formerly malleable and entertainingly mobile mouthpiece of those voices that we now know for certain to have been supplied only by others finally disappears. It is rather like observing the figure of a voiceless ventriloquist's dummy being returned to the confines of some dark trunk, secured tightly inside by various complicated locks and strapped by heavy cordage, unlikely ever to be opened and allowed to speak again.

(I)

It is important to emphasize, however, that this final scene of what still stands as Jonson's finest and funniest humours comedy remains – at least in terms of its sheer power as a theatrical event – extraordinarily successful. It constitutes one of those dismissive Jonsonian conclusions that works particularly well on the stage. Quite apart from the tricks and revelations that resolve any other aspects of the play's central plot, the sight of the more absurd pretensions of Matthew's poetic ambitions being reduced to ashes within the finality of a violent if still comically effective conflagration, although of course (as one can tell from Matthew's dejection) rendering either the specific verses or their grander ambitions ever worth pursuing again, Clement's purgatory flames further add to the scene – and yet retain in its air – a certain odd and lingering scent of greater significance. In fact, if we examine the passage more closely, we can see exactly how Jonson has enhanced the spectacular theatrical effectiveness of his presentation. We can also note precisely how the dramatist manages at the same time – through the character of Kno'well, who accepts the judgement of Clement with an air of acting with grand and scrupulous complicity – to complicate this initial startled articulation of parody in English. Parody is to be regarded by the playwright, one soon comes to see, as 'a kind of miraculous gift' indeed.

Jonson begins by playing with concrete particularity on the very real anxieties of his original audience. The language and imagery of the passage have in fact been chosen with painstaking care. The scene is overlaid with a startling number of contemporary references and points of specific legal significance. When, for example, Matthew initially refuses to submit to any physical search conducted by the court officers, he is swiftly warned that any resistance to the Queen's Justice could result in a 'Writ of Rebellion' – a writ, that is, issued for the arrest as a rebel of any individual who fails to appear before the bar of the court, although summoned to do so by public proclamation.[5] Perhaps Jonson, who made a point of inserting the reference in his Folio revision of the comedy (c.1607), meant for his readers specifically to recall such dramatic rebellions as the futile revolt of the Earl of Essex in 1601.

Although Jonson's own loyalty to the late Elizabethan court would doubtlessly have forestalled any genuinely deep sympathy for Essex's ignominious fall from grace, there yet remains, one suspects, something about the desperately theatrical histrionics of the Earl's attempt that would have appealed to Jonson's own flair for self-promoting public drama. Jonson refers on more than one occasion to the 'noble and high' Essex elsewhere in his work – and such references at the very least demand that we entertain the possibility of such a deliberate allusion on the part of the playwright.[6] Early audiences of the play, at all events, would have been very much alive to such an allusion. Even more telling in the same reference, however, is a sidelong glance at the more recent Gunpowder Plot of 1605. Jonson, who was himself for several years an unlikely convert to Roman Catholicism, had not only associated with such conspirators as Robert Catesby and Thomas Winter prior to the timely discovery of the Plot, but had even, himself, been called before the Privy Council and the Secretary of State on behalf of the government in the investigations that followed the attempted treason.[7] Jonson was to be summoned before the Privy Council at the instigation of the Earl of Northumberland on the supposed evidence in his work of 'popery and treason'. The character of Cob, earlier in Jonson's comedy, even cries out at one point in the work for 'vinegar revenge' (F *EMI* III.iii.45) – the adjectival specificity of which constitutes a bluntly explicit reference to the Vinegar House, the Westminster building through which the fresh gunpowder was supposed to have been conveyed before being positioned for explosion beneath Parliament House.[8]

Yet the precise specifics of Jonson's timely allusions, for all the resonance they may originally have added to the scene, are finally less integral to the drama's meaning than the indictment of the more general political and literary-cultural environments he seems intent on conjuring. Even the oblique reference to the very *possibility* of armed rebellion in an era that had already witnessed more than its fair share of such insurrections is itself far more consequential. By threatening his character with a Writ of Rebellion, Jonson's representative of justice slyly equates Matthew's parodic-poetic activity with those forms of seditious treachery that posed a genuine threat both to the authority of the government and to the safety and the well-being of the entire state. To be designated a deliberate 'parodist' in the world of Jonson's drama, in other words, is tantamount to being identified as a treacherous rebel – as a conspiring traitor. And, we should note, the same penalties apply. Justice Clement, playing upon the words 'subjects' and 'realm' (pronounced, of course, 'ream', as in a ream or bundle of paper), acknowledges in his own language that poetry or literary endeavour itself constitutes a form of 'commonwealth'. The trope of the 'republic' or 'kingdom' of letters is an ancient one, yet Jonson on this occasion would appear idiosyncratically and deliberately to have turned the conventional analogy to a very particular purpose.[9] These parodies of Matthew's, Jonson's authorities insinuate, are not isolated acts of textual misappropriation. On the contrary, such writings constitute an urgent matter of national aesthetic security – they pose a full-fledged terrorist attack against what Jonson elsewhere in the play characterizes as 'sacred invention' (Q *EMI* V.iii.322); they represent an abuse of the genuine 'gift', in other words, that inspires writing of sanctioned moral and literary merit. Open the window of linguistic vulnerability just a crack, warns the playwright by means of his draconian punishment of Matthew and his parodies, and who can begin to predict *what* might come flying in. Better, it would appear, to be rid of them altogether, and at once.

If Jonson's barely veiled allusions to treason and armed conspiracy would consequently have heightened the audience's sensitivity to the theoretical and political dangers of Matthew's parodies, and if those same parodies would indeed have underscored the potential figurative significance of Jonson's scene, the spectacle of the actual bonfire itself presents the dramatist with an opportunity to effect yet another turn of the screw. Justice Clement's impromptu conflagration, in which Matthew's supposedly misguided efforts are at once consigned to the flames, would inescapably have recalled for many members of the playwright's original audience the actual public book-burnings of June 1599, on which occasion the satires, epigrams, and 'obscene' erotic poetry of authors including Christopher Marlowe, John Marston, Thomas Nashe, and Everard Guilpen had been publicly destroyed by the orders of the Bishop of London, Richard Bancroft, and the Archbishop of Canterbury.[10] Although the circumstances behind the ban on such writings by the ecclesiastic authorities – and the reasons for singling out certain works and authors, in particular, from the veritable flood of contentious satire that was then pouring forth from the popular press to be burned – have been interpreted over the years in a wide and surprisingly complicated number of different ways, critics such as John Peter noted some time ago that whatever else may have motivated such a spectacular response on the part of the established church, their actions constituted an explicit 'act of literary criticism'.[11] These dangerous new upstarts of 'Satyre' and parody needed swiftly to be put in their places while there was yet the possibility of their even being identified, shackled, and confined. Indeed, rather than risk any chances when dealing with such appropriative and mockingly mimetic materials, it was better simply to burn them. To do so, it was hoped at the time, might rid the world of such a corrosive parodic potential for once and for all. Better, in other words, to nip the buds of such supposedly festering flowers that were to be borne of these noxious literary weeds before they had yet had the opportunity to blossom.

Yet exactly *why* – the modern reader is still left to wonder – were these same satires and parodies considered to have been so monstrously dangerous? In what way did they represent or otherwise embody a new and more potential sort of threat than had yet been encountered? Why were they posited as constituting an assault not merely on textual and authorial ethics, but as betraying in their purpose an even greater danger to ecclesiastical or moral rectitude so catastrophically disruptive as to be greeted with a response very close to hysteria? After all, various forms of personally directed satire had long been popular among the South- wark theatres. Londoners by all accounts enjoyed few things so much as the enactment of dramatic feuds and quarrels that involved both personal and institutional satire on the stage. Some critics have argued that the most threatening aspect of such works (and the most radically destabilizing features of the work of Christopher Marlowe, in partic- ular) was precisely their unprecedented potential for explicitly *political* volatility; on some level, it was the easy accessibility to their meaning that rendered them a radically new and hitherto unconsidered form of opposition to established political power. Some contemporaries stressed the peculiarly worrisome possibility that the erotic and satiric power of such writing was itself merely the logical – if unforeseen and uninten- tional – result of an increasingly standardized and officially sanctioned classical education.[12] Might not works such as the *Amores*, the *Ars Amat- oria*, and the *Remedia Amoris* of Ovid (43 BC–AD 17), for instance, only inevitably lead to the ambiguous sexuality of modern works such as Marlowe's own *Hero and Leander* (1598)? Could the Virgilian present- ation of Dido and Aeneas as a private, erotic threat to the *res publica* in Book IV of the *Aeneid* somehow have been construed, in a similar manner, casually to have anticipated the divine paedophilia and sexual 'perversion' so much in evidence in that same author's *Dido, Queen of Carthage* (1594)? Was it not, finally, inconceivable that the playful eroti- cism and the intensely self-conscious artificiality of the popular Ovidian redactions of classical mythology (the narrative details of which would have been inescapably familiar to any schoolboy) could also lead, after a period of long intimacy and often intense memorization, to a creative- imitative impulse – an imaginative *desire* – to push such material 'one step further', as it were, and transform the narrative acts included in those sanctioned redactions into the stuff of absolute parody? These were no mere hypothetical questions. Such a scenario, in fact, would appear precisely to have been the impulse that prompted Thomas Nashe's own transformations of the very same Hero and Leander narrative in his volume of *Lenten Stuffe* (1599). In Nashe's version of the well-known tale (a legend so familiar, he reminds his readers, that 'every apprentice in Paul's churchyard will tell [it to] you for your love, and sell [it to] you for your money'), the story first presented in Musaeus' original poem is degraded into a farcical romp, in which the drowned Hero is unceremoniously described towards the poem's conclusion in his hitherto lamentable state as having been 'sodden to haddock meat'.[13]

Yet still further possibilities remained – some of them almost too dismaying even to be considered. Although Nashe's self-conscious cheapening of classical narrative currency in his *Lenten Stuffe* could obviously afford amusement, such inconsequential playfulness can hardly have formed the main concern of the bishops. Such an apparent disrespect for the work and the achievement of one's classical predecessors was perhaps disheartening, but it was in no way truly dangerous. Indeed, far more disturbing to the educated clergy was the very suggestion that their *own* pedagogical practices and programmes had in some way themselves been responsible for the recent outpouring of parody and satire in England. There was something profoundly unsettling in the realization that the 'corrupting sensual charms of classical literature', if not strictly governed or supervised in their teaching and instillation, could in actual fact have long concealed within their lines those very same – and formerly long-sanctioned – 'charms' that had come to generate the new collateral line of licentious and morally (as well as formally) unacceptable writing: parody.[14] If Jonson was among the first to characterize parody in *Every Man in His Humour* as treacherous merely by associating the mode with unstable commonwealths, Writs of Rebellion, and the potentially deadly consequences of political rebellion or dissent, his scene's obvious allusion to the Episcopal orders of 1599 drew a further connection between the literary activities of parody and satire, on the one hand, and the political threats posed by acts of treason, betrayal, and those insidious enemies that lurk within the inner world of the Court, on the other. What could possibly have been more stable or more circumscribed, the authorities would have asked themselves, than a conservative, classical education founded on the belief that the primary functions of poetry and of the poet were precisely those that involved drawing a line, as Jonson was himself to put it

later in his career, between 'things sacred' and 'things profane' – of
parting 'scurrility from wit'?[15] Typically, Jonson himself was – even in
the act of making such distinctions – drawing on the educational aims of
higher classical study as they had been posited by his Italian Renaissance
humanist models; he was emulating a humanist system and concept
of education that had looked to cultivate a realizable goal by means of
which, as the influential scholar Vittorino da Feltre was to have it, the
purpose of any master was to inspire in his students a 'consciousness
of re-entering upon a forgotten and long-lost possession'.[16] Some older
European traditions may still have dismissed classical studies as matters
fit to be pored over only by *magistri puerorum* – to be looked upon as
matters of sporadic, scholastic, or grammarian interest; yet the 'new'
methods of education had already effectively instigated a move away
from such a view – had they not? – as anathema to their own larger
efforts to instil an infallible morality in young students. Not surprisingly, the ecclesiastical authorities even in England would have been
stunned to discover that their apparently stable centrepieces of classical linguistic and rhetorical authority would appear inherently to have
harboured those very same enemies to authoritative discourse that were
even at that moment evolving and transmuting themselves into various
modes of satire, parody, and indecent eroticism. Indeed, the curriculum
had in actual fact worked somehow to sustain them and, in due course,
had likewise permitted or encouraged such derivative forms to pursue
active inter-textual lives of their own. Parody, in particular, was to be
regarded as profoundly threatening to any sense of linguistic stability,
insofar as it was a mode that quite literally relied not only on its difference, but on its conformity – on its infective and insidious mimeticism –
to subvert language, and to undermine the rhetorical authority that was
previously thought unalterably to have inhered in official forms of religious and political discourse. It is noteworthy that some of the more
recent studies of Jonson's own legacy as a dramatist have themselves
begun to concentrate on the assembly and reception, in subsequent eras,
of critical editions of Jonson's dramatic and poetic writing – editions
such as that produced by William Gifford as late as 1816 – and the
manner in which such later critical estimations of the dramatist's reputation often served as excuses to explore the significance of allusive and
parodic-imitative responses to his *own* work within the criticisms of,
say, Samuel Taylor Coleridge, or the rather more creative products of
writers including the Poet Laureate Robert Southey.[17] Might Jonson's
expressed antagonism to parody and to related literary-imitative forms
be connected to his *own* penchant for copious literary allusion and

imitation – connected to his own predisposition for forms of parody, travesty, cento, and pastiche? Was Jonson the harbinger of a mode that was to flourish in his lifetime and within his own writing, whilst at the same time a writer who cultivated a (possibly deliberately) misleading vendetta against others who attempted merely, in their own manners, to accomplish much the same thing?

The mere possibilities of the earlier references and allusions noted above are in themselves forceful enough to explain Jonson's use of such a book-burning scene to conclude his play. There yet remains to be identified, however, at least one even more powerful resonance informing the cultural information of the passage. The bonfire and the accompanying metaphorical language of disease and contagion that figures so prominently in Jonson's drama would instantly have recalled to contemporary viewers the devastating plague of 1603–04 – a visitation that ultimately consigned more than 30,000 Londoners to their graves, and one that may very possibly have claimed the life of the playwright's own three-year-old son.[18] Despite the decline of the infection in many of the London boroughs in 1604, the plague continued almost unabated in several other areas of the country throughout the earliest years of the reign of King James I. The ominously high if fluctuating bills of mortality would again shut down theatres around the city and postpone the official business at nearby Westminster several times before the end of the decade. As a playwright, Jonson appears to have had little hesitation in exploiting the current threat in the interests of his drama. If the plague yet remained a sustained threat to the members of Jonson's company, the scene of (quite literally) flagrant anagnorisis in *Every Man in His Humour* presents a vivid re-creation of those familiar protective measures that would so often have been taken in the city against the threat of contagion. The lighting of stone-pitch bonfires to purge the 'rotten Air', the firing of similar bonfires of oak, ash wood, and juniper 'in places low and near the River', the wholesale burning of bedding, blankets, mattresses, and household stuffs in the streets: such precautions against the disease would have been all too common to Jonson's earliest spectators and readers.[19] Jonson's epidemiological language in the scene not only echoes the anxiety of the Privy Council in the official plague orders issued in 1603 by the Lord Mayor and the aldermen and councillors of the City, but also mimics the precise language of plague pamphleteers such as Thomas Lodge, James Godskall, and Frances Herring. Herring, for example, had argued in one pamphlet with which Jonson may well have been familiar that the bodies of plague victims were 'very dangerous for spreading the contagion, and poisoning the whole city'; the plague corpses, he warned, 'corrupt the air with their ill quality'.[20] Justice Clement's concern that Matthew's verses be destroyed before they have the opportunity of '[infecting] the whole city', and his insistence on the necessity of '[cleansing] the air' of any such parodic effluvia quite explicitly echo Herring's emphasis on preventative measures such as purification and fumigation when contemplating the sustained communal health of London itself.

The imagery that enlivens this otherwise slight passage from *Every Man in His Humour* – its tone, its vocabulary, and the cultural resonance of the allusions that cluster within Jonson's language – appears finally to indicate that, for all the seeming 'comedy' of the scene, we are meant to understand that something of vital importance to the country and to its literary and cultural ideals is at stake here. Matthew's seemingly innocuous parodies have unsuspectingly precipitated a national textual crisis. His deliberately imitative verses, on closer examination, are pointedly connected by the dramatist – and through a surprisingly complex cluster of references – to the greatest possible threats faced by contemporary English society and, indeed, to its foundational notions of culture and civilization itself. Matthew himself, again, is perceived to be a form of textual terrorist, and his literary parodies are seen to participate, if only by means of their metaphorical language, in the crimes of treason and sedition. Even more ominously, parody constitutes a threat comparable to that of a devastating textual plague. Should this epidemic of parody ultimately prove successfully, or without concerted opposition, to effect its formal and substantive transformations – should its textual revisions, however seemingly slight, ephemeral, or even risible prove finally and insalubriously to 'infect' the health and purity of a valued classical tradition – then its permutations might very well signal the beginnings of a literary-cultural apocalypse. It is the end of the world as we know it, Jonson seems almost to be shouting at his audience with prophetic abandon, and he, for one, does *not* feel fine.

In the earlier Quarto version of Jonson's play, one of the characters responds to Clement's reading of Matthew's verses by protesting that were one even tentatively to label Matthew's parodies 'poetry', then one might just as well 'call blasphemie, religion; call Devils, Angels; and Sinne, pietie'. 'Let all things', he cries in resignation, 'be preposterously transchanged' (Q *EMI* V.iii.305–7). Parody, such a reaction implies, is not only bad in and of itself; it is a mode that operates as an analogical catalyst for the forces of anarchy and disruption throughout every level and within every institution of civilized society. In her influential exploration of the role of the masquerade as a social phenomenon in eighteenth-century English culture and literature, Terry Castle emphasized the proximity of certain forms of hierarchically disruptive social activity; her work focused in particular on the masked assembly and other institutionalized festivals of 'misrule'. Yet in so doing, Castle pointedly stressed the connections between such public and ritualistic displays to explicitly *literary* forms of subversion and disguise such as satire and burlesque. The main point of Castle's argument was that such quintessentially eighteenth-century textual forms as parody, satire, and burlesque, like their social equivalents, 'made hierarchies explicit by dramatically suspending them; . . . the temporary collapse of structure intensified awareness of the structure being violated'.[21] Jonson's drama both anticipates and betrays much the same sort of 'intensified awareness' of the threat of similar 'violations'. As is often the case within similar manifestations of carnivalesque activity, the hierarchical inversion accomplished by the perverse mimesis of literary parody is presented in Jonson's comedy as paving the way for a complete obfuscation of precisely those political, moral, and religious boundaries and *schema* that make for order, harmony, discrimination, and unity. The formal and linguistic distortions of parody, much like the calculated social violations of the eighteenth-century masquerade explored by Castle, are recognized by the dramatist as arguably (and hence tolerably) healthy yet also potentially *dangerous* expressions of rebellion. The transformations accomplished by textual parody by their very nature intrinsically challenge the authority of the literary and cultural *status quo*.

(II)

It is no mere accident, therefore, that one of the very first times the 'miraculous gift' of parody is even mentioned by name within the classically based traditions of English literature, its products are instantly and unceremoniously consigned to the flames. Parody is most clearly perceived by those who first identify it for what it is and what it might become as a potential contagion that needs to be eliminated lest its influence infect the triumphant 'right and natural language' that typically concludes Jonson's dramas; in this particular instance, it is a threat to the privileged discourse of closure and authority located in the terminating, judgemental language of Justice Clement in the play's final scene.[22] Jonson in fact, in the final moments of his comedy, defines or depicts the foundations of an entire critical tradition within which parody will eventually be characterized as a noisome, literary plague –

an observable, pestilential contagion – the very nature of which implies the worst excesses of communicability and multiplicity. It is derided as maintaining itself by means of a self-generating, mirroring *in*substantiality that could eventually contaminate *all* language – one, moreover, that perpetuates itself only by means of its own derivative and parasitic brand of *in*-essentialism. Much like physiological plagues, parody is presented as a danger to a larger collective community (in this case, the entire linguistic community at large). It heralds a potential catastrophe that is threatening the English language from the 'outside'. It is telling that we tend even today to refer to any author whose work has been parodied as having been singled out as the hapless 'victim' of some sort of crime. Parody is not only, as the American essayist Susan Sontag observed in one of her several studies of the plague metaphor, something that is in itself 'disgracing, dis-empowering, and disgusting'; it is alienating in the worst possible sense, if only because it seems to act so corrosively upon the literature of 'true' poets, and to denigrate the work of Jonsonian 'true Artificers' in much the same manner as a transformative and perversely transmogrifying disease.[23]

Parody, this prevalent strand of our literary tradition further stipulates, is a parasitical force that systematically infects, deforms, and eventually kills *real* language – a viral force that feeds in the manner of some linguistically voracious vampire on the efforts of *real* poetry. Curiously, Middle English had often employed the homonym *parodi(e)* or *paradoie* (a distorted form of the Old French *periode* or, formerly, the Medieval Latin *periodus*) to signify 'death' or 'termination of life'.[24] Admittedly, such usage soon fades from use. When the time finally arrives for designating parodic literary activity in English, the language itself appears to have demonstrated an atavistic impulse to reach back in time so as to create an appropriately distanced and foreign source (plagues of any kind, incidentally, are inevitably blamed on and named after neighbouring dominions). As already touched on in Chapter 2, the otherwise vaguely designated terms *parodos* or *parodia* – combinations, clearly, of the (Greek) preposition *para*, in the sense of, among other things, 'alongside' or 'against', either with *aeido* (meaning 'to voice') or, more likely, with the noun *aoide* ('song' or 'ode') or its verb form *aeidein* (to sing) – lead in time predictably by means of their subsequent Latin and French manifestations to our own Modern English 'parody' or 'beside song'. The aurally proximate Greek word *odos* was itself used to signify a 'pathway', an 'entrance', an 'approach'; metaphorically, *odos* connoted not only a 'journey' or a 'voyage', but also 'the way' or 'the method, as in 'a method of thinking' or 'a mode of belief'. It could also signify the 'way' or 'manner' of doing a thing, or the 'meaning' that was to be gleaned from a particular prophetic sign or omen.

The first of the etymologies suggested above is likely to be the more historically accurate of the two.[25] Even so, we are left at least to entertain two possible interpretations – one slightly dismissive, the other contradictorily and even slightly complimentary – of the original connotations of the word 'parody'. According to the legacy of the first such interpretation, parody is eventually considered less the sign of the 'miraculous gift' of Jonson's comedy than it is to be considered as resting among the unsightly pustules of a scabrous curse; the ulcerous, self-replicating sores of parodic imitation pose an immanent threat to all 'healthy' or 'genuine' literature – literature that would yet seem to exist for its early critics in a state that remains (somehow) essential, straightforward, non-imitative, non-parodic, whole. Just as the bubonic plague (as Daniel Defoe was to describe that disease in his famous reconstruction of the 'Great Visitation' of 1665) demonstrated an unwholesome ability to insinuate itself from its earliest incubation into the – as he puts it – 'ordinary discourse' of unsuspecting people, so too the literary plague of parody is thought without invitation to effect its unsavoury transformations on 'ordinary' (and somehow 'innocent') literary language.[26]

It is possible, therefore, that Jonson himself could be posited as the instigator of an astoundingly pervasive literary-critical tradition that posits parody from its very first appearance in the language as mere *para*-literature. The chastening fire of linguistic exclusivity that kindles the flames at the conclusion of Jonson's drama is merely the first of many such attempts (not all of them by any means so spectacular, nor so intrinsically successful) to rid the world of parody forever. It is among the earliest efforts to exclude the parodic impulse from the taxonomies of valued literary creation as extra-literary and parasitic. Subsequent to such usage, at least, one can say that even those occasions on which parody is not being openly stigmatized as a literary plague, it is (as a literary mode) almost always derided as somehow low, foul, illegitimate, and base. Parody is at best an excrescence; it is at worst the premature and often abortive progeny of an immature literary mind. As we shall see, there may in fact have been a great deal more to Jonson's understanding of parody – to say nothing of the understandings of his contemporaries and those who followed in their footsteps – than is constituted by such a wave of contemptuous dismissal and distaste. We should not yet forget, after all, that a second possible connotation of a word such as 'parody', should it have been encountered in its original Greek, might at the very least have brought to mind the parallel 'path' or 'way' alongside of which one travelled towards the truth of an oracle or presentment of some kind.

As Chapter 2 made clear, critics for far too long sided against parody in its supposed war against 'legitimate' or 'creative' writing. It was F. R. Leavis, again, who had commented earlier in the twentieth century that 'people who are *really* interested in creative originality regard the parodist's game with distrust and contempt'.[27] More recent writers on the subject have remained no less eager to remind us that parody is nothing more than 'the first phase of comic invention'; such critics tend likewise to stress that, as such, parody is an embryonic 'phase' of creative development – the primary and distinctive feature of which is 'destruction and reductiveness'.[28] Parody, we have so often been informed, remains a literary phenomenon that occurs (or ought properly to occur) early in a writer's career – preferably in the *juvenilia* to which even the most devoted reader or specialist need rarely, if ever, seriously return. Henry Fielding, for example, may very well have *begun* his career as a novelist with the open parody and burlesque imitation that ridiculed the popularity of Samuel Richardson, in his slight *Shamela* (1741), but he very soon – and very wisely, it is understood – cultivated a more 'mature' and less obviously derivative style in his major achievements as a writer, *Tom Jones* (1749) and *Amelia* (1751). Jane Austen's earliest work, to note another popular example, is often overtly and consciously parodic. Yet as she matured as an artist, we are led to believe, Austen, too, similarly put away childish things and developed a narrative style that eschewed the broad and open parodic imitation of works such as 'Lesley Castle' (*c.*1790–93) and 'Love and Freindship [sic]' (*c.*1790–93), or even of *Northanger Abbey* (pub. 1818) for the sophistication of more inherently creative approaches. Charles Dickens and William Makepeace Thackeray, too – and even, to some extent, the George Eliot of *Adam Bede* (1859) – may similarly have *begun* their respective careers with novels that, if not consistently parodic of particular authors or works, engaged in frequently explicit parodic dialogues with out-of-date or hackneyed literary styles and techniques.[29] But these authors also, we are confidently informed, had the good sense very quickly to move on. In fact, an unfortunate tenet of such a potentially enabling model of literary-stylistic maturation and development fatally necessitates an eventual graduation from 'parodic' to 'creative' activity; parody and creative originality, we have invariably been led to conclude, are inimical activities, incapable ever of existing harmoniously within one and the same work.

Surprisingly enough, parodists themselves have tended often to legitimize a self-defeating insecurity regarding the value and the supposedly
diminished status of their own work. Max Beerbohm, a designedly
belle-lettristic amateur who even today remains perhaps the most
renowned parodic stylist in English, protested in the prefatory 'Note'
to his *Christmas Garland* (1912) that although, when younger, he may
have fallen into the shameful habit of 'aping . . . this or that writer', the
Garland itself bears witness to the fact that his 'own style' had, at length,
been 'more or less formed'.[30] (The guilty sigh of relief that unwittingly
testifies only to the strength of Beerbohm's continued awareness of his
formal and stylistic indebtedness, however, is close to audible in such
remarks.) It is nevertheless striking that even a writer who is considered
among the most proficient of English parodists was ready and even
eager to renounce his own considerable parodic gift as a 'dreadful little
talent', and to mock parody itself as 'a subsidiary art' – a derivative
form dismissed condescendingly as 'the specialty of youth'.[31] While
remaining imitative and dependent, then, parodies are at the same
time appropriately (if somewhat paradoxically) literary 'first fruits'; they
represent tentative attempts at authorial emulation that fledgling writers
need to 'get out of the way', as it were, before embarking on their professional careers as writers, and developing distinct literary voices of their
own. According to such a view, parodies are akin to the sketches of an
amateur or an apprentice; in much the same manner that a graphic artist
must first, before commencing his own professional career, labour long
and hard over painstaking copies of his chosen 'Masters', so too the qualified writer must learn first to speak in a voice that echoes the tones and
cadences of his predecessors. The suggestion always remains, however,
that the masturbatory self-absorption of parody – a self-absorption that
necessarily manifests itself if an apprenticeship within the mode is unad-
visedly carried on for too long – renders its products inherently self-
defeating and doomed to a certain and very peculiar kind of failure.
A concomitant implication is that parodies are (inevitably) historically,
biographically, and topically 'bound'. Parodies are in fact to be classed
among those literary productions that suffer most from what Michael
McKeon once styled the 'generality theory of value' in literature – that
is, the supposition, still widely maintained among general readers, that
'good' or 'valuable' literature manages somehow to transcend the local
details and the particular occasion of its composition.[32] Poetic excellence, according to such an interpretive theory, is constituted by a
reference to larger, transcendent (and hence typically non-political or
ideologically neutral) concerns, rather than to historical realities, or to

any determining cultural contexts. Parody, it need hardly be pointed out, provides a perfect example of the kind of literary phenomenon that is typically seen as being trapped by its own circumstantialities; parody, to echo the words used by Samuel Johnson when criticizing what he mistakenly predicted to be the supposedly short-lived novelty of Laurence Sterne's *Tristram Shandy* (1759–67), will never – indeed, *can* never – 'do long'.[33]

We should not be all that surprised by the attempts of both authors and literary critics alike to relegate the creative growing pain of parody to such a troublesome if unfortunately necessary 'phase' of literary apprenticeship. Nor should we express any great amazement at similar attempts to quarantine parodists themselves as the not-yet-glorious denizens of the wider heavens of poetic creativity. Scholars and critics of the literature of antiquity – to extend the scope of our inquiry for one moment beyond the English tradition – have long sought to discredit the referential activity of parody by dismissing the first practising *parodoi* either as relatively untalented amateurs who mocked the efforts of those professional bards who recited epics at times of public festival and communion or, conversely, by treating them as *rhapsodes* who themselves attempted misguidedly to interpolate crowd-pleasing curiosities into their own recitations, if only as a means of maintaining their audiences, or of periodically distracting those audiences from the otherwise unrelieved intensity of their more serious work.[34] In either case, parody is peremptorily pushed to one side; its status as a creative art is diminished – if not entirely eliminated – and its function is trivialized as providing the necessary formal or substantive leaven desired only by undemanding consumers of *panem et circences*. Such a perceived dichotomy between the *rhapsodos* and the *parodos* – the divide that separated the 'high' epic from the 'low' and lowly mock epic, the non-negotiable stylistic chasm that distinguished creative innovation, on the one hand, from echoing imitation, on the other – has of course been an influential distinction. Parody has continually been postulated as a mode productive only of 'impure' poetry – a slavish and even servile form of mimetic expression lacking the essential qualities and aesthetically redeeming properties of more central traditions of versification and canonical literary endeavour.

(III)

If the response to parody I have been sketching above (given its destined reputation in the English tradition as a dangerous and *para*sitic activity) is in many ways emblematic of its emerging status in the era as a literary mode, it is entirely fitting as well that the initial instance of *naming* in English – an instance that comprehends elements of both frightful wonder and suspicious amazement – should occur in the work of Ben Jonson. By creating a name for something – by the solid and solidifying act of denotation – the collective human mind signifies a profound cultural recognition that the new and hitherto unspecified has suddenly made itself felt as something present and localized. The first appearance of the definite form of the written or spoken word for a concept indicates nothing less than, as Ernst Cassirer put it, 'a sort of turning point has occurred in human mentality'.[35] The fixed historical and linguistic articulation of the word 'parody' in English gives a local date to the designation of an activity that will stand out among the most confrontational practices of a new literary-critical era. Writers such as Jonson were clearly of an age, eagerly beginning (though following, as usual, in the steps of their Italian Renaissance predecessors decades earlier) to make precisely these sorts of distinctions between various types of imitations, emulations, and copies in their own tongue. Many would move on to equate parody with poetic insipidity or *failure*. No less significant, however, is the fact that Jonson himself seems at the same time anxious to assume an unassailable air of superiority with regard to the new appropriative ethic of composition implied by the parodic mode. Jonson seeks in this early comedy, at least, to claim this 'remarkable gift' of parody for his own, and, in so doing, to exert some form of control over its worryingly wayward and possibly voracious textual potential.

One could even argue that there was something of the parodic ethos that for Jonson, at least, was bred in the bone. Readers familiar with the dramatist's early life will recall that following the death of Jonson's natural father just one month before his birth in late 1572 or early 1573, his widowed mother left their home in the north of England.[36] Acknowledged by many of his readers to stand head and shoulders alongside the likes of Samuel Johnson or Charles Dickens as one who might conspicuously and with pride be pointed to as a writer '*of* London' – as one of the very *creators* of the vision, history, and soul of the metropolis itself – Jonson was not, in fact, a Londoner by birth. In fact, we do not even know exactly where Jonson was born, although his mother had soon settled in Hartshorn Lane, near Charing Cross. Shortly thereafter, she married for a second time. Jonson's own father had been a minister – perhaps even one of some distinction – and the possibility that both the writer's natural father and his grandfather before him had been members of the gentry was a fact that he himself was only naturally inclined later in life to make rather much of. The second husband of the young boy's mother, however, was by trade a bricklayer – and this, of course, was something that Jonson's various antagonists would throughout his life never for one moment allow him to forget. This is not to suggest that bricklaying was in any way generally considered to be a particularly mean or lowly trade. The practical availability of the excellent London clay had dictated that since as far back as Roman times by far the better part of the city's buildings had been constructed of brick and timber rather than of stone, and to be a bricklayer was at least to be considered a skilled artisan.[37] Although Jonson himself later professed that he realized almost immediately that he 'could not endure' what he perceived to be the ignominy of pursuing his stepfather's trade, his failure to qualify as one of Westminster's Queen's Scholars, and so to continue his studies at university, demanded that from about the age of 16 he would have been compelled to leave his schooling completely.[38] In about 1589, therefore, he resigned himself to being apprenticed as a manual labourer. Deeply dissatisfied by such a situation, Jonson appears almost immediately to have abandoned his craft to join the army, then stationed in the Netherlands. Eventually, however, having returned from Flanders probably sometime late in 1598, he was compelled grudgingly once again to return to the trade; he even went so far as to redeem his earlier apprenticeship (for a fee), and became a journeyman member of the Worshipful Company of Tilers and Bricklayers at some point between October 1598 and January 1599.[39] Consequently, in the months just before he managed somehow to insinuate himself into Pembroke's fledgling acting company at the Swan and so embark on his career as an actor and, later, a writer, Jonson may in fact have been so dispirited as to have foreseen for himself little more than an undistinguished career in his guild as a craftsman.

Much has been written regarding the burning sense of shame that Jonson later confessed to having felt when he was publicly labelled as a bricklayer. The occupation had a profound effect on his own sense of self and self-worth for the remainder of his life. The repetitive monotony of such a physical task would no doubt have been maddeningly frustrating to a man of his intellect and abilities. Yet, without making too much of the matter, it is not at all inconceivable that the very physical activity of bricklaying – the activity, over and again, for literally years, of placing the weight of one, nine-inch object (the precise size of London bricks was carefully regulated) against the side of still another, very similar, and in all probability identical object – may itself subtly or subconsciously have worked in some oblique way to his greater advantages as a writer: as a dramatist and a poet. Whilst Jonson had yet been a student at

Westminster, William Camden, we know, had managed to instil in him a comprehensive vision of the ancient world that posited the classical ideals of its writers and philosophers – Quintilian, Horace, Cicero, and Seneca – as having provided a crucial civilizing pattern upon their civilization as writers and moralists in the world of letters. Yet just as significantly, they were not merely stylistic models but, as Marchette Chute put it, 'great men who had provided [Jonson with] the ambition . . . to be such a writer himself'. As teachers, Camden and his assistants instilled in Jonson a sense of the moral dignity and the value of poetry, and encouraged him by 'force of example to bring back the ancient days of order and reason, and rebuild in England the massive glory that had once been Rome's'.[40] For Jonson the whole of antiquity was perceived, mentally, not to exist simply as a body of work or chronicle of histories that belonged merely to or in the past, but to be a living legacy that potentially existed and even thrived *alongside* his own life and times. They were not just literary models or patterns, but were looked upon as a body of work that was somehow quite literally to be placed beside his own achievement – quite literally to be echoed and parodied – in his own era. They would be set up so as to be looked upon side by side. Such a method of comparison could often be taken quite literally; as we shall see, Jonson's highly supervised Quarto version of *Everyman in His Humour*, first printed in 1601, would look to emphasize the perceived simultaneous existence of the world of the classical past and that of the present age by means of precise and detailed passages that paralleled the dramatist's own text alongside those of his various sources.[41] In such a sense, parody could emphasize the very synchronicity of history and human experience itself. Some few critics were capable of recognizing this perception and quality of mind even as Jonson and his reputation continued to be contested in the nineteenth century. Thomas Campbell, writing in his *Specimens of the British Poets* in 1819 on *Sejanus* and its 'parodic' revitalization, in particular, noted that the work was not, as some had claimed, 'a lifeless mass of antiquity'. Of the 1601 Quarto, he noted:

> Ben Jonson forestalled [criticism] by footnotes citing the authority for all that he had worked into [his] harmonious and very noble play. Because the footnotes were there, and looked erudite, the superficial thing to do was to pronounce the play pedantic. Jonson was no pedant. He had carried on for himself the education received at Westminster School, was a good scholar delighted in his studies, and accumulated a large library . . . But he was a true poet and true artist.[42]

Although it is obviously to some degree a fanciful speculation to entertain, there may very well be no small degree of truth in the observation that in whatever professional capacity Ben Jonson was destined to be employed – were he to be a dramatist and a court poet, or, like his stepfather, a bricklayer and labouring mason – his particular task would inevitably have benefited not only from those habits of patience, concentration, and diligence that he had been fortunate enough to learn as a younger man in the crowded classroom of William Camden's Westminster School, but, with a similar rigour, to have been strengthened, and to no incidental or insignificant extent, such habits of mind as had been instilled in him as a trained artisan: habits of mind that specifically called for a flawless sense of parataxis and balance, an eye for secure and measured alignment, a close to intuitive feel for those sometimes elusive dual elements that only his eye could perceive were capable of fitting together with flawless precision, and an instinct with regard to the intrinsic harmony that draws together such objects as demand perfectly to be set against one another side by side, or one atop the other, with an infallible sense of symmetry and of balance. For all his protestations later in life to Drummond that he could never have 'endured' the life and work of a bricklayer, Jonson oddly found himself throughout his early career as a dramatist in a position that asked him no less patiently and harmoniously to place one item of his own or of a colleague's craftsmanship alongside yet another and very close to exact copy of it – to match it with its seemingly (but never just quite) identical partner. The paratactic integrity of a brick wall was not all that different, however loath Jonson himself would have been to acknowledge it, from the semblance of symmetrical coherence that united apparently similar dramatic or poetic artefacts together in the façades of parodic imitation. Ben Jonson, the early dramatist, in other words, was not yet quite so far removed from his training as a fledgling journeyman – a member of the Worshipful Company of Tilers and Bricklayers – as he most assuredly must have consoled himself at the time to have been.

(IV)

Did Jonson's contemporaries have any similar legitimate cause to be so worried about the possibilities – the worrisome capacities for predatory co-option or even the possible advantages – of parody as a comprehensive literary technique? Indeed, could parody really develop to the extent that it seems genuinely to have done to have posed such a potentially appalling threat to the playwright and his work? One might certainly argue that at bottom the fundamental, referential 'idea' and impulses of parody – its inescapable and emphatic reliance as a literary mode that pointedly acknowledged its own textual and verbal antecedents, its ritual use of formal and textual derivation, and its *modus operandi* of explicit, extrinsic literary reference – were, in actual fact, nothing all that new to English writers. The poets of the early sixteenth century, after all – poets such as John Skelton and Sir Thomas Wyatt, for example – had already perceived themselves to have been working within a literary tradition that had absorbed in the course of its own development not only the recognized classics of ancient parody (the Old Comedies of Aristophanes, for example, or the Homeric burlesque of the *Batrachomyomachia*), but extended to include a viable if rather less influential tradition of medieval parody as well: the parodic-travestying tradition of the *parodia sacra,* and of the *Cena Cypriani,* of the goliards and the *Carmina Burana,* of soties and Saturnalia. Still earlier, in the fourteenth century, Chaucer had himself, of course, contributed to the native English parodic tradition a work that many critics still recognize to be one of the most fundamental cornerstones of that tradition, in the form of his humorous imitation of the many 'romances of prys', in his *Rime of Sir Thopas* (*c*.1387). One could also contend that Middle English works as rich and as varied as *Sawles Warde* (*c*.1175), *The Owl and the Nightingale* (*c*.1225), *Dame Sirith* (*c*.1250), Middle English lyrics such as 'Alysoun' and 'Wynter wakeneth al my care' (*c*.1314–25), *Sir Gawain and the Carl of Carlisle* (*c*.1475), and even the masterfully constructed and openly humorous *Sir Gawain and the Green Knight* (*c*.1375) stood in potentially and at times even explicitly parodic relationships *vis-à-vis* earlier literary works.

In the late sixteenth and early seventeenth centuries, however, the airy nothings of such casual inter-textual playfulness and polyglossia that characterized this tradition of classical and later medieval dialogue were finally and with good reason given a local habitation and a name. The terminological shift that occurs in Jonson's drama arguably indicates the punctual emergence of parody – of a new *kind* and of a new *potential* of parodic exploitation – as a force to be reckoned with in the living modes of the English literary tradition.[43] Thus, while non-dramatic parody can, once again, claim to have occupied a modest place in English literature prior to Jonson's first use of the actual word 'parody' in his early humours comedy, the particular *dynamic* of wholesale and text-specific parodic appropriation we see Jonson fretting over in *Every Man in His Humour* does, indeed, signal the arrival of an entirely new practice at work among both poets and dramatists. The method of parodic reference we might trace in the satires, sonnets, and elegies of John Donne (or, for that matter, in his religious sonnet sequences *La Corona* [1633] and the *Holy Sonnets* [1635]) can serve as a useful point of comparison here. The twentieth-century critic John Peter memorably highlighted Donne's 'originality' in his works ('Donne', Peter emphasized, was in such works 'much more than a product of his general situation' and less a poet 'responding' to particular textual cues). It is certainly true that the intensely personal style of Donne's early satires tends to transcend and to overreach the conventional targets of those satirists and 'parodists' who preceded him in English – writers amongst whom we might include Edward Hale and George Gascoigne.[44] Yet Donne's work, however intimate or personal, necessarily took shape at the same time that it maintained a point of parodic contact with the larger traditions of the sonnet sequence; its indebtedness is arguably most notable with regard to the images and conventions of the form's Italian originator, Petrarch. The grotesque catalogue of features articulated, for example, in Donne's 'Elegy 8: The Comparison' (1633) superbly parodies the predictably hyperbolic praise bestowed by the Petrarchan poet persona on his mistress, Laura. Yet the referential strategies that shape Donne's parody of Petrarchanism in the 'Elegy' remain inescapably generic. They are emphatically *not* textually specific references. Such strategies are in fact indebted not so much to a literary mode as they are to an intellectual movement (one that would have to comprehend works such as John Marston's *The Metamorphosis of Pigmalion's Image and certain Satyres* [1598] and Joseph Hall's *Virgidemiarum Sex Libri* [1597]) that sought to appropriate and render literal the latent eroticism of its 'parodic' or imitative models. (Donne's parodic echoes of and references to Petrarch are not, in any case, meant to be read as anti-Petrarchan. Rather, as critics such as Thomas P. Roche, Jr., have argued, they are, rather, parodies that further endorse 'the subtext of [Petrarch's] poems, stating explicitly what Petrarch was trying to accomplish through the persona of the poet-lover'.)[45]

The seemingly parodic strategies inherent in the verse satire of poets such as Hall, Marston, and Donne, in any event, precede the far more rigorously text-specific parodic techniques we begin to see only in the years immediately following Jonson's dramatic comedy. The targets of earlier parodists, should we chose to designate them as such, had typically been a genre (popular English versions of the romance in *Sir Thopas*, for example), or a literary style somehow divorced from any particular author (such as Skelton's parodies of the various services for the dead in his well-known mock-elegy 'Phyllyp Sparowe' [1505]).[46] On those rare occasions when readers *do* encounter text-specific parody in English prior to the late sixteenth century, such parody is typically engaging in an extended dialogue with past or alternative traditions, as is the case with Chaucer's parodic-imitative conversation with an established Petrarchan tradition in the 'Canticus Troili' that closes Book One of the *Troilus* (*c*.1385). Other similar instances from roughly the same period might include the casual or incidental 'Christianizing' of tales from the *Gesta Romanorum* (*c*.1275), John Lydgate's idiosyncratic reappropriations of Chaucerian verse forms, metres, and even particular lines in his own *Siege of Thebes* (1420–22), or Wyatt and Surrey's individually idiosyncratic reformulations of the Petrarchan tradition in sonnets such as 'Whoso list to hunt' or 'Set me whereas the sonne dothe perche the grene' (1557).[47] Some very few other text-specific incidents remain matters of purely *internal* parody, much like the kinetic, parodic relationship established between the fabliau of 'The Miller's Tale' and the more serious romance of 'The Knight's Tale' within Chaucer's *Canterbury Tales* (*c*.1387–1400), or the frequently complex inter-relationships that entwine several of the secular ballads included in the Harley collection (*c*.1314–25) with some of the religious lyrics set to similar melodies in the same volume. The medieval tendency for creating literary hybrids of this sort continued well into the seventeenth century in the work of authors such as George Herbert, who can frequently be found transforming and parodying the conventions of secular love poetry within his own rather more seriously intentioned lyrics.[48]

The inter-textual relationship at work in instances such as these is perhaps best described as ancestral; it constitutes an imitative-referential connection rooted in a concept of textual dialectics that depends in almost all cases on an essential element of temporal *distance* and on a process of literal translation or at least cultural assimilation. Moreover, it is a derivational link that also encourages and often demands a similarly interpretive distance of a patient and considered response. It is a relationship, that is to say, that relies on both temporal and reflective elements that appear to readers to have been rooted *in* and *of* the past. The gestation period of such 'parodies', in other words, was more often than not an extraordinarily extended one. The tense staccato quality of the rapid-fire exchange that begins to characterize parodies from the late sixteenth century onwards is almost nowhere to be found in the more established traditions of medieval verse satire; only very rarely indeed does one encounter in the literature of the Middle Ages or of the Renaissance an author who is writing an ostensibly creative text that is engaged in an explicitly parodic dialogue with styles contemporary – or nearly contemporary – with his or her own efforts. The exemplary narratives of John Gower's *Confessio Amantis* (1390), which frequently echo the stories of Chaucer's *Canterbury Tales*, arguably constitute some of the few possible exceptions to such a general rule. More typically, complicated imitative responses – such as that of William Langland in his *Piers Plowman* (1367–86) to the homiletic tradition and to the scholastic philosophy and theology of the period – are much less usefully recognized as instances of stylistic indebtedness and specific parody than they are as examples of a more general, inter-textual debate or cultural conversation structured on an imprecise and (more often than not) emphatically leisurely pattern of intellectual dialogue.

For the authors of the late sixteenth century, however, what had hitherto constituted only a rare and barely recognizable element of the creative process was transformed (and in a breathtakingly short period of time) into one of the unavoidable *facts* of poetic composition. From the late 1580s and 1590s onwards, the ethos of parody is consistently oriented in the direction of text-specific responses to particular authors and to particular works. It must have seemed to the forgivably shaken survivors of this new form of parodic 'attack' that the linguistic specificity of 'answering' poems, such as those included in Tottel's popular *Miscellany* ('Against women either good or bad,' for example, and its paired 'answered'), or Sir Walter Raleigh's more widely known reply to Marlowe's 'Passionate Shepherd' (1599), had suddenly and with dramatic energy been combined with the personal mockery and often naked vitriol of a Skeltonic 'flyting' match.[49] Skelton himself, in his own day, railed against those individual upstarts such as Sir Christopher Garnesche who looked to usurp the exclusive 'auctoryte' of the laureate; the poets of succeeding generations (and the seventeenth-century satirist John Cleveland would be an excellent example of a poet who was to operate in this particularly furious line of wit) would find themselves confronting a veritable legion of such 'Garnesches' – parodic 'critics' who attacked their targets not, like Skelton, in the public forum of the 'kynges noble hall', but assailed them from within the sheltered anonymity afforded by the technological revolution of the printing press.

Literary-historical models such as those proposed by John Peter in the twentieth century that reconstructed the gradual displacement, throughout the Middle Ages, of Latin satire by its tamer and more generalized medieval counterpart – complaint – and that then charted the eventual re-emergence of a fierce satiric tradition in England in the late sixteenth century can serve as a useful point of comparison here. Peter had argued that the classical Roman mode of satire exemplified within the work of authors such as Horace, Persius, and Juvenal had effectively been displaced by the Christian Latin literature of the early Middle Ages. This later tradition, coloured as it was by the ethics of Christianity, favoured a decidedly more conceptual, allegorical, and corrective brand of satire; it claimed to chastise not the individual, but the abuse – the sort of satire still distinguished as 'complaint'. The principal factor in this historical transformation of satire, Peter maintained, was nothing less than 'the nature of Christianity itself'.[50] The principles of sufferance and restraint (in other words, the ideals and doctrinal standards of Christian ideology) worked effectively to tie the hands of early Christian 'satirists' such as Jerome and Tertullian – satirists who, it often seems, would willingly have pursued the more rigorous and scornful techniques of their own Latin models, had their own temperaments not been bound by Christian doctrine. The long-forgotten methods of personal or private satire re-emerged in England only in the late sixteenth century, when the poets and dramatists of that era began actively to cultivate an awareness of their existence as part of a larger cultural and literary-critical continuum; such methods re-emerged only, that is to say, when the rediscovered satires of the older civilization were redistributed and recognized as long having constituted an integral part of a textually accessible poetic tradition. Jonson himself, possessed as he was of the advantages of an excellent education, would have been very much aware of this greater and more comprehensive tradition of imitation and parody within which he, too, was participating.

(V)

The critical traditions of parody, again, are notoriously less clearly articulated within our literary-historical vocabularies than those of satire. Although the recurring themes of classical satire may, as critics such as Peter contended, have been deflected and transmuted by the homiletic and reprobative strain of the Middle Ages, it is arguable that classical parody had in fact never truly enjoyed any comparable status as a marked and recognizable literary mode, in the first place, ever to have been subject to a similar pressure of critical self-examination and scrutiny. It is also noteworthy that the abuse and raillery – the Juvenalian *saeva indignatio* – that had constituted perhaps the most prominent characteristic of ancient satire was likewise a stance or authorial 'attitude' that had never really extended to the ethos of parodic literary appropriation. Although Sir Thomas Browne, writing in the mid-seventeenth century, may himself have recognized (with an eye, specifically, to the work of Hipponactes and Hegemon Sopater) that the parodies being produced in his own age were 'but old Fancies reviv'd', there was in fact surprisingly little effort to retrieve (or to construct or formulate) a full-blown, ancient parodic 'tradition'.[51] The classical monuments of parody were considerably less conspicuous than their satiric counterparts; in marked contrast to the re-emergence of satire, there was never to be any discernible 'slow seepage' of truly catalytic parodic 'masterpieces' into English in the course of the sixteenth century.

It might initially appear, then, that the sudden proliferation of parodic activity in English in the late sixteenth and early seventeenth centuries was in many ways the result of transformations that were, quite simply, rather more commercial and technological than profoundly cultural or ideological. The establishment of printing presses in England in the sixteenth century for the first time facilitated the rapid appropriation of the text, and obviously sustained the means for parodic manipulation of recently published material within the space of a few weeks – or even days – of its first appearance. The more significant question that has yet to be answered, however, involves the momentous issue of precisely *why* this sort of rapid appropriation and parodic abuse was so suddenly recognized by writers as a dominant (if frighteningly powerful and trans-formative) poetic technique. The printing press, in other words, may admittedly have provided the mechanical *means* of such parodic appro-priation; yet the revolution of the printed word itself offers no truly comprehensive and explanatory ideological framework within which we might then account for the fundamental cultural conditions that facilitated such changes in the literary-critical environment in the first place. What *kinds* of tensions could conceivably have initiated and then sustained such a far-reaching crisis in the practical use of language, and in the dynamics of poetic activity and of the creative imagination in general? While the answers to questions such as these can be articu-lated more properly within the pages of a more comprehensive cultural critique, rather than in a study (such as this) that looks primarily to elucidate some of the strategies of particular authors in the subsequent *practical* crisis of authorship in the period, it should at least be observed that historical circumstances in England – most prominently the disaster of the English Civil Wars, the resulting disruption of many traditional societal bonds and loyalties, the concomitant destabilization of long-accepted traditions of linguistic and rhetorical authority, and the even-tual proliferation of weekly newspapers, journals, magazines, and other literary ephemera – worked eventually to encourage this new form of literary energy. The role of the poet in a society that had moved so rapidly from the old aristocratic order to the inherent instability of new societal structures based on rather more pragmatic and often contingent relationships of power (and patronage) was bound to be problematic. If assertions of poetic 'authority' were beginning to become troublesome or dubious, naturally the poets themselves became at once more aggressive and defensive in their efforts to secure and to protect their own claims to literary dominion and competency. Parody no longer extended to ancestral or parental echoes and imitations; it was a mode that – in sharp contrast to such temporally extended references – was now a relentlessly literary and contemporary affair. Poets began 'looking out for their own', in other words, and they began also to develop literary strategies that might conceivably work to prevent any possible parodic textual abuse of their own works. 'Verse satire directed explicitly at public figures and institutions', George de Forest Lord commented in his monumental collection of *Poems on Affairs of State*, 'first occurs in England as the Civil war breaks out'.[52] A similar revolution in the textual basis of literary parody and its targets had emerged only a few decades earlier, in the work of Ben Jonson and his contemporaries.

(VI)

As one of those poets and dramatists who was to be a defining and determining figure in the creation of the very concept of 'professional' authorship in the English tradition, Ben Jonson was himself very much capable, on occasion, of the most comprehensive reappropriations and redactions of his chosen classical progenitors within his own work.[53] Jonson's assumed role (a role he had, again, assumed partly by virtue of his education at the Westminster School) suggested that he was himself a singularly capable if self-appointed representative of the classical tradition. He conceived himself to be the 'British Horace' who alone possessed both the learning and the moral authority to act as mediator between the monarch and society – a role that necessitated not only the many explicit imitations and parodies of Roman poets such as Horace, Juvenal, and Martial in volumes like the *Epigrams* (1616) and *The Underwood* (1640), but similarly required an extensive understanding of Roman Augustanism and its possible relation to the early Stuart court. In their influential study of the politics of poetic transgression, Peter Stallybrass and Allon White observed that although the exalted notion of professional authorship that Jonson so carefully constructed and to which he devoted his entire career as a writer was 'in every way in contradiction' to the spirit of Saturnalia and parody, the subsequent inclusion of the debasing and vulgar concept of authorship embodied in the popular discourse of parody and the theatre within Jonson's own work constitutes merely one very obvious example of what was to become a recurrent pattern in cultural representation.[54] Although professing a whole-hearted rejection of the 'contagion of the low', and attempting to construct an authorial identity that stood in calculated opposition to the discursive tactics of popular dramatic culture, Jonson invariably included something of the 'clamour of the market place' in his own work.[55] No matter how hard Jonson might try, and no matter how committed to its purity he may claim to have been, the high traditions of classicism that were to provide the genuine patterns for imitation could not help but be infected by their lowlier cultural enemies. However much one wished to lock the plague out of the house, it would manage always, somehow, to find its own way in.

Stallybrass and White seemed, convincingly enough, to have demonstrated the extent of the avowedly 'classical' Jonson's transgressions into the chaotic world of Bakhtinian carnivalesque. Yet the degree to which Jonson sought to suppress such acts of literary hybridization in his own works remains intriguing. The question of precisely how large a role this new 'gift' of parody might be permitted to play within a redefined classical aesthetic is one that is raised again and again in Jonson's plays. Richard Helgerson once observed that the 'lack of the usual genre markings' rendered Jonson's laureate self-presentation – his effort to distinguish himself *from* the new literary marketplace of the theatre at the very same time that he was writing *for* that market – particularly problematic.[56] Helgerson's observation holds true in more ways than one. Jonson not only lacked the proper generic qualifications of a 'natural' laureate (the crafting of a body of early pastoral and bucolic poetry, for example, and the carefully staged progression towards the achievement of a grand heroic poem), his own undertakings tended in actual fact towards a parodic conflation of generic distinctions. Parodies and parodic play, in other words, pervade nearly all of Jonson's work. The arc of the Virgilian model of poetic progress did not merely elude Jonson – he seemed consciously, for all his avowed professional ambitions, to avoid it. As some of his earliest critics acknowledged, not only was Jonson aware of his own literary borrowings, he seemed at times deliberately to flaunt them (one recalls the 'victorious thefts' that Dryden would later ascribe to Jonson – to whom the former poet memorably referred as the 'learned plagiary').[57] The issue of Jonson's comprehensive thefts has been addressed over the years by a number of critics, including Stephen Orgel, who have together stressed the range and multiplicity of Jonson's borrowings.[58] Another critic, Robert Watson, argued that *all* of Jonson's comedies are – if one were to be absolutely honest about the issue – based on parodic structures that were 'more extensive and subversive than have commonly been acknowledged'.[59]

In a play such as *Every Man in His Humour*, the focus of Jonson's parody is trained not so much on the substance of the classical past as it is on the abuses of contemporary, English society. Jonson launches his parodic-satiric attack not against linguistic absurdity in general, but on carefully chosen instances of particular excess – the inflated language of Kyd and Marlowe, for instance, or the perceived plagiarisms of Samuel Daniel. In some of his later plays the *loci* of such attacks would become even more specific; Jonson himself would briefly get caught up in the so-called 'War of the Poets' – a once famous altercation that, in the series of plays including *Cynthia's Revels* (1601), *Poetaster* (1602), and *Satiromastix* (1602), witnessed the most textually specific parodic exchange in English to date. Dramatic poetry (and particularly parodic poetry) was suddenly being conceived as a tool to be employed in a larger struggle – as a formal means to both aesthetic and ideological ends.

Jonson was especially afraid of the new breed of writers whom his predecessor Sir Philip Sidney had first characterized as 'Poet-Apes' – 'Empty spirits' who seemed capable of making 'each men's wit [their] own' in what nevertheless remained a 'barren and infected age'.[60] He professed instead to emulate an age 'when wit, and artes were at their height in *Rome*'.[61] And with good reason, too. Jonson was among the earliest 'victims' in English of the kind of literary ventriloquism that was to become a salient feature of the poetry of the late seventeenth century and, of course, much of the most memorable work of the first half of the eighteenth century as well. As to the critics themselves, Jonson confessed only an impatient disgust; 'they fly buzzing, mad, about my nostrills', he complained in his response to the public reaction to one of his comical satires.[62] In other words, Jonson lets his audience know, they quite literally stink. Jonson was certainly among the first poets to learn – from his heated participation in the rapid-fire exchanges and reappropriations of his own material in the above-mentioned *Poetomachia* – that the linguistic specifics of his own text (its vocabulary, syntax, imagery, tropes, and structures) could be used against him with alarming ease and effectiveness.[63] From the early seventeenth century onwards, it is inconceivable that an author would even think of setting pen to paper without first contemplating the possibility that the very words he was about to write – *his* words – would, in a matter of months, weeks, or even days, be thrown back in his face.[64] Parody quickly becomes an integral part of the poetic process, and it is the element the poet chooses to ignore at his peril. In the move from a smaller controlled group of readers to a claim to a larger public purpose, and to a more comprehensive audience, the language of poetry was about to be destabilized. The authority of authors was to be snatched from beneath their very feet. Language, simply put, was no longer 'safe'. *All* poets would now be faced with the possibility that whatever they wrote could and would be used against them – transformed, transmuted, reflected, and distorted. Such language was the author's own and yet at the same time so obviously *not* his own. The potential for parodic response was not only to affect the ways in which the poets of the seventeenth century wrote – it was to influence what they wrote about, how daring they felt they could be in addressing certain subjects, how they might make use of and acknowledge their source material, and even how they worked to shape the anticipated responses of their target audience. The imitative parodic models nascent in the broad-based inter-textual dialogues of the early sixteenth century were suddenly to be transformed into an identifiable threat – a clear and present danger – to the writing author.

Jonson's anxiety regarding parody was to some degree only a practical extension of his deeper and more far-reaching anxiety concerning the inherent instability of language itself. In his *Timber, or, Discoveries* (1640), Jonson several times declared his love of 'plain' language, and repeated his conviction that one can always judge the moral quality of a man by his language. 'Language', he noted in one well-known passage,

> most shewes a man: speake that I may see thee. It springs out of the most retired and inmost parts of us, and is the Image of the Parent of it, the mind. No glasse renders a man's form, or likeness, so true as his speech.[65]

In an earlier discussion on decorum, he had observed in a similar vein that:

> I would rather have a plain, downe-right wisdome, than a foolish and affected eloquence. For what is so furious and *Bethl'em*-like, as a vaine sound of chosen and excellent words, without any subject of *sentence*, or *science* mix'd?[66]

Jonson's reiterated concern for 'plain' and proper usage – for the unsullied 'purity of language' (*Volp.* Epistle, 121) – was, again, the legacy of his education under Camden at Westminster; it was a recollection of Camden's insistence that good writers make good politicians. The values of language were equally the values of reticence and clarity.

It is worth noting, too, that Jonson's antipathy to much contemporary usage was also rooted in part in a genuinely felt reaction against what we might still today call 'inkhorn' terms – the playwright was responding to the same historical phenomenon that prompted Shakespeare's mild satire of those who 'hath... eat paper, as it were', in *Love's Labours Lost* (*LLL* IV.ii.25). Although he was himself by no means reluctant or even, it would often seem, the slightest bit hesitant to use newly imported French and Latin words in his own work, Jonson launched a virulent attack on the obvious abuses to which wholesale or indiscriminate linguistic borrowing could lead. ('We must not be too frequent with the mint', he says at one point in his *Timber, or Discoveries*, 'every day coining. Nor fetch words from the extreme and utmost ages'.[67] His own attempt at an English Grammar – first published in the 1640 Folio – reflected the playwright's sustained desire to schematize English etymology and syntax in the face of the perceived threat of possible and perhaps even imminent linguistic chaos. Jonson reveals in all his writings a constant anxiety regarding this new potential for linguistic misappropriation; he also acknowledges a pervasive distrust of all forms of language play outside his own. Chief among his anxieties was his fear relating to parodists and imitators of his own work. The new legion of 'Tinkling Rhymers' who purposefully distort the works of others are, he says (once again finding rhetorical strength in the language of contagion), an '*Epidemical* Infection' (*Timb.* 349; 360–61), the victims of 'an itching leprosy of wit' (*EMO*, Induction, 68). Jonson's plays are filled with poetasters such as Matthew in *Every Man in His Humour*, or Antonio Balladino in *The Case Is Altered* (1598), who foolishly profess to believe that good poetry is like old bread 'which the staler it is, the more wholesome' (*CA* I.ii.46). It is particularly telling that throughout Jonson's plays when characters create alternative selves in a fallen world that all too readily accommodates the deceptive and illusory, they typically attempt to form those identities *through* language, rather than through some easier disguise of costume, or any form of physically observable behaviour.

To illustrate Jonson's concepts of linguistic 'disguise' and transformation, we need only turn briefly to another scene from the early *Every Man in His Humour*. We have already seen that Jonson's fears regarding language and parodic appropriation are reflected in the figurative language of the drama. The playwright's anxieties about parody are present not only in the comedy's final scene, they can be traced throughout the drama. The central deceiving character of Brainworm, for example, is in the course of the play disguised by pretending to have been 'translated' from a servant into a soldier (F *EMI* II.iv.1–2); Brainworm soon finds a suitable mark in his master, Kno'well, a man who relies far too heavily upon the stability of language and appearances to remain long untroubled in Jonson's comic world. Kno'well's very name is in fact singularly inappropriate to his character; when he first engages the disguised Brainworm as his follower, he typically does so on false linguistic evidence. Kno'well, the audience soon discovers, knows little about the world, and even less about himself. Brainworm begins to praise his offer of employment 'by the place, and honour of a soldier', yet Kno'well protests,

> Nay, nay, I like not these affected oaths;
> Speak plainly man: what think'st thou of my words?

BRAINWORM: Nothing, sir, but wish my fortunes were as happy as
  my service should be honest.
KNO'WELL: Well, follow me, I'll prove thee, if thy deeds
  Will carry a proportion to thy words.
> (F *EMI* II.v.122–27)

Kno'well, who himself maintains a Lear-like faith in the prelapsarian unity of action and expression, is destined to find out the hard way that there is, after all, a parodic discrepancy – a fatal duality – between the 'words' and the 'deeds' of his follower. Later in the play, when Brainworm's oddly motiveless deception is revealed, Kno'well is shocked most not by his own overall gullibility, but rather specifically by his auditory credulity. 'Is it possible!', he exclaims in wonder to Brainworm, 'that thou should'st disguise thy language so, as I should not know thee?' (F *EMI* V.iii.70–1). Yet Kno'well's folly is close to excusable in Jonson's world; few of the characters in the play speak in their proper tongues. Matthew and Captain Bobadil for instance, are nothing if not purely linguistic creations. Justice Clement testifies to their corporeal insubstantiality by his initial refusal to judge them, on the grounds that they have 'so little of man in 'em' (F *EMI* V.v.2). And although, as we have seen, Matthew is symbolically consumed by the flames that destroy the language of his parodies, Bobadil himself is ultimately dismissed as little more than an empty signifier – he is merely the 'sign o'the soldier' (F *EMI* V.v.49) and not, in fact, a true or in any way substantial 'soldier' at all.

Throughout his career Jonson remained troubled by the fact that although he frequently took care to acknowledge his own indebtedness to others (his own *Timber, or Discoveries*, in which he praises the ability of a poet to 'convert the substance of another poet to [one's] use' is on its title page itself unappetizingly described as the 'reflux' of his 'daily Readings'), he pretended at the same time to deplore the '*fox-like*' thefts of those poets in whose writings 'a man may find whole pages together usurp'd from [another] Author'.[68] Jonson was of course given to including entire passages from the classics in his own works (the speeches of Cicero in *Catiline* [1611], Horace's complaints against contemporary poets in the satires in *Poetaster*, or, as we shall see, Juvenal's description of the fall of Sejanus in his tenth satire in Jonson's own version of that tragedy), while at the same time loudly insisting on his own status as a 'true Artificer'. He resented the necessity of having to relinquish interpretive authority to the ironically designated 'understanding Gentlemen of the ground' (*BF* Induction, 49–50) – as he characterizes his hostile critics in the Induction to *Bartholomew Fair* (1614) – the inattentive yet still fractious spectators who 'dislike all, but mark nothing' (*NI* Dedication, 11). The Intermezzos between the acts of his late play *The Staple of News* (1626) include characters with names such as 'Tatler', 'Expectation', and 'Censure', who seem purposefully to misconstrue the action of the drama, or lament the absence of anti-quated dramatic conventions. Nor was Jonson even beyond creating 'attorneys' who attempt to control the critical response in the theatre itself. Jonson was, we should remember, the first author conspicuously to supervise the printing of his own *Works*. By some accounts, the playwright even went so far as to sit in the printing house, wrangling in his later years with incompetent printers such as John Beale, and attempting to maintain authorial control over his writings even as they went to press.

(VII)

In his analysis of the problems of poetic imitation in *The Anxiety of Influence*, Harold Bloom memorably cited Jonson as an example of one of those fortunate authors who had few significant problems when dealing with the psychological burden imposed on the modern author by the existence of past literary traditions. Jonson's relation to the past, Bloom had argued, was one of 'filial loyalty' – the playwright had 'no anxiety as

to imitation, for to him (refreshingly) art [was] *hard work'.*[69] Jonson was –
in Bloom's own terminology – a predecessor of those 'strong' poets who
were able successfully to manipulate the authority of their forerunners,
and turn the oedipal anxiety of the intra-poetic relationship to their
own creative advantage.

Bloom's reading of Jonson is surprisingly partial, and to some extent
even wrong-headed. Any reader who has made their way through
Jonson's dramas soon realizes that nothing could be further from
the truth. Not only was Jonson constantly anxious about his own use
of the past, he was caught up in a complex cluster of anxieties that
placed the author in a creative position that spun and collided uneasily
between aspects of the past, the present, and the future. In the very act
of making his work public – in the act of turning it over to a critical
audience – Jonson not only exposed both himself and his poetry (and
hence exposed to those who might be aware of its influences) and the
extent of his own indebtedness to past tradition, but further left himself
open to the charge of being too derivative a writer, or even a plagiary. At
the same time, he was aware of the very real possibility that he was not
only rendering his *own* work open to his critical enemies and detractors,
but that he was also making it available as an elemental substance for
subsequent plagiarists, imitators, and parodists.

There would obviously be little purpose in attempting to replace
or otherwise to demolish Blooms's chronological starting point that
posited Milton as the great Sphinx who plagued all subsequent poets
only to replace him with an earlier victim of poetic anxieties in the shape
of Ben Jonson – particularly when generic parody and its concomitant
authorial concerns can be argued in a great many respects to have operated as pervasive if unacknowledged and often marginalized elements
to different degrees in the literature of almost *any* period in literary
history. Jonson and the poets of his generation – not merely the so-
called Tribe of Ben, but the great many others who followed in their
footsteps and continued to write throughout the seventeenth century –
arguably *do* seem to stand, however, at the beginning of the intense and
often intensely personal text-specific parodic dialogues that result in the
more pervasively ventriloquistic literature of the later seventeenth and
eighteenth centuries.

All this is not to suggest that Jonson himself, as one can to some
degree sense even in the darker humour that shadows scenes such as
that which sees Matthew's own parodies disappear in flames, was incapable of recognizing some of the potentially positive aspects of such
an ethos of poetic reappropriation. Many of the more recent critics of

parody and its traditions – Simon Dentith foremost among them – allow within their analyses of the mode ample scope for those senses in which the admittedly polemical rejoinders and transformative techniques of which parody stood capable of encouraging responses of playful or cleverly interrelated rejoinder, but likewise cultivated positive attitudes of transformation; at best, parodies could compel all writers to consider the ways in which they necessarily dealt with past accomplishment when they 'made language their own', and the extent to which they invariably participated in a series of evaluative responses to previous chains of utterance and alluded with evaluation to previous texts.[70] Reconsiderations such as these – those that draw together the insights of critics from Bakhtin to those such as Genette, Rose, Hutcheon, Dane, and a great many others – help expand our notions of parody so as to render it not merely a two-dimensional weapon of polemical attack, but to see it as a mode that has played both conservative and subversive roles within a much wider extent of literary culture than has previously been acknowledged. Ben Jonson happens to be a poet and a parodist who stood in a particularly peculiar historical position, and one whose own abilities rendered him capable of recognizing the significance of that position, and (to whatever extent he finally thought possible) attempting to effect or at least to emphasize its place and pivotal role in literary and dramatic invention. In Jonson's earliest humours comedies and comical satires we witness the response of a man who is himself deeply concerned but not yet dangerously worried; he would throughout his career admittedly be a great deal less capable than others of acknowledging some of the more positively creative aspects of parodic play and response. Even we, today, seem to react with much less anxiety than an author such as Jonson might have done to the possibilities of parody and its tendencies to cultivate an interrelatedness of certain often more established and authoritative forms or poetic 'kinds' with, or between, other less elevated levels of discourse. Recent critics such as Harold Love, for example, have begun to explore the curious relationships that could exist in the period (as, indeed, they do now) between such trends of discourse that connect private and often personal gossip, on the one hand, to the formulation of public or state lampoon and satire, on the other. Love is one among many who have started to examine the ways in which the latter types of formal parody and satire were within a few short decades – among a single generations of poets – to develop 'from being the product[s] of isolated disaffection', into something that was rather 'the work of a circle of recognized poets, frequently operating in collaboration'.[71] Other recent studies have continued to explore this shift of interpretive and critical power from the individual to a larger public sphere, and the growth of what critic Mark Knights has now described as the growth of a national political culture, and have turned to examine in 'the shift towards a representative society, a crisis of public discourse and credibility, and a political enlightenment rooted in local and national partisan conflict'.[72] It is within such very crises of discourse, credibility, and partisan conflict that parody was to play such a significant role. As a younger man, and in the very earliest of his creations, Jonson perhaps remained capable of remaining open to some of the more positive aspects of such a shift. Within the space of only a very few years, however, his attitude would appear distinctly to have darkened – and to have darkened to such an extent that the way ahead was to be not merely perilous, but very probably fatal.

(VIII)

Having begun this chapter with a look at the bonfire that concludes Jonson's early *Every Man in His Humour*, and having noted that one of the responses available to the already shaken and even slightly hysterical guardians of linguistic authority in that play when faced with Matthew's parodies was to burn them, I find it is useful to move towards a conclusion with an examination of a similar book-burning scene in one of Jonson's slightly later dramas. The brief examination of one important aspect of his 1603 *Sejanus, His Fall* that follows – and of the contrast that the playwright seems to make between the even slightly imaginative if dangerous possibilities of text-specific parody in the first humours play and the rather more ominous sense of linguistic instability that he depicts in the subsequent tragedy – is intended in this instance merely, if only anecdotally, to anticipate some of the more wide-ranging concerns and anxieties that will begin to characterize a new literary era. I have chosen to look at *Sejanus*, in particular, because there seems to be a fundamental, underlying similarity between the ironically 'miraculous' and transformative 'gift' of parody as it is first defined by Kno'well in *Every Man in His Humour* and the grimly pessimistic linguistic apocalypse that concludes Jonson's later tragedy.

It is generally acknowledged that *Sejanus* itself represented a significant turning point in Jonson's dramatic career. Some critics have gone so far as to argue that the tragedy is in fact among the first of the dramatist's works that explicitly (and not always with any great deal of restraint) explores the relationship between 'the playwright and his public'.[73] More specifically, the play is thought to have heralded a change – and a change of the sort that would in time grow to be characterized by a great deal of animosity – in that same relationship. Clearly, Jonson – although he had been led somewhat arrogantly to anticipate in the Prologue to the work that had immediately preceded *Sejanus*, his *Poetaster, or the Arraignment* (1602), that he was capable of standing 'above [the] injuries' of his critics – had in fact been fiercely angered by the public failure of the earlier *Poetaster*, which had appeared on the stage early in 1601.[74] Clearly, he had begun that same work – one in his series of three similar plays in the *poetomachia* that had been written in such quick succession, and that dealt largely with the issues of legal satire – with high hopes. Even the allegorical figure of 'Envy' herself, who addresses the audience in that play's Prologue, professes to be distraught when she learns that the new drama is to be set in Rome. How could a work the action of which was to take place within the Augustan age – the great Golden Age of Classical Literature and one that was, moreover, to feature in its action figures no less illustrious than Ovid and Horace themselves – prove, among the discriminating audience that had been assembled at Blackfriars, in any way to be a failure? Be that as it may, the spectators on that occasion appear to have been rather less than completely entertained by the personal vendetta of the dramatist's Chapel play. Jonson's drama (which would later be grouped as one of those works frequently described as his 'Classical Satires') proved a peculiarly odd combination of romantic comedy, straightforward classical translation, and highly personal satiric portraiture. The plot was complicated and confused, its action was not particularly engaging, and the entire effort appeared to be completely obsessed with issues of poetic authority, ownership, and appropriation. In the *'Apologetical Dialogue, To the Reader'* that was later published alongside the text in 1602, Jonson (presented in the guise of a 'character' designated simply as the 'Author') engages in a post-mortem regarding the work with two of his colleagues, Nasutus (whose name indicates that he possesses a taste for satirical wit) and Polyposus (possibly meant to suggest that he is one capable of judging matters from many different points of view). As the Author bitterly complains of the play's public reception,

> Oh, this would make a learned and liberal soul
> To rive his stained quill, up to the back,
> And damn his long-watched labours to the fire;
> Things that were born when none but the still night,
> And his dumb candle saw his pinching throes:

Were not his own free merit a more crown
Unto his travails than their reeling claps.
This 'tis, that strikes me silent, seals my lips,
And apts me, rather to sleep out my time,
Than I would waste it in contemned strifes
With these vile *Ibides,* these unclean birds,
That make their mouths their clysters, and still purge
From their hot entrails. But I leave the monsters
To their own fate.[75]

Nasutus and Polyposus have strikingly little to argue against the author's angry renunciation of the stage. By the end of their discussion, however, Ben Jonson the 'Author' appears for all the vehemence of his complaint suddenly to have been inspired (as he so often is and will continue to be) by the sense of a new resolve. He announces his intention to 'try/If Tragedy have a more kind aspect' than comedy. 'Leave me', he immediately instructs his two companions,

> There's something come into my thought
> That must, and shall be sung high and aloof,
> Safe from the wolves' black jaw, and the dull asses' hoof.[76]

Jonson, in other words, has decided that the time has come for him to write a proper tragedy. And it was no simple accident, of course, that parody was to play such a critical role in this new work.

Others, too, have noted that *Sejanus* 'represents a crucial point in Jonson's development as a dramatist'.[77] As his editor Philip Ayres has observed first with reference to the dramatist's general outlook, and then with regard to the direction from which he approaches his historical source material in the proposed tragedy,

> It is the first play of Jonson's to express a thoroughly pessimistic outlook on the human condition, and the first to concentrate its actions exclusively about a central intrigue. It is the criminal or quasi-criminal mind, in *Sejanus*, as in *Volpone* and *The Alchemist*, that now fires Jonson's imagination. . . . The villains have the power in *Sejanus*, and in this respect it anticipates the . . . earlier comedies. Jonson is no longer a strong presence on his own stage.[78]

A considerable amount of debate has been devoted to the question as to whether Jonson – in his stated desire to underscore the play's moral criticism that the end of the republic was brought about by a combination of immorality, excess of luxury, and calculated distortions of the truth of political and historical matters – made more effective use of his original material in his capacity as a historian, or as a poet. As Ayres, again, notes of the nature of this debate,

> This material is handled creatively, and Hazlitt's description in his lecture on Beaumont and Fletcher, Ben Jonson, Ford and Massinger of the play as a "mosaic" of "translated bits" does it an injustice. It has been estimated that no more than a quarter of the play is translation or paraphrase.[79]

Even so, such an apparent re-evaluation yet manages to emphasize the degree to which much of the play seems indeed to a large extent to stand as a cento-like collection of various pieces that have been positioned so as primarily to emphasize messages that were new and different from those that they had, at first, argued, or for which they had stood in their original contexts. One reviewer of a recent (2005) and unexpectedly successful production of the play by the Royal Shakespeare Company at Stratford observed: 'Though it could never please the asinine mob, its thick marginalia showed it to be a work of profound scholarship, a mosaic of subtle translations from Tacitus and others.' As the same reviewer noted laconically, 'Funny things never happen on the way to Tacitus' Forum.'[80]

The only actual dramatic models to which Jonson would have turned when recalling his studies of Latin tragedy, of course, were necessarily those of the surviving works of Lucius Anneaeus Seneca (*c*. AD 5–65). Only nine of Seneca's tragedies had been preserved, and although they had each themselves been written as adaptations modelled on those of his Greek predecessors, they were in truth increasingly acknowledged as rather slow-moving if rhetorical sophisticated pieces. They were unlikely ever to have been performed before an audience on the Roman stage. In fact, much of the style and structure of these examples of the Senecan tragic mode had been the subject of some significant controversy in Italy not very many years earlier in the fifteenth century, when those same, several models that Seneca appeared to have handed down to posterity as the pattern for any respectably serious drama had been attacked onstage by one Giangiorgio Trissino in his own vernacular tragedy, *Sofonisba* (1515). Trissino's dramatic principles had eventually, themselves, suffered something of a counter-attack thanks to the popularity of Giambattista Giraldi Cinthio's more traditional *Orbecche*

(1541), and, somewhat surprisingly, the success of the latter's revenge tragedy – one that more closely and pointedly followed the established Senecan model – seems to have won the day.[81]

Jonson's own instincts as a classicist, of course, were unlikely to have led him in any direction other than Seneca in the first place. The well-known humanist educator Aeneas Sylvius Piccolomini, afterwards Pius II, in his *De Liberorum Educatione,* written in 1450 on a Latin model and particularly concerned with issues of possible styles of writing, had reiterated to his readers precisely the sort of advice that might very well have come from the mouth of Camden himself. 'In tragedy, a most valuable discipline', the humanist noted,

> we have Seneca alone. In speech, we aim at dignity and grace. Tragedy present us with the one, comedy with the other. Moreover in reading the Dramatists, let the master win his pupil to judge characters and situations, with grave warnings against all pleadings in favour of wrong-doing.[82]

The form of a Senecan tragedy demanded a structure of five acts, with the actions of the principal figures remarked upon by a chorus – an entity reduced by the Roman author, however, to a single individual rather than (as in his Greek precedents) a larger group of commentators. Senecan drama similarly emphasized lengthier speeches and mono-logues as the most effective means of forensic address. His work helped further to develop the creation of dramatic characters as exemplifying certain 'types' of individuals; similarly, it encouraged the use of specific and still-recognizable dramatic devices (such as the use of stage 'asides') and allowed for the presentation of supposedly confidential conversa-tions among certain characters similarly to be 'overheard' by members of the audience. Perhaps the most significant aspect of Senecan tragedy for Jonson, however, was, as noted above, the emphasis his plays placed on strong issues of proper ethical action and morality (*sententiae*), and the related dangers posed by any unrestrained passion, or any such similar submission to the hazardous extremes of human emotion. The specific passage of *Sejanus* that I wish to consider in the pages that remain can at the very least serve as a heuristic stimulus to a further considera-tion of Jonson's own acute awareness of the problems related to the precise manner in which literary (and political) society was preparing itself to deal with the linguistic instability and the aggressive parodic potentialities of the new poetic age.

The substance of the basic plot of Jonson's *Sejanus* is itself, in actual fact, relatively straightforward. Although the dramatist's concern for the efficacy of his moral rhetoric and his faithful adherence to the techniques of his dramatic precedent can obscure the work for some modern readers, it has legitimately been asserted that 'the good and evil characters are just as easily identifiable as in [Jonson's] earlier works'.[83] The drama draws on its obvious and relatively well-known historical sources (primarily Tacitus' *Annals* and the *History of the Romans* written in the later Greek of Dio Cassius) to detail some of the specific events that had taken place in the reign of the Roman Emperor Tiberius Caesar Augustus (AD 14–37). The death of the emperor's adopted son and heir apparent, the popular Germanicus, whilst in Syria in AD 19, was suspected by many to have been undertaken so as to allow for the succession, rather, of Tiberius' own son, Drusus. The subsequent death in AD 23 of Drusus senior himself, however (he was later revealed to have been poisoned with the help of his own wife Livilla), led to a period dominated by one of Tiberius' most trusted aides and the closest of his advisers, Sejanus. Sejanus, however, remained only a knight, but not a senator (an important distinction). Although the court of noble Romans seemed content, initially, to stand by passively as the influence and power of Sejanus grew to a degree unprecedented in one of his status, the widow of the hugely popular Germanicus, Agrippina (herself mother to Drusus junior, Nero, and Caligula – each of whom stood in line to the throne), was quick to warn her own friends of the threat posed by Tiberius' favourite. She specifically counselled her sons to stand bravely against the ambitions of the corrupt Sejanus. Tiberius himself had been encouraged by Sejanus to retire from Rome to Campania in AD 26, where he famously settled on the island of Capri – a retreat that he was rarely ever to leave again. Sejanus had by this stage established himself in an unrivalled position above both consuls and senators; suspicions circulating within the court that he looked to attain supreme power for himself were further aroused by his attempt to marry Drusus' widow (a match that Tiberius refused to allow). A group of nobles associated with the clan of Germanicus – the husband of Agrippina who had been poisoned at Antioch – eventually succeeded in arousing Tiberius' suspicions regarding the man whom he had only recently appointed as his colleague and consul. In October AD 31, thanks to a clever scenario arranged in part through the actions of a group of senators under the secret leadership of the new prefect Naevius Sutorius Macro, Sejanus was arrested. He was soon executed. His son and daughter were likewise killed within a matter of days; his wife Apicata committed suicide.

Sejanus' followers were tracked down and massacred with a violence that shocked even those of his contemporaries who might otherwise have remained rather blasé about such carnage. In Jonson's version of the story, which remains to almost all extents fairly close to his original sources, the lines that separate the good from the bad, again, are drawn with absolute clarity. The noble friends and followers of Agrippina constantly lament the loss of the republic and of its former heroes – the likes of Brutus and Cato. The voice of the satirist is frequently located in characters such as that of the senator Lucius Arruntius, who – with colleagues that most prominently include his associates Lepidus, Sabinus, and Silius – cannot refrain from castigating the ambitions of Sejanus and the illicit and licentious passivity of Tiberius.[84]

Another significant and particularly devious critic of Sejanus and his tactics, however, is notably present in Jonson's play in the guise of the writer and historian Cremutius Cordus. It is worth recalling that in his *Poetaster*, Jonson had attempted more openly, and in the guise of the poet Horace, to position himself on the stage as a satirical poet – an open critic of the stage language and contemporary usage. Moreover, as Jonson's editors Herford and Simpson likewise noted of the playwright's technique in that work, he had no less obviously 'used the court of Augustus as a vehicle for unmeasured personal ridicule of his contemporaries'.[85] In his subsequent tragedy, however, if, as later critics and editors such as Ayres note, 'it is impossible to establish beyond all doubt that in *Sejanus* Jonson intentionally presented any historical analogies for specific contemporary political events or realities', he certainly appears through the character of the writer Cordus to attempt to do precisely that (although it remains true that the Earl of Northampton in 1604, before the Quarto version of the play was published, noted the contemporary relevance of the work as well, particularly charging Jonson with creating a play that was in its sympathies 'popish').[86] Cordus, admittedly, is presented specifically as a historian, and not a poet; yet all the techniques that are said to charac-terize his work align him with the new kinds of parodist and parody that Jonson had begun to see all around him. Jonson, that is to say, deliber-ately aligned the positive possibilities of 'parody', in its grandest sense, with the blunt and controversial historical chronicles that were being written by Cordus, in which the nobility of the men of the past was to be contrasted with the present degenerate age of Sejanus. 'Throughout the relevant section of the [Quarto text] we have, of course', Ayres reminds the modern reader, 'Jonson's marginal notes reminding us of his "integrity in the story" – and immediately after the trial of Silius we have Cremu-tius Cordus, the historian accused of shadowing present times in his treatment of past times, insisting on the integrity of his presentation of history'.[87] Jonson's own visual presentation, in other words – itself structured in his volume quite literally as a parody in its dense presentation of parallel literary texts – works if only to underscore the fact that within the play itself Cordus is similarly rendering the absurd and dangerous present to be little more than a parodic and farcical re-enactment of the genuinely noble achievements of the past. (In most modern editions of the tragedy, of course, the marginal notes indicating Jonson's original Latin sources have been eliminated. The Manchester 'Revel's Plays' edition points the reader to these sources with admirable thoroughness, however, though noting that the Quarto's 'marginal annotations are useless to most modern readers, who cannot go to the early editions Jonson cites, and may not read Latin'.)[88] 'As Cordus learns to his cost', as Katherine Duncan-Jones commented simply, 'historical parallels are risky'.[89]

Act I of *Sejanus* serves largely as an extended portrayal of the manner in which Sejanus' followers will ape and cater to the lawlessness of the emperor and his second-in-command in any manner necessary to their own self-advancement. In so doing, they are presented as quite literally imitating, cringing, and – yes – parodying their deplorable masters. Their self-conscious mimicry nicely sets the stage for the accusations subsequently to be made against the morally upstanding Cordus, who is however no less capable, as noted, of using his own techniques of parodic reference and imitation to make the necessary salient points regarding the current state of political affairs. In Act III of *Sejanus*, the writings of Cordus are gathered before the Senate and – in a scene strikingly reminiscent of the bonfire that had taken place in Jonson's earlier humours comedy – destroyed. Cordus, who has been writing a historical account that justly praises Germanicus and condemns the ostentation of Sejanus, has in other words found it impossible even to laud the Roman virtues of the past without awakening the fears of the corrupt court of Tiberius' Rome. In a persuasive speech in his own defence, Cordus protests that his words are 'innocent' (*Sej* III.407), yet the Senate, operating under direction from Sejanus himself, decrees that the torch be set to his recently completed annals:

> COTTA: [G]ive order, that his books be burnt,
> To the *Ædiles*.
> SEJANUS: You have well advised.
> AFER: It fits not such licentious things should live
> To upbraid the age.
> ARRUNTIUS: If the age were good, they might.

LATIARIS: Let 'em be burnt.
GALLUS: All sought, and burnt, today.

(Sej III.465–9)

Again, the scene is remarkably similar to that presented in *Every Man in His Humour*. Yet the situation dramatized finally and with humour in the earlier play has been completely turned on its head. The language that ultimately dominates Jonson's tragedy is not the unhesitating truth of Cordus or his associate Arruntius (nor is it even, as in the early humours comedy, the temporary linguistic authority represented by a figure such as Justice Clement), but the obviously false and insidious dialogue of – at first – Sejanus, and then of Tiberius and, finally, Macro himself. Observers such as Sabinus and Lepidus may well remark that the mere censorship of Cordus' writings will only increase the power and forcefulness of their message:

LEPIDUS: Let 'em be burnt! Oh how ridiculous
           Appears the *Senate's* brainless diligence,
           Who think they can, with present power, extinguish
           The memory of all succeeding times!
SABINUS: 'Tis true, when (contrary) the punishment
           Of wit, doth make the authority increase.
           Nor do they ought, that use this cruelty
           Of interdiction, and this rage of burning;
           But purchase to themselves rebuke, and shame,
           And to the writers an eternal name.

(Sej III.471–80)

Nevertheless, the 'brainless diligence' of the Senate appears, in this instance at least, initially to have been quite effective. Although Cordus' writings are, admittedly, not designated as parodies but exist more as parallel histories that make use of deliberate techniques of parodic comparison to underscore their message of morality, the threat of *any* inscripted alternative to the stability of the dominant, tyrannical linguistic mode is significant. In the earlier comedy, Jonson had allowed for the possible efficacy of 'the punishment of wit'. The burning of Matthew's parodies in the bonfire in the closing scene of *Every Man in His Humour* was a harsh but arguably necessary act carried out by the appointed guardians of linguistic authority. By the time Jonson came to write *Sejanus* a mere five years later, that very same bonfire has itself become problematized. On the one hand, Jonson seems clearly to be acknowledging the vicious nature of a more hostile literary climate. He seems even to be admitting the futility of any such brutal attempts at literary discipline and censorship. In the five years that separate the two plays, Jonson appears to have lost almost all of his faith in the ability of poets or writers of any kind to maintain at least *some* kind of authority over their own work. He seems also to have lost faith in his earlier supposition that a 'true and natural language' will perforce emerge victorious in any struggle with linguistic duplicity, or in any contest against – at least – the unabashedly appropriative proclivities of the new literary aesthetic.

On closer examination, *Sejanus* presents us with a vision of a world wherein the proper relationship between words and meaning has been broken down only to be conveniently reassembled to serve the purposes of faction and deceit. The Rome of *Sejanus* is a Rome wherein the most threatening possible combinations (in Jonson's eyes) of the parodic dynamic between form and content have, as in an incoherent and incomprehensible nightmare, prevailed. The inherent instability of 'the popular air,/Or voice of men' (*Sej* V.695–6) has been further weakened by the efforts of Sejanus – pointedly described as the 'voice' of Caesar's world (*Sej* II.56) – to blur the linguistic boundaries that had formerly worked to separate truth from falsehood. Arruntius at several points in the play laments Sejanus' tendency to flatter the sounds of words 'ere their sense be meant' (*Sej* I.507). He particularly comments on his enemy's canny ability to take parodic advantage of 'the space/Between the breast, and lips' (*Sej* III.96–7) – the same space that serves, in no small measure, as the active sphere within which the parodist himself operates. Latiaris also observes that Sejanus' grace is 'merely but lip-good' (*Sej* I.410), and notes with regret that he does not have 'a mind allied unto his words' (*Sej* I.401). Indeed, so great is the disjunction between words and meaning in the apocalyptic world of this play, that it has become dangerous to commit one's self to writing, or even to casual, open speech. 'Our words/How innocent so ever, are made crimes', Silius observes nervously in the play's opening lines, 'We shall not shortly dare to tell our dreams/Or think, but 'twill be treason' (*Sej* I.67–70). In Act III, of course, Silius himself acknowledges the 'words' (*Sej* III.299) that the rhetorician Afer has manipulated and misconstrued so as to convict him of treason. Cordus is likewise condemned in the Senate for having written historical annals on times 'somewhat queasy to be touched' (*Sej* I.82). Sabinus finally voices his disdain for his own time:

> When our writings are,
> By any envious instruments that dare
> Apply them to the guilty made to speak
> What they will have, to fit their tyrannous wreak?
>
> (*Sej* IV.132–5)

Arruntius is shortly thereafter driven to despair by the restrictions imposed by Tiberius and Sejanus upon all means of expression:

> ARRUNTIUS: May I pray to Jove,
> In secret, and be safe? Aye, or aloud?
> With open wishes? So I do not mention
> Tiberius, or Sejanus? Yes, I must,
> If I speak out. 'Tis hard, that. May I think
> And not be racked? What danger is't to dream?
> Talk in one's sleep? Or cough? Who knows the law?
>
> (*Sej* IV.300–6)

Throughout the play, the characters of Sejanus and Tiberius – assuming the roles of actors, dramatists, and theatrical managers – have monopolized the sources of truth and discourse; it is they who remain at all times the internalized poets and parodists of the drama. The rhetorical eloquence of Tiberius in the Senate, for example, is characterized by Arruntius as a 'well-acted' performance (*Sej* III.105). Sejanus, in the same scene, openly takes control of and parodically appropriates the language of the drama when he provides Varro with a carefully scripted set of accusations against Silius. 'Here be your notes', he tells Varro as he passes him the pages and assumes the role of a demonic coach, 'What points to touch at, read: / Be cunning in them' (*Sej* III.6–7). Tiberius, too, manipulates the action of the play through language when he finally orchestrates the downfall of Sejanus himself through the superbly crafted rhetoric of his letter to the Senate in Act V. Although in private Tiberius' language can operate with the same fast-paced tension of Sejanus' dialogue (as in *Sej* II.163–330) – or even break down to the point of inarticulation (*Sej* III.515) – the emperor's public discourse remains at all times a fluid and tightly controlled flow of speech that (parody-like) anticipates and incorporates potential responses. The latter half of the play even finds Tiberius assuming the offstage role of an all-powerful actor-manager; Arruntius continues the parodic theatrical metaphor when he tells us that Tiberius remains at Capri, '[a]cting his tragedies with a comic face' (*Sej* IV.379).

Yet as poets and parodists, both Tiberius and Sejanus appear to lack the creative skill required for the production of truly convincing drama – *and* of truly creative parody. Their dual control over the dialogue of the play may be confident and certain, but it is at the same time strictly mechanical. The metaphorical language of the drama subtly matches the roles played by Tiberius and Sejanus as poets, dramatists, and parodists, with the less imaginative tasks of 'building', 'weaving', and 'forging'; individuals are reduced to mere tools or, more accurately, 'instruments' in their hands. Livia chooses Lygdus as the most suitable 'instrument' to administer poison to Drusus (*Sej* II.11) – someone to be 'wrought/To the undertaking' (*Sej* II.18). Macro is referred to as a 'new instrument' raised against Sejanus (*Sej* Arg. 28) or, alternatively, as the 'organ' through which Tiberius must work (*Sej* III. 649). Tiberius is even at times reduced to an unthinking agent of destruction – a plodding juggernaut – who can 'turn aside those blocks' that stand in the way of Sejanus' political progress (*Sej* II.392).

Moreover, the drama itself begins to assume the status of a complic-ated engine – it becomes a machine that relentlessly but calculatedly plots the annihilation of its own *dramatis personae*. Sejanus suggests to Tiberius that they allow Agrippina and her supporters to proceed as usual until 'in the engine, they are caught, and slain' (*Sej* II.269). Shortly thereafter Silius suggests that he and his companions attend the Senate to 'see what's in the forge' (*Sej* II.495); upon discovering the Senate's purpose to destroy his own life, Silius then dismisses their hypocritical adherence to the law as a mere 'engine', or a 'net of Vulcan's filing' (*Sej* III.245). Sabinus and Silius had opened the drama with the comment that their success at court had been hindered by the fact that they were 'no good engineers' (*Sej* I.4). Arruntius later describes Sejanus as an artisan 'weaving/Some curious cobweb to catch flies' (*Sej* III.23–4), while Tiberius observes to himself that Sejanus has been 'wrought into our trust;/Woven in our design' (*Sej* III.625).

This mechanical control over the action and the language of the play is destined to continue – through the character of Macro – even as the stage drama itself draws to a close. The language of truth – the language of (among others) Cordus, Arruntius, and Lepidus – is never allowed to emerge with any positive force in the course of the play. Although Arruntius and Lepidus predict (in the passage quoted earlier) the ultimate triumph in time of Cordus' writings over their unjust censorship, Jonson himself offers no real hope in *Sejanus* that such a victory is inevitable or even likely. Indeed, on almost every level, the play works to thwart the possibility of any such ending; the drama systematically undercuts the hopes and the predictions that history has anything more to offer than an unending cycle of greed, flattery, and persecution. *Sejanus* also functions to undermine the hopes that the myriad possibilities of a textually appropriative aesthetic can ever be employed to any purpose other than that which is destructive.

In a provocative discussion of Shakespeare's *King Lear*, the critic Stephen Booth once proposed that what finally makes Lear's tragedy so unnerving, so unendurable, and so outrageously unacceptable to us as theatregoers is what Booth himself chose to call its 'indefinition'. Booth was referring to the play's purposeful violation of its own audience's eminently reasonable expectations as to just where and how its tragedy should end – its relentless and catastrophic breaking of dramatic delimitations and theatrical boundaries.[90] Lear's tragedy continues with painful intensity *after* the dramatic action and language that ought formally to have marked its conclusion has taken place onstage. The semi-ritualistic speech announcing social and political reformation that finally does close the drama, articulated by Albany at V.iii, rings false and ineffective in our ears. *Sejanus* resembles the Shakespearean tragedy in nothing so much as in its similarly daring and self-conscious manipulation of dramatic form – in its willingness to press beyond those formal boundaries ostensibly intended structurally to delimit and to confine its own tragic action. In *Sejanus*, as in Shakespeare's *Lear*, the choric response that pretends to announce the positive values of the drama falls short of the ruthless horrors depicted in the play (or specifically, in Jonson's tragedy, the outrages daily committed in the name of Caesar). The familiar and normally reassuring voice of the chorus is in fact a response that is appropriated and parodied towards the end of Jonson's drama by Sejanus himself. A brief look at the final moments of the tragedy will demonstrate precisely what I mean.

The closing scenes of Jonson's play depict the popular regret and political confusion that immediately follows the death of Sejanus at the hands of the Roman mob. Nuntius arrives among the assembled veterans of Sejanus' intrigues and ambition, announcing further news of their former enemy. 'What can be added?', a doubting and seemingly uninterested Lepidus asks, 'We know him dead' (*Sej* V.823–4). The harrowing account of the fate of Sejanus' son and daughter then follows (*Sej* V.828–44). Their mother Apicata, Nuntius further informs the gathering, herself had evoked the language of apocalypse to question the cruel injustice of her children's death:

> Her drowned voice gat up above her woes:
> And with such black and bitter execrations,
> (As might affright the gods, and force the sun
> Run backward to the East, nay, make the old
> Deformed Chaos rise again, to o'erwhelm
> Them, us and all the world) she fills the air; . . .
>
> (*Sej* V.855–60)

The sickening see-saw movement or oscillation that has characterized both the action and the rhetoric of the drama, however, now infects the Roman mob itself. No sooner have they killed Sejanus than they begin to regret the gruesome outcome of their riot. 'Part are so stupid, or so flexible', Nuntius says of the mob,

> As they believe him innocent; all grieve:
> And some, whose hands yet reek with his warm blood,
> And grip the part which they did tear of him,
> Wish him collected, and created new.
>
> (*Sej* V.873–7)

The people's desire for a Sejanus thus 'created new' testifies to a like desire to rebuild the state in his image. The rise of the equally unscrupulous Macro (and the dubious promise of Caligula) suggests to Jonson's audience, at least, that they will have very little difficulty indeed in doing so. The stoic response to the play's catastrophe – the sum of the values posited by characters such as Arruntius, Cordus, and Lepidus in the face of Macro's immanent rise to power and the increasing tyranny of Tiberius – had already been voiced prior to Nuntius' account of the violent death of Sejanus himself (*Sej* V.705–35). As the drama draws to a close Arruntius and Terentius can do little more than reiterate their ineffective platitudes about the vagaries of Fortune, and once again warn against such avoidable sins as pride and blasphemy:

> ARRUNTIUS: Forbear, you things,
>   That stand upon the pinnacle of state,
>   To boast your slippery height; when you do fall,

> You pash your selves to pieces, ne'er to rise:
> And he that lends you pity, is not wise.
> TERENTIUS: Let this example move the insolent man,
> Not to grow proud, and careless of the gods:
> It is an odious wisdom, to blaspheme,
> Much more to slighten, or deny their powers.
> For, whom the morning saw so great, and high,
> Thus low, and little, 'fore the, even doth lie.
>
> *(Sej* V.883–93)

Jonson might well have protested that in ending the drama on such a distinctly sombre note, he was merely remaining faithful to the narrative of his several historical sources. In the account of the death of Sejanus' children, for example, Jonson had drawn with little alteration from Book LVIII of Dio's *Roman History*. In his *Annals*, Tacitus included not only a more fully detailed embellished account of the murder but a more general consolation regarding the uneven distribution of Fortune's rewards as well – a consolation that seems in many ways to provide the only possible response to the conclusive despair of the drama.

Yet the most compelling explanation for the fact that the traditional Roman virtues announced by Arruntius, Terentius, and Lepidus at the end of *Sejanus* fall so far short of the audience's demand for a moral ending to the play does not lie chiefly in the simple observation that Jonson was anxious to remain faithful to the historical truth of his source-texts; nor, one might add, is such a 'conclusion' unsatisfactory because the very qualities of balance and restraint that are meant to characterize stoicism are, in and of themselves, of a fundamentally anti-dramatic nature. Strikingly, Jonson's primary source for the actual description of the death of Sejanus was neither Tacitus nor Dio, but Juvenal. Juvenal's tenth satire contains a vivid description of Sejanus' fall that Jonson translated directly into the dialogue of his drama (*Sej* V.786–98) – indeed, the prevalence of the dismemberment imagery in the play both to anticipate Sejanus' particular fate and to point to the faction that has torn apart the Roman 'body' politic itself works to make Juvenal's satire a thematic and imaginative cornerstone of Jonson's tragedy. The *positive* response that Juvenal had finally offered in the face of human vanity and folly, however, is placed in the tragedy not only in the mouths of Arruntius and Lepidus, but is echoed parodically in

Jonson's drama by no one other than Sejanus himself. Juvenal's central stoic response to the mutability of fortune –

> nullem numen habes, si sit prudentia, nos te,
> nos facimus, Fortuna, deam caeloque locamus.[91]

– is parodically and very specifically echoed in Sejanus' *own* avowed scorn for the divinity of Fortune:

> Tell Proud Jove,
> Between his power and thine, there is no odds.
> 'Twas only fear first in the world made gods.
>
> (*Sej* II.160–2)

The only possible 'answer' in a world that truly illustrates the vanity of human wishes, in other words, is in Jonson's tragedy pre-empted and parodied by Sejanus, to be replaced only by a gesture of despair. In having Sejanus mimic and parodically echo these crucial lines of Juvenal's satire, Jonson effectively replaced the Roman poet's single potentially hopeful response to the question as to whether or not there is, ultimately, anything worth praying for ('Nil ergo octabunt homines?') with the sardonic maxims and displaced parodies of his own tragic antagonist. The dark and nihilistic mood that shrouds Jonson's tragedy is, finally, countered (or complemented) only by the grim prediction that human affairs are once again about to embark on the Tacitian cycle of history that has only just witnessed the rise and fall of Sejanus. The names may have been changed (now it is Macro, not Sejanus, who will play the role as the minion of Tiberius), but the elemental stuff of the tragedy remains – absurdly and inevitably – much the same. The possibilities of parody and linguistic appropriation, Jonson's drama would seem likewise to conclude, are now firmly in the hands of the literary enemy. Parody has for Jonson, and within only a matter of a few years, developed from being a potential threat into constituting a truly deadly enemy – an enemy now woven by the casual appropriations of the warnings of Juvenal within the very fabric of society, and within the language through which it is compelled to express itself.

Jonson would until the end of his life remain close to desperately anxious and certainly pessimistic as to just how the final outcome of what he continued to view as this deeply consequential struggle against the forces of parody was to be played out. The catastrophic destruction of his own famous library in the autumn of 1623 in a fire that almost

completely destroyed his lifelong and painstakingly acquired collection of volumes of Greek and Roman writers, antiquities, Renaissance
volumes, manuscripts, and a tremendous amount of other scholarship
cannot but further help underscore the less visually spectacular but by no
means less insidiously damaging and increasing threat posed by literary
parodists and their so-called 'work' – the threat of writers who, after all,
in a like manner 'consumed' the work of others. As if again to remind
him of such dangers, the little material that remained in his collection
only narrowly escaped a similar conflagration just ten years later. The
older Jonson pretended to be capable of joking about such events. In his
well-known 'Execration upon Vulcan', in which he seems only naturally
and personally to blame the ancient master of fire for having instigated
the destruction of his collection, he initially dismisses the deity with the
half-hearted curse: '[a] Pox on your flameship'. He ends the poem with
the simple request, referring perhaps to his country's foreign enemies
but more pointedly to his detractors and literary rivals, that in future
Vulcan at least

> On both sides do your mischiefs with delight;
> Blow up and ruin, mine and countermine,
> Make your petards, and granats, all your fine
> Engines of murder, and receive the praise
> Of massacring mankind so many ways.[92]

Parody, Jonson would insist till his dying breath, should be among the
very first of those dangerous enemies to learning and to the emulations
inspired by genuinely creative endeavour that ought more properly to be
set to the torch in this world. Otherwise, he suggests, the mode and its
many accomplices had already established themselves in a nearly perfect
position to begin their distastefully unoriginal scheme of effectively
'massacring mankind'. Vulcan himself could afford sit this one out.

4
Minding True Things by Mock'ries: The *Henry V* Chorus and the Question of Shakespearean Parody

> [W]hat I publish is no true Poëme ... in the want of a proper Chorus, whose Habite, and Moodes are such, and so difficult, as not any whom I have seene since the Auntients ... have yet come in the way off. Nor is it needful, or almost possible, in these our Times ... to observe the auld state and splendour of Drammatick Poëmes, with preservation of any popular delight.
>
> – Ben Jonson, *Sejanus*, 'To the Reader'[1]

In the first edition of his *Dictionary of the English Language* (1755), Samuel Johnson defines a dramatic chorus as 'the persons who are supposed to behold what passes in the acts of a tragedy, and sing their sentiments between the acts'.[2] The quotation that Johnson has chosen to illustrate this usage is drawn from the opening lines of Shakespeare's *Henry V* (1599), in which the Prologue offers a general apology for the supposedly inadequate resources of the theatre, and humbly solicits the assistance of the audience in transforming the unworthy scaffold of the stage into a venue respectable enough to represent the epic splendour of Henry's continental victories. 'For 'tis your thoughts', the Prologue reminds the audience at the beginning of Shakespeare's history,

> that now must deck our kings,
> Carry them here and there, jumping o'er times,
> Turning th'accomplishment of many years
> Into an hourglass – for the which supply,
> Admit me Chorus to this history,
> Who, Prologue-like, your humble patience pray,
> Gently to hear, kindly to judge, our play.[3]

Johnson's powerfully synthetic intellect appears in this particular instance, however, to have led his normally sound lexicographical instinct for clarity slightly astray. The definition itself, insofar as one can even make sense of it, seems specifically to refer to the functions and conventions of the dramatic chorus as they were first set out in antiquity. Johnson's terms would appear specifically to define the sort of chorus that his classically trained reader might encounter in a continuous Greek tragedy (such as Aeschylus' *Agamemnon*, for example, or Sophocles' *Oedipus Rex*) and even in Greek comedies (such as Aristophanes' *The Frogs*) in which an otherwise passive and unified group of spectators literally *sing* and *dance* their editorializing comments (their 'sentiments') throughout the course of the play; the chorus in an ancient Greek theatre might count anywhere from 12 to 15 members in a tragedy, and as many as 24 in a comedy.[4] Within the contexts of such a definition, the reference to the neo-classical division of 'acts' remains something of a mystery. The illustrative quotation that Johnson chooses to offer as an example of proper usage, on the other hand, appears no less clearly to evoke the choral conventions of a less ritualistic, insular English theatrical tradition, wherein an individual actor often delivered a spoken chorus that, rather than commenting on the action of the drama, more often than not undertook to assist in the exposition of the play, or to supplement the alleged narrative and dramatic *representational* inadequacies of the stage itself. In the classical tradition, the chorus looked usually to underscore and often to anticipate the moral lessons of the drama; in the English tradition, by contrast, the figure of the chorus attempted more commonly to expedite the dramatic action, or to ease such narrative misapprehensions and confusions as were supposed to have been entailed by the physical limitations of the theatrical environment. One facilitated interpretation, in other words, whereas the other facilitated exposition.

Not surprisingly, Johnson's uneasy conflation of these two notions of the chorus results in a definition that raises a great many more questions than it answers. Why, for instance, should he choose a speech from what is arguably Shakespeare's *least* tragic history play (and one that was in fact introduced generically to its original audience neither as a 'History' nor a 'Tragedy', but rather as a 'Life') to illustrate what has just been defined as a specifically tragic convention? Moreover, if the illustrative quotation is meant to serve as a precise example of the function of a chorus, why then are its exhortations immediately described as 'Prologue-like' in the text? What is the relationship between the two? And how might one account for the role of the chorus in, say, Aristophanic comedy? Johnson's own lack of clarity is further compounded by a curious printer's error in the second edition of the *Dictionary*, in which the plural verb of the definition's second clause is replaced by its singular counterpart – the 'persons' now 'sings' their sentiments – leaving the entry, in its final form, an unintelligible muddle, uneasily suspended between the traditions of two widely divergent and often irreconcilable theatrical cultures.[5]

The imprecision of Johnson's definition is worth dwelling on, if only because it reappears as a more influential if slightly reformulated bit of chaos in his 1765 edition of Shakespeare's *Works*. Johnson begins his analysis of *Henry V* with a number of glosses on the same opening speech of the Prologue that he had earlier used as an illustrative quotation in the *Dictionary*. It is clear from his observations towards the beginning of the drama that Johnson accepts the apologies of the Chorus at face value – he accepts them, that is, as making the necessary excuses for a dramatic mode of performance that frequently fails to measure up to its heroic subject. When, for example, the Chorus – speaking on the part of all the players – exhorts the audience to

> Piece out our imperfections with your thoughts:
> Into a thousand parts divide one man
> And make imaginary puissance.
>
> (Prologue, 23–5)

A confident Johnson, in his most approving and authoritative manner, observes:

> This passage shews that Shakespeare was fully sensible of the absurdity of shewing battles on the theatre, which indeed is never done but tragedy becomes farce. Nothing can be represented to the eye but by something like it, and 'within a wooden O' nothing very like a battle can be exhibited.[6]

Most of Johnson's early notations regarding the Chorus continue in this magisterial tone. He chastises Shakespeare for retaining 'mean' metaphors, adds generously to Warburton's explanatory glosses, and confidently disputes the earlier transpositions that had been made by Pope and Theobald.

An uncharacteristic note of uncertainty, however, begins to creep into Johnson's remarks on the second act. Faced with the textual confusion of the Chorus's speech at the beginning of Act II, he reluctantly admits that everyone who reads the lines 'looks about for a meaning which he cannot find'.[7] Johnson himself searches, in vain, for 'connection of sense' and 'regularity of transition' in the passage. Having finally decided that the text of the Chorus has been obscured by accidental transpositions, Johnson rearranges the lines in an effort to restore what is 'probably' the true sense. Yet this retreat into the subjectivity of 'what pleases me best' – particularly in light of his own high-handed dismissal of the 'improbable conjectures' of Sir Thomas Hammer in the *Preface* – has what can only be called a demoralizing effect on his subsequent criticism.[8] The authoritative, apodictic tone that had characterized Johnson's earlier pronouncements is notably absent from his later remarks regarding the speeches of the Chorus. Indeed, it is not until his final commentary that any reference is made to the place of the Chorus in the larger design of Shakespeare's drama, and at that point Johnson seems rather too eager to discredit it altogether:

> The lines given to the chorus have many admirers; but the truth is, that in them a little may be praised, and much must be forgiven; nor can it be easily discovered why the intelligence given by the chorus is more necessary in this play than in many others where it is omitted.[9]

Johnson recovers just enough rhetorical authority in this passage to allow his dismissal to ring with some degree of conviction. His repeated impatience with Shakespeare's descriptive narration – the playwright's 'disproportionate pomp of diction', as he terms it elsewhere in the *Preface* – goes some way towards explaining his apparent lack of interest in a dramatic device that was, after all, rooted not in 'the power of nature', but in the contrived world of theatrical convention and spectacle.[10] The discomfort and uncertainty of his earlier comments yet ring in our ears, however, and one senses that the order and pattern that Johnson sought invariably to impose on literature and personal experience – that defiant act of positive assertion and design in the face of potential meaninglessness – has been, on this small point of the dramatic Chorus, baffled, and a minor victory claimed for the forces of inscrutability.

(II)

Critics since Johnson have for the most part persisted in a remarkably reductive reading of the *Henry V* Choruses. Coleridge professed himself content with the explanation that the Chorus was the voice of 'Shakespeare himself', apologizing, again, for the inadequate resources of the popular theatre.[11] Similarly Hazlitt, who dismissed *Henry V* as 'but one of Shakespeare's second-rate plays', mentions the Chorus only in passing, and then only to draw the reader's attention to a single redeeming moment of visual imagery.[12] In our own day, a standard critical response appears to have evolved within which the Chorus, despite the fact that it conspicuously *fails* to perform the duties of a connecting device with even moderate proficiency, is at least seen as contributing to the 'epic sweep' of Shakespeare's drama.[13] Few rigorously systematic attempts have been made to connect the presence of the Chorus in *Henry V* to other choric figures in Shakespeare's work (e.g., the allegorical figure of 'Rumor' in *Henry IV: Part II*, Gower in *Pericles*, Time in *The Winter's Tale*, or even Thersites in *Troilus and Cressida*), and although some of the most recent literary interpretations of the play have finally, as Ivo Kamps has written, moved away from 'a protracted critical tradition preoccupied with the personality of Henry V' to pursue issues of more interest to cultural and materialist critics, the Chorus tends to have played only the smallest of roles in such revisionist interpretations.[14]

Only towards the end of the twentieth century did a number of scholars, more concerned with the structural and thematic unity of the play, turn to the circumstances surrounding original Elizabethan productions in their efforts to explain why Shakespeare felt it necessary to include a choral figure in *this* play, in particular. Warren D. Smith, for example, had earlier argued that the speeches of the Chorus were not even included in the playhouse version of *Henry V* – thus explaining their absence from the Quarto publication of 1600.[15] Smith suggested, instead, that the lines were added for a specific court performance at the Royal Cockpit in Whitehall. The otherwise 'un-Shakespearean' vocabulary used by the Chorus – for example, specific words such as 'scaffold', 'cockpit', 'wooden O' – was employed with reference not, as one might have thought, to the public playhouses of the Globe or the Curtain Theatre, but rather to the unusually cramped circumstances that marked the conditions within which the play had been presented on a particular festive occasion. Smith's analysis was seconded by G. P. Jones, who similarly observed that the obsequiousness and exaggerated rhetoric of the Chorus – to say nothing of its anxiety regarding standards of professional decorum and artistic standards – was more easily accounted for when it was understood as having originally been directed towards a sophisticated and demanding court audience.[16] Lawrence Danson, on the other hand, was quick to point out that 'there is no reason to think that a court audience would have been more intolerant than Shakespeare's usual audience'.[17] Danson set out in turn from the premise that *Henry V* was the first of Shakespeare's plays to have been acted at the Globe theatre in 1599, and read the self-deprecating remarks of the Chorus as a sly tactic for actually drawing attention to the splendour of the new theatrical environment. The humility topos of the Chorus is thus in some ways analogous to Henry's own feigned humility – 'I speak to thee plain soldier' (*HV* V.ii.148) – when wooing Kate in the play's final act. Just as Henry remains fully aware of the fact that just beneath his clumsy lovemaking and fumbling attempts at French lies his real status as a 'maker of manners' (*HV* V.ii.296), so too the Chorus, though supposedly emphasizing the 'rough and all unable pen' (*HV* Epi. 1) of the dramatist, points instead to the genuine transformative capabilities of the playwright's imagination, and to the stunningly effective power of the dramatic illusion at the new Bankside theatre.

While the scholars have thus sought typically to explain the presence of the Chorus in *Henry V* with reference to the original occasion of the play's performance, the role and function of the Chorus has itself been parodically transformed by modern productions of the play – productions that would appear consistently to have reflected a deepening reaction in the West against the wastefulness and brutality of wars in general. As the critic Michael Quinn observed some time ago,

> Our attitude towards war has changed. The experience of two world wars and innumerable other wars involving innocent civilians as well as fighting men has made us less nationalistic and even less patriotic, and certainly more pacifist, and far less inclined to be enthusiastic about wars of aggression.[18]

Far less susceptible, too, to the flamboyant and jingoistic rhetoric that so often accompanies such conflicts. Dean Frye noted in a similar vein that 'the rather obvious heroics of Agincourt inevitably grate on generations for whom there is no poetry in war'.[19] However much Laurence Olivier's mid-century film version of the play may have responded to the rise of nationalistic spirit in the wake of the Battle of Britain and in the midst of the Second World War, it became less and less possible to prescribe a viewing of *Henry V*, as Charles Lamb had once been able to do, as a restorative of national orthodoxy.[20] Productions of the play mounted within the last 40 years or so, at least, have generally preferred to undercut the glamour and 'sacred obligation' of Henry's struggle by emphasizing the play's dark undertone of political intrigue and nationalistic militarism. The parodic-ironizing power of Bardolph, Nym, and Pistol (one thinks in particular of Bardolph's deflating and textually self-referential 'On, on, on, on, on! to the breach, to the breach!' at III.ii.1–2, or Fluellen's 'Up to the breach you dogs!' at III.ii.18) has been rendered practically superfluous by a series of productions that have typically presented even the grand speeches of Henry himself at II.i and IV.iii in an atmosphere of smoke, bloodshed, and ominous metallic clamour.

In such productions the Chorus itself has often been presented as an outsider, a beleaguered civilian in a military world who is at best a gullible tool manipulated by the political establishment or, at worse, an informed and active apologist for that establishment, fully aware of his own propagandizing role.[21] Adrian Noble's successful and in many respects trendsetting 1984 production of the play at the Royal Shakespeare Theatre in Stratford (the values and ironies emphasized in Noble's production would continue to exert a considerable influence on subsequent stagings of the play both in England and in America for at least 20 years or more) provides an early but still excellent case in point.[22] Noble's presentation encouraged a necessary distrust of all figures of political power – and seemed to motivate a distrust in particular of figures such as Henry, who seem (but *only* seem) to retain something of the naiveté of their pre-political existence. Such productions are typically a spectacular combination of blood, guts, and technical thunder; audiences are constantly provoked into drawing possible connections between the wars of Henry V and the wars of the late twentieth century and of the new millennium. The King's reading of the list of the noble dead at III.viii, for example, was in Noble's own production presented in front of a backdrop that listed the fallen in a continuous, unpunctuated pattern of names and titles – an apparently deliberate attempt to recall the (then) recently unveiled Vietnam War Memorial in Washington, DC, in which the mind-numbing sequence of the original's hard, polished granite was both mimicked and anticipated in the deceptively florid script of an Elizabethan scribe. The Chorus was accordingly transformed from a periodic commentator on the presentation of the drama, into an ever-present monitor of the onstage action and audience response. Pale, nervous, and constantly alive to the deceit implicit in the very activity of the theatre, he soon emerged as a conscious deceiver in whose mouth conceivably ennobling invitations to the audience, encouraging a positive and creative complicity, were made to sound more like the soap-box exhortations of a rabble-rousing hypocrite. A similar role was consequently assigned to the Chorus (played by Derek

Jacobi) in Kenneth Branagh's 1989 film production of *Henry V*.[23] The Chorus is portrayed in Branagh's film as a dark, surreptitious, and manifestly untrustworthy figure. He is dressed in twentieth-century clothing, his civilian garb announcing him as an outsider to the action of the drama – a figure not only excluded from the inner circles of power, but one who is in actual danger himself. The scenes representing the siege of Harfleur, for example, find the shouts of this Chorus – already having lost much of his authority and looking for all the world like a trench-coated correspondent or film spy – competing with the deafening explosions of the ammunition; his own shouting, against the thunder of the siege, is hollow and ineffective. Film critic Pauline Kael accurately captured the tone of feigned authority and false enthusiasm in the voice of Jacobi's Chorus when she compared its timbre to that of 'a radio announcer at the racetrack trying to crank up the listener's excitement'.[24]

There is perhaps little use in protesting against such popular and – indeed – such theatrically compelling revisions of the 'significance' of the Chorus in Shakespeare's drama, yet it is worth considering the extent to which modern producers and directors have had (quite literally) to deconstruct and reassemble *Henry V* simply in order to achieve this ironizing and essentially extra-textual parodic effect.[25] The full transformation of the Chorus from imaginative agent to parodic Brechtian narrator in Noble's original, ground-breaking Stratford production, for example, entailed the displacement of the second act Prologue to follow II.i – the Chorus's description of Henry's 'dreadful preparation' was thus made to endure the more forceful, proleptic irony of Nym and Pistol's trivial wrangling outside a London tavern. Likewise, the Prologue to Act IV was presented before III.vii, so that the effeminate courtliness of the French noblemen similarly gave the lie to the Chorus's announcement of the 'dreadful' note of preparation in the military camps at Agincourt.

Given extensive textual restructuring of this sort, it is eminently reasonable to argue that subsequent to even more polemical productions that have managed to accommodate the presence of the Chorus within the limits of a 'modern', more cynical reading of *Henry V* have done so only at the risk of disassembling the original structure of Shakespeare's play altogether. In their efforts to replace the eager surrogate poet who yearns for a Muse of fire with a more informal (and emphatically mute) 'chorus' of common soldiers and war-weary civilians, these productions have in fact flattened the voice of the Chorus into insubstantial two-dimensional parody – a parody, moreover, that does justice neither to the complexity of Shakespeare's own already parodic construction nor (on a more obvious level) to the genuine supra-cinematic effectiveness of its narration and description. The responses of audiences to this dissatisfying interpretation have been not very far removed from the puzzlement shown by Johnson when editing the play over 200 years ago; the bewildered spectator is now confronted with not one but two 'choruses', one of which is perforce burlesqued as a positive hindrance to the more legitimate informal choric response inherent in the action of the drama and in the unspoken criticisms of the many Michael Williamses and John Bateses who only together make up the body of Henry's army. In our efforts to refashion Shakespeare as our contemporary, in this instance at least, we have only further muddied waters not very clear to begin with.

I would suggest that it is only by reconstructing the meaning-constitutive context of *Henry V*'s original theatrical environment on a wider, much more inclusive scale than critics have yet attempted that we can begin to relate the presence of the Chorus as a legitimate parody to the larger thematic concerns of Shakespeare's play. By focusing our attention on the drama's 'moment of socialization' (to borrow a term from Jerome McGann) and by relating the Chorus to the particular meta-dramatic conventions and alienation techniques of the Elizabethan theatre, we can at least begin to see why it occupies such a prominent role in a play that concludes a dramatic tetralogy so often concerned with pageantry and ritual. Resetting the drama in its historical contexts, in this instance, may not yield any fixed or universal meanings, but we may at least be able to work beyond the questions that our own cultural environments have led us to ask of the play, to discover those issues to which the text itself was responding in its own 'dialogue with history'.

(III)

In her important 1967 study *Shakespeare and the Idea of the Play*, Anne Righter, quite some time ago, made use of Francis Fergusson's notion of the 'idea' of a theatre – 'the picture of the human situation which the whole culture embodies and which the stage itself represents' – to examine the changing relationship between actors and audience in sixteenth-century English drama.[26] One of the central points of Righter's study was that the arrival of professional players and of a distinctly secular drama in the early part of the century effected a profound change in the audience's assumptions about the stage and, more particularly, in their assumptions about the boundaries of the theatrical environment itself. The earlier religious drama had encouraged the audience to play a central role in the activity of the theatre. The very impulse of the mystery play as a 'reaccomplishment' of sacred history, as opposed to a mere reflection of human nature, relied upon a dynamic relationship between actors and audience. The spectators, as Righter noted, were themselves the most indispensable actors in the mystery plays, because it was for their spiritual benefit that the pageant of sacred history was being re-enacted in the first place. The indistinct boundaries between the players and the audience only further helped to emphasize this participatory role. The appearance of the morality play towards the end of the four-teenth century, however, signalled the initial disruptive change in this relationship. Although the audience still participated vicariously in the onstage action through 'Mankind' and 'Everyman' figures, its members were, for the first time, clearly *outside* of the dramatic environment.

The secular drama of the mid-sixteenth century took this develop-ment one step further and, seeking to overthrow what Righter described as the 'tyranny of the audience', emphasized a more classical notion of the play as a bounded illusion not to be broken by the interference of the spectator. The development of the theatre from the mid-sixteenth century onwards moved further and further away from the medieval tradition of the audience as actor towards an assertion of the autonomy of the stage, so that by the time Shakespeare was writing his comedies and histories for a late Elizabethan audience, the self-contained status of the stage had been completely established. The appearance of dramatic techniques such as the soliloquy – which replaced the overt moralizing of the medieval drama with a more indirect means of reference to the audience – was a typical manifestation of this new theatrical environ-ment that constantly guarded itself against audience intrusion.

Such an analysis of this complex and important moment in the history of the English drama is doubtlessly a persuasive one. Few critics would wish to deny that one of the characteristics of the sixteenth-century theatre is this fundamental displacement of the audience from the central privileged position that it had enjoyed in the ritual of the earlier theological drama. Yet this same argument tends to oversim-plify the swiftness and the extent of the transformation, and in so doing denies both the sheer persistence of the meta-dramatic play in late Tudor and early Stuart theatre and, perhaps more significantly, the degree to which the old meta-dramatic traditions remained avail-able for parodic exploitation. In fact, throughout the drama of the sixteenth and seventeenth centuries, playwrights continued to manip-ulate the mechanics of dramatic illusion; far from being discomforted by the presence of spectators or the supposed 'tyranny of the audience', Elizabethan dramatists seem just as eager as their predecessors to draw those spectators into the play, and engage less often in what Righter described as 'bold affirmations of dramatic distance' than in remarkably cheerful and enabling admissions of dramatic *intimacy*. The dialectical possibilities of this simultaneous intimacy and distance provide, as I have suggested earlier in these pages, an ideal condition for parodic exploitation.

Indeed, there are several significant counter-examples to the suggestion that the relationship between audience and actors centred exclusively on the distancing possibilities of the new dramatic environment. One thinks, for example, of those elaborate framing devices – traceable from the early *Fulgens and Lucrece* (c.1519) through to *Jack Drum's Entertainment* (1601), *Wily Beguiled* (1606), Beaumont and Fletcher's *Knight of the Burning Pestle* (1613), and any number of Ben Jonson's early comedies – in which actors pretending to be members of the audience or subordinate workers in the theatre or tiring house introduce and comment freely upon the dramatic action. Other framing devices include those often elaborate structures wherein a single figure – St. Dunstan in *Grim the Collier of Croydon* (pub. 1662), for example, or Revenge in Kyd's *Spanish Tragedy* (1592) – announces the subject of the drama, and remains an onstage spectator throughout the course of the play. There were also, of course, many straightforward addresses to the audience, as in *The Pardoner and the Frere* (c.1530), or Thomas Preston's *Cambises* (1570). Indeed, rather than being a period of dramatic isolation or withdrawal, as analyses prompted by interpretations such as Righter's would lead us to believe, the late sixteenth and early seventeenth centuries (as such events as the celebrated War of the Theatres might bear out) were more obviously a time when the playhouses related on a very matter-of-fact level both to the 'real' life of the audience and, inter-textually, to the existence of a reproducible body of dramatic work, openly drawing attention to the central elements of artifice and illusion inherent in theatrical presentation. The most significant devices of the mature Elizabethan theatre, such as soliloquies and expository dialogues, did not simply appear *ex nihilo* as resentful enclosure acts against audience intrusion or extra-dramatic address, but were themselves the much more natural developments of a rich and deeply rooted meta-dramatic tradition.

This context of alienation techniques can help us, I believe, to gain a better understanding of the kind of expectations that would have been raised among an Elizabethan audience when an individual calling himself a Chorus or a Prologue stepped onto the stage of the Globe theatre. Most critics seem to take for granted that all English choruses prior to Shakespeare's obsequious and often confusing figure were instead, themselves, rather clear-spoken and almost dictatorial in their apparent control over the theatrical action. Yet while some few choruses still maintained the homiletic voice of their predecessors in the sacred drama, one of the more verifiable effects of the secularization of theatrical material was in fact to shatter the authoritative monotone of choral commentary. Deprived of the theological substance that had legitimized the commentaries of the Vexillators in *The Castle of Perseverance*, for example, or the messenger who serves as Prologue to *Everyman* (1510), the figure of the chorus soon finds itself emptied of particular significance, and is more often than not solicitous as opposed to admonitory. The Prologue to Thomas Tomkis's late *Lingua* (1607) is one of the few choral figures to retain the authoritative 'take-it-or-leave-it' tone that one can trace at least as far back as the riding of the banns for the so-called N-town cycle of mystery plays. The *Lingua* Prologue tells the audience:

> Our Muse describes no lovers passion,
> No wretched Father, no unthriftie Sonne:
> No craving subtl Whore or shameless bawde,
> No stubborne Clowne, or daring Parasite,
> No lying servant, or bold sycophant.
> We are not wanton, or Satyricall.
> These have their time and places fit, but we
> Sad houres, and serious studies, to reprieve,
> Have taught severe Phylosophy to smile.
> The Senses rash contentions we comp,
> And give displeased ambitious Tongue her due:
> Heres all judidious friends; accept what is not ill,
> Who are not such, let them do what they will.[27]

Far more characteristic are those Prologues and Choruses that humbly request the patience and forbearance of the audience, and remain acutely aware of their tenuous dramatic position. Note, for example, these representative Chorus-Prologues from a selection of sixteenth- and seventeenth-century plays:

> [S]ith nothing but trifles may be had
> You shall hear a thing that onlie shall make you merie and glad

And such a trifling matter as when it shall be done
Ye may repose and say ye have heard nothing at all.
Therefore I tell you all, before it be begun
That no man looke to heare of matters substancyall.

(*Jack Juggler* [1553] Pro.69–74)[28]

Both merry and short we purpose to be,
And therefore require your pardon and patience,
We trust in our matter nothing you shall see,
That to the goodly may give any offence,
Though the style be barbarous, not fined with eloquence
Yet our author desireth your gentle acceptation,
And we the players likewise, with all humilitie.

(*The Triall of Treasure* [1567] Pro.50–6)[29]

My dutie first in humble wise fulfill'd,
    I humbly come, as humbly I am will'd,
To represent and eke to make report,
    That after me you shall hear merrie sport.
To make you joy and laugh at merrie toyes,
    I mean a play set out by prettie boyes.
Whereto we crave your silence and good will,
    To take it well: although he wanted skill
That made the same so perfectly to write,
    As his good will would further and it might.

(*Tom Tyler and his Wife* [c.1540] Pro.1–10)[30]

By the late sixteenth century, the Chorus was perceived both by playwrights and by audiences as an element of antiquated theatrical ritual
that – though kept alive through the momentum and vitality of the
meta-dramatic tradition of the Elizabethan theatre – was now available
for creative parodic exploitation. No longer a figure who automatically
commanded the respect of spectators through his own supra-dramatic
comprehension of the sacred theatrical presentation, the Chorus could
be used by dramatists in any number of innovative ways. This new,
subordinate position of the Chorus is at times reflected in a certain
deference to the controlling power of a particular dramatist, or even to
the response of the popular audience itself. The Prologue to *The Tide
Tarrieth No Man* (1576), for example, places both the Chorus and the

author at the mercy of the clapper-clawing palms of the vulgar, and solicits their assistance in the construction of a drama that is seen as an ongoing and cumulative process:

> Thus worshipfull Audyence, our Author desyreth,
> That this his acte you will not deprave:
> But if any fault be, he humbly requireth,
> That due intelligence thereof he may have,
> Commiting himself to your directions grave,
> And thus his Prologue, he rudely doth end,
> For at hand to approache, the Players intend.

> (*The Tide Tarrieth No Man*, Pro.50–6)[31]

It is striking, too, that the Chorus here is likewise seen as somewhat superfluous to the action and comprehension of the drama; the entrance of the actors quite literally pushes him offstage and into the clutter of the tiring house. Other Choruses complain more vehemently about this recent necessity of ingratiating themselves with the spectators of the loathed stage – a complaint with which Shakespeare might certainly have had some sympathy. The Chorus to *The History of the Two Valiant Knights Sir Clyomon and Clamydes* (1599), which appeared in the same year as Shakespeare's *Henry V*, disdainfully regards the 'filthy Swine' and 'babler's tongues' before whom he must perform.[32] The Prologue to *Wily Beguiled* (pub. 1660) similarly chastises the 'paltrie players' and berates the 'barme-froth poet' who has thus made him 'supply the place of a scurvy Prologue'.[33] Still other Choruses offer strictly expository speeches detailing necessary narrative background, as in *Weakest to the Wall* (1600), or *The Bloody Banquet* (1620), or even make a point of concerning themselves with what will *not* be presented in the play, as with *Nobody and Somebody* (*c.*1592), or Christopher Marlowe's *Doctor Faustus* (1604). Marlowe is in fact one of the few dramatists to place his Choruses within the contexts of larger structural parodies of the earlier morality plays. He thus allows them to perform in the face of a unique and comprehensive parodic environment that recalls, more emphatically, the genuine position of commentary that the Chorus had maintained within the moral structures of the older drama. The Chorus in Marlowe's *Doctor Faustus*, like that included in the anonymous 'domestic' tragedy *Arden of Feversham* (*c.*1591), pointedly draws connections between its own function in the drama and the traditions of the earlier morality plays.

Elizabethan dramatists thus exploit the ritual of the chorus to suit a wide and ever-changing variety of dramatic needs. Rather than being completely buried as an obsolete element of a more primitive dramatic past, the choral ritual was being alternately interred and exhumed, examined, and dissected, and (in some cases) parodically torn to pieces – all according to the requirements of a particular dramatic action. It is worth noting that although many choruses good-naturedly draw attention to the failings of inept dramatists or to the clumsy acting of the popular playhouse, very few lament the inadequate resources of the theatre in the manner of Shakespeare's *Henry V*. Only one major chorus – that of George Peele's *David and Bethsabe* (1599) – evinces any sustained anxiety regarding the efficacy of the dramatic represent-ation itself, and consequently calls upon Apollo

>   to conduct
> Upon the wings of [his] well-temper'd verse
> The hearer's minds above the towers of heaven,
> And guide them so, in this thrice haughty flight,
> Their mounting feathers scorch not with the fire
> That none can temper but thy holy hand.[34]

Shakespeare's Chorus, on the other hand, spends much the better part of its time perversely emphasizing the hopeless nature of theat-rical representation, and paradoxically recounting with no little degree of ostentation the many elements of Henry's campaigns that cannot possibly be represented on the stage – betraying, in other words, a start-lingly Derridean lack of faith in the possibility of 'presence'. One need hardly rehearse the complaints of Shakespeare's Chorus at great length; the play is said to be a 'mockery' of Henry's history (*HV* IV.Cho.53); the actors themselves are 'flat unraised spirits' (*HV* Pro.9), who stand only as 'ciphers' to the account of his reign (*HV* Pro.17); the spectac-ular battle of Agincourt is of necessity represented only by 'four or five most vile and ragged foils' (*HV* IV.Cho.50) – in short, the 'huge and proper life' of the action can emerge only as a mangled and diminutive glory that severely diminishes its actual worth. The emphasis thus falls on the contribution that the viewer is required to impart in order to allow the large and hollow ritual of the drama to come to life at all – what Hazlitt called the 'very splendid pageant' of *Henry V* can only achieve its status *as* pageant through the efforts of the individual spec-tator. Fill the ritual with meaning, and thus 'create' the meaning of the play.

It is of course entirely fitting that the drama that points at every possible moment to the elements of role-playing and exploitable, manipulative ritual inherent in the activity of kingship itself should be guided and, in effect, masterminded by a cipher recently emptied of significance and opened to the possibilities of parodic play.[35] Throughout the play – throughout the entire tetralogy, in fact – Henry reveals a profound understanding of the socially fabricated ritualistic nature of what it actually *means* to be a king. Richard II had fallen precisely because of his inability, except in infrequent moments of pathetic self-analysis, to come to grips with a perception of kingship not founded in a concept of absolute legitimacy, while Henry IV – although very much the skilful politician concerned with his 'public image', and the one who in fact fashions the calculating political world that Hal is left to bring to order – was nevertheless himself wearied quite literally to death under the pressure of maintaining some sense of an integrated self in this new environment. It is Henry V who is finally able to deal with the element of role-playing and formalism involved in kingship, and thus re-establish the order that had given way in the opening scenes of *Richard II* on the basis of a new, more individualistic structure of power.

The ritual and pageantry that had characterized the world of *Richard II* have been similarly transformed. Meaning no longer resides in the act of ritual itself, but remains to be added, manipulated, and controlled by the King himself in a well-timed, well-ordered, and carefully constructed moment of self-presentation. The parodic fate of the chorus-as-ritual reflects in the analogy of the dramatic action of the fate of the King: just as positive value no longer adheres in the activity of kingship except as it is defined by its relationship to the other warring elements of the social structure, so too the Chorus now stands a signifier effectively cut off from its signified – the ritual of kingship and the ritual of the Chorus can now be filled in any number of self-serving ways, and the Chorus, like Henry himself, keeps a constant eye open to the advantages of apparent unity, continuity, and self-effacement.

5
John Dryden and Homeopathic Parody in the Early Augustan Battleground

> Our times are much degenerate from those
> Which your sweet Muse with your fair Fortune chose,
> And as complexions alter with the Climes,
> Our wits have drawne th'infection of our times.

> – Andrew Marvell, 'To his Noble Friend
> Mr. Richard Lovelace, upon his Poems'[1]

The preceding chapters have maintained that the earliest years of the seventeenth century witnessed a fundamental shift in established attitudes towards derivative imitation and text-specific parodic appropriation in English. I have suggested that this same shift in attitude – a transformation that can already be seen manifesting itself (albeit in significantly different ways) in the writings of both Ben Jonson and William Shakespeare – precipitates a deeply consequential change in the conditions that govern poetic activity throughout the subsequent decades. The textual anxieties that so clearly evince themselves for the first time in the early years of the seventeenth century can in fact serve as an analogical model for the more wide-ranging literary instability that characterized the work of a great many writers in the years immediately following the Restoration. The breakdown of a particular *kind* of literary standard – the collapse of a generally accepted ethic of authorial possession and authority – resulted in the bewildering hyper-demoticization of literary and journalistic discourse in the latter half of the seventeenth century.

Parody, most noticeably, itself becomes an entrenched part of the new literary system. Not only does parody now serve as an offensive weapon against the language of political opponents and literary rivals;

it emerges as a necessary defensive and creative tool in its own right – a prerequisite for any author looking to 'protect his own', as it were.[2] The mid-seventeenth century witnessed the emergence of poets such as John Cleveland (standing in the line of satire as a direct descendant of John Skelton), who together seem systematically to take earlier poetic forms and styles to explicitly parodic lengths in their efforts to pre-empt any logical or common-sensical objections to their own religious or political positions (or, for that matter, to any criticisms of their own poetic styles). A reader cannot very well take issue with Cleveland's indictment of the Westminster Assembly in a poem such as 'The Mixt Assembly' (1656), for example, by appealing to the poet's sense of even-handedness or 'fair play'. Cleveland deliberately prohibits access to certain traditions of deliberative oratory by *parodying* those traditions – by relying primarily (as he puts it) on the incantation of 'the Magick of [his] words', rather than on the strictly logical or rhetorical coherence of his argument in order to disarm his literary and political opponents.[3]

Cleveland was far from alone in turning to such strategies. Just as poems such as 'The Mixt Assembly' or 'The Rebell Scot' (1658) calcu-latedly make systematically decadent use of metaphysical conceits, and pointedly take other elements of the earlier traditions of court poetry to snarling new lengths in their efforts to avoid the vagaries of poetic misconstruction and misappropriation, so too the earliest works of the Restoration – such as Robert Wild's *Iter Boreale* (1660) – similarly depict the fate suffered by Royalist poets under the recent Commonwealth by deliberately parodying the style of those earlier poets. In the immensely popular *Iter Boreale*, for example, Wild portrays himself as a frustrated and imprisoned Royalist who has for years been denied access to the respectable public language of political encomium:

> I he who whilom sat and sung in cage
> My King's and country's ruin by the rage
> Of a rebellious rout ...
> I that have only dar'd to whisper verses,
> And drop a tear by stealth on loyal hearses;
> Had gnawed my goose-quill to the very stump
> ...
> Now Sing the triumphs of the man of war.
>
> (ll.23–39)[4]

In this instance, Wild's verses deliberately recall the opening lines of works including the prologue to Spenser's *Faerie Queene* ('Lo I the man, whose Muse whilome did maske/As time her taught in lowly Shepheards weeds... '). In so doing, they likewise evoke, at the same time, the lines often prefixed to the beginning of Renaissance editions of Virgil's *Aeneid* ('Ille ego, qui quondom gracili modulatus avena/carmen ... at nunc horrentia Martis').[5] Wild's point is that this same language of martial and political praise that had been so readily available to Virgil or to Spenser and, even more particularly, the step-by-step generic demands of the straightforward poetic career that had also been open to those poets, have been denied the writers of his generation. In fact, the Restoration poet, in his recollections of 'whispering' his verses in secret and 'gnawing' on his pen in lonely seclusion, emphasizes the extent to which he has been denied both a political dynasty *and* a poetic voice. He is compelled now to parody earlier poetic formulations, in part because the previously clear and well-defined path of loyalty, subject, and patronage that had previously outlined the arc of any professional poetic career has been erased. It is only by means of parody that Wild can draw attention to (and perhaps temporarily transcend) the unprecedented degree of competition and divisiveness among the new generation of poets in such self-acknowledged 'small-drink times' (l.17), because only a mode such as parody can simultaneously invoke and dissolve the formal parameters of any competing communities of discourse. By so obviously parodying the lines of Virgil and Spenser, Wild – a dissenting minister who found himself on the side of the Royalists in the Civil Wars – reminds his readers that the forms of poetry available in a time of less troubled loyalties have been thoroughly obscured. Both the political and the rhetorical imperatives of the Restoration dictate a poetic style that takes into account the possible duplicities and 'doubletalk' of late-seventeenth-century poetics.

In a manner typical of the period, Wild concludes his *Iter Boreale* with a question – with an uncertainty. His pen has attempted to negotiate the current poetic scene whilst praising General Monck as the infallible architect of Charles's return to the throne. Yet Wild admits that he is far from certain that when Monck himself dies, there will be any poet remaining who will be willing or even competent enough to praise his achievements. What pen, Wild asks, can possibly 'make posterity believe [Monck's] story?' (l.407). In questioning the ability of future poets to perpetuate and to sustain the magnitude of what he wishes to present as Monck's achievement for the nation, Wild implicitly calls into question the literary vitality (and longevity) of his *own* verses, by highlighting the transient and necessarily politically ephemeral occasion of their composition. Such a matter-of-fact admission of uncertainty with regard to the fate (and, for that matter, the simple value) of one's own poetry becomes an increasingly common theme in the verse produced in the late seventeenth century. Writers who are apt to make themselves the 'Fiddle[s] of the Towne', in the words of the Earl of Rochester's 'Artemiza', after all, might with good reason be expected to demonstrate some self-conscious anxiety regarding the possible, subsequent parodic appropriation of their own work.[6] The opening lines of poems such as Edmund Waller's 'On Saint James's Park' ('. . . who knows the fate/Of lines that shall this paradise relate?') or of his 'Of English Verse' ('. . . who can hope these lines should long/Last in a daily changing tongue?') rejuvenate and help to redefine some familiar classical tropes regarding the possible fate of any poetic document once it has passed from the hands of its creator.[7] Such subtle yet often urgent variations on the traditional poetic *envoi* (from the French 'a sending on the way'), but increasingly connoting a form of literary abandonment, raise some disturbing questions concerning the possibilities of poetic influence, imitation, and response. Moreover, they do so with a heightened sense of anxious sensitivity to the combined threats of literary misappropriation, misinterpretation, diachronic linguistic transformation, and parody. They betray an awareness of their participation in a new age of imitation – a new age of parody – and the writers of the period produce their work with a nervous understanding that the 'rules of the game', as it were, have somehow, since the days of their poetic forefathers, radically been changed.

One explanation for this change, again, can be located simply in the new possibilities of textual reproduction and accessibility within the rapidly expanding print culture of the late seventeenth and eighteenth centuries. I have already suggested that the sudden proliferation of parodic activity in the late seventeenth century was related, at least tangentially, to these new possibilities of textual reproduction and, by consequence, to the concomitant possibilities of textual allusion and appropriation within the new literary system. It is worth our taking a moment, therefore, before turning explicitly to the poetry and the parody of John Dryden, to examine this connection just a bit more closely.

(I)

Certain aspects of the rhetorical and technological shift that begins in the years immediately following the Restoration and that continues throughout the seventeenth and eighteenth centuries – certain aspects, that is, of the new cluster of anxieties surrounding the so-called Augustan author – have been subjected to close and intelligent critical scrutiny. A wide range of critics in the latter decades of the twentieth century (among them Terry Belanger, Natalie Davis, Elizabeth Eisenstein, David Foxon, John Guillory, Alvin Kernan, Jonathan Brody Kramnick) surveyed what has been variously described as the 'rise of print' and the 'decline of courtly letters' in the period from a point of view that placed a great deal of emphasis on the changing status of the literary or printed text itself – on the changing status of the printed artefact – at such a moment of combined rhetorical and technological crisis.[8] Kernan, for example, saw the print revolution of the late seventeenth and early eighteenth centuries not only as profoundly affecting the hard facts and actualities of literary production (the systemization of habits of composition, for example, or the standardization of literary texts), but as altering the very concept of 'literature' itself. In fact, some commonly held ideas regarding the authority and status of printed texts – of their uniqueness or 'aura', to use Walter Benjamin's term, or of the respective 'performance' of printed and manuscript materials, to refer rather to Samuel Johnson's earlier formulation of much the same notion – date precisely from this particular technical and epistemological crisis.[9] Perhaps most influentially, with relation to the changing world of writers, booksellers, and printers in the era, Jürgen Habermas postulated the development early in the eighteenth century of what he designated to be 'the public sphere' – a conceptual discursive space that evaded both the strictures of the State and the Court, on the one hand, and the 'private realm' of the family and polite or civilized society, on the other. Such a space, Habermas suggested, permitted and even encouraged within its more liberal confines a hitherto unrecognizable mode of disinterested and rational conversation and discussion, although his position has been subject to some considerable criticism in recent years.[10]

Just as the status of the printed text was shifting in this period, so too was the role of the author in this new print culture undergoing some far-reaching transformations. More conservative critics such as Kernan tended to emphasize (as a consequence of the 'fall of patronage') the emergence of a new *kind* of public writer, a writer who acknowledged the fact that he was writing for a reading public created *by* and increasingly catering *to* the demands of a market-centred print culture. We have already had occasion to note, in passing, the uneasy mingling of a fading system of courtly patronage, on the one hand, with the more utilitarian demands of such a print culture, on the other, in the work of Ben Jonson.

Many critics would locate the crucial point of contact between these two literary cultures somewhat later in the eighteenth century. Kernan, for example, read Boswell's memorable account of Samuel Johnson's chance encounter with King George III in the library of the Queen's House in 1767 as an emblematic moment in the decline of courtly letters, a moment that enacted the shift in the literary system from traditional royal authority over discourse – the system of patronage – to the newer, more 'democratic' authority of print circumstances.[11] The juxtaposition of the emphatically physical and even grotesque Johnson with the demanding and autocratic King in the elegant Octagon library, Kernan suggested, emblematized in ritual the transfer of power from the old aristocratic order of 'gentleman amateurs' to an author (such as Johnson himself) who accepted the market-based reality of his position. Johnson was – by his own proud acknowledgment – himself the 'author' of print culture, the unhesitating initiator of a new literary era.

I have suggested that some of the more central developments in this decisive shift in the literary culture occur earlier, and that the process captured so strikingly in Kernan's reading of Boswell's *Life of Johnson* (1791) is in actual fact perhaps better looked upon as the end stage of a process that had been going on, to some degree, since at least the very beginning of the seventeenth century. The writers of Dryden's generation are the authors who most dramatically confronted the kinds of rhetorical destabilization occasioned by such a shift. The writers of the Restoration – more so than the writers of the mid-eighteenth century – were the first to come to grips with the anxieties of the new literary age. Dryden – not Johnson – stood *primus inter pares* among that first generation of authors who found it inescapably necessary both to admit and to defend their collective status as 'professional' authors.

The emphasis of many more recent critics on the shift from patronage to the new sense of authorial self (and seeming self-sufficiency) in the Restoration and in the eighteenth century at least serves to focus our attention on one important aspect of the changing literary culture of the period: the status of the author and the concept of authorship itself. Many would probably concede that the gradual emergence of the concept of 'professional' authorship in the Restoration and early eighteenth century not only necessitated a desire to distance and to distinguish one's self from the passing system of polite letters and courtly patronage – to distinguish one's self from that which yet remained 'above' one's self, as it were – but instigated at the same time an unprecedented anxiety regarding the newly threatening and expanding 'Grub

Street race' (the concomitant 'below' – the seething underside of the new literary system).

It is perhaps only obvious that the generation that saw the first stirrings of the idea of literary copyright, and that first emphasized the enhanced status and authority of the printed as opposed to the manuscript text, would likewise experience a debilitating *loss* of control over the text as a *physical* object. Critics such as Peter Stallybrass and Allon White were among the first to emphasize the extent to which the symbolic domain of the new professional author and of professional authorship itself, in the period, 'emerges *over against* the popular'.[12] The cultural (and, indeed, social) chaos of a changing literary system produced a legion of writers from whom the new professionals – Dryden (at least the Dryden of the 1700 *Fables*, for example), Pope, Fielding, and Johnson – constantly tried to separate themselves. These writers were early on characterized as intrusive insects and plague-carrying rodents ('Paper-rats' and 'Book-scorpions', Andrew Marvell was quick to call them).[13] They are later stigmatized as barbaric hordes, hacks, dunces, and inept pseudo-literary bullies.[14] The primary charges against them, of course, remain accusations of plagiarism and parody.

The efforts of the new professional author, such as Dryden, to keep himself clean of the kinds of cultural and literary pollution – to keep himself clean, that is, from the contagion of the new literary *diseases* that were seen to be transmitted by the appropriative authors from whom the new professional has only tentatively and temporarily distinguished himself – are in some measure doomed to failure. Such efforts refuse to acknowledge that the distinctions between the 'high' and the demotic, between literary artists and literary 'Mechannicks', are themselves largely specious, and that the two 'classes' of writers are in fact mutually dependent, and both rooted in the competing literary system that they ostensibly oppose.[15] A number of critics, picking up where scholars such as Belanger and Kernan seem to have left off (e.g., Stallybrass and White, Terry Castle, Stuart Hall, and Brean Hammond, Frank Donoghue, and Jeremy Black), all touched on these fictions of cultural pollution and transgression, and the cultural conditions that encouraged their development. Literary figures from Dryden through Pope and Fielding (and, indeed, Johnson) are forever detailing the distinctions to be drawn between high and low art forms, between the demotic and the classical, the grotesque and the courtly. Dryden himself, early in his career, seeks to impose a distinction between his own professional activity, on the one hand, and the products of an author such as his aristocratic friend and brother-in-law, Sir Robert Howard, on the other, whose 'Musick uninform'd by Art' boasts a 'native sweetnesse', yet reveals 'no signe of toil, no sweat' (ll.1–18).[16] In his early poem 'To my Honoured Friend, Sr. Robert Howard' (1660), Dryden pretends to flatter the unpretentious ease and artlessness of Howard's lines, but in fact concludes by privileging the hard-won craftsmanship and artistry of his own prophetic verses. He similarly attempts to distinguish himself from what he sees to be the growing literary underclass (including Denham, Marvell, and those other poets who participated in the 'Advice to a Painter' exchange); in the account prefaced to *Annus Mirabilis,* he calls attention to the 'Historical' aspects of his own work, and explicitly places himself (as Jonson did before him) in a long line of classical rather than modern or contemporary authors. *Mac Flecknoe* (1682), of course, is a more obvious example of Dryden's attempts to separate himself from the growing population of the sons of Non-sense, whose works, in Dryden's apocalyptic vision, threaten to choke the very streets (the mercantile and political corridors of power) of London.

Dryden's instinctive response to the cultural seepage that seems to be approaching him *both* from above (from the gentlemen amateurs such as Howard or Rochester who imposed their writing on the public by means of their rank) and from below (from the Shadwells and Flecknoes lampooned in *Mac Flecknoe*) is an attempt to establish his own culturally clean and untainted literary space or property. It is the response of quarantine. He is nevertheless compelled to encounter a constant competition – a veritable Babel – of discourses. The unrivalled degree of cultural and literary mobility not only produces diverse and competing literary forms, but instigates a seemingly inescapable cycle of literary creation and repossession – a particular 'pattern of reversal', to adopt a phrase of Michael McKeon's – a cycle that draws all authors into a constant re-enactment and redefinition of the encoded fictions of authorial status, dependency, and self-sufficiency.[17] The new professional, in an effort to inscribe his own work as high art, may initially attempt to adopt a pose of disdainful distance towards the so-called literary hacks. Yet more often than not he is compelled towards a final capitulation (or, more accurately, re-capitulation) to the 'low' and 'vulgar' standards of his literary parodists and detractors – he is forced to join the sphere of the parodic idiom himself. Attempting to escape the parodists, Dryden himself *becomes* a parodist. In *Mac Flecknoe*, for example, we again hear a parodic echo of the very same Spenserian lines that Wild had imitated in his *Iter Boreale*. Dryden has Flecknoe proclaim to Shadwell,

> My warbling Lute, the Lute I whilome strung,
> When to King *John* of *Portugal* I sung,
> Was but the prelude to that glorious day,
> When thou on silver *Thames* did'st cut thy way,
> With well tim'd Oars before the Royal Barge

> (ll.35–9)

Dryden, like Wild, here indicates that he too is standing at a parodic distance from the epic and lyric tradition conjured by the cluster of pseudo-Spenserian and Shakespearean language. Unlike Wild's more defensive poem, however, Dryden's lines make use of a parodic idiom *not* to indicate his *own* relationship to an inaccessible or otherwise pre-empted lyric tradition, but precisely to demonstrate that such a tradition, while denied to Flecknoe and Shadwell, remains (comparatively) open to him. Dryden's parody of Spenserian diction in *Mac Flecknoe* seems to indicate that while the competent poet can use parody creatively and fruitfully, the incompetent poet will use it only to belittle and deride or – like Wild – to suggest the poetic possibilities denied to the earlier Restoration author.

Although inextricably caught up in this literary cycle that consists, in essence, of a series of emphatic, self-congratulatory separations or divisions and uneasy rapprochements, John Dryden evinces one possibly sustaining response to this cycle early in his career. He institutes the practice of what might be called 'homeopathic' parody to keep his rivals and enemies at bay. While the hyperbolic language and ingratiating dramatic spectacle of Dryden's earliest dramas (one thinks, for example, of *The Indian Emperor* [1665] or *Tyrannick Love* [1669]) appear to leave those dramas unprotected from the possibilities of parodic exploitation, his occasional verse, and particularly his political satires, consistently includes elements of self-conscious parody and self-parody that work to ward off the threat of subsequent parodic exploitation of his own language. Dryden administers homeopathic doses of parody – moments of purposefully induced bathos or perhaps linguistic self-consciousness – that act as a preventive measure against subsequent exploitation.

The most rhetorically successful of Dryden's early poems, *Mac Flecknoe* and *Absalom and Achitophel* (1681), refuse on some level to take themselves entirely seriously, or – as is the case with *Annus Mirabilis* (1667) or *The Medall* (1682) – they look constantly to emphasize the distance between themselves and the works (and in the case of *The Medall* this work is the actual physical artefact of George Bower's medal) to which they are in some measure responding. What had remained in the hands of poets such as Cleveland and Wild a sporadic and intuitive urge towards self-protection becomes for the poets of Dryden's generation nothing less than a full-fledged *strategy* of parody.

One very specific example of the type of homeopathic self-parody that consists not so much of linguistic self-consciousness as of an awareness on the part of Dryden regarding how vulnerable his own verse satire could be to subsequent appropriation and attack can be found in *Absalom and Achitophel*. Critics have long sought to explain and account for lines 180–91 of the poem. The verses were not included in the first (1681) edition, and appear to have been added to the poem only by the printing of the third London edition. The passage seems to qualify the harsh censure of the character of Achitophel/Shaftesbury by praising his honesty and ability as a judge:

> So easie still it proves in Factious Times,
> With publick Zeal to cancel private Crimes:
> . . .
> Where Crouds can wink; and no offence be known,
> Since in anothers guile they find their own.
> Yet, Fame deserv'd, no Enemy can grudge;
> The Statesman we abhor, but praise the Judge.
> In *Isreals* Courts ne'r sat an *Abbethdin*
> With more discerning Eyes, or Hands more clean:
> Unbrib'd, unsought, the Wretched to redress;
> Swift of Dispatch, and easie of Access.
>
> (ll.180–91)

These lines, no doubt, have variously inspired various minds. The editors of the California Dryden note that contemporary estimates of Shaftesbury's record as Lord Chancellor oscillated between the extremes of disdainful condemnation and warm praise (praise that is echoed, it would appear, in these lines) for his supposed impartiality. The lines can either be read ironically (and thus add 'a fillip to the satiric portrait') or as an honest qualification of Shaftesbury's character that works to soften the satire of the passage as a whole.[18] Dryden might also, in attempting to appeal to the 'more Moderate Sort', as he puts it in the preface to the poem, likewise be attempting to moderate his own condemnation of Shaftesbury – he might, that is, be living up to his claim of having '[rebated] the Satyre (where Justice woud [sic] allow it) from carrying too sharp an Edge' ('To the Reader': 22–4).

While the precise intent of the passage – and the reasons why it was omitted from the earliest editions of the poem, or added to later ones – must remain obscure, I would suggest that Ian Jack, who argued that the lines actually work to sharpen the attack on Shaftesbury 'by making a show of impartiality', is perhaps closest to the truth.[19] Although it is certainly arguable that Dryden's vigorous condemnation of Shaftesbury as a false councillor and traitor in the poem is too strong to be convincingly mitigated by such a relatively modest defence of a single praiseworthy virtue, the passage nevertheless effectively throws a spanner in the works of monologic satiric condemnation. Dryden establishes a potentially ironic (and potentially self-parodic) distance between text and meaning; a gap opens in the poem as its author backs off from a wholehearted party-political engagement, and stands for a moment outside the acknowledged debating space of such conflict. Any parodists who in turn attempt to use Dryden's *own* words against *him* will be forced to interpret a difficult passage, and will likewise be confronted with the possibility of unconsciously parodying *themselves* if they misinterpret their original. Dryden's homeopathic parodic technique thus permits him to dislocate himself within his own text. He purposefully 'plants' a parody in his own work, so to speak, in the hopes of throwing his parodists and detractors off the trail.

Making use of the extended definition of literary parody formulated earlier, I would like to use the remainder of this section to talk *generally* about the concept of parody in Dryden, and to examine the close relationship between yet-emerging concepts of literary allusion, plagiarism, and parody. Dryden's verses are so many (over 20,000 lines), and his critical insights so various (and so occasional) that while it is virtually impossible to do justice to the scope of his formulations regarding individual literary and critical endeavours and their relationship to past achievement and contemporary literary production, it is at least necessary to review the salient features of his own ruminations on such subjects as 'burlesque', 'parody', 'plagiarism', and 'lampoon'. We will briefly need to examine Dryden's own relation to the troubled critical taxonomies and lexical imperatives that would become increasingly hard-pressed to accommodate these new 'kinds' of literary production, ranging from authorial emulation, to literary theft and plagiarism. There exists a close relationship in Dryden's criticism between concepts of parody, on the one hand, and concepts of plagiarism, on the other, positions that have since evolved into discreet literary categories. Making use of the more text-specific aspects of our earlier definition of parody – returning, that is, for a moment to a more conservative conception of the parodic as 'a kind of writing in which the words of an author are by a slight change adapted to some new purpose', I would like to turn to an examination of the parodic responses to Dryden's most successful political satire, *Absalom and Achitophel*. Dryden's poem provoked a series of text-specific parodies that can serve as a 'test case', so to speak, to isolate some very specific aspects of Dryden's provocation of and response to literary parody. What, precisely, provokes Dryden in a literary parody? What is the proper response to the many parodies now pouring from the printing presses; when, in fact, *is* a response proper? We shall see that in Dryden's case the various contemporary parodies of *Absalom and Achitophel* fail, to a large degree, to excite the poet's attention not because they lack the sufficient *animus* – the personal and political weaponry – of a negative parodic attack but because they fail *as parodies* precisely where Dryden's parodic-appropriative activity is most successful and most aware of the necessity of maintaining parodic distance. Dryden's own homeopathic parody eventually traps his opponents into flattening and weakening their own parodic attacks. I would like to begin with a close examination of a very short prologue that seems to capture and to crystallize Dryden's anxieties regarding the new poetic atmosphere of parodic inter-textual activity, in much the same manner that the early *Every Man in His Humour* scene underscored the similar, emerging anxieties of Ben Jonson a generation before.

(II)

In early February 1668, John Dryden prepared a prologue for a revival of Thomas Tomkis's university comedy *Albumazar*, to be staged later that month at the Duke's playhouse.[20] Dryden, mistakenly supposing Tomkis's 1614 play to have been the source of Ben Jonson's *The Alchemist* (1612), accordingly structured his induction to the drama on an elaborate contrast between Jonson's 'noble' and enabling poetic appropriations (which he saw as typical of the last age – 'When few men censured, and when fewer writ'), and the more rapacious practices of a new generation of poets operating in the prevailing 'Anarchy of witt'.

The prologue begins with a spirited defence of Jonson's supposed borrowings:

> To say this Commedy pleas'd long a go,
> Is not enough, to make it pass you now:
> Yet gentlemen, your Ancestors had witt,
> When few men censurd, and when fewer writ.

>And *Johnson* (of those few men the best) chose this,
>As the best modell of his master-piece;
>*Subtle* was got by our *Albumazar,*
>That *Alchamist* [sic] by this Astrologer.
>Here he was fashion'd, and we may suppose,
>He lik'd the fashion well, who wore the Cloaths.
>But *Ben* made nobly his, what he did mould,
>What was another's Lead, becomes his Gold.
>
>(ll.1–12)

Dryden's decision to open the prologue on this note is itself a bold move, particularly when one considers that he ought more practically to be advancing – in the face of a potentially antagonistic crowd at Lincoln's Inn Fields – the claims of Tomkis's original. Although Dryden quickly characterizes Jonson as the 'unrighteous conqueror' of Tomkis's material (a phrase that recalls his earlier reference to Jonson in the *Essay of Dramatic Poesy* [1668] as a 'learned plagiary'), he is at the same time careful to grant a sense of legitimacy and necessary refinement to Jonson's later, more famous comedy. Dryden, who had just two years earlier, with Sir William D'Avenant, transformed *The Tempest* (1611) into the elaborate opera *Th'Enchanted Isle* (1666), and who would, in the course of his career, work similar transformations on such plays as *Troilus and Cressida* (1603) and *Antony and Cleopatra* (1608), was in some measure using the occasion of Tomkis's play to offer an apology for his own redactions (both recent and anticipated) of Elizabethan and Jacobean dramas. Dryden employs an alchemical imagery that anticipates his own justifications for reworking Shakespeare's plays to suit the particular tastes of the Restoration audience ('What was another's Lead' becomes, in Jonson's abler hands, 'Gold'). While there yet remains some sense of a dark and huddled sexual intrigue in the propagation of the two plays (*'Subtle* was got by our *Albumazar*/That *Alchamist* [sic] by this Astrologer'), Dryden's lines smack at the same time of the more strictly logical language of patriarchal self-sufficiency, and even spontaneous generation. The sexual imagery of the passage is, in any case, immediately qualified by a sartorial metaphor ('Here he was fashion'd, and we may suppose/He lik'd the fashion well, who wore the Cloaths') that transforms the supposed sexually dependent relationship between the two plays (and the concomitant suggestion of literary schizophrenia) into one of simple and healthy typological fulfilment. Utilizing a familiar comparison between tailoring and writing, between the code of the garment and the code of rhetoric, Dryden makes it clear that Tomkis's comedy is merely the innocuous pattern – the base model – of Jonson's more substantial 'master-piece'. Complicating his metaphors even further, Dryden similarly suggests that Tomkis's university comedy is the shapeless, passive substance from which the sculptor Jonson 'moulds' his own play.

This self-interested vindication of an appropriative and revisionist dramatic method is precisely what Dryden is seeking to advance most forcefully in the opening lines of the *Albumazar* prologue. While legitimizing his own revisions, Dryden at the same time compliments the more advanced and sophisticated tastes of the current generation. (Dryden's 'To say this Comedy Pleas'd long ago/Is not enough to make it pass you now' would appear to be a deferential compliment to his audience at the expense of their Jacobean forebears.) Yet – having justified Jonson's method and, indeed, his *own* method, to his audience – Dryden quickly moves on to a related topic that is obviously his main concern in the ensuing prologue: a vigorous indictment of the poetic standards of what Hugh Ormsby-Lennon once aptly called the 'Early Augustan Battleground'.[21] In contradistinction to the comparative appropriative decorum of Jonson's day, Dryden observes:

> [T]his our age such Authors does afford,
> As make whole Playes, and yet scarce writ one word:
> Who in this Anarchy of witt, rob all,
> And what's their Plunder, their Possession call;
> Who like bold Padders scorn by night to prey,
> But Rob by Sun-shine, in the face of day;
> Nay scarce the common Ceremony use,
> Of stand, Sir, and deliver up your Muse;
> But knock the Poet down; and, with a grace,
> Mount *Pegasus* before the owners Face.
> . . .
> Yet it were modest, could it but be sed,
> They strip the living, but these rob the dead:
> Dare with the Mummeys of the Muses Play,
> And make love to 'em, the *Aegyptian*, way.
> Or as a Rhyming Author would have sed,
> Joyn the dead living, and the living dead.

(ll.15–32)

The essential necrophilia of the poetic practices of the current generation is thus contrasted to what Dryden presents as the reproductive purity of Jonson's age. The current climate, Dryden tells his audience in no uncertain terms, is one of robbery, plunder, and parasitism. Whereas the poets of Jonson's age were able 'conquerors' (however unjust) and transforming alchemists, the current rabble are merely 'padders' and 'thiefs'. Dryden's evocation of the cultural abuse and pollution of Hellenic classicism ('Pegasus') by an intrusive and competing ancient tradition (represented here as a plague-bearing kind of Egyptian darkness) works to posit the previous generation of English poets as operating in a kind of Saturnian Golden Age of literary borrowing and imitation.

It is of course ironic that while Dryden is busy lamenting a lost ethic of decorum and professionalism, his language in passages such as these recalls nothing so much as Jonson's own repeated complaints regarding contemporary theatrical practice. If the plagiary Matthew in Jonson's early *Every Man in His Humour* had been characterized by Jonson as being 'all for the pocket-Muse', the poets and dramatists of Dryden's day are similarly described as being 'Poets not of the heart, but of the hand'. Both Jonson and Dryden deplored in their respective literary climates an ethic of composition and of literary invention that was purely digital, mechanical, and appropriative in the worst possible way. Yet, whereas in one of his earliest plays Jonson had been concerned with a single idiolectic transgressor who haunted the liberties and the outlying suburbs of London, Dryden is now worried about a pack of literary highwaymen who seem to have infected the entire countryside and 'rob all'. More to the point, the literary-imitative offences that had before been circumscribed by the narrow confines of a court-centered literary culture have now been set free to find their way into *public* affairs. Plagiarism and parody, like unscrupulous vagabonds, have taken to the road.

The prologue to *Albumazar* is, like almost all of Dryden's literary and dramatic criticism, occasional. Far from formulating any comprehensive theory of poetic creation, Dryden was addressing a number of very specific concerns when writing the piece. George McFadden suggested that Dryden's more general attack on literary plagiarism and appropriation is on this occasion directed in particular at his former friend and patron, Sir Robert Howard.[22] McFadden pointed out that Dryden's indictment of literary misrepresentation and plagiarism constitutes a reaction to Howard's printing of *The Indian Queen* (1664) 'without any mention of a collaborator' – without any mention, that is, of Dryden. James Anderson Winn reiterated McFadden's suggestion that Dryden was likewise outraged that Howard had appropriated yet another drama and transformed it into a dangerous piece of political propaganda.[23] Winn's scenario is thoroughly convincing. Howard had recently produced *The Great Favourite, or The Duke of Lerma* (1668) for the King's Theatre. Winn suggests that the older play that Howard had used as a basis for his drama (perhaps, originally, the work of John Ford or Henry Shirley) may also have been regarded by Dryden himself as a likely candidate for revision for a popular audience. Dryden thus saw Howard's play as 'an infuriating double theft'. That is to say, his privileged familiarity with the original source of Howard's play led him to view the *Duke of Lerma* as an unscrupulous and perhaps perfunctory revision of an older manuscript. He likewise suffered the humiliation of seeing some desired dramatic material snatched from his own hands, and placed in those of someone who he would be increasingly inclined to regard as (at best) an aristocratic dilettante, and (at worse) a threatening literary and political rival. The fact that Howard's *Duke of Lerma* had eventually used that material as a weapon in the increasingly bitter feud between the Yorkists (including Dryden's benefactor, Clarendon) and Buckingham can only have made Dryden more frustrated and uncomfortable. It is certainly arguable that Dryden used his next opportunity to write for the popular theatre as an opportunity to revenge himself upon Howard's seeming literary ingratitude.

As with the original *Essay on Dramatic Poesy*, however, it is possible to read Dryden's criticism in the *Albumazar* prologue as both occasional *and* general.[24] Upon closer examination, in fact, the larger concerns that Dryden addresses in the prologue are those to which he shall return again and again in his critical writing. The sense of generational conflict that so motivates the *Essay of Dramatic Poesy* itself (and seems to find its way into all of Dryden's prose criticism), the anxiety regarding the possible dramatic superiority of the preceding age (which we encounter in the 1694 poem to Congreve), the uneasy derivative status of his *own* age, even – in ll.31–2 – an early doubt regarding the propriety of rhyme on the stage: *all* are present in this early prologue to *Albumazar*. Dryden ends the prologue with the suggestion that since it is only the audience who can approve or disapprove of any dramatic effort in the theatre by the show of their own applause, they are all potential accomplices to these new acts of poetic misappropriation and parody. They, too, literally, have a 'hand' in its failure or success. 'Gentlemen', he observes,

> y'are all concerned in this,
> You are in fault for what they do amiss:

> For they their thefts still undiscover'd think,
> And durst not steal unless you please to winck.
> Perhaps, you may award by Your Decree,
> They should refund, but that can never be.
> For should you letters of reprizall seal,
> These men writ that, which no man else would steale.
>
> (*Alb.* Pro.41–8)

Dryden's 'y'are all concerned in this' is both characteristic and significant. This final attempt to draw the audience into the artistic process as discerning and responsible critics evinces Dryden's typical desire to create and to foster an inclusive sense of community and critical consensus.[25] These artistic conflicts, Dryden implies, are like the Civil Wars that have affected them *all*. Just as the political and religious quarrels have to be worked out through an informed acknowledgement of a shared destiny and common concerns, so too questions of literary quality and propriety are emphatically *public* questions, and need to be resolved in a public forum. (It is interesting, too, that the language of political chaos, 'anarchy', that appears earlier in the prologue is conjured again in the legal language of reparation so familiar to the displaced nobles of Dryden's generation – 'letters of reprizall' – that concludes the passage.) The penchant of the age for literary theft and abuse – for plagiarism *and* parody – is not limited to the authors themselves, who are represented here as violent and lawless highwaymen, but is pervasive and inclusive. There is, at least, some hope for redemption here; the audience still holds over the appropriative writer the power of approval and disapproval, and can justly censure the poet or dramatist who imitates or borrows irresponsibly. It is up to the responsible author, the responsible audience, and the responsible reader together to set the proper bounds of parodic and poetic appropriation.

(III)

The *Albumazar* prologue is just one early example of Dryden's persistent efforts to situate his own work within the context of past literary achievement. If I have dwelt on this passage at the expense of some of the poet's other, lengthier ruminations on the subject, I have done so in order to underscore the several connections he appears to be drawing between the combined threats of plagiarism, parody, and political chaos – threats that are linked in turn to the political and rhetorical trauma of the recent past. It is now something of a critical commonplace to say that the poets of Dryden's generation were among the first writers in the English literary tradition to feel an overwhelming and compelling need to differentiate themselves – generically, stylistically, and linguistically – from their immediate predecessors. From the vantage of the 1660s and 1670s, the poets and dramatists of Shakespeare's generation were, to use Dryden's own language in his poem 'To my Dear Friend Mr. Congreve' (1694), like the 'Gyant Race before the Flood'. While they may lack the sheer imaginative strength of their forefathers, the current generation of poets, Dryden argues, have at least been able to best their 'Syres' in the 'wit' and 'sweetness' of their verse. (There is perhaps, in Dryden's comparison of the poets of the last generation to the Biblical Nephilim – the Titans of *Genesis* 6:1–4 – likewise some indictment of the behaviour that precipitated the subsequent deluge of poetic and civil strife.) Dryden and the poets of his generation would refer again and again in their work to this sense of periodization – and of distancing – in their attempts to formulate a systematic response to the achievements of the past and, at the same time, somehow to incorporate those achievements in their own work.

This unprecedented generational self-awareness is of consequence in a number of ways. It may, as both Walter Jackson Bate and Harold Bloom maintained, facilitate an anxiety-producing sense of filiation and indebtedness. It may likewise result, in George Steiner's less psychologically coherent formulation, in 'the anarchic bitterness of the latecomer'.[26] Or, indeed, the so-called burden of the poet can, on occasion, actually be looked upon as a positive gift; the poets stand, after all, as the legitimate heirs to a valued and valuable tradition. Whatever the particular pattern of response, this kind of literary self-consciousness tends to foster and to promote subsequent attempts to create a 'new' language of poetry suitable to the concerns and preoccupations of a new generation of poets – a generation for whom the achievements of the past are emphatically *past* and *achieved*. The novel pressure of periodization – the sense of distance and ancestral and paternal filiation – leads as well to a self-conscious questioning of the relationship between poets *within* a single literary 'era'. Writers find themselves in competition not only with the past, but with one another. Who will best succeed in the task of cultural revision? Who most possesses that rare ability to balance imitation and innovation? Writing after the achievements of the generation that produced Shakespeare and Jonson (and acknowledging, at the same time, the grand culmination of the English literary Renaissance in their *own* generation in the figure of John Milton), the poets of the Restoration were among the first to have these questions thrust upon them. If Jonson's articulation of the word 'parody' in *Every Man in His Humour* marks a new era in the critical discourse of parody and the parodic, the taxonomies of parody – the taxonomies of literary imitation and emulation in general and the distinctions between 'parody', 'burlesque', 'imitation', 'pastiche', in particular – are formulated by a generation of poets for whom these distinctions had become increasingly meaningful and important.

Dryden's own relationship to parody, libel, and lampoon could be extraordinarily complicated and at times inconsistent. His encounters with the new literary order ranged from his own casual and frequently dismissive responses to contemporary parodies and lampoons, to some emphatically physical reminders of just what it meant to be a poet in this new, competitive generation. Returning to his home one evening in December 1679, Dryden was attacked and beaten by three unidentified assailants in Rose Alley, a dark and circuitous passage extending between Covent Garden and Dryden's house in Long-acre. The *London Gazette* ran a notice a few days later stating that the poet had been 'barbarously assaulted and wounded', and the attack obviously left Dryden badly shaken. A reward of 50 pounds was offered for information regarding the attackers. The King himself offered to pardon any principal or accessory who came forward to divulge information regarding whatever 'divers men unknown' were behind the incident. The 'Rose Alley Ambuscade', as it was soon called, remains something of a mystery to this day.[27] Although James Winn sensibly argued that the attack was just as likely to have been the result of political rivalry or class hostility as it was the fallout of a strictly literary quarrel, we have already had occasion to mention that these categories were, in this period, far from being mutually exclusive. Blame for the assault has traditionally fallen on John Wilmot, Earl of Rochester. It is in fact eminently likely that Rochester, whose just pretensions to being a 'witty man' Dryden had recently mocked in the Preface to *All for Love* (1678), and who was convinced that Dryden himself had a hand in Mulgrave's 1679 *Essay upon Satire* (which had been circulating in manuscript in the months before the attack and which characterized Rochester as leading 'a life so infamous it's better quitting'), was the man behind the attack.[28] The ambuscade was, in any event, only the most violent and the most emphatically physical of the repeated attacks that Dryden sustained during his laureateship and his years as the most outspoken apologist for the Tories.

Dryden had been an obvious target for abuse by political enemies and literary rivals since mid-1668, when the quarrel with Howard (begun, perhaps, with the preface to *Albumazar*) culminated in the *Defence of the Essay of Dramatic Poesy* (1668). Dryden may at times sound unusually beleaguered in his early defence of rhymed heroic drama ('Intending to assault all poets, both ancient and modern', Dryden whines of Howard, 'he seems only to aim at me, and attacks me on my weakest side'), but in the years to come he would have far more than his fair share of opportunities to develop a more detached and condescending tone of reply.

The Rehearsal (1671) is of course the most memorable of these early attacks, and the one that has most often attracted the attention of subsequent generations of critics. Years after the drama appeared Dryden would comment that he had never bothered to respond to Buckingham's burlesque 'because I knew the author sate to himself when he drew the Picture, was the very *Bays* of his own Farce' (IV.8). Buckingham in fact scores some palpable hits against the excesses of Dryden's heroic style, and frequently employs an explicitly parodic method in his satire of the dramatist. While the laureate himself is satirized as a less than scrupulous plagiary whose one rule of invention when confronted with the task of composition is to consult his 'Book of drama commonplaces' and have 'in one view, all that Persius, Montaigne, Seneca's tragedies, Horace, Juvenal, ... Plutarch's lives and the rest, have ever thought, upon the subject', *The Rehearsal* itself operates on a similar principle of constant, parodic appropriation.[29] Lines from Dryden's dramas *The Indian Emperor, Tyrannick Love*, and – most pointedly – *The Conquest of Granada* are likely to reappear in Buckingham's piece in a calculatedly ruthless light. The result is an often elaborate layering of textual reference and parody. Some of those parodies that cut to the heart of the posturing bluster of Dryden's most 'ranting' heroes such as Maximin and Almanzor contain, at the same time, concealed jibes at Dryden's own appropriative-imitative method. In his determination to be of service to Almahide in the second part of *The Conquest of Granada*, for example, Dryden's hero declares:

> Spight of my self I'le stay, fight, love despair;
> And I can do all this, because I dare.

> (II.iii.5–6)

Dryden includes a translation of Virgil's 'possunt quia posse videntur'. The passage is reduced in *The Rehearsal* to Drawcansir's resolve:

> I drink, I huff, I start, look big and stare;
> And all this I can do, because I dare.

> (IV.i.213–14)

The passage is in many ways a double-barrelled, self-consuming parody. The gaseous vacuity and wide-eyed attitudinizing that characterizes Buckingham's language here seems to draw attention not only to the parody of Dryden's language in *Granada*, but to the grand and airy distance between the belittled Dryden and his own (justly) praised Virgilian original.[30] The passage, condemning Dryden and implicitly praising Virgil, thus functions as an indictment of the simultaneous excesses and limitations of Dryden's own parodic-imitative practice.

There is a great deal of excellent text-specific comedy in Buckingham's parodic redactions of Dryden's originals. Buckingham's parodic drama would have many successors, including Fielding's hilarious *Tragedy of Tragedies* (1730), Stevens's *Distress upon Distress* (1752), and Sheridan's *The Critic* (1779), which appeared just over a century after Buckingham's original. Unlike these later efforts, however, Buckingham's *Rehearsal* succeeds less frequently when it is echoing specific passages of Dryden's heroic drama than when it is personally ridiculing the character of Dryden. Bayes/Dryden is presented as a hack dramatist whose definition of poetry appears to have less to do with invention and craftsmanship than parody and appropriation ('the chief art of poetry', Bayes comments at one point in a definition of poetry that sounds much more like a definition of parody, 'is to elevate your expectation, and then bring you off some extraordinary way'). Indeed, the vindictive and hyperactive pasquinades of the 1660s and 1670s – the products of 'the new way of writing' – seem just as frequently to ridicule Dryden's personality, family, and reputation, as his literary or political convictions. Each new product of Dryden's pen seems to provoke *some* sort of parodic, inter-textual response; the Howard–Dryden controversy of 1668 and the *Rota* pamphlets a few years later initiate a constant pattern of censure and parody that would last until Dryden's death in 1700.

The fiercely predatory atmosphere of inter-textual appropriation and abuse in the 1660s and 1670s makes it particularly difficult to begin deciding precisely what, in this era, constitutes parody, and precisely how parody is to be differentiated from 'answering poems' and other derivative imitations. Dryden, while obviously not considering his own borrowings and imitations as 'parodic' in the larger sense of inter-textual activity in which I have been using the term, nevertheless, felt himself close enough to the issues of parody, lampoon, burlesque, satire, and other 'defamatory writings' (260) to attempt to formulate his own definitions of such terms, and to place his own work within the newly formulated taxonomies of literary appropriation.

In the *Discourse Concerning the Original and Progress of Satire*, dedicated to the Earl of Dorset and prefixed to a collection of translations of Juvenal and Persius published by Jonson in 1693, Dryden avowedly traces the history of the satiric mode from the Greeks to his own day. Dryden's own tone of 'vicious modesty' is at times wonderfully self-deprecatory and even wistful ('I ought to have mentioned him before', Dryden says of a certain author at one point, 'but by the slip of an old man's memory he was forgot'). The whole is something of a personal vindication and an *apologia pro vita sua*. 'Tis no shame to be a poet', he tells Dorset at one point, 'tho tis to be a bad one' (225). While claiming to define the 'art of satire' as a precise verbal art, Dryden persistently defers committing himself to designating any 'primacy of honour' among the ancient satirists, and is constantly drawn from his ostensible subject to a contemplation of the larger issues of poetic borrowing and emulation; there is again a constant pressure to justify the genius and capability of his own age, and a condemnation of the 'multitude of scribblers' who 'daily pester the world' with their 'insufferable' poetry (212).[31] While directing the reader's attention towards felicitous examples of literary appropriation ('great contemporaries whet and cultivate each other, and mutual borrowing and commerce, makes the common riches of learning, as it does of civil government'), Dryden at the same time flicks aside the 'dull makers of lampoons' who seem to give the lie to his claims for the current age. The closest Dryden gets to an actual definition of the lampoon parody with which he has been so pestered is to classify it as a subset of satire, and call it 'a dangerous sort of weapon, and for the most part unlawful' (253). He deliberately excludes from the proper genealogies of satire the *silli* of the Greeks, which he defines as 'satiric poems, full of parodies; that is, of verses patched up from great poets, and turned into another sense than their author intended them'. Satire itself comes in for a more extended treatment a few pages later when it is defined as 'a kind of poetry, without a series of actions, invented for the purging of our minds'. Dryden also notes that the satiric method consists 'chiefly in a sharp and pungent manner of speech, but partaking also, in a facetious and civil way of jesting'. While conceding Boileau's imitations and parodies in his *Lutrin* to be 'the most beautiful, and the most noble kind of satire' (273), Dryden obviously sets contemporary parodic abuse and appropriation in a different category altogether – such attempts are little more than slanders that have no way of attaining the majesty of classical originals.

Dryden's scornful dismissal of contemporary imitations and parodies (and his easy equation between plagiarism and lampoon parodies in the *Discourse on Satire*) are again complicated by the fact that Dryden himself was several times in his career accused of literary plagiarism. Thomas Shadwell's *Medall of John Bayes* (1682) had charged of Dryden,

> No piece did ever from thyself begin;
> Thou can'st no web, from thine own bowels spin.
> Were from thy works cull'd out what thou'st purloin'd
> Even *D – fey* would excell what's left behind
> . . .
> Thou plunder'st all, t'advance thy mighty Name,
> Look'st big, and triumph'st with thy borrowed fame.
> But art (while smiling thus thou think'st th'art *Chief*)
> A servile imitator and a thief.[32]

> (ll.65–78)

Later in his career, Dryden was similarly attacked by Gerard Langbaine, who criticized him for 'taxing others with stealing characters from him, . . . when he himself does *the same*, in almost all the Plays he writes'.[33] Dryden several times claims never to have paid much attention to the doggerel of the 'dull makers of lampoons' (217) who had attacked him and parodied his own poetry throughout his career. 'I complain not of their lampoons and libels', he explains to Dorset,

> though I have been a public mark for many years.
> I am vindictive enough to have repelled force by
> force, if I could imagine that any of them had
> ever reached me; but they either shot at rovers,
> and therefore missed, or their powders were so
> weak, that I might safely stand them, at the
> nearest distance. (212)

He returns to the subject later in the essay (abandoning the colourful martial imagery) noting:

> I have seldom answered any scurrilous
> lampoon when it was in my power to have
> exposed my enemies, and being naturally

> vindictive, have suffered in silence, and
> possessed my soul in quiet. (254)

An older generation that included Louis Bredvold smiled at Dryden's 'public claims to some of the nobler virtues' in passages such as these, and Dryden's superbly casual insistence in both passages on his own 'naturally vindictive' temperament is amusing.[34] Although he continues the passage with a return to the *topoi* of excessive personal modesty, which is one of the distinguishing thematic features of the essay as a whole, Dryden is obsessed with his own perception of the decorous restraint he feels he has maintained in the face of numerous parodic slanders. The discrepancies between Dryden's two 'defences', however, is telling. In the first passage he insists that the lampoons and parodies never reached him; in the second he observed merely that he has 'suffered in silence' and 'possessed [his] soul in quiet'. The latter phrase – recalling as it does the language of *Psalms* 4:4 – would further seem to suggest the emotional, almost spiritual nature of the wounds suffered through such attacks.

Dryden's claims of restraint are in a sense perfectly legitimate. Following the lessons of his initial, exasperated outburst against Howard in 1668, Dryden rarely displayed any anger against such antagonists openly. He endured the attacks of Settle and Rochester – and the numerous parodies of *Absalom and Achitophel*, *The Medall*, and *The Hind and the Panther* – in comparative silence; he certainly never answered attacks with *quid pro quo* perfunctory parodies even when, as was the case with Montague and Prior's *The Hind and the Panther Transvers'd* (1687), we have solid evidence that those attacks affected him at a deeply personal level.[35]

Yet in another sense Dryden's protestations that he never dirtied his hands with the business of parody and lampoon is an obvious falsification of his literary record. There are numerous instances of Dryden's engaging in attacks on 'the reputation of other men' (253). James Winn points out that the *Discourse on the Original and Progress of Satire* itself – in which Dryden continually denies the *animus* of parodic activity – is the essay in which, tellingly, Dryden first admits publicly to the authorship of *Mac Flecknoe* (1682). Likewise, the scathing characters of Doeg (Elkinah Settle) and Og (Thomas Shadwell) in *The Second Part of Absalom and Achitophel* (1682) might surely be counted as examples of Dryden's being revenged upon the 'reputations' of his enemies.

Dryden – who claimed in the *Discourse on Satire* to have 'given up [his poetry] to the critics' (254) – perhaps remained anxious regarding the expansive and appropriative power of parody because his own work, while not necessarily lampooning his contemporaries, was so thoroughly 'parodic', in the larger sense with which we have been using the word. Dryden's earliest poetry, for example, is the product of a 'conceited' Westminster style that draws heavily upon the language and the images of Royalist propaganda; yet the excessive critical self-consciousness of poems such as the elegy 'Upon the death of Lord Hastings' – and the frequent over-extension of the Royalist idiom to bathetic lengths – leads the reader to wonder if the visual and mythological imagery of that Royalist style is purposefully being taken to parodic or self-parodic lengths. Dryden's earliest poems – the poems prior to his catalytic reading of D'Avenant's preface to *Gondibert* – comment again and again on the 'second-hand' nature of his own poetic imagery, and constantly work to attain a balance between the standard Royalist language and metaphysical conceits of the poetry of the last age, and the new poetic language of social and political commitment. Even after his earliest justifications (in the 'Preface' to *Annus Mirabilis*) of a new poetic idiom that gradually eschews the 'jerks or sting of an Epigram' (46), Dryden continues to write a poetry that is in some way both responsive and reactionary. It was, for example, for a long time supposed that *Annus Mirabilis* derived not only its title but, to some extent, its *modus vivendi* from the Fifth Monarchy *Mirabilis Annus* tracts that had begun appearing in the early 1660s. Michael McKeon has argued convincingly that the conventions of eschatological prophecy employed by Dryden in the poem were 'universally acceptable and universally employed' by both Royalist and anti-Royalist writers, and that there is 'no reason to suppose... that Dryden owed any real debt to [the *Mirabilis Annus*] tracts'.[36] If Dryden's poem is not an explicitly ironic reflection of the Fifth Monarchy tracts, however, it remains parodic in the larger sense of engaging in an explicit text-specific dialogue with an already existing body of writing. If Dryden is not specifically 'answering' the dissenting prophecy of *Eniagtos terastios* (1661) and *Mirabilis Annus Secundus* (1662), he is at least using the shared language and imagery of political prophecy in the 1660s, which renders his poem, as McKeon is himself anxious to demonstrate, a function of already existing rhetorical and ideological strategies; Dryden's poem is quite literally a complementary 'beside-song'. One might argue as well that the Biblical typology of a poem such as *Absalom and Achitophel* depicts contemporary events as in some way 'parodying' the archetypal myths of the past. Dryden is picking up on a number of English antecedents, including sermons and several popular poems, that characterize Charles as David, and Monmouth as Absalom.[37]

Almost all of Dryden's critics have recognized, on some level, the essentially parodic character of his work, employing a selection of literary-critical terminology ranging from 'imitation' and 'allusion' to 'parody' and 'burlesque'. Samuel Johnson commented on Dryden's mimetic 'habit of reflection', and noted that he was in certain ways 'if not always a plagiary, at least an imitator'. He noted too that Dryden was likely to 'ease his pain by venting his malice in a parody', and just as likely to descend into self-parodies 'of which perhaps he was not conscious'.[38] T. S. Eliot, noting the parodies of Cowley in *Mac Flecknoe*, observed that Dryden's poetic method was at times 'something very near to parody', and suggested that one of Dryden's most conspicuous qualities as a poet was his 'capacity for assimilation'.[39] Eliot's phrase is an intriguing one: Dryden's 'assimilation', in Eliot's estimation, seems to consist primarily in his ability to enhance his borrowed or derivative material – to create complementary beside-songs, 'and to employ parodic techniques not to belittle', but to 'make his object great in a way contrary to expectations'. Ian Jack noted that the particular parodies of Cowley in *Mac Flecknoe* serve as analogical models for 'the mock-heroic conception of the whole poem'.[40] Hugh Macdonald observed that *The Rehearsal* was undertaken to burlesque Dryden's heroic plays 'which were themselves burlesques'.[41] David Hopkins noted that Dryden was in his dramatic work always hovering 'on the border of burlesque and self-parody'.[42] Reuben Brower praised Dryden's 'allusive irony' (often consisting of close imitation and parody of other authors), and noted that Dryden's parodic redactions of his classical originals can at times themselves be so 'noble' as to be 'hardly recognizable as parody'.[43]

The excessively dependent and 'parodic' nature of Dryden's own work might then go some way towards explaining his own anxiety regarding the possibilities of parodic attack and response. In order to see precisely what Dryden's reactions to parody were, however, it is worth taking a closer look at a specific instance. When preparing his invaluable bibliography of Dryden in the early twentieth century, Hugh Macdonald undertook a survey of the many attacks on the poet. Macdonald examined the literary assaults on Dryden ranging from the early attacks of Ravenscroft and the *Rota* pamphlets (1673) to the falsely attributed pamphlets of the later 1680s and 1690s primarily as a source of biographical information.[44] Macdonald's descriptions remain a valuable complement to his bibliography, yet fall short of any rigorous analysis of the pamphlet attacks themselves. Although they are frequently referred to in passing by Dryden's critics, very few of the attacks have been the subject of any detailed critical attention. James M. Osborn, while dismissing most of the attacks on Dryden as 'painfully dull reading', made an exception for *The Medall of John Bayes*, but never offered any justification for his praise of Shadwell's piece as 'deservedly the best known and most quoted' poetical assault on Dryden, and merely skimmed the piece for biographical information. A more comprehensive example than the single Shadwell parody can be found in Dryden's most important political poem, *Absalom and Achitophel*, which provokes a number of text-specific parodies and which, ultimately, leads to Dryden's *The Medall*. What – precisely – provokes Dryden to react to parodies, and *how* he responds to his parodic detractors will be the concern of the remaining pages.

(IV)

Absalom and Achitophel was published in the third week of November 1681 – just one week before Shaftesbury's trial. Although the piece initially appeared without a name on its title page, Dryden's authorship was within days of the poem's appearance an open secret. The laureate's vigorous vindication of 'the King & his friends', as Narcissus Luttrell comfortably put it, formed part of the larger paper war between the Whigs and the Tories that had been going on since the first rumours of actual popish treacheries had reached the ears of the public in the mid-1670s.[45] More specifically, Dryden's poem took its place in the dialogue that had followed Charles's dissolution of the Oxford Parliament in April 1681. The King's own *Declaration*, vindicating his conduct to Parliament, had appeared shortly after the brief session at Oxford, and had in turn been followed by a sharply critical Whig retort in *A Letter from a Person of Quality*.[46] Dryden's own defence of the King's *Declaration* had likewise appeared in June.[47]

Predictably, Dryden's political satire in turn provoked a wide range of responses in verse and prose. At least eight of these responses are direct text-specific parodic reactions to Dryden's poem. These include 'Towser the Second, A Bull-Dog' (Dec. 1681), 'Poetical Reflections, on a late poem Entitled *Absalom and Achitophel*' (Dec. 1681), 'A Panegyrick on the Author of *Absalom and Achitophel*' (Dec. 1681), 'A Whip for the Fool's Back' (Dec. 1681), 'A Key (with the Whip) to open the mystery and iniquity of the poem call'd *Absalom and Achitophel*' (Jan. 1682), 'Azariah and Hushai' (Jan. 1682), 'Absalom's IX Worthies' (March 1682), and *Absalom Senior* (April 1682). Of these pamphlet attacks on Dryden only two can be attributed to authors with absolute certainty: 'Azariah and Hushai' to Samuel Pordage and 'Absalom Senior' to Elkinah Settle. Editors since Malone have speculated on the authorship of the other attacks, with attention focusing most frequently on Buckingham, Settle, Shadwell, Henry Care, and Christopher Nesse. A number of other attacks on Dryden followed the publication of *The Medall* on 16 March 1682, and the appearance of the *Second Part of Absalom and Achitophel* in November of that same year. These attacks can more accurately be described as responses specifically to those two subsequent poems, and are best discussed with reference to the paper wars that surrounded those works, rather than those that sprung up immediately around *Absalom and Achitophel*.

The four initial attacks on *Absalom and Achitophel* all appeared within just over a month of the publication of Dryden's poem. The angry sputtering of these parodies within days of one another is just one indication of how volatile the Augustan parodic battleground could be. 'Towser the Second, A Bull-Dog' is dated 10 December in Luttrell's copy.[48] It has been attributed (since Malone) to Henry Care, a fanatic anti-Royalist hireling who, in July of 1680, had been placed on trial for editing the *Weekly Paquet of Advice from Rome*, a paper that regularly accused the church of England with charges of popery; on the accession of James II, Care himself would in turn write for the Roman Catholic party.

'Towser' may well be Care's production. It displays all the characteristics of the confused and clumsy invective of the Whig publisher. The title draws a connection between Dryden – who is described in the satire as a mad dog 'Snarling and Biting every one he meets' – and Roger L'Estrange, the Tory journalist who had earned the sobriquet 'the dog Towzer' in 1680, and who had been attacked once before by Care in the epistle to his *History of the Damned Popish Plot* (1680). 'Towser' begins with a text-specific parody of the opening lines of Dryden's *Absalom and Achitophel*:

> In pious times when Poets were well-bang'd
> For sawcy Satyr and for Sham-plots hang'd
> A learned Bard, that long commanded had
> The trembling Stage in Chief, at last run mad,
> And swore and tore and ranted at no rate.

(ll.1–5)

Rather than developing the Biblical typology and scriptural allusions of Dryden's Davidic original, however, Care dismisses his own reference to the 'pious times' of Dryden's metaphor to describe a 'classical' debate between '*Apollo* and his *Muses*' regarding what is to be done about this poet gone mad. One of the Muses suggests bleeding him, another recommends burning a Peruvian balsam to fumigate the head; 'Clio', the satirist dryly tells us, 'was more for Opiates'. Not having received very sound advice from his muses, Apollo then turns to a 'noble Friend' who opens the poet's infected head, and ministers to his fevered brain. Although this has the beneficial effect of preventing the poet from swearing all the time, it is not enough to restore him to his wits. 'For since', Care notes,

> he has gin' ore to Plague the Stage
> With the effects of his poetick rage,
> Like a mad Dog he runs about the Streets,
> Snarling and biting every one he meets.
> The other day he met our Royal CHARLES,
> And his two Mistresses, and at them Snarles.
> Then falls upon the Ministers of State
> And treats them A-la-mode *de Billingsgate*.

(ll.30–8)

Apollo – 'vext to see there was no more/Effect of Medicine' – then sends some surgeons to 'annoint' the poet with 'Oyl of Crab tree', an obvious reference to the Rose Alley Ambuscade. This does little good, however, and the poet is soon said to be running up and down the town 'crying out against an Absalom and Achitophel'. Apollo concludes the poem with a determination to worm Towser and, opening the poet's mouth, draws out a worm 'which of the Jebusite smells very strongly'. If the worming does not succeed in rendering Towser docile, Apollo concludes, the dog of a poet will be hung. It is perhaps too over-ingenious to suggest that Care's own open ending is parodic of Dryden's own historically incomplete narrative.

Care's versification throughout this parodic response to *Absalom and Achitophel*, lamentable, to begin with, deteriorates even more the further he moves from the formal strategies of his target text. If Dryden's own early, heavily end-stopped verse and aphoristic syntax could at times render his poetry susceptible to parody, this stylistic weapon is lost on Care, whose own lines tend to suffer from hopeless enjamb-ment, inconspicuous rhymes, and awkward use of caesurae that – at their worst – weaken his verse and threaten to render the thread of his muddled argument invisible. Indeed, once moving away from the preformed literary language of Dryden's original, Care loses sight as well of Dryden's arguments and imaginative sympathies. Earl Miner has argued that one of the central strengths of Dryden's poem is its 'closed metaphor'. 'The Biblical air', Miner notes, 'is maintained throughout. If it be allegory, it is more tightly shut than any other modern English allegories'.[49] Care's failure lies precisely in his willingness to open Dryden's sacred history, to offer an obvious 'key' to his meaning, to pinpoint the metaphorical vehicle. Unlike the sustained distance that Dryden himself attempts to maintain throughout his own parody of Biblical history, Care leaps – or rather stumbles – from specificity to specificity, and over-situates his poem in the actual events and personalities of the contemporary party-political conflict.

The main indictment of Care's parody is reserved until the very last lines of the satire, when the mad poet is accused of Roman Catholic sympathies. Dryden's lines on the 'native right' of the patient Jebusites might in fact be construed by a dissenting reader to reveal his own support of the Roman Catholics. The suggestion of Roman Catholic sympathies at least makes comprehensible Care's pointed coupling of Dryden with L'Estrange (who was throughout 1681 battling the attacks of Whigs and dissenters who accused him of attending mass and receiving the sacrament) more understandable. Yet Care's suggestion of Dryden's Roman Catholic bias gains nothing from his withholding it until the end of the parody; rather than being a calculated attack on Dryden's religious beliefs (an attack of which Care was surely capable), the slur of Roman Catholic affiliation comes across as an afterthought to an already rambling and imprecise account of Dryden's (supposed) poetic vagaries.

Following Care's 'Towser' by only a few days was a poem called 'Poetical Reflections on a late Poem Entitled *Absalom and Achitophel*'.[50] The piece is attributed on the title page only to 'a Person of Honour'. Although attribution has traditionally been made (on the basis of Wood's *Athenae Oxoniensis*) to the Duke of Buckingham, there is little internal evidence that the work is in fact his. Both the 'Poetical Reflections' and the next response to *Absalom and Achitophel* to appear, the 'Panegyrick on the Author of *Absalom and Achitophel*', concern themselves to some extent with Dryden's early poem on Cromwell, and the charge of political apostasy.[51] The 'Heroic Stanzas on the Glorious Memory of Cromwell' (1659) had been reprinted late in 1681 by

Dryden's Whig antagonists, seeking to discredit his subsequent efforts in verse, and attacking Dryden himself as a hireling with a 'nauseous mercenary pen'.[52]

The 'Poetical Reflections' begins with a preface 'To the Reader' that denounces Dryden's 'scandalous pamphlet' as a 'Capital or National Libel' rather than a merely personal attack. The author is concerned most that the characters of Shaftesbury, Monmouth, and the King himself have been irreparably abused in Dryden's work, and accuses Dryden's 'impious poem' (perhaps justly) of attempting to influence the outcome of Shaftesbury's trial, and exchange Shaftesbury's more 'prudent deserts' for the 'Hangman's axe'. 'I suppose the poet thought himself enough assured of their condemnation', the author writes, '. . . that his genius had not otherwise ventur'd to have trampled a person of such eminent abilities, and Interest in the nation'. The poem itself is admittedly poor stuff. Like Care's effort of a few weeks earlier, the 'Poetical Reflections' begins with a precise parody of Dryden's poem:

> When late Protectorship was Canon-Proof,
> And *Cap-a-pé* had seiz'd on *Whitehall*-Roof.
> And next, on *Isrealites* durst look so big,
> That *Tory-like*, it lov'd not much the *Whigg*:
> A Poet there starts up, of wondrous Fame; . . .

(ll. 1–5)

The 'pious times' of David/Charles II's reign are here exchanged for the more explicit era of the 'late Protectorship' and the rule of Nimrod/Cromwell. Whereas Dryden's poem had in its opening lines addressed the central questions concerning the legitimacy of rhetoric and authority, the anonymous author of the 'Poetical Reflections' concerns himself only with a desire to accuse Dryden of being a sycophant and a hireling:

> A Grace our might *Nimrod* late beheld,
> When he within the Royal Palace dwell'd,
> And saw 'twas of import if Lines could bring
> His Greatness from *Usurper*, to be King:
> . . .
> And tho no Wit can Royal Blood infuse,
> No more than melt a mother to a Muse:
> Yet much a certain Poet undertook,
> That Men and Manners deals in without-Book.

> And might not more to Gospel-Truth belong,
> Than he (if Christened) does by name of *John*.

(ll.15–26)

Although the poem affects to enter the same 'judaic trance' that colours Dryden's poem, the poet here – like Care – misses the opportunity to impose the biblical metaphor with any consistency, and the poem subsequently veers recklessly between thinly veiled typology on the one hand (Queen Catherine is presented as Bathsheba, for example, while Amiel is Finch, Lord Chancellor) and an open naming of the Whig's antagonists (i.e., 'Tory Roger' L'Estrange) on the other. The body of the poem consists of a defence of Monmouth and Shaftesbury ('Thou did'st no honour seek', the poet assures the young Duke, 'but what's thy due'), and a half-hearted attack on the 'filched allusions' of Dryden's 'judaick sham'. Unlike Care's piece, which pointedly accused Dryden of a Roman Catholic bias, the 'Poetical Reflections' only suggests that the 'evil poetry' of the 'Tory-writer' might appropriately be burnt with the effigies of the pope on 17 November. The poetic energy of the 'Poetical Reflections' is directed primarily at a vindication of the Whigs, and a pretended scorn of Dryden's apostasy, and a similar scorn directed at his attempts to prophecy 'against the sense of Heaven and Men'.

The 'Panegyrick' focuses even more intently on the Whig accusation that Dryden is a turncoat and, as the postscript to the recently reissued 'Heroic Stanzas' put it, 'a turd . . . to men in pow'r'.[53] Although certain phrases of *Absalom and Achitophel* are invoked, and Dryden's biblical typology is again turned to serve the Whig cause (Cromwell, for example, is here represented as Moloch), the main charge is Dryden's supposed sycophancy to men in power, and the piece appears to function less obviously as a text-specific parody of *Absalom and Achitophel* than as a general indictment of Dryden's inclusive and indiscriminate poetic method. The power of appropriation and abuse granted to the poet is depicted as the counterpart to the 'pow'r unlimited' defended (it is alleged) by Dryden in both 'Heroic Stanzas' and *Absalom and Achitophel*.

'A Whip for the fool's back,' and 'A Key (With the whip)' – the next two responses to Dryden's poem – appeared in late December. Both have been attributed to the Calvinist preacher Christopher Nesse.[54] They ask to be read as a single attack. Nesse's first pamphlet is one of the oddest responses to Dryden's poem insofar as it takes offence not at Dryden's political agenda, but his supposed advocacy of promiscuous polygamy.

The full title of Nesse's pamphlet is 'A Whip for the Fool's Back, Who Styles Honourable Marriage a Cursed Confinement'. The opening line attacks 'Dirty Jack' as a 'prince of Pimps'. As Nesse writes in the second pamphlet:

> First *one to one* was the first *blest* Confinement;
> *More* is a *Monster*, and a Curs'd consignment;

(ll.29–30)

'The Key' is, on the whole, a slightly more interesting attack on Dryden, as Nesse particularly glosses the typology of Dryden's 'Jewish allegories'. Like Dryden's other attackers, Nesse concentrates on the supposed injustice of Dryden's attacks on Monmouth and Shaftesbury, and on Dryden's seeming apostasy in light of the recently republished verses on the death of Cromwell. 'Must brave *Monmouth* be his [Absalom's] parallel', Nesse laments, 'By Renegade Wits of old Cromwell?' Nesse's lines at times perceptively respond to the seemingly parodic extension of Royalist imagery to Cromwell in Dryden's own 'Heroic Stanzas'. Nesse revived that imagery to refer to Monmouth's own unjust succession, as postulated by Dryden:

> From *Davids* Carkass he might step to th'Throne.
> With many more insinuating Tricks,
> Impatient of delays, th' *Mock Sun* to fix
> In's Royal Orb before th' *True Sun* was set,
> Present Possession of the Crown to get . . .

(ll.132–6)

Nesse also – like the author of 'Poetical Reflections' – accuses Dryden of attempting to influence the outcome of Shaftesbury's trial, and recommends Shaftesbury's forgiving nature; he likewise styles Titus Oates as 'England's saviour' and applauds his saving the country 'from that Damned Popish Plot'. Nesse's main point of attack, however, lies in what Dryden would later (in the 'Epistle to the Whigs' prefaced to *The Medall*) scornfully style his 'skill in Hebrew derivations'. Nesse obviously prides himself on his supposed ability to correct the errors of Dryden's typology. In the 'Epistle to the Whigs' Dryden ventures to suggest that Nesse went no further in his learning than the Index to Hebrew Names and Etymologies, which is printed at the end of English Bibles.

Of the three remaining responses to *Absalom and Achitophel*, one – 'Absalom's IX Worthies' – is a positive reaction to Dryden's 'Incomparable Poem', and is to be classed rather with the commendatory verses to that work by poets such as Nathaniel Lee and Nahum Tate (it was in fact prefixed to later editions of *Absalom and Achitophel*).[55] The author attempts to make some of the details of Dryden's Davidic myth more obvious, yet the attempt at praise is surprisingly clumsy. The poet suggests, for example, that the author of *Absalom and Achitophel* (as yet professedly 'unknown' and 'concealed' in these recommendatory pieces) is either

> Satyr or Statesman, poet, or divine,
> Thou any thing, thou everything that's fine.

This statement recalls nothing so much as Dryden's own indictment of Buckingham as 'everything by starts, and nothing long'.

Pordage's 'Azariah and Hushai' is one of the most coherent attacks on Dryden, and far and away the best written parody of Dryden's verse. Although Pordage has been mocked by subsequent critics from Malone and Scott to Macdonald for – in Dryden's own words – resorting to 'the utmost refuge of notorious blockheads' and using Dryden's 'own language' against him, Pordage perhaps realized better than any of Dryden's other literary assailants the value of the tactics of text-specific parody and even *cento* technique in response to a poem as powerful as *Absalom and Achitophel*. Pordage begins the barrage of parody in the prefatory 'To the Reader', virtually paraphrasing Dryden's own admonitory account of his own work. As he will do throughout the parody itself, Pordage lifts phrases from Dryden's own poem ('Wit and Fool be the consequences of Fool and Tory', 'I know not if my poem has a Genius to force its way . . .'). He styles his own parody not as an 'answer' to *Absalom and Achitophel* ('I call not this an answer to Absalom, I have not much to do with . . .') but rather as a complementary corrective reflection of Dryden's work. 'The Ancients', Pordage writes, 'say that everything hath two hands, I have laid hold of that opposite the author of *Absalom and Achitophel*. As to Truth, who has the better hold, let the world judge; and it is no new thing, for the same Persons, to be ill or well represented by several parties' (73–4). Pordage suggests that his own poem is a 'better' work than Dryden's *Absalom and Achitophel* if only because his Azariah is 'more agreeable to the virtue of a Heroe'. 'I could wish,' Pordage suggests, that the same hand that drew the Rebellious Son with so much Ingenuity and Skill, would outdo mine, in shewing the virtues of an obedient Son and Loyal Councellor, since he may have as much Truth for a Foundation to build upon, the Artful Structure of the heroes glory, with his own Fame and Immortality.[56]

The narrative of 'Azariah and Hushai' is loosely adapted from II Kings 14–15. The biblical story forms a small part of the history of the kingdom of Judah under the Davidic dynasty in the eighth century BC. Both Amaziah (800–783 BC) and his son Azariah (783–742 BC) continue the tendency of their predecessors such as Jehoshaphat (873–849 BC) and Joash (837–800 BC), insofar as they fail to prohibit worship in local shrines and in 'high places', even while they repudiate the more reprehensible predecessors such as Athaliah (842–837 BC), who had allowed the substitution of the worship of Baal for the worship of the Hebrew God.

Pordage takes advantage of the tolerant and – it might be construed – forgiving nature of these rulers to forge the following narrative: The Canaanites [Roman Catholics] or worshipers of Baal [the Pope] are encouraged by the fact that Amaziah [Charles II] had not, in the early years of his reign, 'cast out Baal's Priests, and cut down every grove'. The Chemerarins [Jesuits] accordingly see the time as fit to contrive some sort of plot to bring destruction upon Judea [England] and its King, and return Judea fully to the worship of Baal. Until the plot Amaziah's reign had been a 'long, happy, peaceful' one. The plot – 'the Nation's bane and curse, so bad no man can represent it worse' – fails only because one Libni [Titus Oates] has proven himself the 'glorious Saviour of the Land', and brought the plot to light. In spite of all evidence to the contrary (in particular, the murder of Azrid [Sir Edmund Bury Godfrey]), the protestations of the convicted conspirators leads many of the Jews to (wrongly) suspect that the plot was, perhaps, no more than a fabrication. The virtuous Hushai (Shaftesbury) is the man among the King's Counsellors who is most distressed by such suspicions, particularly since they work to support the claims of Eliakim (James, Duke of York), to the throne in favour of those of Amaziah's son, Azariah (Monmouth). Although the Jews are a sober and patient race, the ensuing struggle divides their number into two opposing camps. Azariah in particular is distressed to find that he and Hushai have been styled Absalom and Achitophel by the 'creatures' of their political enemies, and turns to Hushai for advice. Hushai can only advise him to 'Let Virtue be your Guide alone'. Hushai himself was a loyal councillor to Amaziah who is now forced into exile by slander. Hushai also uses the occasion to lament the fact that a loyal son so like his father should be estranged from that father by the 'venom'd Tongues' of his enemies. Hushai asserts Azariah's legitimate right to the throne, yet notes that it would be better 'without the Crowne to die/Than quit your virtue and best Loyaltie'. He advises Azariah to divert himself with 'country sport' and absent himself from the court political struggle. Many lords stand beside Azariah in his 'loyalty', including Nashai (Essex), and Elshima (Macclesfield).

The Royal Court is, meanwhile, in disarray, and finds its supporters from a drunken group of 'roaring bullies'. Foremost among the supporters of the crown is Shimei (Dryden). Pordage's caricature is worth quoting at length:

> *Shimei* the Poet Laureat of the Age,
> The falling Glory of the *Jewish* Stage,
> Who scourg'd the Priest, and ridicul'd the Plot,
> Like common men must not be quite forgot.
> Sweet was the Muse that did his wit inspire,
> Had he not let his Hackney Muse to hire:
> But variously his knowing Muse could sing,
> Could *Doeg* praise, and could blaspheme the King:
> The bad make good, good bad, and bad make worse,
> Bless in Heroicks, and in Satyres curse.
> *Shimei* to *Zabed's* praise could tune his Muse,
> And Princely *Azarai* could abuse.
> *Zimri* we know he had no cause to praise,
> Because he dub'd him with the name of *Bays*.
> Revenge on him did bitter Venome shed,
> Because he tore the Lawrel from his head;
> Because he durst with his proud Wit engage,
> And brought his Follies on the Publick Stage.
> Tell me, *Apollo*, for I can't divine,
> Why Wives he curs'd, and prais'd the Concubine;
> Unless it were that he had led his life
> With a teeming matron ere she was a Wife
> Or that it best with his dear Muse did sute,
> Who was for hire a very Prostitute.

The poet goes on to conclude – parodying Dryden's own lines in *Absalom and Achitophel* – that 'Innovation is a dangerous thing/Whether it comes from People or from King'. The power-hungry traitors attempt to persuade Amaziah to use open force against the supporters of Azariah, and seek 'to fright him with his father's fate'. The Jews are distressed when Hushai is sent to prison. Azariah, in a speech that eclipses Amaziah's final blessing, extols the Jews to pay their loyal duty to their sovereign. Amaziah concludes the poem by banishing all the priests of Baal from his kingdom, and acknowledging Azariah as his rightful heir. Pordage concludes the poem with a gesture of divine recognition and approval familiar from Dryden's original:

> He said: Th'Almighty heard, and from on high
> Spoke his Consent, in Thunder through the Skie:
> The Augerie was noted by the Croud,
> Who joyful shouts returned almost as loud:
> Then *Amazia* was once more restor'd,
> He lov'd his People, they obey'd their Lord.

The central concerns of Pordage's parody in 'Azariah and Hushai' are obvious, and all these concerns work to correct the factual and sympathetic errors of Dryden's original. The Popish Plot is presented not as a shady and imprecise conspiracy 'dashed and brewed with lies' but rather as a truly threatening conspiracy so bad that 'no man can represent it worse'. The Catholics are an absolute danger to the English Church and State. Like Dryden, Pordage emphasizes the essential goodness of Charles, yet in Pordage's poem it is the King himself and not Monmouth who is susceptible to the 'whispers' of unscrupulous advisers. The behaviour both of the legitimate Monmouth and of the sage councillor Shaftesbury – and, indeed, of the English people – is vindicated throughout the poem, and the burden of treacherous behaviour falls, rather, on unscrupulous 'journalists' like the protean Dryden.

(V)

The parodies and attacks on *Absalom and Achitophel* apparently failed to shake Dryden. It is striking that the particular slanders on the poet's own family (Pordage's designation, for example, of his devoted wife Elizabeth as 'a teeming matron ere she was a Wife'), on his religion, and on his own seeming political apostasy – the unhesitating cries of 'turncoat' and 'traitor' – were in themselves insufficient to bring Dryden to comment adversely, or at length, on any of his detractors in print. It is even arguable that what finally provokes the poet to respond in this particular instance is, in fact, not the rhetorical slings and arrows of his outraged political opponents but the actual sight of

Shaftesbury riding triumphant through the streets of London following his acquittal in November 1681. In the 'Epistle to the Whigs' prefaced to *The Medall*, Dryden's furious anger at the political reality of Shaftesbury's acquittal threatens to fragment the detached, scornfully 'civil' tone that he attempts to maintain throughout his preface to the poem. Dryden makes a point of inviting his opponents to again use parody as a tool against him, pointedly suggesting that the parodies and imitations of *Absalom and Achitophel* conspicuously failed to achieve their desired end. 'If God has note bless'd you with the Talent for Rhiming', he suggests,

> make use of my poor Stock and wellcome: let your Verses run upon my feet: and for the utmost refuge of notorious Block-heads, reduc'd to the last extremity of sense, turn my own lines upon me, and in utter despaire of your own Satyre, make me Satyrize my self.

While it has been argued that Dryden is only distancing himself from the parodists here in a pretended scorn of their appropriative and 'unoriginal' poetics, I suspect that his casual dismissal of the possibilities of an effective parodic assault against *The Medall* is in no small degree genuine. Dryden, himself an appropriative and assimilative poet at heart, was no mean judge of the effectiveness of those parodies appearing in the popular press, and had every reason to believe that his own efforts remained carefully inoculated against this particular kind of parodic infection.

In his excellent study of Dryden's poetry and drama, the critic David Hopkins has offered a possible framework within which we can measure the success or failure of these several parodies. Hopkins makes substantial claims for Dryden as a poet whose best work transcends the boundaries of specific topical and party-polemical reference, and addresses questions of general nature, or, as he puts it early in his study, offers 'penetrating general speculations about Man and Nature'.[57] Hopkins goes on to note a number of Dryden's strong points, emphasizing the later translations as opposed to the earlier poetry and prose, and suggesting that Dryden's most powerful heroic verse is to be located not in the early drama (which he dismisses as frequently melodramatic and, by Dryden's own admission, dull), but in the later non-dramatic translations. Hopkins' discussion of the satirical poems of the early 1680s deserves our particular attention, as he points out that poems such as *Absalom and Achitophel* gain an inner depth and peculiar imaginative life only when Dryden is freed from the particular constraints of his biblical allegory, or when he chooses to complicate them. 'Dryden's strategic purpose', Hopkins observes,

> necessitated his aligning Charles II and his cause with the absolute moral authority of the One True God of the Bible. But his deeper imaginative inclinations were prompting him to see Charles/David as a figure closer to the glorious lecher-gods of classical myth. The aspects of Charles which kindled Dryden's poetic imagination most vividly could not be made to feature too prominently in a piece of Royalist propaganda. The polemical task of Dryden the Laureate, though undertaken with genuine commitment, can, in this respect, be thought of as having exercised a constraint upon the imaginative flights of Dryden the Poet.[58]

Thus not only can it be argued that Dryden's poem lacks the allusive coherence of, say, Pope's *Dunciad*, but it is precisely when, as John Aikin noted, he is 'freed from the shackles of a political or polemical task' – when he is allowed some degree of imaginative independence – that he is most successful in the poem. 'The poet stands back', Hopkins concludes, 'uncommitted to any of the suggestions as they stand (or perhaps committed to them all), inviting us to entertain speculations rather than take up a point of view'.

The primary failure of the parodies of *Absalom and Achitophel*, which we have examined in this chapter, lies precisely in their unwillingness to allow this degree of *distance* between themselves and their parodied original. Whereas Dryden's own parodic method revels in the options of poetic and imaginative choice – of multiplicity of meaning – the decidedly second-rate parodists of Dryden's satire insist on flattening the poem out, on crushing that distance for the sake of an uncompromised, two-dimensional, party polemic.

I have attempted in this chapter to present a very broad view of one poet's response to parody. We have seen that in the case of John Dryden, the threat of parody is intimately related to the enhanced anxieties of plagiarism and imitation that had surfaced in the years following the Civil Wars, and the Restoration of the Monarchy in 1660. Dryden himself develops a strategy of self-parody in the face of numerous parodic appropriations of his own texts. In Chapter 6, I will focus my attention on a single parody of a single poet: Richard Owen Cambridge's 1756 *Elegy Written in an Empty Assembly Room*, an early response to Alexander Pope's 1717 *Eloisa to Abelard*. While I have been concerned in these pages on Dryden to range as widely as possible among the poet's work, I shall in Chapter 6 attempt to concentrate more rigorously on a closer reading of a single poem, and again stress the advantages – and indeed, the necessity – of taking the literary mode of parody into account as a legitimate response to a poet's work. The focus of Chapter 6 shall, accordingly, be on what might be termed the sympathetic dialectic of parodic appropriation.

6
Parodying Pope's *Eloisa to Abelard*: Richard Owen Cambridge's *An Elegy Written in an Empty Assembly Room*

> The Athenians were so fond of Parody, that they eagerly applauded it, without examining with that propriety or connection it was introduced. . . . This love of Parody is accounted for by an Excellent French Critic, from a certain malignity in mankind, which prompts them to laugh at what they most esteem, thinking they, in some measure, repay themselves for that involuntary tribute which is exacted from them by merit.
>
> – Richard Owen Cambridge,
> 'The Preface' to *The Scribleriad*, 1751[1]

Current studies of the poetry of the eighteenth century seem only to have just begun to redress a perceived imbalance in the depth of interest and attention that has recently been devoted to the various works of the first great poet of the era, Alexander Pope.[2] Not surprisingly, the last decade or so of the twentieth century proved to have been something of a golden age of Pope criticism. The long-awaited appearance of Maynard Mack's massive biography of the poet in 1985 marked the mid-point of a decade that saw more serious scholarly interest in Pope's work than ever before. The tercentenary of the poet's birth (in 1688) prompted not one but two impressive collections of commemorative essays, both of which quickly took their place among the numerous articles and the dozens of full-length studies relating to Pope's work that had appeared since 1980. If, as Margaret Anne Doody lamented in 1988, it was still 'very hard to find lovers of Pope outside the classroom', there were nevertheless some substantial indications that his status *in* the classroom – despite the increased demand to represent hitherto less canonical voices and modes on university reading lists – had grown ever more secure. Charles Kerby-Miller's fine edition of the *Memoirs of*

Martinus Scriblerus (1741) was reissued in 1988, and Steven Shankman's scrupulously detailed edition of Pope's *Iliad* (1743) – a model of academic scholarship – finally made it to bookstores in 1996.[3]

It is hardly surprising – particularly given the often explicitly political agenda of much post-modern and contemporary criticism – that in such a flurry of critical activity, some of Pope's works proved to be more popular than others. Indeed, whilst Pope's later satiric and didactic poetry (and his self-mythologizing and the highly politicized construction of himself as an urbane and impartial Horatian satirist) was scrutinized more closely than ever before, works that had received the generous attention of previous generations of critics were pushed, somewhat unceremoniously, from the critical spotlight. *The Rape of the Lock*, for example, which perhaps still, if only for reasons of pedagogical convenience, continued to receive its fair share of attention in the classroom, appeared often to be of less interest to some of the most influential of Pope's late-twentieth-century commentators than his satires and 'imitations'. The 'new' Pope criticism at the turn of the century tended to value the cultivated, allusive voice of the poet – the public poet, the Tory satirist – sometimes at the expense of the arguably more delicate ambiguities that exerted such a strong hold on critics such as Cleanth Brooks and J. S. Cunningham earlier in the twentieth century.[4] The early pastoral poetry and the *Essay on Criticism* (1711), seem in a similar manner to have been set to one side, for some time, to make more room for the *Moral Essays* of 1731–35 – the work of Pope's self-designated 'Opus Magnum'.[5] Above all, it has been the Horatian Pope – 'Alexander Pope of Twickenham', the Pope of the 'Epistle to Augustus' (1733) and the *Epilogue to the Satires* (1738) – who appears most to have interested commentators within the last two decades; critics seemed particularly eager to reacquaint themselves with Pope the 'professional' author, and to engage themselves more fully with the precise details and actualities of the poet's unprecedented rise both to financial independence and to critical pre-eminence.

Of all Pope's major works, the verse epistle of *Eloisa to Abelard* (1717) – a poem that Samuel Johnson once dubbed 'one of the most happy productions of human wit' – perhaps fared worst in the course of such a revaluation.[6] The flow of Pope criticism in the latter decades of the twentieth century produced only a relatively slow and desultory trickle of articles on *Eloisa to Abelard*, and the attention given to the work in many lengthier studies seemed on occasion perfunctory.[7] As early as 1984, David Fairer (whose subsequent work has done much to reposition *Eloisa to Abelard* in the eyes of modern readers) observed that while contemporary critical theorists had continued to place a particularly high value on Pope the satirist, there had likewise grown 'a dislike for the histrionics of *Eloisa to Abelard*, for its unironic wholeheartedness, its imaginative commitment to the woman's predicament, and what is seen as Pope's unhealthy interest in its heroine's self-arousal'.[8] Other critics have echoed (and in some cases anticipated) Fairer's observation. David Morris, for example, suggested that the objections to *Eloisa to Abelard* could be conveniently divided into three essential categories: aesthetic, ethical, and moral. The first centre around the charge that the epistle fails to measure up to the standards of poetic decorum – the necessary harmony 'among subject, style, and form' – that Pope himself set for any production in verse.[9] Eloisa, critics commonsensically object, would simply not have written an emotionally charged response to Abelard's epistle within the careful rhetoric and artful elaboration demonstrated in Pope's rhymed heroic couplets. A second, more substantial series of objections have been levelled against the poem by critics who lament what they see to be Eloisa's histrionic and self-dramatizing 'defence of the indefensible', that is, her refusal to offer any ultimate assurance regarding her duty towards God in the face of her unmastered (and unmastering) passion. Furthermore, it might be argued that Pope's epistle carries with it no coherent moral purpose; that while, as Morris writes, 'she is hardly a pattern for imitation . . . she is equally inappropriate merely as an *exemplum* of culpable misconduct'.[10]

We might add to such a perceptive summary of the possible exceptions to be taken to Pope's poem a fourth and more comprehensive difficulty facing any critic wishing to make sense of *Eloisa to Abelard*, and that, quite simply, concerns the matter of precisely how we are to make sense of this admittedly bravura performance within the context of the larger body of Pope's work. Although it has often been pointed out that in the eighteenth century the heroic epistle constituted one of the poetic 'kinds' that, as Geoffrey Tillotson observed, had 'long been accorded an almost fulsome popularity' (and was thus one of the forms of poetry over which the young Pope would have been eager to demonstrate his mastery in his 1717 *Works*), it is likewise true that even the most authoritative and knowledgeable of Pope's twentieth-century critics – Maynard Mack, for example – had a difficult time resisting the suspicion that the work 'consorts somewhat oddly with the rest [of Pope's poetry]'.[11] The most persuasive defenders of *Eloisa to Abelard* (Mack included) have accordingly attempted to reintegrate the poem into the larger body of Pope's work. Pope's biographer, for example, read the poem as a double-edged autobiographical exploration of the poet's own sense of sexual frustration. If the crippled Pope found in Abelard a convenient representation of his own feelings of sexual ostracism (particularly, in late 1716 and early 1717, with regard to the Blount sisters and to Lady Mary Wortley Montagu), he likewise created an Eloisa who could 'express his [i.e., Pope's own] angry sense of imprisonment in a fate he had never asked for and done nothing to deserve'. 'The Eloisa and Abelard story', Mack suggested, 'offered latent possibilities of identification with both lovers'.[12]

A reading such as Mack's at least allows the poem to participate in the continuing biographical drama of Pope's work. It roots the unusually intense (and artfully 'feminine') emotion of *Eloisa to Abelard* – along with what is usually considered to be its 'companion' piece, the *Elegy on the Death of an Unfortunate Lady* (1717) – more firmly in the specific details surrounding its production and publication in 1717, as well as connecting the verse epistle to those other aspects of Pope's poetic output that tend to explore the difficulties posed by social, physical, and religious exclusion. David Morris had contributed to this sort of coherent reading of Pope's work by arguing that Eloisa's status as a tragic heroine is wholly reflective of the 'irreconcilable claims of divided human nature' that are elaborated upon at greater length in the *Essay on Man* (1733) and its darker counterpart, the *Dunciad* (1728; 1742). The personal and emotional struggles between reason and passion – between duty and impiety, logic and faith – that are depicted in *Eloisa to Abelard* resolve themselves into one small redacted example of the more comprehensive dichotomies at work in the human condition of 'deviating Man' in the larger body of Pope's verse.

The comparative lack of interest in *Eloisa to Abelard* – or the admission that it is possible to draw the poem into critical consideration only by associating it with Pope's work as a whole – is of no small significance. Previous generations of poets and critics, who consistently devalued Pope's satirical and didactic work, naturally had no such desire to tie the privileged and seemingly 'proto-Romantic' *Eloisa to Abelard* to Pope's other writings. From the late eighteenth century onwards, the poem had attracted attention precisely *because* it seemed to stand apart from Pope's other work – precisely because its highly eroticized subject matter allowed the poet momentarily to transcend the small-minded 'Augustanism', the occasional specificity, and the backbiting rancour that (critics argued) characterized and constrained the didactic poems and the Horatian imitations of Pope's later career. In his empathetic depiction of Eloisa's revived and impossible passion for her disabled

lover, as in his evocation of the sublime solitude of the highly
Gothicized Paraclete, Pope for once, romantic critics liked to think, got
things right. The sincerest form of flattery is reflected in no fewer than
nine separate 'answering' poems and parodic imitations of Pope's own
amatory epistle in the second half of the eighteenth century, compared
with only three text-specific replies prior to 1747.[13] The poets of the
mid to late eighteenth and early nineteenth centuries in fact kept *Eloisa
to Abelard* very much alive at a time when Pope's other work was beginning to be dismissed as unnecessarily bitter and vindictive. Although it
is perhaps a disservice to the complexity of the late-eighteenth-century
attitudes towards lyric poetry to state, as Lawrence Wright had once felt
himself able to do, that *Eloisa to Abelard* and its imitations, replies, and
parodies, were 'by far more popular during the decades in which the
Romantic point of view dominated' (what, after all, is comprehended
by the term "the Romantic point of view" when referring to the critical
attitudes of the mid-eighteenth century?), it is nevertheless true that
Pope's poem attracted far more inter-textual activity in the way of
parodies and 'response' poems in the middle and final decades of the
eighteenth century than ever before or since.

It is time that such parodies and imitations – too often dismissed as
mere 'curiosities' – be taken into critical account. If recent critics have
been eager to reintegrate *Eloisa to Abelard* (thematically, biographically,
or stylistically) into the larger body of Pope's work, they have, unfortunately, frequently been so at the expense of these earlier commentators;
it would seem that very little attempt has been made to examine the
parodies and responses to *Eloisa to Abelard* if only because a generation
of critics who have studied the possible stylistic and thematic harmony
of the poem within the context of Pope's larger achievement is apt to
be considerably less interested in what has haphazardly been designated
as a 'Romantic' or 'proto-Romantic' response to its subject matter. The
mid- and late-eighteenth century responses to Pope's poem are labelled
as mistaken or, at least, partial, and a series of imitations and parodies
are dropped from critical consideration. A seemingly non-negotiable
gap is thus opened in the critical heritage of Pope's work, a gap that
divides the insights of parodists from playing any role in the subsequent
judgements of more 'legitimate' critics.

Parody can in fact be used to close this gap. It is worth taking a
moment to remind ourselves that Pope was himself a poet who –
consciously emulating the achievements of the past and strategically
placing himself with reference *to* those achievements – effectively began
his career as a parodist and imitator. His earliest verses were imitations

of poets such as Waller and Cowley; he likewise set out on his path as a
poet with paraphrases, imitations, and translations of Homer, Boethius,
Chaucer, and even the Psalms. One of his earliest pieces is the parody
entitled simply 'Spenser: The Alley', a Swiftian description of London's
straggling Thames suburbs that sees the final, potentially forceful alexandrine of the Spenserian stanza used, rather, to superb bathetic effect.
Describing a street scene that one might encounter in Deptford or
Wapping, Pope writes,

> The snappish Cur, (the Passengers annoy)
> Close to my Heel with yelping Treble flies;
> The whimp'ring Girl, the hoarser-screaming Boy,
> Join to the yelping Treble shrilling Cries;
> The scolding Quean to louder Notes doth rise,
> And her full Pipes those shrilling Cries confound:
> To her full Pipes the grunting Hog replies;
> And grunting Hogs alarm the Neighbours round,
> And Curs, Girls, Boys, and Scolds, in the deep Base are drown'd.

(ll.19–27)[14]

It is surprising to recall that the lively alexandrine that closes Pope's
verse here was actually written *before* Swift's own similar and more
familiar Virgilian parody 'A Description of a City Shower' (1710). Pope
of course parodies the vagaries of Spenserian diction in his pseudo-
antiquated vocabulary (in this stanza 'Quean' and 'doth', for example),
as well as Spenser's frequent inversion and repetition. Yet even as Pope
parodies his model, he picks up on the light-hearted tone – the fantastic
inclusivity – that already characterized Spenser's own designedly parodic
stance with regard to the epic seriousness of, say, Boiardo or Tasso. It is
Pope's particular gift as a parodist truly to comprehend his originals; he
possesses the intuitive, sympathetic identification of the great translator
and the great imitator, and uses both his ear for verse and his larger
understanding of a poet's meaning (here, for example, Spenser's own
love of surface play and narrative proliferation) effectively to parody his
target texts. I would further suggest that Pope's easy grasp of Spenser's
language is matched in this brief early parody by the emphatic *absence*
of any 'darke conceit' or allegorical meaning in his humorous redaction.
Pope seems to be suggesting that the multiplicity of meaning inherent in
Spenser's own allegory was at times simply obscured by – or at least less

important than – what he would later in life call the 'vast... delight' of his Spenserian model.[15]

Critics have long recognized Alexander Pope's use of text-specific parodic techniques to enhance the force of his satire in many of his mature poems, including both *The Rape of the Lock* and, of course, *The Dunciad*. In *The Rape of the Lock*, Pope not only included many explicit echoes of his classical models (the game of Ombre, at iii.25–100, is patterned after the funeral games of *Aeneid* V.286–603, for example, whilst the description of the Cave of Spleen [iv.25–54] recalls the Hall of Vulcan in *Iliad* XVIII.440–4), but gained the added dimension of *self-parody* by effectively referring his English readers to the language of his own 1715–20 *Iliad* translation for his Homeric models. Clarissa's famous speech at V.9–34 – which, as Pope himself specifically noted, is 'a parody of the speech of Sarpedon to Glaucus in Homer' – perhaps best exemplifies the kind of depth Pope could gain from such a doubly parodic/self-parodic technique. Pope had in fact first translated the 'Episode of Sarpedon' (a combination of passages from Books XII and XVI of the *Iliad*) for inclusion in the sixth volume of Tonson's 1709 *Poetical Miscellanies*. 'Pope's choice of the Sarpedon episode for his first published essay at Homer', as Maynard Mack observed in his biography of the poet, 'shows how well he already [understood] the poem without which *The Rape of the Lock* would be unimaginable, and how deeply he [was] laying the groundwork, though as yet unconsciously, for his brilliant reinterpretations of contemporary by past experience that so distinguish his later work'.[16] In Clarissa's speech, Sarpedon's emphasis on 'Fame' and 'Glory' is transmuted into a common sense exhortation towards 'good Sense' and resignation in the face of time, death, and decay. Whilst there may be something in what she says, Clarissa's choric speech, unlike its Homeric original, does not offer any answer in the face of an overwhelming human question, although Pope's understanding of his original again allows him effectively to parody his classical original. Here, Sarpedon's heroic claims for a shared humanity in the face of death are transformed into Clarissa's injunction to Belinda to renounce plenty for singularity – to give up her momentarily privileged world for subjugation to one single individual. Whereas Homer's original had suggested an ennobling fortitude in the face of a shared 'inexorable Doom', Clarissa's equivalent 'good humour' parodically argues for Belinda to resign herself to the common lot of woman, for purposes that are ultimately not philosophical or soundly reasoned, but merely self-seeking.

The Rape of the Lock is a poem typical of the era that produced it insofar as it was constantly rewritten – even well after its initial publication in 1712. The speech of Clarissa, for example, was not added to the piece until its third appearance (and third correspondingly substantial revision) in 1717. The focus of Pope's greatest parodic achievement, *The Dunciad*, rests precisely on this impulse to rewrite and re-craft the poetic object – to encourage almost endless alterations in the direction of greater expansion and depth. *The Dunciad* itself, of course, exists in several widely different versions, yet Pope uses his familiar Homeric, Virgilian, and Miltonic models to create a mock-epic parody that highlights and emphasizes the impossibility of pinning down the author or, for that matter, pinning down the text: *The Dunciad*, the poem that develops out of control, relentlessly pursues a path far beyond the control of its posited (and frequently disguised and erased) author. It is the ultimate parody, insofar as it acknowledges the plurality of voices that work to produce the literary text, at the same time that it self-parodically pokes fun at the vision of a single identifiable and definable 'author'.

The text-specific parodies included in poems such as and *The Rape of the Lock The Dunciad* have, again, received the detailed attention of both critics and editors. What has *not* been recognized, however, is the extent to which Pope had refined his parodic art so that even those poems that readers would not normally identify as parodies incorporate elements of text-specific parodic technique in their larger structures. Critics have likewise slighted the possibility that subsidiary parodies can in fact transcend mere stylistic critique and formal mimeticism, to engage in a genuine dialectic with a targeted text. In the pages that follow, therefore, I will undertake a closer examination of a single parodic response to Pope's *Eloisa to Abelard*, in an attempt to demonstrate the manner in which a parody roughly contemporaneous with its original can be in a unique position to 'understand' its target text and inform our reading of that poem. Such a reading can at least perpetuate some sense of diachronic critical coherence; far from existing as a series of isolated and irrelevant documents relating to a peculiarly 'proto-Romantic' interpretation and appreciation of *Eloisa to Abelard*, such parodies and imitations can and must be taken into account in subsequent readings of the poem, if only because they very frequently represent historically situated and responsible attempts to engage the poem *on its own terms*. The case to be made for parody is particularly strong with regard to *Eloisa to Abelard*. In the analysis that follows, I hope to demonstrate that the parody in question affords an informed reading of Pope's original, and in fact mimics on an explicitly literary level the epistemological struggle for individual identity – a struggle rooted in the negotiation between memory and imagination – that lies at the heart of Pope's poem.

(I)

In a genial reference to his friend's various abilities as a poet, an essayist, a decorator, a historian, a naval engineer, a landscape artist, and a conversationalist, Horace Walpole once dubbed his Twickenham neighbour, Richard Owen Cambridge (1717–1802) 'the everything'.[17] Cambridge was, as Walpole further observed, 'an officious intelligencer ... who would rather than not be the first to trumpet a piece of news'. Edward Gibbon, in much the same spirit, nicknamed him 'the Cambridge Mail' because of his 'dedication to the collection and dissemination of news and gossip'.[18] Cambridge achieved the most fame in his own lifetime both as a host to the literary and political elite of his day (he counted among his friends and acquaintances not only Walpole and Gibbon but also Thomas Gray, Soame Jenyns, William Pitt, Henry Fox, and Lord Chesterfield) and as the author of the mock-heroic poem, *The Scribleriad* (1751). Much like its immediate inspiration – Alexander Pope's *The Dunciad* – Cambridge's six-book poem satirized false learning and pedantry in heroic couplets, appropriating as its outspoken hero the Scriblerian figure of Martinus Scriblerus himself.

Cambridge's only modern biographer, Richard D. Altick, observed rather dismissively that in works such as *The Scribleriad*, the poet was only doing 'what Swift and Pope had done long before him'.[19] Other twentieth-century critics, among them Eric Rothstein, similarly described *The Scribleriad* as 'refined but dull', and 'acceptable rather than excellent'.[20] Cambridge's admittedly eccentric parodies are deserving of closer critical attention, however, not only because they stand out among the more popular and intelligent of the many parodic responses to more widely available works such as Pope's *Dunciad*, but also because they form part of the long line of later unexamined documents participating in the notoriously divisive controversy of the Ancients and the Moderns; in his Preface to the poem, Cambridge addresses the issue of parody in a strikingly straightforward manner, acknowledging his own debts to (among others) Cervantes, Bouileau, and Samuel Garth. Indeed, although long neglected by readers of eighteenth-century poetry, Cambridge himself has in fact been the incidental subject of some relatively recent critical attention. While Altick's own passion for literary detective work failed to turn up any material that had been left spectacularly unexamined in Cambridge's career, renewed interest in the writings of the novelist Frances Burney has highlighted that same author's romantic interest in Cambridge's son, George, and has again emphasized Cambridge's own important role as a seeker-out and promoter of literary talent.[21] More significantly, some of Cambridge's own work and the role that he played more generally in creating the peculiar climate of the literary world in the mid-eighteenth century has once again been subject to scrutiny. Michael Suarez, in his Introduction to a facsimile reprinting of Robert Dodsley's widely circulated and unusually saleable six-volume *Collection of Poems, by Several Hands* (1748–58), observed that the essays Cambridge contributed to the journals published by Edward Moore in *The World* under Dodsley's supervision were easily among those 'that should be numbered among the best in that collection'.[22] James Sambrook, even more strikingly, has noted that certain portions of Cambridge's mock-epic work constitute something more than a *de facto* sequel either to *The Dunciad* or to the 1741 *Extraordinary Memoirs and Discoveries* of Scriblerus. In a revised entry on Cambridge in the latest (2004) edition of the *Dictionary of National Biography,* Sambrook expressed his own hope that the *Scribleriad* and – in particular – its 'references to aerial combat, submarines, and electricity' might help bring the work to the attention of some modern readers.[23] In this respect, too, it is worth observing that Cambridge's interests in such relatively fantastical innovations seems even to bear some relation to the visionary new technologies brought to life in the magic realism of Robert Paltock's astonishing Enlightenment novel *Peter Wilkins* (1750).[24]

Along with *The Scribleriad*, Cambridge's *Elegy Written in an Empty Assembly Room* was easily one of his most popular productions. One of the few such parodies to be printed with his approval in his own lifetime, the work was to see itself through three editions in quick succession in the spring of 1756.[25] The *Elegy* was likewise one of those poems written by Cambridge that was to be included in the 1758 edition of Dodsley's *Collection.* Walpole sent a copy of the poem to his cousin Henry Seymour Conway just five days after its initial publication, recommending it to his attention as one of only 'two new fashionable pieces' then circulating around town.[26] Although the wide, occasional popularity of the piece was short-lived, the *Elegy* (which again appeared in Cambridge's collected *Works,* published posthumously by his son in 1803) continued to be a generally well-known parody of Pope's original 1717 *Eloisa to Abelard.* Cambridge, whose admiration for Pope's own poem shines through in his own parodic imitation, had actually engaged in some business with Pope in 1741 (he had prevailed upon his relation Thomas Edwards to ship 'minerals' for Pope's grotto at Twickenham from Bristol), although he and Pope appear never actually to have met face to face. Much like Pope, Cambridge – a fellow native of London – was eventually to spend much of his life in Twickenham, where he lived in a Thames villa close to Richmond

Bridge (originally Twickenham Meadows, later renamed Cambridge Park), not very far from Pope's own more modest house and grotto.

(II)

As is the case with so many of the text-specific parodies of the mid-eighteenth century, the socio-cultural contexts of Cambridge's *Elegy* are inextricably linked to its possibilities of meaning. The subject of Cambridge's Assembly Room *Elegy* can be identified as the notoriously quarrelsome Viscountess Townshend (Etheldreda [Audrey] Townshend, née Harrison).[27] Lady Townshend, who had formally separated from her husband (Charles, Baron Lynn, afterwards 3rd Viscount Townshend) in 1741, maintained her own household near St. James's Street, Westminster, where she gained a considerable reputation in the mid-eighteenth-century for hosting extravagant evening entertainments, often for visiting dignitaries. She was no less famously known in some circles for her pursuit of high-profile lovers, including politicians and high-profile figures such as Lord Baltimore, Thomas Winnington, William Boyd, Lord Frederick Campbell, and Henry Fox; she was dismissed by at least one rival for having 'gained to herself as infamous a character as any lady about town for her gallantries'.[28] Later generations – including, not surprisingly, her own descendants – have attempted to rehabilitate her popular reputation as 'one of the most beautiful, fascinating, and witty women of a witty and fascinating age'.[29] As a social hostess in the mid-eighteenth century, at least, Viscountess Townshend thrived on her own reputation as a compelling and often controversial social presence.

It is all the more damaging, therefore, that in Cambridge's parody of Pope's epistolary original, Etheldreda Townshend is among those very few high-profile individuals who has been snubbed by the Duchess of Norfolk, Mary Blount (Blount had married the Hon. Henry Howard in November 1727). Townshend has not been invited to the grand entertainment being held at Blount's spectacular new London showcase, Norfolk House.[30] The 'drums' or evening entertainments at Norfolk House would very soon establish themselves as being particularly fabulous and well-attended events. The Norfolks' entertainments had become far more extravagant since the long-awaited completion in February 1756 of the new Norfolk House, designed by Matthew Brettingham the elder, who had only recently designed Holkham Hall in Norfolk. The new Norfolk House in London was built on the site of the couple's earlier residence in St. James's Square (a dwelling that had – subsequent to his ejection from St. James's Palace in 1737 – served for three years as home to [in the words of his own mother] 'the nauseous little beast', Frederick, Prince of Wales). It is a further testament to Blount's skills as a social operator that she managed at the same time to remain on good terms with Queen Caroline herself.

The couple's purposefully impressive and over-awing new showplace in St. James's Square had taken years to complete. Although their earlier residence on the same site (purchased by the 8th duke in 1722, and dating from the 1660s) had already functioned as a centre for the distribution of London scandal and gossip, the new structure was decidedly more fabulous; Norfolk House was soon attracting a glittering company of guests, and formed the focus of a number of celebratory occasions featuring illuminations and bonfires that carried its allure well beyond its own walls and into the surrounding neighbourhood. Although the new home presented to the street only a relatively simple brick façade, the revitalized Norfolk House somewhat uncharacteristically concealed its treasures behind its unimposing front; it boasted an interior described by Walpole as 'a scene of magnificence and taste'. 'The tapestry, the embroidered bed, the illumination, the glasses, the lightness and novelty of the ornaments, and the ceilings', he marvelled in his correspondence, 'are delightful'.[31] The masquerades, parties, and entertainments held at Norfolk House, he confided to yet another correspondent 'are wonderfully select and dignified; one might sooner be a knight of Malta than qualified for them'. As Rosemary Baird has observed, with Norfolk House, the Duke and Duchess 'had helped to create a new standard of interior design'. The highly decorative style of Norfolk House – which, although long popular in France was anticipated in England almost exclusively by Chelmsford House, in 1749 – set an influential trend in domestic and interior design in the country.[32] The elegance of Brettingham's structure and elaborate circuit of rooms was further highlighted by decorative works deriving from the rococo designers, Gilles-Marie Oppenard and Juste Aurele Meisonnier. The attention to detail was scrupulous; William Farington (brother to the diarist John Farington) designed specific layouts for the table arrangements. An elaborate scheme of rooms laid out in different colours and themes – the 'Flowered Velvet Room', the 'Green Damask Room', the 'Crimson Drawing Room', and so on – beckoned visitors through the house, and beneath the hybrid rococo ceilings were gilt-wood looking glasses, matched with gilt-bronze pier tables and serving tables.

Whether or not one admired the flamboyant style of the new furniture and decorations, there was little point in denying that to be in with the

Norfolks, so to speak, was to be in with the 'in' crowd. Referring to a ball held by the Duchess for the brother of the Prince of Wales – the Duke of Cumberland – early in 1756, Walpole's correspondent Mrs Patrick Delany (although crediting the Duchess's husband with the event's success) wrote: 'The Duke of Norfolk's ball and the supper that he gave were magnificent; our Whitehall friends danced till four in the morning. The supper and dessert were the prettiest that have ever been seen; the dessert, besides the candles on the table, were lighted by lamps in fine green cut glasses'; the *Daily Advertiser* of 2 April noted that the Princess Dowager of Wales and 'the rest of the royal family' were the guests of honour.[33] The Norfolks had earlier, in 1742, played a significant role in the late reconciliation between George II and his eldest son; the pointed exclusion by Norfolk of the equally celebrated society hostess Etheldreda Townshend from the March entertainment of 1756 was perhaps all the more striking because of the Duchess's reputation for helping likewise to reconcile or act as a kind of go-between amongst English Roman Catholics, generally, with members of the Protestant ruling élite. According to Christopher Simon Sykes, Townshend was 'for political reasons . . . quite deliberately not invited'.[34] In any event, from the window of her own, decidedly more modest establishment near St. James's Street, Lady Townshend held what would in any other circumstances have been an enviable view of the lively and glittering parade of guests making their way along the illuminated streets to nearby Norfolk House. As matters stood, she was rumoured instead to have 'sat at home alone in the darkness, with not a candle burning and the shutters tightly closed so that no passer-by should guess she was within'.[35]

The contrast between the ostentatiously plain exterior of Norfolk House that faced St. James's Square, on the one hand, and the veritable riot of embroidered silks, gilt-wood ensembles, carved woods, and self-consciously stylish decorations that deliberately set out to ravish anyone privileged enough to set foot beyond the 'regular rows and windows' that alone broke its 'insipid' length of exterior wall, on the other, was both pointed and dramatic.[36] The comparative famine of the building's stoically classical façade served further to emphasize the veritable succession of 'feasts' (the figurative language of consumption was invariably invoked by early guests) that so surprisingly followed once one had entered into the grand circuit of Norfolk House itself. The structure, in other words, drew attention in a concrete manner to the oppositions of interior and exterior – of outward form to internal substance, of the diurnal and obviously *mundane* to the sequestered and privileged *exotic* – and the role of the viewing subject as a possible negotiator between the two. Indeed, the House itself figured in some ways as a model or representation of its mistress's own role as an adept facilitator of reconciliation and communication within the fashionable world. The Duchess was a societal force who skilfully linked the oddly confluent yet often conflicting lives of the influential few who moved in the very highest echelons of what the American writer Nathaniel Willis would in the next century dub the 'Upper Ten Thousand'. As a self-styled healer and reconciler, the Duchess herself was a strategist who necessarily linked both sides of a conversation, as it were, and helped to draw the two speakers together, or at least to place them side by side. The parallels between the structures of architecture and design, on the one hand, and the language of poetry, on the other, are in this instance exceptionally nice ones. Norfolk House, curiously, comes close to the playfulness of the parodic itself, insofar as it pointedly and paradoxically *internalizes* that which is exotic – that which is quite literally 'outside' itself – much in the manner that Townshend might be posited as a socio-cultural 'parodist' herself.

And what better literary form within which to dramatize further the tensions inherent within such dichotomies and societal oppositions than that of the verse-epistle? In his excellent survey of the English poetry of the eighteenth century, David Fairer very aptly draws his readers' attention to the observations contained in a two-volume guide to *The Art of Poetry on a New Plan* published by John Newbery in 1762; of the formal epistle or 'verse letter' of the period, the guide observed: 'This species of writing, if we are permitted to lay down rules for the examples of our best poets, admits of great latitude . . . for as the Epistle takes [the] place of discourse, and is intended as a sort of distant conversation, all the affairs of life and researches into nature may be introduced'.[37] Those epistles that describe 'in a familiar and humorous way . . . the manners, vices, and follies of mankind are the best; because they are most suitable to the true character of epistolary writing, and (business set apart) are the usual subjects upon which our letters are employ'd'.[38] Fairer himself justly notes that the verse letter is a form of mediation – a form that 'develops strategies for working under cover', and speaks 'in two directions simultaneously'. 'In this genre', Fairer continues, 'the potential for irony is considerable and available for satiric use'.[39] And it is precisely this use to which Cambridge puts the form in his parodic *Elegy*. In doing so, he creates a complex sense of literary and biographical echoes that signal his own comprehension of the multilayered dialogues implicit in Pope's original poem, and their possible relevance to those presented parodically in his own.

(III)

The recognizable epigraph to Cambridge's *Elegy* – 'semperque relinqui/sola sibi' ('and always she seemed to be left alone' – is taken from Book IV of Virgil's *Aeneid* (ll.466–7), and describes the condition of Dido (who significantly reappears at line 76 of Cambridge's poem) following the departure of Aeneas. The text of the *Elegy* reproduced here is taken directly from a copy of the first (11 April) edition currently in the British Library.

ADVERTISEMENT

THIS Poem being a Parody on the most
remarkable Passages in the well-known
Epistle of *Eloisa* to *Abelard*, it was thought
unnecessary to transcribe any Lines from that
Poem, which is in the Hands of all, and in the
Memory of most Readers.

AN
ELEGY
WRITTEN IN
AN EMPTY ASSEMBLY-ROOM[i]

IN Scenes where HALLET's[ii] Genius has combin'd
With BROMWICH[iii] to amuse and chear the Mind;
Amid this Pomp of Cost, this Pride of Art,
What mean these Sorrows in a Female Heart?
Ye crowded Walls, whose well enlighten'd Round   5
With Lovers Sighs and Protestations sound,
Ye Pictures flatter'd by the learn'd and wise,

---

[i] An assembly room was a venue for public gatherings, that is, public assemblies, defined by Chambers 1751 *Cyclopaedia* as 'a stated and general meeting of polite persons of both sexes, for the sake of conversation, gallantry, news, and play'. The *OED* further notes that 'private assemblies correspond in some respects to the modern "reception" or "at home"'. The assembly or 'drums' was an eighteenth-century term for an evening assembly of fashionable people at a private home.

[ii] William Hallet, a cabinetmaker, once accused by Walpole of practising a 'mongrel Chinese' style of design.

[iii] Mitford Bromwich, a decorator and wallpaper manufacturer, mentioned by both Walpole and Thomas Gray in their correspondence.

Ye Glasses ogled by the brightest Eyes,
Ye Cards, whom Beauties by their Touch have blest,
Ye Chairs, which Peers and Ministers have prest,   10
How are ye chang'd! like you my Fate I moan,
Like you, alas! neglected and alone —
For ah! to me alone no Card is come,
I must not go abroad — and cannot *Be At Home.*
    Blest be that social Pow'r, the first who pair'd   15
The erring Footman with th'unerring Card.
'Twas VENUS sure; for by their faithful Aid
The whisp'ring Lover meets the blushing Maid:
From Solitude they give the chearful Call
To the choice Supper, or the sprightly Ball: 20
Speed the soft Summons of the Gay and Fair,
From distant Bloomsbury to Grosvenor's Square;
And bring the Colonel to the tender Hour,
From the Parade, the Senate or the Tower.
    Ye Records, Patents of our Worth and Pride!   25
Our daily Lesson, and our nightly Guide,
Where'er ye stand dispos'd in proud Array,
The Vapours vanish, and the Heart is gay;
But when no Cards the Chimney-Glass adorn,
The dismal Void with Heart-felt Shame we mourn;   30
Conscious Neglect inspires a sullen Gloom,
And brooding Sadness fills the slighted Room.
    If but some happier Female's Card I've seen,
I swell with Rage, or sicken with the Spleen;
While artful Pride conceals the bursting Tear,   35
With some forc'd Banter or affected Sneer:
But now grown desp'rate, and beyond all Hope,
I curse the Ball, the D — ss and the Pope.
And as the Loads of borrow'd Plate go by,
Tax it! ye greedy Ministers, I cry.   40
How shall I feel when SOL resigns his Light,
To this proud splendid Goddess of the Night!
Then when her awkward Guests in Measure beat
The crowded Floors, which groan beneath their Feet!
What Thoughts in Solitude shall then possess   45
My tortur'd Mind, or soften my Distress!
Not all that envious Malice can suggest
Will sooth the Tumults of my raging Breast.
(For Envy's lost amidst the numerous Train,
And hisses with her hundred Snakes in vain)   50

Though with Contempt each despicable Soul
Singly I view, — I must Revere the Whole.
   The Methodist in her peculiar Lot,
The World forgetting, by the World forgot,
Though singly happy, tho' alone is proud,   55
She thinks of Heav'n (she thinks not of a Crowd)
And if she ever feels a vap'rish Qualm,
Some *Drop of Honey*,[iv] or some holy Balm,
The pious Prophet of her Sect distils,
And her pure Soul seraphic Rapture fills;   60
Grace shines around her with serenest Beams,
And Whisp'ring WHITF — D[v] prompts her golden
   Dreams.
And now convinc'd all human Pow'rs are vain,
Alike the IRISH and the BRITISH Swain;
An heav'nly Spouse alone she deigns t' approve,   65
And melts in Visions of eternal Love.
   Far other Dreams my sensual Soul employ,
While conscious Nature tastes unholy Joy:
I view the Traces of experience'd Charms,
And clasp the Regimentals[vi] in my Arms.   70
To dream last Night I clos'd my blubber'd Eyes;
Ye soft Illusions, dear Deceits arise:
Alas! no more; methinks I wand'ring go
To distant Quarters 'midst the Highland Snow:
To the dark Inn where never Wax-light burns,   75
Where in smoak'd Tap'stry faded DIDO mourns;
To some Assembly in a Country Town,
And meet the Colonel — in a Parson's Gown —
I start — I shriek —

[iv] [The Title of a Book of Modern Devotion]. Original note. The reference is specifically to *A Choice Drop of Honey from the Rock Christ: Or a Short Word of Advice to All Saints and Sinners* by Thomas Wilcox [also Wilcocks](1622–87); the pamphlet had passed through close to 50 editions by the mid-eighteenth century.
[v] George Whitfield (1714–70), populist preacher and early friend of John Wesley (1703–91), evangelist and founder of Methodism. Lady Townshend had herself gone to hear Whitfield preach in Chelsea, at the home of Lady Huntingdon, on at least one occasion, in 1748. Although she attempted to cultivate a relationship with Lady Huntingdon's circle of Methodists – a group known as 'Lady Huntingdon's connexion' – she later referred to Whitfield's style of preaching as 'canting'.
[vi] Uniforms.

O! could I on my waking Brain impose,   80
Or but forget at least my present Woes!
Forget 'em — how! — each rattling Coach suggests
The loath'd Ideas of the crowding Guests.
To visit — were to publish my Disgrace;
To meet the Spleen in ev'ry other Place;   85
To join old Maids and Dowagers forlorn;
And be at once their Comfort and their Scorn!
For once, to read — with this distemper'd Brain,
Ev'n modern Novels lend their Aid in vain.
My MANDOLINE — what Place can Musick find   90
Amid the Discord of my restless Mind?
    How shall I waste this Time which slowly flies!
How lull to Slumber my reluctant Eyes!
This Night the Happy and th' Unhappy keep
Vigils alike, — N * *vii *has murder'd Sleep.*   95

Although Cambridge's *Elegy* was – simply by virtue of its title – long mistakenly identified in bibliographical studies as a parody of Thomas Gray's 1751 *Elegy Written in a Country Church-Yard*, the poet quite clearly states that the piece is a text-specific response to Pope's *Eloisa to Abelard*. Cambridge has in fact provided his readers with a knowing parody of his original – a parody, as we shall see, that remains at all times alive and alert to the structural, formal, and thematic oppositions of its model text.

(IV)

From what direction does Cambridge approach his parodic target? To what effect, to use the terminology of critics such as Simon Dentith, is the 'polemical' stance of the mode being used in his work; or, to use the earlier parodic vocabulary of Linda Hutcheon, what is its 'ethos' towards its 'target' text?[40] Alexander Pope's own *Eloisa to Abelard* is a poem of consistently maintained oppositions. From a desired unity of thought and action (described at one point in the poem as that state of mind in which 'souls each other draw/When love is liberty, and nature, law' – a unity that, Eloisa further laments, 'was once the lot of *Abelard* and me') the dramatic heroine of Pope's poem has fallen into the 'craving Void' of a divided and perpetually dividing world.[41] The opening verse paragraph of *Eloisa to Abelard* introduces us to this dualistic universe:

---

vii Clearly, the reference here is to Norfolk herself.

In these deep solitudes and awful cells,
Where heav'nly-pensive, contemplation dwells,
And ever-musing melancholy reigns;
What means this tumult in a Vestal's veins?
Why rove my thoughts beyond this last retreat?
Why feels my heart its long-forgotten heat?
Yet, yet I love! – From *Abelard* it came,
And *Eloisa* yet must kiss the name.

(ll.1–8)

The sober, weighty 'contemplation' of the divinity is immediately contrasted to the erratic 'tumult' in Eloisa's veins; the confinement and solitude of the cloister is held against the dangerously wandering and 'roving' thoughts of the agitated vestal; the chill of the Paraclete's 'deep solitude' and 'awful cells' is balanced by the erotic heat, long smouldering, now leaping into flames, raised again by the epistle that has fallen into Eloisa's hands. The volatile emotions of an impassioned young girl have been reawakened after a period of 15 years in the 'veins' of a 31-year-old Abbess. Even the necessary decorum of Eloisa's outward response and appearance before her convent subordinates would have been dramatically at odds with the emotions reawakened in the reader by the epistle, the historical Latin original of which had addressed her as *'dilectissime'* – 'my beloved'. From the moment Eloisa first sets eyes on the opening lines of the epistle from Peter Abelard that has managed somehow to find its way into her hands, a dynamic tension is brought to life between the outer and the inner, between reality and appearance.

It will be Pope's method throughout his own version of *Eloisa to Abelard* to advance the argument of his poem – to project Eloisa's psychological oscillation between religious 'duty', on the one hand, and erotic 'desire', on the other, between 'law' and 'rebel nature', 'virtue' and 'impiety' – precisely by means of these multiple sets of mirroring, binary oppositions. He mimics, in the homological structure of the poem itself, the dualities of Eloisa's own moral, ethical, and religious dilemmas. The second verse stanza of the poem, the reader soon discovers, rather than resolving any of these tensions, only continues and amplifies the structured oppositions and contrasts of the first:

Dear fatal name! rest ever unreveal'd,
Nor pass these lips in holy silence seal'd.
Hide it, my heart, within that close disguise,
Where, mix'd with God's, his lov'd Idea lies.

Oh write it not, my hand – The name appears
Already written – wash it out, my tears!
In vain lost *Eloisa* weeps and prays,
Her heart still dictates, and her hand obeys.

(ll.9–16)

Silence is here at once contrasted to speech and utterance; concealment
and disguise to truth and revelation; God is held (as He is almost exclusively throughout the poem) only as a relatively ineffective counterpoise
to Abelard. Most significantly, writing – and specifically the writing of
letters or epistles – is offered as a corrective to acts of obliteration and
effacement. The world inhabited by Eloisa is a world in which each idea
or action can no sooner be mentioned, before it is absorbed within its
opposite, or at least haunted by the trace of that opposite (a notion
that twentieth-century literary theorists have often claimed as uniquely
their own).

   One could continue to pick apart the larger thematic, structural homologies posited throughout Pope's poem: starvation is set against sexual
appetite, austerity against indulgence, friendship against love, and love
itself against liberty. Such paradigmatic opposition on the structural
level is of course entirely appropriate to a poem that takes as its subject
the struggle of a single individual – torn at times by the explicit threat
of schizophrenia (cf. ll.153–54) – for some sense of individual identity
and coherence in the face of a suddenly revived and potentially over-
powering passion. Alternatively, we could trace these oppositions on
a more precise metrical and rhetorical level, and note the continuous
use of such devices as antithesis, caesura, and balanced repetition in
a poem in which, as Jacob Adler has observed in his study of Pope's
prosody, almost everything mentioned is mentioned 'in conjunction
with something else'.[42] Adler himself attributed the remarkably balanced
oppositions, homologies, and rhetorical devices of Pope's poem to the
psychological bias of its heroine. Eloisa's own relentless attempts to apply
her learned logic to 'affairs of the heart' are continually deconstructed
and washed away in the 'deeper tide of feeling' that will, eventually
and without fail, resist the subordination of passion and emotion to
rhetorical logic. Yet Adler's analysis of Pope's versification, however
correct in its discussion of the rhetorical particulars and actualities of
the text, tends to leave the reader with the larger picture of an Eloisa
who is a 'hopelessly entrapped' and stereotypically 'feminine' hysteric.
The reasoned, binary oppositions and repeated contrasts of the poem

are in fact, Adler argued, set up only to alert the reader to their final collapse in the hysterically emotional imagining by Eloisa of her own triumphant death and union ('May one kind grave unite each hapless name/And graft my love immortal on thy fame') with Abelard.

Readings such as Adler's – readings that attempt to analyse Eloisa's rhetoric as *speech* (a speech, moreover, that finds its own logic in a gender-based notion of psychological realism) – tend to obscure the fact that the epistle of *Eloisa to Abelard* is just that: an epistle. The poem is not meant to represent a spontaneous, emotional, and unpremeditated effusion on the part of Eloisa. It is, rather, a letter addressed to a partic-ular individual, and as such partakes in the characteristics of all such missives in that it both draws, to some extent, on the character of the person to whom it is addressed and likewise (as both H. Jacobson and R. D. S. Jack have pointed out) 'has the advantage of both monologue and dialogue'.[43] The dualities of the poem's structure are thus carried into and magnified by the larger opposition and dialectic inherent in the form of the heroic epistle itself.

Moreover, Pope's Eloisa not only relies on the 'image' of Abelard when addressing her letter to him; she draws specifically upon the body of writing attributed elsewhere in the tradition of Eloisa and Abelard (most pointedly in the 1713 Hughes version of the correspondence) to Abelard himself. As R. D. S. Jack observed, a close study of Pope's source, the 1713 Hughes version of the letters,

> reveals that many arguments used by Eloisa are in fact based on letters there attributed to Abelard. The conflict, though largely within herself, is usually determined to some degree by the way she believes her correspondent views it.[44]

D. W. Robertsons, Jr., in his survey of the Abelard and Heloise myth as it has manifested itself in various aesthetic forms and in various literary cultures throughout history, had pointed out that this kind of rhetorical borrowing and cross-referencing within these later versions of the medieval epistles was in fact an important and significant component both of the original correspondence and of subsequent retellings and representations of the tragedy.[45] Eloisa typically – and at times amusingly – employs the arguments of Abelard, the determined dialectician and logician, against him. We could even say she parodies his learning, and the use of that learning in the interests of her own deliberative oratory. When confronted with an offer of marriage from Abelard soon after her initial abduction from the residence of

Canon Fulbert, for example, Eloisa, in earlier versions of the legend,
launches into a neat little sermon (later recounted by Abelard himself)
demonstrating the manner in which such a marriage would not only
ruin Abelard's career in the church, but damage the reputation of
Church philosophers everywhere. The sermon is particularly ironic (and
oddly persuasive) insofar as it relies almost exclusively on rhetorical
strategies advanced by Abelard himself.

Pope explicitly invokes and works within this tradition that posits
Eloisa as a parodist of Abelard, and a letter-writer ready and even eager
playfully to employ Abelard's own arguments against him. Pope's Eloisa
is one who works with an existing body of writing upon which she
draws in her own memory. She drafts her own epistle so that it stands
at a coherent point of dialogue with relation to this earlier body of
correspondence. In lines 177–94 of Pope's version of Eloisa's epistle,
for example, his heroine laments the fact that while she would willingly resign her guilt and 'past offence' to forgetfulness, she cannot
yet bring herself to let go of the 'phantom' image of Abelard himself;
while she regrets her 'crime' and its consequences, she remains, to
an odd yet powerful degree, in possession of its sensual benefits. The
passage in which Eloisa delineates this paradox is again presented as
a tightly structured series of dualities, positing Man against God, piety
against despair, frozen 'chastity' against the forbidden fires of Love,
crime against pleasure, guilt against innocence:

> I ought to grieve, but cannot what I ought;
> I mourn the lover, not lament the fault;
> I view my crime, but kindle at the view,
> Repent old pleasure, and solicit new:
> . . .
> How shall I lose the sin, yet keep the sense,
> And love th' offender, yet detest th' offence?
> How the dear object from the crime remove,
> Or how distinguish penitence from love?
>
> (ll.183–94)

The arguments employed by Pope's Eloisa are of course those of Abelard
himself, taken by the poet from Abelard's reply to Heloise's first epistle
in John Hughes's 1713 redaction:

> What abhorrence can I be said to have of my Sins, if the Objects of
> them are always amiable to me? How can I separate from the person

I love, the Passion I must detest. . . . 'Tis difficult in our sorrow, to distinguish Penitence from Love.[46]

Pope adds yet another level to these dialogues and redactions, by creating an Eloisa who not only draws upon the previous epistles of Abelard in her own writing but echoes and condenses the arguments of the historic Heloise in this later heroic epistle.

The letter that has fallen into Eloisa's hands at the Paraclete at the opening of Pope's poem is thus the immediate textual cue for her own inter-textual activity; it is the starting point, as it were, for Eloisa's own attempts to negotiate between the past and the present (and in fact bring the past *into* the present) through the memory of that earlier body of writing, as part of her attempt to locate and describe precisely *who* she is, and how she stands in relation to the various forces that seek, ask, or demand to control her own life and language.

Critics have often pointed out the manner in which eighteenth-century authors tended to view memory as 'providing the basis for coherent reasoning and of substantial identity'. 'Not to remember', David Morris has noted with reference to eighteenth-century epistemology, 'is not to exist'.[47] Individual identity, as philosophers such as David Hume would note, is itself a negotiation between memory and imagination – a negotiation that allows us to perceive a 'self' within the 'perpetual flux and movement' of momentary perception; memory 'discovers personal identity', or, as Morris puts it, 'orders the individual'.[48] Hume's conception of personal identity – and the notion that memory and imagination actually work together to make a 'self' possible – was of course one of several responses to a question that had been keenly debated throughout the late seventeenth and early eighteenth centuries, a question that might simply be stated as 'what is a person?' or, alternatively, 'what *is* human identity?' In his 1651 *Leviathan*, Thomas Hobbes had placed a great deal of emphasis on the idea of 'improvising'. Hobbes suggested that as persons we 'represent ourselves acting' in the social world (*'Persona'*, he reminds his readers, 'in latine signifies the *disguise*, or *outward appearance* of a man, counterfeited on the stage. . . ').[49] John Locke, emphasizing the language of accountability, had later countered Hobbes's notion of human identity as a façade or 'fiction' by emphasizing the continuity of consciousness, and calling attention as well to the 'business' of memory to 'furnish the Mind those dormant Ideas, which it has present occasion for . . . '.[50] The endeavour to write about the 'self' and the search for the self becomes noteworthy in the eighteenth-century predilection for literary genres such as autobiography and – perhaps best equipped to detail the internal movements of a personality – the novel itself. Needless to say, modern thinkers have further complicated this long-sustained interest in the internal and external standards by which the self is evaluated by emphasizing, even more than the British empiricists, the discrepancies between what social psychologists have described as how we think we would like to be (the *ideal* self) and how we think we ought to be (the *ought* self).

Much of the poetry of the period likewise attempted to respond to the philosophical questions raised by the search for the self. One of the central struggles of Pope's *Eloisa to Abelard* – a poem which, as Morris further observes, 'varies between [Eloisa's] excursions into fantasy and her vivid recollections of the past' – is precisely this contest between memory and imagination for 'a coherent identity and a fully human self'.[51] By drawing upon an existing body of knowledge in her own memory, while allowing that memory to be balanced by a creative, self-sustaining (yet at the same time outward-looking) imaginative vision of personal identity – Eloisa can achieve some kind of personal coherence. The structurally balanced homologies of Pope's poem consequently mirror not only the thematic oppositions inherent in the work (the struggles, however articulated, between reason and passion, duty and impiety, love and honour) but reflect on an explicitly rhetorical level the epistemological struggle for coherence and identity that is, in fact, the central issue of Eloisa's epistle. This struggle or dialectic has been obscured by subsequent readers of Pope's *Epistle*, who have tended, for the most part, to concentrate only on the larger thematic contrasts at work in the poem at the expense of this formal, structural level of the poem's meaning.

Parody, then, is arguably in a unique position to 'understand' Pope's *Eloisa to Abelard*. Pope's poem suggests that the individual identity of Eloisa is itself a negotiation between memory and imagination – that personal identity is in fact the meeting point, in the present, of a memorial reconstruction of 'pastness' with a projected, free openness to the (possibly providential) design of human affairs. What better literary form to understand such a structure than one that itself explicitly relies upon the meeting and cooperation of memory and imagination – that simultaneously rests, that is to say, upon the cusp of existing perceptions and formal structures, and that which extends our identity beyond memory? If Eloisa must construct herself by negotiating the textual and memorial cues of the past, and the possibilities of the present, so too does the meaning of any parody create that meaning through a similar negotiation between an existing body of textual cues (the literary past) and the as-yet barely suggested possibilities of the imagination. The most successful parodies of *Eloisa to Abelard* mimic on an explicitly literary level the struggle for epistemological coherence rooted in memory, a struggle that is the focus of Pope's own poem. While engaging in a good-natured parody of Pope's work, subsequent parodies and imitations of *Eloisa* can simultaneously assert positive continuity with past traditions, containing as they do the notion that the interpretation of such textual cues provides the essential inherited basis of critical understanding and coherence.

(V)

The 'Advertisement' that prefaces Cambridge's poem explicitly announces its parodic involvement with the same struggle between memory and imagination that forms the basis of individual identity and lies at the heart of Pope's original. The notice alerts modern readers to the fact that many eighteenth-century parodies appeared in editions that either printed the targeted text on the bottom of the page or on facing pages. Cambridge seems unusually more eager in this partic-ular instance, however, to conjure the reader's 'Memory', and to alert the reader that the comprehension of his own piece relies at every moment on the *memorial* reconstruction of his original model – on Pope's own *Eloisa to Abelard*. Rather than following the custom of printing that model alongside his own text, however, Cambridge asks his readers to bring it with them in their own minds, and to allow his own parody (like Eloisa's letter from Abelard in Pope's epistle) to act as the constant textual cue for *their* own inter-textual activity. Although labelled an 'Elegy', Cambridge's parody falls into the hands of the reader – and requires the same kind of epistemological activity of the reader – in much the same manner that the letter that prompts Eloisa's own epistemological crisis falls abruptly into the hands of Pope's tragic heroine.

The narrative of Cambridge's own 'heroine', of course, forms a dramatic and (initially, at least) humorous contrast to that of Pope's Eloisa. The subject here is a fashionable London lady, who, far from being trapped in the stony-cold surroundings of Pope's Paraclete, is lamenting her own isolated 'fate' in an elegant, if empty, London assembly room. Again, it is generally accepted that Cambridge's representation is meant particularly to be Etheldreda Harrison, who is among those slighted by the Duchess of Norfolk, who has purposefully not invited her to one of the evening assemblies being held at her new London home. Cambridge is careful to present in the poem many parallel images that parody Pope's original model. If Eloisa's emotional situation is reflected in Pope's epistle by the weeping statues of the 'pitying Saints' who witness her involuntary impris-onment, so too is Lady Townshend's social disgrace witnessed by the mute 'Pictures . . . Glasses . . . Cards . . . and Chairs' that decorate the normally crowded and elegant assembly room. There is a similar element of sympathetic identification in Cambridge's work; just as the Paraclete's moist stones are said to mimic Eloisa's tears, for example, the chairs in Cambridge's parody comically echo the groans of the female exile, when they are pressed with the weight of 'Peers and Ministers'.

Yet where Pope's poem had focused on Eloisa's need to shape some sense of personal identity through the negotiation of memory and imagination, the heroine of Cambridge's parody is confronted not by a personal epistemological crisis, but rather by a social one. The letters and correspondence that had provided Eloisa with the textual basis of her own memory (as well as the theoretical arguments of her current expression) have dwindled here in the *Elegy* into invitations and calling cards, the visible evidence, ranged on the mantelpiece of social respectability and acceptance (ll.26–32). The 'craving Void' of Pope's Eloisa is of course mimicked here in the 'dismal Void' of social ostracism, the 'sullen Gloom' of the empty assembly room similarly mirroring the 'solitary gloom' of the convent. The substantial corres-pondence between the two lovers in Pope's poem is in Cambridge's parody reduced to the mere ciphers announcing and displaying the social manifestation and credentials of the individual. While acknow-ledging in the parodic form of his own work the dialectic between memory and imagination that gives meaning to Pope's poem in the first place, all that is left in Cambridge's lines of the actual substance of Pope's work is an obsessive and self-centred materialist concern. The speaker is, again, troubled not by a crisis of personal identity but rather by the threatened damage to and diminution of social status and respectability.

On closer examination, in fact, Cambridge's *Elegy* begins to appear more and more misogynistic. If the poet is eager to demonstrate his understanding within the parodic form of the fundamental tensions of Pope's original – his understanding, that is, of the dialectic between memory and imagination that simultaneously parodies both Pope's heroine and her epistle – he unfortunately seems just as eager to dismiss the ultimate significance of that dialectic, at least for the society women such as Lady Townshend herself with whom he is surrounded and, to some extent, for whom he is writing. The opening lines of Cambridge's parody, rather than setting up the significant ideational oppositions that suggest the thematic tensions of Pope's original, place his own dramatic heroine within the superficial trappings of contemporary societal fashion, the monologic dictates of 'the Ton' (ll.1–14).

The references in Pope's opening lines to William Hallet, a cabinet-maker, and – even more to the point – Mitford Bromwich, a wallpaper manufacturer, are conjured as the craftsmen of Lady Townshend's contemporary 'prison'. Both deal in lacquers and surfaces – in the fashionable appearances of things – and the rich (if gaudy) objects of the assembly room's furnishings are of course meant to stand in parodic contrast to the genuinely spare, ascetic, and sepulchral austerity of Eloisa's surroundings. Lady Townshend's social dilemma is rooted not, like Eloisa's, in the fiercely re-awakened internal reality of her situation, but in pride, social niceties, outward decorum, and the necessarily duplicitous phrasing of contemporary custom (e.g., 'I must not go abroad – and cannot *Be at Home'*). Cambridge's parody dwells on and exploits the possibility of female loneliness in eighteenth-century society. The woman who is excluded from the realm of the socially correct is thrown into an existential crisis that parodies Eloisa's potential schizophrenia. (The isolated, masturbatory potential of Pope's original is similarly and obviously exploited in Cambridge's parody.)

The poet ironically goes on to praise the higher power – 'the social Pow'r' – that first created the use of invitations and epistles. Here, however, such epistles are the means of purely social intercourse, not personal expression. They are by no means the catalysts for the kinds of personal epistemological crises of the sort that grips Pope's Eloisa. Cambridge explicitly evokes the Methodist 'in her peculiar Lot' who has the power to dismiss the cares of the world and the pressures of social conformity with the aid of devotional literature. The potential opposition between passion and piety that is internalized in Pope's Eloisa is here fractured into two separate individuals, in two very different social situations; the threatened schizophrenia of Pope's original is to some extent realized. Eloisa's Spartan and pointedly Roman Catholic religious discipline is re-presented in Cambridge's parody in the figure of a passionate Methodist who is visited in her dreams by 'Whisp'ring WHITF—D'. The unnamed narrator herself complains that her own nights are troubled by the sensual visions brought to her bed by her own darker version of such an evangelical Ariel. The nightmare vision of ll.67–79 conjures the false marriages persistently avoided by the heroines of eighteenth-century novels, yet the predicament of Dido (recalled here at line 76, and evoked as well in the Virgilian epigraph to the poem) works again to diminish the threat of the purely social disenfranchisement facing Cambridge's heroine. Dido, like Pope's Eloisa, was ostracized not only socially, but sexually, emotionally, and politically as well – and the power that provoked that banishment or abandonment was the power that mattered, that is, masculine authority. Lady Townshend's exclusion and the exclusion of others like her from the sisterhood of Norfolk's drum, Cambridge tells us, is in truth rather laughable, and worthy only of a belittling amusement.

The poem would appear to end on a lighter note, however, as Cambridge's heroine remains trapped in her own bare assembly room, while Norfolk's social space crowds with guests and admirers. 'How', Townshend asks,

> shall I waste this Time that slowly flies!
> How lull to slumber my reluctant Eyes!
> This Night the happy and th' Unhappy keep
> Vigils alike, —- N * * *has murder'd Sleep.*

(ll.92–5)

Those included within the realm of the social and public sphere in the end suffer a fate no less tortuous than its sustained enforcement of deference and *ennui*. Even so, while Cambridge's parody thus seems to pick up on the larger structural dialectic posited by the heroic epistle in the formal patterns of his own parodic imitation, he seems consistently to attempt to diminish and to flatten the dialectic crises that lies at the thematic or substantive heart of Pope's poem. Contemporary society ladies such as Townshend, Cambridge seems to be saying, are not confronted with the epistemological crises of heroines such as Pope's Eloisa, if only because they operate within the eternal 'now' – the persistent present – of the contemporary fashionable world. Eloisa's passionate struggle for individual coherence in a world in which reason clashes with emotion, love with duty, and passion with piety, Cambridge suggests, is inappropriate or at least irrelevant to a society that offers only choices of social conformity or social ostracism. Cambridge's understanding of the structural implications of Pope's own poetic form paradoxically allows him to lead a misogynistic attack against the significance of the concomitant thematic dialectics of *Eloisa to Abelard*. The very same understanding would appear to have afforded him unfortunately little in the way of any genuine insight into the seemingly inescapable dilemma of the eighteenth-century female self, trapped within a suffocating, schyzotypal crisis of identity.

7
Parody, Autobiography, and the Novel: *A Narrative of the Life of Mrs Charlotte Charke* and *The History of Henry Dumont, Esq., and Miss Charlotte Evelyn*

> Writing is a way of turning the unhappiest moments of one's life into money.
>
> – J. P. Donleavy[1]

Early one morning in the autumn of 1755, an eager young Irishman named Samuel Whyte set out with a friend on a business errand in central London.[2] Having quickly left the more familiar precincts of St. Paul's Churchyard and Paternoster Row behind them, the two men were soon wending their way among the neighbouring streets of nearby Clerkenwell. The nascent stirrings of restless urban activity (the full flowering of which would later prompt the novelist Arnold Bennett to dub the area one of the truly 'great metropolitan industrial districts' of London) were becoming increasingly noticeable within the increasingly over-burdened lanes and byways of the once rural community.[3] Although an ancient settlement, Clerkenwell might until recently have been dismissed as little more than a rustic cluster of cloistered nunneries and medicinal springs. By the later decades of the seventeenth century, however, fashionable pleasure gardens, spas, and music houses had spread across the hamlet's former meadowlands. The thriving cottage industry that supplied the capital's watch and clock-making trade (the craftsmen of Clerkenwell produced some 120,000 watches each year) soon transformed the small country parish of open fields and one-room cottages into an industrial quarter of closely packed settlements and often noisome tenements. Unwholesome garrets typically served both as home and workplace to many of the neighbourhood's artisans.[4] Indeed, the concentrated centre of jewellery and precious metal work in London, the area was considered by some to have long possessed a mysterious alchemical quality that was uniquely its own. The inhabitants of Clerkenwell, Peter Ackroyd has even suggested, seem throughout history 'to have imbibed the quixotic and fevered atmosphere of the area; somehow by being beyond the bars of the city, strange existences [have been] allowed to flourish'.[5] Radicals, occultists, outcasts, incorrigible individualists – any number of inherently marginal elements of the great and varied human congregation of London seemed to thrive in the vicinity. Over the years, the idiosyncratic territorial impulse of Clerkenwell was memorably to nourish such singular characters as Margaret (a.k.a 'Mad Madge') Cavendish, Duchess of Newcastle, as well as the notorious miser, Thomas Cooke, and the once locally famous 'musical small-coal man', Thomas Britton (an itinerant vendor of coals whose musical aspirations managed to attract to the tiny residence above his coal shed some of the most celebrated composers and performers of the day, including Handel).[6] Topographically liminal with respect to the proper boundaries of the City of London (Ackroyd's reference to its being 'beyond the bars of the city' reminds us that the neighbourhood lay quite literally outside the barriers marking the entrances into the territory of the capital), Clerkenwell provided a conveniently proximate and adjacent refuge for those who refused to conform to the acceptable, the permissible, or the otherwise 'confined'. It was tantalizingly close to (but never itself quite a part of) the urban centre; its precincts seemed to survive by virtue of their resourceful ability to offer a space for difference, and to supply the unpredictable on demand.

As it happened, Samuel Whyte chose to make his journey through Clerkenwell on a particularly inauspicious day. Heavy rains the preceding evening had saturated the household trash deposited in the area's open sewers and 'dust-holes'. The ensuing torrents quickly dissipated the notorious communal rubbish heap (euphemistically dubbed 'Mount Pleasant' by the local residents) into something that might more accurately have been described as a quagmire. The downpours that continued throughout the morning further confused the district's already maze-like thoroughfares into a single wretched and impassable swamp. Every conceivable species of refuse mingled with the mud and dust of the streets to swell the kennels into malodorous torrents of near-Swiftian proportions. By the time the two visitors managed finally to pick their way among the wretched footpaths, the clean stockings in which they had set out, Whyte observed with some chagrin, had long since been encrusted with mud 'up to the very calves'.

Later to be remembered as the respected principal of the successful English Grammar school in Grafton Street, Dublin, Whyte would eventually have among his pupils the playwright Richard Brinsley Sheridan (the son of his first cousin, the novelist Frances Sheridan) as well as Arthur Wellesley (the Duke of Wellington), and the poet Thomas Moore.[7] He was also to achieve some minor celebrity as a writer of treatises on educational reform and elocution, and would gain some further renown as the author of several volumes of poetry. (his defence of the acting profession, entitled simply *The Theatre* [1792], enjoyed a modest success in his own lifetime.)[8] As we shall see, there is every reason to believe that the close relationship that Whyte enjoyed with his novelist cousin Frances until her untimely death in 1766 may have a small but significant role to play in the story that follows.

In the waning months of 1755, however, the literary fortunes of Whyte's companion – an enterprising young bookseller named Henry Slater, junior – seemed more auspicious than his own. Slater's father was an established bookseller who had long operated a modest but successful circulating library near Drury Lane. His son – who had until then contented himself only with assisting in the family concern – had recently begun to consider increasing his own stake in the book trade, and was now eager to begin book-selling and publishing for himself. Convinced that the success of any ambitious young man of business depended on his ability aggressively to seek out potential best-sellers and to snatch them up before the competition had been given the chance to make any counter-offers, Slater had managed recently to locate – in the muddy purlieus of Clerkenwell – a possible prize: Mrs Charlotte Charke, the daughter of the celebrated actor, theatre manager, and Poet Laureate Colley Cibber.

Charke's lively autobiography, *A Narrative of the Life of Mrs Charlotte Charke*, had appeared in eight weekly parts in April and May of 1755. The *Narrative* passed through two single-volume editions by the end of that same year. Several times in the course of the work, the author had pointedly referred to a novel – *The History of Henry Dumont, Esq., and Miss Charlotte Evelyn* – which she claimed already to have completed and made ready for publication. Charke went so far as to insist that the popular *Narrative* relating the story of her own life had itself emerged merely as the incidental by-product of this more ambitious effort in fiction – a fiction, she emphasized, that had yet to find a publisher. Having intended initially only to write a straightforward fiction, Charke claimed that she had unintentionally unlocked the storehouse of her own most personal and intimate memories. (A connection might here be made to the manner in which other novels of the period – Samuel Richardson's *Pamela* would be the most striking example – emerged only 'accidentally' or inadvertently, on occasions when their authors were

engaged in other enterprises; in some sense, too, all such works participated in a *literal* tradition of parody, insofar as they were initially ancillary
or somehow 'supplemental' works.) 'When I first came to Town', Charke
protested in her autobiography, 'I had no Design of giving any Account
of my Life, farther than a trifling Sketch, introduced in the Preface to
Mr. DUMONT's History, the first number of which', she confidently
asserted, 'will shortly make its Appearance, and I hope will be kindly
received. . . '.[9] The young Slater – with an eye, no doubt, to the considerable advance publicity that the successful *Narrative* had already provided
Charke's work – was eager to get his hands on the novel and publish it
himself. And so, with this intention in mind, he had persuaded Whyte
to accompany him on the short journey from the bookstalls of St. Paul's
Churchyard to hear Charke read aloud from her work, and to settle on
a price for the volume.

Having negotiated their way among the sodden carriageways of
Clerkenwell, however, the pair – by now considerably the worse for
wear – were surprised to discover Charke's residence to be little more
than a miserable thatched hovel. As Whyte would later recall in an
account of the visit published in the *Monthly Review*: 'we knocked at
the door, which was opened by a tall, meagre, ragged figure with a
blue apron, indicating what otherwise might have been doubted, the
female gender'. The dark interior of the home, as best they could tell,
was meanly furnished, containing the sort of movables that Edmund
Burke would elsewhere characterize as 'much fitter to be lamented than
described'.[10] A dresser decorated with a few coarse delft plates, a small
earthenware jug, a broken black pitcher: these seemed to be the only
substantial objects distinguishable in the gloom. On one side of the
chamber, Whyte recalled, a fire smouldered ineffectually on a small
hearth. A chattering monkey snatched at one hob; a disconsolate tabby
cat sought to warm itself at the foot of the other. The author herself
sat in a maimed chair pulled close to the same hearth, precariously
positioned (or so one gathers from Whyte's description of her appearance) to collapse at any moment, rather in the manner of Dickens's
Mrs Skewton, into a sordid and unseemly bundle in one corner of the
room. Charke's emaciated dog, Fidele – which appeared to Whyte to
be 'almost a skeleton' – lay stretched at its mistress's feet. A magpie
perched on the upper rung of her chair. 'On her lap', Whyte observed of
Charke,

> was placed a mutilated pair of bellows: the pipe was gone, an
> advantage in present office: they served as a succedaneum for a

writing desk, on which lay displayed her hopes and treasures, the manuscript of her novel. Her inkstand was a broken teacup: her pen worn to stump: but she had one! A rough deal board, with three hobbling supporters, was brought for our convenience, on which, without further ceremony, we contrived to sit down and enter upon business.[11]

Judging from Whyte's description, everything about Charke appears somehow to be shattered, broken, smashed, or fragmented. No single one of the objects that she has gathered around her, if the details of Whyte's account are to be at all credited, has been left undamaged or in any way suitable to its proper office. A cracked teacup stands in the place of an inkwell. A pair of otherwise useless bellows has similarly been requisitioned to perform the service of a writing desk. A dog, a cat, a magpie, and a monkey (figures in their own way as appropriately bizarre and pitiably theatrical as the freakish domestics acknowledged by the protagonist of Ben Jonson's *Volpone* as naturally his 'own' in the comedy that bears his name) seem awkwardly to stand in place of a wholesome and legitimate or even, for what it's worth, *human* family. Both the magpie – a bird of chattering voice and notoriously thievish inclination – and the monkey strike a further note of parodic and anthropomorphic talkativeness or mimicry.

Try as he might in his account to sound encouraging about such details as Charke's worn 'stump' of a pen ('. . . she had one!'), Whyte's desperate cheer of enthusiasm rings hopelessly hollow. His seeming optimism appears on the occasion deliberately to have been roused at least as much in an attempt to shore up his own sinking spirits, as it was to reassure his readers of his support for the efforts of Charke herself. Even the physical manuscript of Charke's novel, the account invites the reader to speculate, may not be quite what it seems. Why, for example, should Whyte choose so pointedly to describe its singular bulk – oddly, and so peculiarly in the plural – as her 'hopes' and 'treasures'? In what way might Charke conceivably have disposed the individual pages of the same tattered manuscript – across the sooty surface of a pair of crushed and fractured bellows, no less – in such a way so as flatteringly to 'display' them for her visitors? Why, for that matter, has the young publisher been compelled to pursue this supposedly fashionable author to such an unfashionably dark and out-of-the-way retreat in the first place? Are we meant in any way to admire the figure of the author presented here, most readers soon find themselves asking of Whyte's depiction of Charke? Or are we meant, rather, simply to laugh at her?

The manner in which Whyte appears very quickly to have begun re-evaluating his own first impressions of Charke – the manner in which he overcame his initial hesitation even to set foot within the splintered menagerie of her world – is no less clearly reflected in the subsequent portion of his account. Whyte soon finds himself confessing an unexpected respect for his hostess. Charke's voice, he tells the reader, even amidst such surroundings, sounded humbled but not harsh – hushed, but not broken. Her fractured speech yet managed to convey, Whyte observes with a nicety that manages neatly to combine the demands of decorum with the impulse of the erotic, 'the mingled effect of authority and pleasure'. The two young men spent several hours in Charke's company on that otherwise dreary morning, sitting with the author and listening to her read from her novel aloud. When Charke finally looked up from the pages of her manuscript, she asked for the novel a price of thirty guineas; Whyte adds a novelistic touch to his own description of the transaction when he describes the reaction of Charke's domestic servant: 'the squalid handmaiden, who had been an attentive listener, stretched forward her tawny length of neck with an eye of anxious expectation!'. The amount would appear to have been a reasonable one; only a few years later, in 1759, Samuel Johnson was to request an advance of thirty guineas from his friend, the printer William Strahan, on the delivery of the manuscript of his slim oriental tale *Rasselas*, and would eventually receive a payment of £100 for the first edition of that tale.[12] Be that as it may, the young publisher countered Charke's asking price with a drastically reduced offer of only five guineas. Charke displayed no outward sign of disappointment. Indeed, so struck was Whyte himself by the resigned tone with which Charke received Slater's reduced payment that he felt compelled (prompted more, he would have us believe, by a true spirit of generosity than by a concern for his own financial security) to double his friend's amount, and run half the risk of the publishing costs himself. Slater agreed to the split. Charke – reserving a somewhat surprising fifty copies of the novel for herself – accepted the offer, and the deal was completed.

Samuel Whyte's initial impulsive venture in the book-selling trade as Henry Slater, Jr's business partner did not fare quite so well as he had hoped. *The History of Henry Dumont, Esq., and Miss Charlotte Evelyn*, which the pair presented to the public in 1756, failed to attract the degree of attention its young publishers had anticipated. Although the novel passed through more than one edition that same year, sales were generally disappointing, and original copies of the novel today remain – along with some of Charke's earlier writings for the stage – comparatively rare. The novel's publication was noted, although the work itself was not reviewed, by the *Gentleman's Magazine* in February 1757.[13]

(I)

The History of Henry Dumont, Esq., and Miss Charlotte Evelyn is likely on first acquaintance to strike those readers more familiar with her earlier *Narrative* as precisely the sort of novel that one might have expected from the pen of a yet defiantly transgressive – as opposed to a truly reformed or penitent – Charlotte Charke.[14] The *History* is a work that demonstrates, if not an immediately obvious unity of structure or design, then at least an uncommon degree of faith in the self-sufficient vitality of its own fictional world. Many of its characters are proto-Dickensian in their sheer comic intensity (although much of that same larger-than-life vitality is the textual legacy of Charke's career as an actor and impersonator – a recollection of her life as a trained as well as a spontaneous or impromptu parodist on the stage). As in the previously published *Narrative*, that same sense of vitality appears to carry both Charke and her fictional characters far beyond the bounds of any dubiously intended 'purpose' or 'intention'. Both life and art, as conceptualized by Charke, have a way of getting quickly and often ridiculously out of hand.

The more obvious strengths of Charke's previously published life would at first glance suggest precisely those areas in which her novel might have been criticized, at least at the time of its first publication, for having somehow fallen short of the mark. In fact, the *History* in many respects stood as an odd kind of textual complement to Charke's life story – a self-reflexive and self-parodic companion piece that begged to be read against its (paradoxically derivative) predecessor for its meaning. Few readers would deny that the success of Charke's earlier *Narrative* had been to a very great extent the result of what can only be described as the sheer and uncompromising *force* of its author's wildly iconoclastic personality. Although protesting that it told a story 'nothing but what may daily happen to every mortal breathing', Charke's compelling autobiography nevertheless boasted of the fact that it chronicled the adventures of a woman who was – by her own unapologetic admission – determined to earn the title of 'a nonpareil of the age' (*Narrative*, 5). The *Narrative* had, in fact, already assumed the status of being at one and the same time both a memoir and a form of novel in itself. Charke's was a hybrid text that constantly protested its devotion to verifiable fact, yet every page of which paradoxically amounted to a seditious handbook of domestic rebellion. Behind Charke's story lay the dynamic of its author's exuberant sense of herself as a powerfully autonomous subject – her fiercely independent sense of personhood or what some modern critics would characterize as female agency – engaged in radical lifelong conflict with cultural structures of conformity and authority. With such possible exceptions as the life and writings of highly unconventional figures such as her (former) fellow Clerkenwell resident Margaret Cavendish and – a little later in the period – Delarivier Manley and Eliza Haywood, or of the gendered narratives related by the self-liberating heroines of equally innovative novels such as Defoe's *Moll Flanders* (1722) and *Roxanna* (1724), and extending to Sarah Fielding's *The Governess* (1749), the traditions of English prose fiction had never seen anything quite like Charke's *Narrative* before.

Admittedly, one could argue that the story related by Charke in her autobiography would in almost any hands have proven itself to be a compelling one. Born into what was even by the time of her arrival one of the most boisterous, energetic, and shrewdly self-promotional families in the history of the English theatre, the infant Charlotte decided very early in life that the quiet paths of feminine domesticity were ludicrously incommensurate with what she already perceived to be her own considerable talents and ambitions. 'I had no Notion of entertaining the least Thought', she had boasted early in the *Narrative*,

> of those necessary Offices by which the young Ladies of the Family so eminently distinguished themselves, in ornamenting a well-disposed, elegant Table, decently graced with the Toil of their Morning's Industry; nor could I bear to pass a Train of melancholy Hours in pouring over a Piece of embroidery, or a well-wrought Chair, in which the young Females of the Family (exclusive of my mad-cap Self) were equally and industriously employed; and have often, with inward Contempt of 'em, pitied their Misfortune, who were, I was well assured, incapable of currying a Horse, or making a Race with me.
> (*Narrative*, 18)

Elegance, decency, and the industry, toil, and craftsmanship of a sheltered domestic world: Charke slyly tells us that she wants nothing to do with these things. Interior hours wasted in the dull routine of domestic female chores – accomplishments, achievements, call such 'necessary Offices' what you will – were hours altogether wasted. Perceiving her own 'Self' to be 'mad-cap' in the great English tradition of anti-authoritarian, topsy-turvy playfulness and Saturnalia, Charke dismissed those same 'young Ladies' who would be so foolish as to submit and conform to the prescriptions of those 'Offices' as melancholy prisoners – prisoners who were to some extent complicit in their own confinement. Some drama critics may try to dismiss Charke's highly self-conscious non-conformity and iconoclasm merely as symptomatic of her otherwise inconsequentially 'zany' mentality, but Charke herself appears rather obviously to have had a larger purpose in mind. The gendered role one plays in society, she suggested with admirable prescience, is at least as much a matter of choice as it is a matter of destiny.

Charke's *Narrative* makes for extraordinarily entertaining reading. The young Charlotte Cibber decided to spend the better part of her own time perfecting her skills in more obviously masculine pursuits such as riding and shooting. When sent to the home of a nearby physician to assist in domestic chores and learn how to maintain an economic household, she characteristically expressed a great deal more interest in the professional activities of the doctor himself. Far from learning anything of a domestic or designedly feminine nature, Charke aspired rather to become accomplished in the arts of medicine and physic. Such an education, Charke wryly asserted, was 'in Fact a liberal one, and such indeed as must have been sufficient for a Son instead of a Daughter (*Narrative*, 10). She further boasted,

> I was never made much acquainted with that necessary Utensil which forms the housewifely Part of a young Lady's Education, call'd a Needle; which I handle with the same clumsy Awkwardness a Monkey does a Kitten, and am equally capable of using the one, as Pug is of using the other.
>
> (*Narrative*, 10)

Again, in passages such as this, Charke not only revels in her perception of the 'necessary' as superfluous, but emphasizes that, in her own case, the ability to conform would be positively unnatural – a grotesque and potentially dangerous incongruity. After a brief and unhappy marriage to a profligate violinist named Richard Charke (by whom she had one child), Cibber decided upon the most obvious option available to her: she turned her attention to the theatre. A born performer, she was soon acting featured roles in plays such as *Antony and Cleopatra*, John Vanbrugh's *The Relapse* (1696), and George Lillo's hugely successful domestic tragedy, *The London Merchant* (1731). In time, Charke also enjoyed considerable success as the male lead in a number of popular dramas. She notably acted the part of Macheath in John Gay's *The Beggar's Opera* (1728), Mr. Townley in *The Provok'd Husband* (1697), and Lothario in Nicholas Rowe's *The Fair Penitent* (1703).

Charke, very early in her theatrical career, took to the habit of assuming masculine attire offstage as well an on.[15] The decision to masquerade in her daily life as a man, Charke would cryptically inform her readers in the *Narrative*, was done 'for substantial Reasons' (*Narrative*, 47). Yet, as critics such as Fidelis Morgan have observed in their own commentaries on Charke's *Narrative*, there would have been a surprising number of eminently practical reasons for any woman living to disguise herself in masculine clothing. Indeed, a steady look beyond the more established and well-known personal histories of the period very soon uncovers the partial narratives of a number of cross-dressers – women whose occasionally even more fragmented and anecdotal stories together form an extended sub-text or supplemental narrative to Charke's own, more fully articulated history. Although some readers will detect explicitly sexual or 'fetishist' elements in Charke's passing as a man in private life, there is no substantial evidence to support such claims. The sexologist Havelock Ellis, writing as early as 1942, concluded that Charke was merely 'boyish and vivacious' and discouraged any suggestion that her cross-dressing was primarily or even partially motivated by sexual factors.[16]

On the whole, modern readers are likely to agree that it is considerably more probable that the actress's initial reasons for deciding to pass on occasion '*EN CAVALIER*' (*Narrative*, 47) were connected as much to her seemingly constant indebtedness and financial insecurity as they were to any more personally complex or psychosexual motives. The many duns, bailiffs, tradesmen, and creditors who had issued writs against Charke would obviously have kept a sharp eye out for those women who answered to her physical description, yet they would of course have had little reason to examine the appearance of any young men of similar age who happened to cross their paths. Moreover, Charke's early professional success in performing in male attire on the stage not only made such a transformation a comparatively easy one but – if her disguise was indeed part of a sartorial strategy assumed primarily if not exclusively for reasons of financial expediency – a psychologically comforting one as well. The logic is mere common sense. As Morgan further observed of Charke's personality and sense of vocation:

> If she took a job as a chambermaid, it would have been a humiliating come-down, an inescapable admission of failure (if only to herself); if

she dressed up as a man and took a job as a *valet de chambre* it would have been much less psychologically damaging, for the acting skill required provided a buffer that made the actual reality of the job like a joke, a trick, brilliantly performed by a consummate actress.[17]

It would be easier for Charke to play at life itself, in other words, than it would have been for her to participate in any activity that denied her what she had already come to regard as her (paradoxically) 'essential' function – the role of flamboyant and histrionic impersonation.

Of course, such tactics could always backfire. Charlotte Charke when dressed in the guise of a man seems never to have surrendered the tendency to display all the flamboyant tastes and attitudes of Charlotte Charke when dressed as an actor or an actress on the stage. Her intuitive propensity to play her dramatic roles – and to play *all* her dramatic roles – to their fullest could lead to some sticky situations. On at least one occasion the singularity of her ostentatious and typically conspicuous and 'handsome' laced hat ('ornamented with a beautiful Silver Lace' [*Narrative*, 50]) was so outlandish as to allow it to be very minutely described by passers-by to a bailiff, and so render his quarry unmistakable. But then again, blending into the crowd would never have sat that well with Charke's sense of personal style. In whatever manner Charke chose to dress, her peculiar sense of decorous indecorum appears never to have worked to obscure or effectively disguise herself, but always vividly to stand apart. Even cross-dressers – indeed, *especially*, cross-dressers, as Charke herself might have argued – would have carried with them some sense of their responsibilities towards upholding, defining, and, on occasion, transforming the dictates of the *ton* – of the fashionable world. It would appear that Charke was no more incapable of cross-dressing with style than she was capable of resisting cross-dressing at all. If, for whatever reason, she was going to be a transvestite, then she would at least see to it that she was an innovative and *chic* transvestite. There was more than a touch of Etheredge's Sir Fopling Flutter – and not a little, for that matter, of his Dorimant, as well as of Colley Cibber's own Lord Foppington and his Sir Novelty Fashion – in Charke's own, more strategically practical representation of the 'Man of Mode'. Charke, however, was not so much a dedicated follower of fashion as she was a sartorial harbinger of the most idiosyncratic kind.

Charke left the London stage in 1737. Her decision to abandon her career as an actress was due in part to larger events then taking place in London's theatre world, as well as to complications stemming from the intrigues of her actor-brother, Theophilus Cibber.[18] Yet her own constitutional inability to conform to the necessary discipline of the world of the playhouse seems also to have contributed to Charke's change of direction. In the several months that followed what amounted to a complete overhaul and restructuring of London's theatre scene, Charke herself began an extended and at times bizarre descent into the activities of the city's underworld. She engaged in an extraordinarily wide range of business ventures, all of which proved in the end to be catastrophic failures. A modest list of Charke's subsequent activities would begin by noting that she operated a puppet theatre, in which she is said to have manipulated the Punch puppet, in particular (Charke's proclivity for ventriloquism necessary to the manipulations of puppetry is a complement to her earlier manifestations of secondary or parodic behaviour). Such theatres managed to take advantage of a technical loophole to evade many of the Licensing Act's restrictions and flourished throughout the period. Later, Charke opened a public house; hawked sausages in the streets; took up, on several occasions, with a number of provincial theatrical touring companies; was on at least one other occasion arrested for debt and released from detention by her Covent Garden acquaintances; worked as a waiter in a tavern; served as *valet de chambre* to an Irish Lord; and – not so very many years before the notorious Mrs Lovett, with the help of her good friend and neighbour Sweeney Todd, was rumoured to have supervised a similar establishment in London's Bell Yard – owned and operated a shop selling meat pies. Finally, and apparently only as a last resort, she decided to try her hand as a professional author of prose fiction.

The chequered events of Charke's own life, as she herself soon realized, had provided her with a priceless store of narrative material and incident – a fictional hoard the likes of which most novelists of the period would have envied. Truth, so the popular saying goes, is stranger than fiction, and here was truth with a vengeance. Charke's story would very probably have provided the stuff of popular tales in almost any era. Yet much of the immediate interest in her *Narrative* – much, that is, of the book's initial popularity and even notoriety – had depended upon Charke's timely and public airing in its pages of the quarrel that had kept her separated from her famous father for over 20 years. Although Colley Cibber – among the most successful writers and performers of the era, however much he may have invited the ridicule of his contemporaries and rivals – appears to have stood by Charlotte through a bitter dispute with the theatrical manager Charles Fleetwood in the early 1730s, there soon afterward occurred a falling-out between father and daughter that left Charke, if not legally disowned, then for all practical intents and purposes expelled from the family and from all its theatrical ventures. After 1735, Cibber took little interest in his daughter's increasingly desperate career, and deliberately avoided any contact with her. Charke was devastated; she probably also felt (although she would have been the last to admit it) frightened, abandoned, and alone. The despair at being so utterly excluded from the life of her family and the sense of rejection she felt at her father's renunciation of her can be felt trembling just below the surface of Charke's writing, and forms the obsessive centre both of her autobiography and of her novel.

In one early instalment of the published *Narrative*, Charke made no effort to disguise her intention of using the autobiography as an open attempt to effect a reconciliation with her father and family. 'Were I to expire this Instant', she declared in the early pages of her history,

> I have no self-interested Views in Regard to worldly Matters; but confess myself a Miser in my Wishes so far, as having the transcendent Joy of knowing that I am restor'd to a Happiness, which not only will clear my Reputation to the World, in Regard to a former Want of Duty, but, at the same Time, give a convincing Proof that there are yet some Sparks of Tenderness remaining in my Father's Bosom, for his REPENTANT CHILD.
>
> (Narrative, 9)

Desperate, she informed the reader, for some indication of her father's favour or forgiveness, she soon afterwards wrote him a letter appealing for a reconciliation – a letter that she subsequently printed in its entirety in the fifth instalment of the *Narrative*. In actual fact, Cibber merely returned the original epistle to his daughter, unopened and with no cover, within a blank sheet of paper. Even Charke herself was taken aback by such a display of *sang-froid*. 'The Prodigal', she cried in seeming grief and indignation,

> according to Holy Writ, was joyfully received by the offended father: Nay, MERCY was even extended itself at the place of Execution, to notorious Malefactors; but as I have not been Guilty of those Enormities incidental to the formention'd characters, permit me, gentle Reader, to demand what I have done so hateful! so very grievous to his Soul! so much beyond the Reach of Pardon! that nothing but MY LIFE COULD MAKE ATONEMENT?
>
> (Narrative, 63)

Making easy use of the dramatically charged language of Newgate and Tyburn, Charke confesses herself to be a domestic offender – a criminal sentenced to a life of family exile. Her theatrical background prompts her quite naturally to picture herself as a literary or dramatic character; she reads the ongoing saga of her own life story in much the same manner that she would have read a novel or a play. She interprets according to rules of genre, precedent, and type. Charke in fact effectively transforms the natural drama of being into one of being-as-drama. Consequently, she reinterprets – and risks *mis*interpreting – the 'text' of her own life. If fictional characters earlier in the period, in novels such as Defoe's *Robinson Crusoe* (1719), had looked to stories such as that of the Prodigal Son to provide them with a narrative model or pattern that could help them to locate precisely where they had gone *wrong* in their lives – where their own transgressions had over-stepped the line of the male tradition's wise and judicious advice – Charke turns to the same familiar narrative of Luke 15:11–32 reluctantly to portray her own father, rather, as a figure of inflexible and sanctimonious self-righteousness. Some of the characters included in the plays in which Charke had performed may necessarily have been dragged, unrepentant, to the gallows (George Lillo's passionate heroine/villainess Millwood may well have loomed large in Charke's imagination here), but what, she asks her reader, of that divine and gentle mercy that was supposed in yet another drama to season justice even in the hearts of kings? Shylock's defiant daughter, Jessica, in Shakespeare's *The Merchant of Venice*, provided yet another pattern for the actress's behaviour; Jessica's cry, 'I have a father, you a daughter, lost' (*MV* II.v.56) is Charke's own lament throughout her *Narrative*. And almost instinctively, it would appear, Charke likewise compared herself to the character of Cordelia in Shakespeare's *King Lear*. She presented herself in the *Narrative* as a comparative innocent, cut off from the affection of a loving if tragically misguided father by a rancorous and vindictive family, the other members of which were united in nothing so much as their determination to deprive her of the rights and even the responsibilities of being a daughter. Cordelia – silent in the face of a baseless accusation, a woman who on some level refuses even to engage in the dangerous, post-lapsarian game of linguistic ambiguity and meaning – paradoxically provided Charke with a model, rather, for becoming a vocal, articulate, and even forcefully outspoken daughter; Cordelia's poignant 'Nothing' (although we should remember that her very silence in the opening scenes of Shakespeare's play is itself to some extent an aggressive act of power and control) is the terse counterpart to and instigation for Charke's own vociferous pleas for mercy, recognition, and understanding. Interpreting *King Lear* in this manner, Charke neglected (uncharacteristically) to read the drama through to its end; so intently was she focused on the aptness of a momentary analogy, she perhaps failed on this occasion to pursue the tragic logic of its larger implications to the play's grim and inevitable conclusion.

Undeterred by the failure of her first attempt to evoke any response from her family, Charke persisted in her efforts to be recognized by her ailing father. Much of what makes her *Narrative* still such engaging reading is the manner in which its author, at the same time that she availed herself of all the dramatic parallels that sprang as readily to her pen as to her lips, seemed still, for the most part, capable of retaining a profoundly ironic distance between her self, on the one hand, and the dogged and stubborn persistence of her activities, on the other. Like all aesthetically successful and engaging autobiographies, Charke's *Narrative* not only offers a subjective recounting of the specific acts and events of a life, but reflects as well – with a carefully contrived distance and, so far as it is possible, dispassion – on the consequences of those same occurrences. Charke is, throughout her work, very much aware that, as Janet Malcolm was to put it when chronicling the legacy of an artistic life even more troubled than Charke's own, the notion that the person writing the life and the person being written about *in* that life are a single 'seamless' entity is, in fact, nothing more than a convenient fiction.[19] Charke's volume chronicles a personal rite of passage – it pointedly details a narrative of multi-layered metamorphoses. And it does so always from the thoughtfully periodic perspective of a narrator who can at least claim to have reached a vantage of rhetorical and experiential authority. Simply put, the reader can perceive the extent of the growth and maturity attained by the adult writer by the very palpable and demonstrable *distance* between past and present.

The schizophrenic impulse inescapably inherent in the very task of autobiography – the recognition on some level that one is not relating the life of a self, so much as the lives of several distinct and separate selves or personae – is dramatically enacted in the course of Charke's *Narrative*. The address prefaced to the single-volume edition of Charke's work that dedicates the volume (rather in the manner of Laurence Sterne) from 'The Author to herself', for example, concludes:

My Choice of you, Madam, to patronize my works, is an evidential proof that I am not disinterested in that point; as the World will easily be convinc'd, from your natural Partiality to all I have hitherto produced, that you will tenderly overlook their *Errors*, and, to the utmost of your Power, endeavour to *magnify their Merits*. If, by your Approbation, the World may be perswaded into a tolerable Opinion of my Labours, I shall, for the Novelty-sake, venture for once to call you FRIEND; a Name, I own, I never *as yet have known you by*.

I hope, dear Madam, as MANLY says in *The Provok'd Husband*, that *'last reproach has struck you'*, and that you and I may ripen our Acquaintance into a perfect Knowledge of each other, that may establish a lasting and social Friendship between us.

(Narrative, 6)

Most striking in this passage is the fact that Charke chooses to echo and include – to parody – the precise language of her father (Cibber had himself written *The Provok'd Husband*, taken from an original play by Vanburgh, in 1728) in her own self-reproach. Cibber had dedicated his own notoriously controversial autobiography in 1740, to Henry Pelham, brother to his friend and patron, the Duke of Newcastle. In so doing, he was merely taking advantage of the possibilities offered by all such dedications; he used it as an opportunity to flatter his patron, and so advance himself socially and professionally. Yet Charke's own cryptic inclusion of a parodically constructed 'dialogue' between her father and herself in her own dedication carefully anticipates the dramatically more personal agenda of her own writing. Her dedication likewise reflects the *Narrative*'s tendency to speak in many voices at once. The parody of the dedication's self-preferentiality reflects the necessarily ventrilo-quistic, histrionic, and self-parodic qualities that, as Charke herself saw it, only when taken together added up to the pretence of an integrated personality in society.

Such irony is very much present from the opening passages of the *Narrative*. In one incident recorded early in the work, the author tells of her youthful attempts to pose as a medical doctor among the neighbouring housewives. Although her father, having subsequently received an outrageous bill for pharmaceutical supplies from the local apothecary, angrily put an end to his daughter's credit, Charlotte appears never to have considered giving up her 'practice' – not, at least, so long as she had an elderly woman on her very doorstep complaining of rheumatic pains and a stomach disorder. Charke writes of her response,

It happened that Day proved very rainy, which put it into my strange Pate to gather up all the Snails in the Garden; of which, from the heavy shower that had fallen, there were a superabundant Quantity. I immediately fell to work; and, some Part of 'em, with coarse Brown Sugar, made a Syrup, to be taken a Spoonful one in two Hours. Boiling the rest to a Consistence, with some green Herbs and Mutton Fat, I made an Ointment; and clapping conceited Labels upon the Phial and Gallipot, sent my Preparation, with a joyous Bottle of Heartshorn and *Sal Volatile* I purloined from my Mother, to add a Grace to my Prescriptions.

(Narrative, 20–1)

The author's gleeful willingness to make do with whatever materials happened to come to hand, the innovation that prompts her to add the extra gasteropodous touch that uniquely distinguishes her own concoction from all other such remedies and – most tellingly – her instinctive and essentially theatrical impulse to stand back and encourage the laughter of her readers at her own expense: all are typical of Charke's cultivation of an ironic and winkingly self-knowing distance from her own work. Throughout the *Narrative*, Charke again and again pokes fun at her tendency to get completely caught up in any activity that she happens to be involved in at the time; she shakes her head at her tendency to allow just one of her many selves to dominate or to dictate to the others at any given moment of her life. When reduced at one point to operating a modest grocery store in Long Acre Street near Covent Garden, for instance, she tells us that she becomes so absorbed in the business of retailing that one might well have mistaken her for one of London's most prosperous merchants. She quips:

The Rise and Fall of Sugars was my constant Topick; and Trading, Abroad and at home, was as frequent in my Mouth as my Meals. To compleat the ridiculous Scene, I constantly took in the Papers to see how Matters went at *Bear-Key*; what ships were come in, or lost; who in our Trade, was broke; or who advertised Teas at the least Prices.

(Narrative, 37)

Note the telling language in passages as short and as otherwise as self-contained as this. The spectacle of Charlotte Charke passing as a merchant upon exchange whose profits depended on the slightest fluctuations of the stock market, or one who (and one again recalls

Shakespeare's own Venetian Merchant), anxiously awaits the news that certain rich argosies had safely 'come to road' is freely admitted to be 'ridiculous'. Charke is equally aware, however, that such a pose is only part of the proper, dramatic attitude she needed to assume to 'compleat . . . the Scene'. Half measures, in life as on the stage, would have availed her nothing. Paraphrasing the techniques of the great Russian drama teacher Konstantin Stanislavski in the last century, the theatre critic David Magarshack once observed that in order for a performer to be able to transform even the most 'barefaced lie' into the truth of real art, the actor must at heart possess, among other talents, 'a highly developed imagination' and 'a child-like naïveté and trustfulness'.[20] Had Charke entered the stage of human drama at a later moment in its history, or had she perhaps acted any one of her roles as daughter, mother, performer, merchant, or writer – each in their proper turn – now rather than then, she might very well have recognized her own strategies of the stage in those of the modern method actor. Her parts, as she put it in the passage quoted above, lay as easily in her mouth – and danced as trippingly on her tongue – as the meals that provided her sustenance; drama, like food, she implies, may be the stuff that dreams are made on, but it was also the 'stuff' that no less surely provided her with a vital sustenance and kept her alive in the face of adversity.

Hand in hand with the sincerity that shaped Charke's intuitive feeling for would-be or imaginary 'truth', the reader soon notices, came a certain singularity of purpose (however paradoxically multitudinous in its forms) that also savoured, in its sheer and uncompromising determination, of the traditions of the drama. The show, whatever the circumstances, *must* go on. Something of the fierce tenacity of such an ethic that so characterized Charke's larger attitude towards life – something of her dogged persistence in the face of adversity – can best be illustrated if we return to Samuel Whyte's description of the actress in her Clerkenwell residence. Always one to appreciate the extravagant dramatic gesture and the generous impulse of *sprezzatura*, Charke would doubtlessly have recognized just how emblematically appropriate Whyte's late anecdotal glimpse of her life would prove finally to be. The seemingly genderless servant (as described by Whyte) is splendidly in keeping with Charke's own personal history. On second glance, too, even the decidedly motley assemblage of animals huddled about her chair ('Fidele' – the 'faithful' dog – we see now is a particularly nice touch) are appropriate companions for the actress. Charke's resilience, however, is best captured in the smallest of details, the impromptu and ingenious 'succedaneum' noted earlier: the inadequate pen, the cracked teacup, the pipe-less bellows. Never one to be conquered by circumstances, Charke only naturally refers to the book-selling trade as her new 'business', and eagerly awaits the success of her novel with a confidence that appears never even to have been acquainted with – much less truly have known – the experience of defeat.

(II)

A Narrative of the Life of Mrs Charlotte Charke, not surprisingly, began to attract the attention of a great many feminist critics. Their focus on Charke's work was not, however, a matter of straightforward literary discovery. Scholars and historians of the theatre had been referring to Charke's autobiography for years. The *Narrative*, much like Cibber's own 1740 *Apology*, was read primarily as a source-book for first-hand information about life, both in front of and behind the curtain. Charke's account also shed valuable light on certain controversial aspects of Colley Cibber's own more practically consequential career as an actor and theatrical manager. The works of both father and daughter, in fact, were looked upon together as a fund of anecdotes and character portraits. Both were oddly mixed and digressive in structure. However much they quarrelled with one another in life, Cibber and his daughter shared, as one modern editor put it, an ability to perceive the individual life itself with a 'multi-faceted sense of event'.[21] The intensity of Charke's belated and often bewildering search for self-definition and for some sense of personal identity recalls nothing so much as Cibber's protestation regarding his own life in the earliest pages of his *Apology*: 'my Appetites were in too much haste to be happy, to throw away my time in pursuit of a Name, I was sure I could never arrive at' (Cibber, *Apology*, 5). Like her father, however, Charke seems to have found herself paradoxically throwing away her happiness in the pursuit of those very Appetites she sought to fill.

Charke's cross-dressing, to say nothing of the concise and convenient contrapunction of her own, seemingly gender-obsessed narrative with the more massive and influential (if equally self-promotional) patriarchal biography of her famous parent, were soon seized upon by students and by a generation of critics eager to exploit the issues of gender and marginality – narrative, social, and sexual – in cultural representation. If one of the goals of early feminist criticism (in America, at least) was to rethink the received and accepted canon of literary history, and to rediscover and re-present women's writing that had been overlooked or deliberately devalued by the patriarchy, Charke's autobiography might yet, therefore, be looked upon by many as little less than a slighted or long-neglected gift. Concealed within what had hitherto been regarded as an eminently practical source-book for theatrical history – an archive to be rummaged, raided, plundered, and excerpted – was the astounding chronicle of a wildly unorthodox female life. Not only did the *Narrative* obviously present the story of a woman who passed her entire troubled existence in the shadow cast by her more famous father, but her work was itself a vivid and remarkably modern exploration of the female experience as Other – of the social construction of the feminine, and the boundaries of sexual identity writ large. Readers including Lynne Friedli, Fidelis Morgan, Felicity Nussbaum, and Sidonie Smith all contributed to a growing body of constructive feminist criticism on Charke's *Narrative*.[22] While necessarily differing in the specifics of their arguments, and in their agenda with regard to their approach to and appropriation of the *Narrative*, all of these critics tended together to read Charke as a designedly transgressive and (consequently) purposefully subversive figure. Charke's career as a cross-dresser – and in particular her career as Mr. Brown, the male name to which she often answered when dressed as man – was read as a carefully crafted challenge to the dominant ideology. Charke's voice was the cry of the liminal in the vast and unresponsive desert of patriarchy. Some objected to such readings as misrepresenting the true nature of Charke's career; still others reinterpreted the documents surrounding the memoir. Sue Churchill, for example, argued that accounts such as Whyte's own 'specifically [parodied] Charke's domesticity, further underscoring the argument that domesticity is precisely where Charke and her *Narrative* posed the greatest threat'.[23]

Erin Mackie, writing in 1991, was among the first to offer a valuable and clear-sighted corrective to the more overtly polemical and increasingly uncompromising readings of Charke's *Narrative*.[24] Mackie noted that the earliest feminist critics dealing with Charke failed typically to include any references in their studies to the several works of fiction and drama that Charke completed before, after, and apparently even during the writing of her own autobiography. In so doing, she suggested, these same critics offered what amounted only to a partial response to Charke's larger and supposedly proto-feminist project. Like Fidelis Morgan's often bizarre co-option and inclusion of Charke's *Narrative* within the pages of her 'own' book, *The Well-Known Troublemaker: A Life of Charlotte Charke* (1988), such readings were necessarily partial and fractured.

Although certain critics have tried to read and – indeed – to highlight such fragmentation within women's lives as one of the 'privileges of femininity' as it opposed itself to destructively linear masculine models of behaviour and of narrative, one could argue that there is a difference between a narrative that deliberately emphasizes an elusive and constantly shifting subjectivity, and one that is simply disordered – one that is inchoate only to be incoherent. In Morgan's 1988 volume, the text of Charke's autobiography was divided into six separate 'chapters'. Each of these revised instalments of the *Narrative* was then followed by a section written by the critic, baldly titled 'The Facts'. Such a devaluation of Charke's work did little to enhance its value in the eyes of the reader, but appeared to presuppose a degree of clinical objectivity on the part of the modern critic that, given the obsessions of contemporary critical discourse, was quaint, at best. The dual but still prioritized attribution of authorship on the title page of Morgan's volume (which reads: 'Fidelis Morgan with Charlotte Charke') was particularly gratuitous and unsettling. The pretence of willing collaboration, co-authorship, and – more particularly – unity of purpose in the volume was spectral, rawly appropriative, and ultimately dishonest; it served in every way to highlight a jarring temporal disjunction rather than in any way to heal it.

Mackie, on the other hand, convincingly argued that in the rush to impose 'feminist aims on Charke's life', readers such as Friedli had rashly overlooked the context provided by Charke's other writings. 'A reading of Charke's fiction alongside her autobiography', she observed, 'discovered Charke's manifold allegiance to the patriarchy and so revises readings of her autobiography'. Simply put, Mackie argued that while Charke may have been 'transgressive in her momentary effects, she [was] not subversive in her aims'. 'Her impersonation of the masculine, which is often an impersonation of the paternal', Mackie asserted, sought 'to reinforce, reinstate, and maintain the value of masculine, patriarchal conventions'.[25] Mackie and those who followed her critical lead proceeded in time to more detailed discussions of the manner in which Charke's several fictions also worked to fulfil this 'compulsion'. Most significantly, *The History of Henry Dumont, Esq., and Miss Charlotte Evelyn*, in particular, can convincingly be analysed as Charke's attempt literally to rewrite her own feminine history. The same gender boundaries that in Charke's own life were apt to become so muddy and obscured are, in her fictions, more rigorously controlled, directed, and policed. As the narrative voice of the *History*, Charke 'espouses the scrupulously proper in her attempt to revise her life and her practices in a manner that might exonerate her from charges of delinquency'.[26]

The logic of closely reasoned arguments such as Mackie's remains close to incontestable. Mackie herself began her own examination of Charke's work by challenging the assumptions central to earlier feminist readings, both of Charke's *Narrative* and of her supposed, extra-textual agenda. She noted: 'Charke's most transgressive gestures – her cross-dressing, her adoption of male roles in life and fiction, her imitation of and challenge to the father – are undertaken not to undermine but to affirm the value of the masculine on which the patriarchy and her own cross-dressing depend'.[27] Calling attention to Charke's significant grounding of her own story within the Biblical story of the Prodigal Son, for example – a story that strengthens and reinscribes the bond between the prodigal and the patriarch – Mackie heretically contended that Charke is 'a cross-dressing failure. ... Her errors are narrated only in order that, with her father's financial backing, they may be abandoned'. 'The scriptural foundation for this pattern is the story of the Prodigal Son', she further observed, 'a story into which Charke explicitly places herself as penitent prodigal with her father as merciful patriarch'.[28] The *Narrative* asks thus to be read not so much as a challenge to, but an extension of, Cibber's own autobiography – an exercise in wish fulfilment. Colley Cibber, in other words, is in his daughter's novel not only shown how a loving and generous parent ought properly to behave to his penitent daughter, but is likewise shown that Charlotte Charke (a.k.a Mr. Brown) has also benefited from some hard-learned lessons in the necessary boundaries of the feminine sphere. Charke's fiction quite clearly reconfigures the events of her own life, rectifying its errors and decorously re-establishing those boundaries that it might have been wiser never to have crossed in the first place.

Such a reading recognizes the multi-layered status of Charke's *History* as parody. Her novel not only insists on being read alongside her earlier *Narrative*, but reminds its readers that that same autobiography had in turn positioned itself as a parodic take on Cibber's own *Apology*. Given the extent to which Cibber's volume had already been subject to a tremendous and repeated amount of ridicule and parody – particularly at the hands of Henry Fielding who, in works such as *Shamela* (1741), *Joseph Andrews* (1742), and *Jonathan Wild* (1743), mocked the pretensions of 'such persons' to trouble the world with their 'apologies' in the first place – Charke's publication of both her *Narrative* and her *History* intimately involved her in a truly furious whirlwind of imitation, ridicule, and parody.[29] Every aspect of Charke's life and writings seems to have been flagged by her own intense awareness of doubleness and alterity – of mockery, and the echoes of multiple response. In the *History*, she attempts definitively to use her talents of mimicry to her personal advantage, and, in so doing, writes the parodic corrective to her own life.

(III)

Charke's novel is one that – in significant contrast to other, generally similar works of the same period – appears to go out of its way to announce the presence of not one but two protagonists in its very title; the work is christened with what would appear to be a gesture of inclusion and reconciliation, a naming indicative of harmony and union. The novel's double-barrelled title is further extended by its additional promise to provide its readers with a 'Variety of entertaining Characters and very Interesting SUBJECTS With some Critical Remarks on Comick *Actors*'. Charke then appends (as yet another element to the title page) an epigraph from Joseph Addison's *Cato* (1713) that quotes a description of the play's virtuous character Marcia (Cato's daughter) from the first act of that hugely popular political-theatrical drama. The lines as cited by Charke read:

> The virtuous Marcia tow'rs above her sex;
> True, she is fair (oh, how divinely fair!)
> But still the lovely maid improves her charms
> With inward greatness, unaffected wisdom,
> And sanctity of manners.

(Addison, Cato I.iv.147–51)[30]

Charke has significantly truncated these lines, however, which are spoken in the play by Juba, the Prince of Numidia, before they reach their actual conclusion in Addison's drama. In the original, Juba continues,

>   Cato's soul
> Shines out in everything she acts or speaks,
> While winning mildness and attractive smiles
> Dwell in her looks, and with becoming grace
> Soften the rigor of her father's virtues.

(Addison, Cato I.iv.151–5)

Addison's tragedy had for years been so popular that Charke would certainly and reasonably have expected a great many of her readers to be able to fill in the missing lines, and so approach the work not only from a point of view that associates Cato's daughter Marcia with her heroine, Charlotte Evelyn, but from one that also parallels the relationship between Cato and Marcia with that of Cibber and Charke herself; the lines implicitly identify Charke as the gentle embodiment of her father's more rigorous 'virtues'.

The primary effect of Charke's extended title, of course, is simply to draw the reader's attention to the fact that hers is a novel with not one but *two* central figures – a novel emphatically with a hero *and* a heroine, both of whom receive equal billing – as well as a supporting cast drawn from its author's experience to supply a perceived need for comic 'variety'. If, as critic Norma Clarke has maintained, one way of defining female authorship in the period was to produce a self-told life that fore-grounded its writer's own ability 'to be remembered' by one's self, then another was 'being able to remember and tell stories about famous authors... at the time when biography, autobiography, and literary criticism were emerging genres'.[31] Yet Charke's extended title – and, more particularly, its promise to offer a variety of 'entertaining Characters' and 'Critical Remarks on Comick *Actors*' – also announces her novel's concern with performance. More precisely, it alerts its readers to the perfomative aspect of self-definition and being, as well as bringing into question a slight but significant anxiety regarding its own status as a text and its possible indebtedness to various literary and discursive modes (history, fiction, drama, the 'characters' of Theophrastus, rumour and gossip, etc.). One could in fact say that if the title attempts to signal for some readers a sense of unity and of inevitable or anticipated marital fulfilment, it no less powerfully suggests an engagement with uncertainty, hesitation, and doubleness; it heralds its own anxious sense of narrative substance 'hovering' between the conflicting generic demands of various literary forms.

This sense of doubleness, doubling, and what we might call textual duplicity can be found throughout the narrative. Charke's *History* is to some degree a multi-generational novel. In this respect, its weighted chronological structure and complicated genealogies significantly anticipate the family sagas incorporated within works such as Sophia Lee's *The Recess* (1783), Frances Burney's *Evelina* (1786), Elizabeth Inchbald's *A Simple Story* (1791), Mary Hays's *Memoirs of Emma Courtney* (1796), and, ultimately, Emily Brontë's *Wuthering Heights* (1848). Charke's multiple and multiplied narratives chronicle the interdependent relationships that connect two separate families – the Evelyns and the Dumonts – and charts the manner in which the various impulses of the individual members of each of those families are finally and only over an extended period of time reconciled within the larger framework of a profoundly comedic domestic harmony. Leo Tolstoy would famously open his 1877 novel *Anna Karenina* with the pronouncement that 'All happy families resemble one another, each unhappy family is unhappy in its own way'. The sense of perpetual, mutual exclusion that would appear to stand as one of the concomitant conditions of Tolstoy's axiomatic observation would never have appealed to the disinherited daughter of Colley Cibber. Not surprisingly, Charke's own novel instead looks prescriptively to chart the erratic narrative course by which unhappy families can themselves be transformed into happy ones. As will again be the case in a work such as Inchbald's *A Simple Story*, a domestic saga of desire, prohibition, loss, and atonement is perceived, through a haze of misrepresentation and hesitation, to have been a series of lost or mistaken opportunities. Echoing mythical archetypes, Charke's narrative begins in the gardens of Versailles, only to fall by the trials of experience into the distinctly post-lapsarian darkness of a world characterized more recognizably by romantic misalliances, sexual confusion, and the noisy haze of sordid, sublunary, and even subterranean urban gambling dens. *The History of Henry Dumont, Esq., and Miss Charlotte Evelyn* ultimately offers its readers the much wished-for story of a domestic paradise regained; yet as much as she tries to lift both herself and her characters back over the walls of Eden and into a lost space of innocence and virtue, the way back to paradise is a notoriously difficult route to negotiate, and places of rest are hard to find when even Providence itself seems to have abandoned the travellers along their way.

Charke crams a tremendous amount of narrative information into the opening pages of her novel, and a brief recapitulation is necessary. The *History* begins by recounting the story of the watchful and benevolent Count Destrades, a French nobleman who introduces his daughter and sole heiress, the Lady Charlotte, into the Royal Court at Versailles. While at Court, Charlotte unfortunately attracts the eye of the King himself; she is pursued by her regal admirer until the disillusioned Destrades, vowing 'never to be a motive of envy by entering into any employment at court' (*History*, 5), rejects the King's offer of a place, and returns with his daughter to the country (the Count's renunciation of the court and its behaviour recalls the similar withdrawal from the *vita activa* of the Marquis, father to the heroine Arabella, in Charlotte Lennox's 1752 *The Female Quixote*). In time, Charlotte marries the young Archibald Dumont, a near neighbour of Destrades and 'a gentleman of immense fortune and good extraction' (*History*, 1), for whom she has confessed a romantic inclination. The pastoral household is completed by the presence of Mr. Evelyn (an Englishman who has been obliged to take refuge in a foreign country because of his financial misfortunes, and who consequently serves as Charlotte's tutor) and by Evelyn's wife. The birth of the novel's eponymous hero, Henry Dumont, and the near-simultaneous birth – after only 12 months of marriage – of a daughter, Charlotte, to the Evelyns, is marred by the subsequent death of Charlotte Dumont from smallpox. Archibald Dumont himself dies soon afterwards. The grieving Destrades decides to move his household to England – more specifically, to his estate at Iver, some 20 miles from London – where the young Henry and Charlotte grow up together as brother and sister.

It is at this point in the *History* that Charke's narrative, already having swiftly covered the events of two generations in the opening chapters of the volume, shifts into a more leisurely and decidedly more epis-odic pace. (This early change in pace and intensity, in fact, to some degree recalls the narrative pattern of Madame de Lafayette's 1678 *The Princess of Cleves*.) The early histories of both Henry and Charlotte are described at some length. Their author seems instinctively to have endowed both characters with a natural inclination and flair for the dramatic. Destrades, for example, refuses to allow his grandson to under-take the Grand Tour of the continent 'customary to young men of the boy's age [now fifteen] and station' since, he claims (sounding rather like stock dramatic characters such as Fainall, in William Congreve's *The Way of the World* [1700], on the subject of Sir Wilfull Witwoud), 'so many of the English youth set out part blockheads, and return accom-plish'd asses' (*History*, 26). In lieu of such continental adventures, Henry and his 'sister' Charlotte decide to set up a theatre 'at the end of a green walk' (*History*, 28) in the park at Iver, where they perform pieces by Shakespeare, Molière, and Terence (Charlotte, the reader is informed, is 'perfect mistress of the Latin tongue' (*History*, 28), and is consequently able to take an active role even in the comedy by the Roman play-wright). Dumont himself is described as a young man possessed of a 'noble virtue' (*History*, 31) that is the direct result of his mixed ancestry and background, and one whose 'whole highest happiness consisted in obeying his worthy grandsire'. Henry, as Charke puts it, 'had the bravery of the English, the politeness of the French, but in the foremention'd virtue he was considerably indebted to the Irish, who are remarkably beneficent to all whose misfortunes have any claim to their pity or redress . . . ' (*History*, 29).

Compelled one afternoon by a violent thunderstorm to seek temporary shelter in a cattle shed within the precincts of Windsor Forest, Henry encounters a 14-year-old who has recently fled the cruel abuse of his uncle. The orphan – referred to only as Jennings – is welcomed into the Count's household and educated by Mr. Evelyn. After five years, he takes up a position as a clerk in a West Indian trading concern. Having at once parted from his friend, Henry, and from his benefactor, the Count, Jennings reveals in a letter that his primary reason for accepting such a far-flung post was his distressing infatuation with Charlotte. Jennings is able in time successfully to transfer his affections to a young native of his new island home. Both Henry and Charlotte are pleased by this resolution, thankful that they will now, at least, no longer stand in any danger of forever having to distance themselves from their friend and companion.

The immediate fortune of Mr. Jennings having thus been settled, the Count decides that the time has now come for Dumont himself to enter society in proper form. Allowing his grandson an income of £1000 a year, Destrades sends Dumont and Charlotte to the fashionable spa town of Tunbridge in Kent, then at the very height of its popularity. The pair are chaperoned on their journey by Charlotte's mother, Mrs Evelyn. Unwilling in life to confine her own behaviour within the narrow constraints of contemporary sexual mores, Charke plunges her fictional protagonists into situations that might very well have driven even the likes of Fielding's Joseph Andrews completely insane. In the course of the visit to Tunbridge, Dumont – 'innocently' pursuing the round of social activities – not only makes the acquaintance of respectable figures such as Lord Worthland and Sir John Generous, but also immediately attracts the attention of 'a strange mortal' (*History*, 57–8), the overtly homosexual Billy Loveman. Charke's inclusion of Loveman in the novel signals her familiarity with what has sometimes been called the 'sodomitical sub-culture' that is said to have flourished in eighteenth-century England.[32]

Dumont receives a billet-doux from Loveman and – immediately thrown on the defensive with regard to his own sexual behaviour – questions just how he has managed to get himself into such a situation in the first place. 'Tis true', Dumont confesses to Charlotte,

> I have heard there are a set of wretches who are shamefully addicted to a vice, not proper to mention to so delicate an ear as yours, but

my behaviour could not in any degree give the smallest hope to the unnatural passion of such a detestable brute. I therefore think it highly incumbent upon me, to make an example of such a villain.

(*History*, 60)

Loveman's semi-literate love letter to Dumont is 'reprinted' by Charke in its entirety. 'Dere Cretor', Loveman writes,

I hop you vont be uffinded at the libarty I tak, in trubling you thes lines, and that the ardunt pishon I have concei'd from your angelack form, will plede my pardun. When you dans'd last night, you gave the fatal blo, which will be my utter ruen, unless you koindly answer my boundless luf; I know you ar a parson of fortin, so um I, and do asure you, vere not my charmer vorth one fardin in the vorld, sush beuty vould make amends for sush a vant. Permet me lufly objeckt, to meet you this evening at the fish-pond, vher I may be happy in paeing my rispex to the divine charmur of my soul.

Believe me lufly cretor my only vish is to convince you, how mutch I am utmurst sincertiy,

> *Your Constant adorer,*
> Billy Loveman

(*History*, 58–9)

Loveman's rustic posturing and his widely idiosyncratic orthography (which would appear to be at odds with some of the artificial and highly literary vocabulary he has cultivated in the service of romance, and in fact owes a great deal to characters such as Fribble in Garrick's 1747 farce *Miss in Her Teens*) stand in sharp contrast to Dumont's own polished diction and discretion. Henry and Charlotte admit the person who has been sent by Loveman to await the answer to his epistle – this is a Mr. Turtle – a 'moppit', Charke calls him, 'whose hair was curl'd in the fashion of a fine lady's' (*History*, 62). Prompted only by the desire for revenge demanded by his outraged sense of pride, Dumont accordingly arranges to meet Loveman at his residence. Arriving at the time appointed for the assignation, he is shown into an empty drawing room and told to wait. 'When he came in', Charke writes of Dumont's entrance into the room,

he saw an elegant cold collation set forth, the window curtains close drawn and pinn'd; but found no body in the room; when asking for the gentleman, the servant sneered, and told him, his lady would wait upon him directly; when immediately there appeared from the inner chamber, this odious creature in a female rich deshabille; who running to Mr. Dumont cried out, 'I come. I fly, to my adored Castallo's arms! my wishes lord!' – stopping here with a languishing air, said, 'Do my angel, call me you Monimia.' then with a beastly transport, kissed him with that ardour which might be expected from a drunken fellow to a common prostitute.'

(*Narrative*, 65)

For such attentions, Loveman is promptly beaten by Dumont, with the assistance of Lord Worthland and Sir John Generous, and then ducked by a mob in the local fish pond. All the while Mr. Turtle runs about the house 'like a distracted thing' (*History*, 67). Loveman is subsequently confined to his bed for a month, at the end of which he and Mr. Turtle 'promise to retire from the world, and live shepherdesses together in some remote country' (68). Their posited homosexual idyll is an unlikely echo of many such withdrawals from the public world of the town to the pastoral retreat of the country to be found in poems throughout the period, from John Pomfret's 'The Choice' (1700) to William Cowper's *The Task* (1785).

Sir John Generous, meanwhile, has confessed his love for Charlotte, and his suit is approved by Dumont; 'I assure you', Generous tells Dumont 'my regard for Miss Evelyn is founded entirely upon a fraternal friendship' (*History*, 72). Sir John's profession of passion, however, is coolly received by Charlotte herself who, 'though she would not presume absolutely to refuse, avoided all opportunities of being alone with her lover; and by a coldness and reserve to him convinced the whole family of her aversion to the match' (*History*, 129–30). Further encounters in Tunbridge include the group's memorable introduction to Sir Boistrous Blunder of Devonshire, and to his son and his daughter, Ursula, all of whom are presented as fat and sweaty rural grotesques (Ursula is said to stomp across the room 'with the air and gentility of a plowman' [*History*, 83]). Dumont and Charlotte, for the sake of a jest, spend time in their company, and are suitably diverted by witnessing the fury aroused by the confession of Sir Boistrous's son that he has been married for six months to one Cicely, a serving maid, and by Ursula's equally disconcerting admission that she too had recently married far beneath her supposed station – to the family's male servant, Jonas.

When Dumont and Charlotte return to the estate at Iver, Mr. Evelyn takes the opportunity to travel to London finally to discharge the creditors who had initially driven him from the country. He discovers one of these creditors – a Mr. Powel – himself to be a prisoner in the Marshalsea. Evelyn promptly rescues him from the prison, and is compelled in his sympathetic generosity to give him a recommend-atory letter to Mr. Jennings in the West Indies. Powel eventually settles, with Jenning's assistance, as a planter on an estate and prospers. Char-lotte, finally, reluctantly gives way to her father's wishes and marries Sir John Generous, although her pleadings with her mother reveal that her heart is 'deeply engaged elsewhere' (*History*, 167) – clearly to Dumont himself. The marriage is short-lived, however, as Sir John dies from the injuries resulting from the fall of his horse, shortly after the birth of a daughter. On his deathbed he acknowledges and approves of his wife's long-standing passion for Dumont.

Though once again free to follow her own 'inclination', Charlotte is unaware of the fact that Dumont has himself during this time been ensnared by a certain Miss Le Roy, a young woman ('of French extraction, though English born' [*History*, 192]) whose addiction to the gambling tables her new husband soon comes to share. Mr. Evelyn engages a friend of his youth – Mr. Allworth – to keep a paternal eye on Dumont, but Allworth can only stand by and watch as the couple's debts begin to spin wildly out of control. Dumont's wife is said to be so shocked by their financial ruin that she takes 'so immoderately to drinking that in about three months she [dies] raving mad (*History*, 241–2). Dumont in his own fashion enlists as a soldier, and is eventually discovered standing guard as a sentinel at the opera by the widowed Lady Generous. Mr. Evelyn buys Dumont's discharge, and the couple are finally free to marry. Charke makes it clear that the conventionally comedic endings of the novel are destined to continue into future gener-ations as well. The now wealthy Mr. Jennings returns to England from the West Indies, and we are told that his son and Charlotte's daughter, Miss Generous, are eventually to be married.

(IV)

It would be easy enough to judge Charke's novel harshly. One could very well argue that the central problem that Charke faced and to some extent failed to resolve in the *History* is quite simply one of narrative drive and organization. Although in her earlier autobiography Charke had dealt with the desired if ultimately irresolvable unity of her own life, her very personality had permitted her, in that same work, to experiment at every turn with the possibilities of narrative profusion. The more restrictive format of the relatively new 'realistic' novel as she conceived it, however, required Charke to focus and to narrow her sights. She needed to build a consistent and believable relationship between her two main characters, and to marshal her subsidiary material so that it supported the linear narrative of the novel as a whole. The difficulty lay in the fact that Charke's particular strength, however, lay in her ability to thrive on the very uncertainty and constant mutability of *lived* experience – to thrive on proliferation. The novel, at least as she saw it, necessitated a concept of the self that – although subject to a constant growth and transformation – is in the end shaped by the teleological impulse of the literary form itself. It is a common characteristic of eighteenth-century novels (one thinks, for example, of *Tom Jones*, or of Richardson's works, or of Clara Reeve's *The Old English Baron*) to assemble the characters of the fiction before the reader in the final pages and to summarize their adventures unto death . . . and sometimes beyond. Charke, in the Dedication to her *Narrative*, had already posited a concept of the 'self' as a wildly amorphous entity that would constantly evade the possibility of definition – an entity, paradoxically, that one's *own* self might well find incapable of knowing, unable to pin down. The possibilities of personal and literary profusion are endless. Charke, we remember, had dedicated the *Narrative* to her *own* self, in the hopes, as she put it, 'that you and I may ripen our Acquaintance into a perfect Knowledge of each other, that may establish a lasting and social Friendship between us' (*Narrative*, 6).

   The same schizophrenic impulse that thus initiates Charke's autobiography – an impulse that remains and even strengthens throughout the volume as Charke begins leading the double life of a cross-dresser – sounds a characteristic note at the outset of her later fiction. Charke's own sense of identity in the *Narrative* is spectacularly insecure; the reader often senses, more particularly, that she is incapable of living in the shadow of her father, that her very presence – 'I came', she writes early in her account, 'an unwelcome guest into the family' (*Narrative*, 9) – is a disappointment, even a criminal offence to Cibber as a parent. Charke had even begun the *Narrative* with an elaborate disclaimer that compares the volume itself to a felon:

> As the following History is the Product of a Female Pen, I tremble for the terrible Hazard it must run in venturing into the world, as it may very possibly suffer, in many Opinions, without perusing it; I therefore humbly move for its having the common Chance of a Criminal, at least to be properly examin'd, before it is condemm'd:

And should it be found guilty of Nonsense and Inconsistancies, I
must consequently resign it to its deserved punishment.

(Narrative, 7)

The links that the *Narrative* establishes in passages such as this with the
flourishing literature of crime in the eighteenth century are never really
picked up explicitly in the text, yet the very implication that Charke's
own 'product of a Female Pen' is related in some way to the criminal
biographies that were being issued to a massively popular response by
authors such as Daniel Defoe encourages a comparison between the
criminal offender and the role of social and sexual outlaw that Charke
enjoyed playing throughout her entire life. Likewise, the format of
the criminal biography that finds the confessed and shriven offender
looking back upon his life with a detached sense of personal identity
finds a parallel in Charke's own concept of the 'self' as a construct that
persistently eludes the grasp of the present-tense writer. Charke often
finds her own fragile identity overwhelmed by the more powerful presence of the dramatic characters she had portrayed on the London stage,
or by the more intimate construct that she had developed with the
assumption of masculine attire and the companionship of 'Mrs Brown'.
At some of the most crucial moments of her *Narrative*, Charke is hidden
or disguised, purposefully transformed from 'Charlotte Charke' as she
might recognizably have appeared as her father's daughter. Our very
first glimpse of the young Charlotte in the autobiography sees her in
what she calls a 'Grotesque Pigmy State' (*Narrative*, 11), parading before
the local townspeople in a ditch by the front of her father's house,
and hoping – with the aid of his wig and of her brother's belt and
sword – to be mistaken for Cibber himself. The incident, which carries
the same novelistic intensity of that first moment of self-knowledge and
epistemological self-sufficiency one recognizes in the opening pages of
Moll Flanders (1722), or Pip's encounter in the graveyard in Dickens's
Great Expectations (1861), works to underscore Charke's abilities as a born
performer, and a master of disguise. 'The Oddity of my Appearance', she
observed proudly,

Soon Assembled a Crowd about me; which yielded me no small Joy,
as I conceiv'd their Risibility on this Occasion to be Marks of Approbation, and walk'd myself into a Fever, in the happy Thought of being
taken for the 'Squire.

(Narrative, 11)

The subsequent pages of the volume contain countless examples of Charke's need to hide behind effigies – her puppet show is a particularly good example – that need to smash and batter their way through the experience of this world. The ease with which Charke shifts from one identity to another, and the consequent 'absurd' state of the self that follows, is noticeable in an incident that takes place in the company of drunken amateurs with whom Charke has found it necessary to perform in the country. As the play lunges wildly out of control – the actors forgetting their lines and shifting their identity from one scene to another – Charke turns the theatrical disaster into an opportunity to run through her entire repertoire. She notes,

> We took a wild-goose Chase through all the Dramatic Authors we could recollect, taking particular Care not to let any Single speech bear in the Answer the least Affinity; and while I was making love from *Jaffier*, she tenderly approved my Passion with a soliloquy from *Cato*.'
>
> (*Narrative* 106–7)

Later, arrested on confused charges with the same group of amateurs, Charke typically entertains her cell-mates with a selection of speeches from Gay's *The Beggar's Opera* so that, in seeing her in the condemned-hold as Macheath, they might 'have the Pleasure of saying, that [she] once performed IN CHARACTER' (*Narrative*, 112).

Yet, for all such observations, one might just as easily contend that the seeming disorder of Charke's arguably 'picaresque' novel is intentional – that there is an aesthetic coherence in the heterogeneity of the novel that reflects the variety of human experience itself. The world of the *History* is a world plagued by romantic and erotic misconceptions; it is a world in which attachments and connections are persistently made that defy reason and order. Much of the novel concerns itself with the manner in which the representation of the various characters attempt, through a painful process of trial and error, to arrive at correct and suitable allegiances even after it seems that mistakes have been made that can never come undone. These attempts to 'get things right' by making themselves available to different combinations and re-workings when first formulations fail anticipate later nineteenth-century novels such as Jane Austen's *Sense and Sensibility* and Emily Brontë's *Wuthering Heights*. Such an openness to the various possibilities of life similarly anticipates Charke's narrative strategy as a writer whose work everywhere reflects her desired goal of achieving some sort of reconciliation with her father.

When direct appeals and their replication in the *Narrative* fail to have any effect on Cibber, Charke returns to her fictional *History* to attempt a rapprochement. When any one formulation fails to work, Charke is ready quickly to toss it aside and try another. A singularity of purpose may remain her aim throughout her work, but such a determination does not necessarily entail a concomitant singularity of design.

The inherent-seeming paradox of Charke's belief throughout the *History* that instability can resolve itself finally into a peaceful and harmonious resolution is to some degree reflected in the amount of physical movement – the amount of peripatetic activity – undertaken by the characters in the novel between different countries, communities, and cities. The characters in Charke's novel, much like their creator herself, find it difficult to remain for any significant time in any one particular place. The novel not only traces their movements from France to England and as far as the West Indies, but finds them ricocheting more specifically between rather unlikely locations such as Versailles, Iver, Tunbridge, Pall Mall, the Marshalsea, and Sir John's seat in Northumberland. The names of both places and characters, too, seem to reflect the heights and troughs of human movement, activity, and experience. Dumont's name rather obviously signifies the extent of the eminence (Fr. *du Mont*) of his family's aristocratic extraction and fortune, a family who are quite appropriately at home at Versailles towards the beginning of the novel, although even Iver – close to the royal parks of Windsor Castle – is a place-name that quite literally means the 'brow' or crowning height of hill. Charke's world is one in which some characters seem naturally to look down upon others; still other figures find themselves plucked from the comfort of their seemingly civilized environments only to be tumbled into mud, hidden in cattle-sheds, burrowed into dens, or thrown into ponds. Nor are Dumont, Versailles, Iver, or even the misleadingly named Miss Le Roy the only signifiers of eminence and prestige. The spa town of Tunbridge Wells in Kent (although not granted the prefix 'Royal' to its name until a great many years later) was likewise, at the time of Dumont and Miss Charlotte's visit, presided over by the famous dandy from Bath, Beau Nash, and was associated with royalty by the presence of the Church of King Charles the Martyr (begun 1678), and by the fact that Henrietta Maria had recuperated there after having given birth to the future King Charles II in 1630. Royal parks and enclosures and the environs of well-bred society are distinguished from the more wildly rural haunts of thieves, outcasts, and societal monstrosities – the unlikely Billy Lovemans and Boisterous Blunders of the world, who are only inappropriately allowed to stray, on occasion, within preserves that ought more properly be retained for those fit to inhabit them. (The significance of Loveman's surname is obvious; yet even 'Billy' would have echoed contemporary phrases such as 'Bill at Sight' – meaning to pay a bill on demand, but by extension, in popular slang, 'to be ready at all times for the venereal act'.)[33] Charke is a novelist who realizes that her fictional world, much like the real world, ought properly to be an environment in which physical boundaries reflect the distinctions of society – where manners, morals, and standing can actually inhibit physical movement; yet it is also a world of transgression and pollution, a place where the clean is made impure. The lines of purity, innocence, obedience, and submission to the 'natural' order and control of society are clearly articulated, yet they are no less likely to be breached and violated as they are to be respected. The *History* is a novel in which almost all of the characters seem to stray from their properly proverbial paths; and in spite of the novelist's own apparent concern not only to represent but to respect such distinctions of order, location, and authority, no one of the figures in Charke's fiction seems capable of 'staying put' in their given or suitable place. All of them end up straying – like the head of King Charles in Mr. Dick's Memorial, in Dickens's *David Copperfield* (1850) – into places where they were never meant to be, and threaten constantly to tumble the narrative completely out of all shape.

The rejection of the Court environment by Charlotte's father at the very beginning of the novel underscores this awareness of the significance of space and location, and reflects Charke's own understanding of the manner in which physical space can impinge on one's psychic, moral, and emotional development. When Count Destrades renounces the Court he rebukes the King,

Consider, royal Sir, your office here is so nice a representation of heavenly power, that one bad action would sully a thousand virtues; and that you are not here as regulator only, but designed an exemplary good to all mankind. I need not be more explicit on the theme which has thrown me under your majesty's displeasure, but shall refer myself to your cooler judgement, whether I have not acted like a prudent father, and a true subject; which characters I shall ever think it my duty to support to a religious strictness.

(*History*, 16–17)

From the very opening of the *History*, Charke thus emphasizes the world of her novel as one in which the 'heavenly' ordered, patriarchal order of things has broken down and is no longer working as it should. The 'prudent father' and the 'true subject' is an isolated figure whose appeal for a restoration of paternal authority and responsibility goes unheard; he is himself compelled to retreat from the world in order to protect his own family with a fierce conviction amounting to 'a religious strictness'.

The Count's rebuke to the King at the opening of the novel sets the tone for the (supposedly) anti-Saturnalian impulse of the *History* as a whole. Charke's indictment of her own father's failure to live up to his paternal responsibilities is fairly obvious in the passage. We live embedded in a world, she seems to be saying, in which the responsibilities of parents to children have been neglected or ignored completely, and the inherent hierarchy both of patriarchy and of domestic order has generally been abandoned. The Count's attempts to redress such a situation by retreating further from society entirely provides only a temporary solution, however, and the post-lapsarian instability of human experience invariably catches up with his entire family. His own son, we remember, is seduced into marrying Miss Le Roy – a figure whose ironically regal name recalls the plight of Dumont's mother when threatened by the attentions of the King of France. You can run, Charke seems to be saying, but no matter how far you run, you cannot hide.

Dumont's alliance with the gambling and eventually alcoholic Miss Le Roy in the latter part of the *History* reinscribes the pattern of romantic mistakes and misalliances that has been present from the beginning of the novel. The reader is confronted by Charke with an unbroken series of cross-purposed and often manifestly inappropriate infatuations and alliances. The love of the fraternal Mr. Jennings for Charlotte; the infatuation of Billy Loveman with Dumont (and to some extent the wifely devotion of Mr. Turtle for Loveman); the misplaced devotion of Sir John Generous for Charlotte (who does not return his affection); and even, of course, the grotesquely comic example of Sir Boistrous Blunder's family, who are indiscriminate enough to marry their own servants: all these unions dramatically emphasize the dizzying multitude of errors it is possible and perhaps even necessary for people to make in their attempts to find romantic, sexual, and domestic happiness. In a world in which the natural order of things has been so violently disrupted, it is little wonder that all such connections are dangerously unpredictable.

Not merely are romantic attachments unpredictable, however, the closest of family relationships are also liable to fracture and even to disappear completely. Many of those parents who would normally be expected to provide for their children die before they can accomplish anything of lasting value. The case of young Jennings, adopted into the Count's family early in the novel, provides a vivid illustration of the manner in which families can at any moment collapse upon themselves even under such common pressure as greed and a simple desire for material gain. Having lost his natural father at an early age, he is left an orphan and his debt-ridden mother dies after an illness of 15 months; his father's property is taken over by a treacherous uncle, who soon dispossesses him of his inheritance and turns him out of the house. As Jennings tells Henry and Charlotte: 'When I ask'd him the reason for this barbarous proceeding, and begg'd him to forgo the wrong he was doing me, he was regardless of my supplication and with brutal rage, cruelly insulted my distress, then with his hardship drove me out of doors to beg or starve' (*History*, 35).

The instability of the world of Charke's novel is further underscored by the manner in which language itself – and hence the possibility of any real means of communication – is destabilized in the midst of such domestic or romantic friction. In her own *Narrative*, Charke seems often to speak in a language ventriloquized from such writers as Nathaniel Lee, John Vanbrugh, Nicholas Rowe, Thomas Otway, Henry Fielding, John Gay, David Garrick, Samuel Foote, and Colley Cibber himself. In her novel, too, characters are compelled to create their own idiolects, and figures are often explicitly compared to characters that would be familiar to readers from the London stage (Charke called attention to her characters' 'Diction' in her Preface to the novel). When Dumont announces to Mr. Evelyn his intentions of marrying Miss Le Roy, Charke writes,

This unfortunate affair occasion'd a great coldness between these two gentlemen; in short; the debate between them rose to such a height, that Mr. Dumont positively affirmed to Mr. Evelyn, all arguments in opposition to his design of marrying Miss Le Roy were fruitless, and (as he through his impatience pleased to add) impertinent; this was a style Mr. Evelyn never had been treated with from Mr. Dumont, and indeed a method of discourse the young gentleman had never been before used to, even to the lowest of his domestics; as his tutor was the first instance of his deviating from that nice decorum he had bred him up to, it struck him deeply to his heart, as he regarded him not only as his pupil, but with the fond eye of a tender parent.

(*History*, 194–95)

The collapse of Dumont's rhetorical standards might just as well be a direct result of the romantic misalliance he is about to make, and the codes of paternal care that he has so flagrantly violated.

Naturally, the 'methods of discourse' used by each of the characters in the novel provide a generally sound indication not only of their standing in respectable or 'polite' society, but tend likewise to reveal something about the nature of their domestic relationships as well. Billy Loveman may wish to masquerade as the romantic heroine of a dramatic tragedy, but his appalling violations of language only match his equally appalling (at least in Charke's conscious representation) predatory and unnatural sexuality. The Blunders provide the most vivid example of the ways in which linguistic defects can highlight or serve as some indication of profound domestic turbulence, while at the same time providing an opportunity for the author herself to display her instinctive understanding of dramatic comedy. The introduction of Sir Boistrous and his family to the assembly at Tunbridge is one of the most memorable moments in the novel:

> The old gentleman was as great a curiosity as his worthy off-Springs; his appearance bespoke him a very old fashion'd country Grazier; his extream broad face and fat jowels, gave the company a perfect and lively idea of a Saracen's head; his bulk and stature very little inferior to the giants in Guildhall; his behaviour was concomitant with the description given of his person. As for example, through the excessive heat of the weather, and the multitude in the assembly, the knight very politely threw off his wig, turning the caul inside out to dry, and slap'd it down by a well-dress'd young lady, who was obliged, from the sickly scent, to have recourse to the other end of the room; then, after rubbing himself down like a cart horse, cover'd his reeking bald pate with a large silk handkerchief, stripping his cloathes open with both hands, shook his sudorifick shirt, which had not a dry thread in it, till he had poison'd all the company, not only with the odious smell, but the beastly sight of his dirty colour'd hairy bosom, that bore a strong resemblance of a leafless hedge in winter. Miss, to mend the matter, undergoing the same inconvenience of heat, began to rub Herself down as her well-bred papa had done just before; and turning to a man of Quality bawlkes out lawk, lawk, measter, do but feel how I swot. Upon this a general laugh succeeded, which Miss conceiving aroused from her having said a comical thing, join'd very heartily in, as did the father, who was proud of his daughter's vivacity, thunders

out his risible applause; assuring the nobleman, that Ursula was a stout wench, and if he would but talk to her he'd find a match for him. I don't know but she might, answer'd the young Lord, but I believe I shan't in a hurry be a match for her.

(*History*, 79–80)

Ursula's monstrous intrusion into the world of 'polite' Tunbridge society, in particular, seems in fact to constitute just as much a grotesque conflation of genre as it does a social gaff of outrageous proportions; it is as though her namesake from Ben Jonson's 1614 comedy – the leprous grotesque, 'all fire and fat', who roasts pigs at Bartholomew Fair, and whose profuse sweat waters the ground 'like a garden pot' – has suddenly wandered into the forest of Arden, or the woods outside Athens haunted by Titania and Oberon in Shakespeare's *A Midsummer Nights' Dream*.[34] Ursula is a female Caliban (or even a Sycorax, Caliban's sister in Dryden's 1670 revision of Shakespeare's romance) in a world properly populated by Mirandas.

But the porcine explosion of Ursula onto the novelistic stage of Charke's world at Tunbridge is an event that seems by this point in the novel almost to be expected. She could no more be restrained from appearing among the spa's visitors than the 'beastly' and 'odious' effusions of Loveman's sexuality could remain hidden behind the drapery and curtains of his effeminate boudoir, or Mr. Evelyn could avoid finding himself in Southwark, confronting the destitute Mr. Powel in the darkness of the Marshalsea. The behavioural precepts of the era's many conduct books, which attempted to proscribe a potentially disruptive female sexuality within the respectable bounds of feminine 'delicacy', seem at times to collide with the more salacious columns of the period's newspapers. The moral programmes soon to be more rigorously codified in the works of writers such as Sir James Fordyce (*Sermons to Young Women* [1765]) and Hester Chapone (*Letter on the Improvement of the Mind* [1773]), are anticipated to the extent that they are already being wildly questioned by the facts of female experience. Characters that ought properly be confined to the farcical world of the stage wander into the streets of our everyday reality.

This is not to suggest that there is any question but that Charke's attempts to *conform* in her novel are genuine; indeed, there is little reason to suppose that throughout her work that same intention (and it is worth reminding ourselves that female novelists of the period would never be afraid to insist that 'a book should be read with the same spirit with which it has been written') is to demonstrate the extent to which she has learned her lesson, and understands that her own volatile energies, like the desires of all men and women, need almost always to be moderated, reigned in, and brought under some form of control.[35] Any stable sense of female agency remains forever beyond Charke's control, however. The invasive and disruptive appetite that characterized the actress's own life works always to shatter the stability of her plans to proscribe desire, or to atone for past indiscretions. Appetite – in such forms as the expression of near-anarchic sexualities, broken families, fatherless children and childless fathers, thieves and highway men, slavery, greed, or even straightforward physical need, cannot – *will not* – remain under control.

The apparently unsuccessful attempt in Charke's work to support the ideology of conduct and female 'delicacy' suggests that the *History* may very well constitute something of a missing link in the history of the eighteenth-century novel. Samuel Whyte and Henry Slater Jr., again, were able finally to present Charke's novel to the public in the spring of 1756. It is more than likely that Whyte would have sent a copy of the volume to his cousin, Frances Sheridan, then living in France; Sheridan herself always kept her 'dear Sam' up to date with the status of her own projects, and the close connection between the two (we remember that she was to entrust the education of her son to Whyte in Dublin) found them in constant contact with one another. Sheridan was to be hard at work on her own hugely successful *Memoirs of Miss Sidney Bidulph* throughout the winter of 1759–60, and the novel was eventually published in 1761; a two-volume continuation appeared posthumously, in 1767. It is doing no disservice to Sheridan's genius or to the accomplishment of the *Memoirs* to suggest that certain elements that first manifested themselves in Charke's earlier work exerted an influence on the latter author's imagination. Both Charke's *History* and Sheridan's *Memoirs* are among the earliest examples of multi-generational novels in the English tradition, and both in fact make use of the possibilities of second and even third generations to correct the errors of the first. Both works significantly follow their two central second-generation characters into first marriages that are manifestly mistaken; in Charke's work, Henry Dumont marries Miss Le Roy and Charlotte Evelyn is united with Sir John Generous before they can be brought together, much in the manner that Orlando Faulkland is compelled to marry Miss Burchell, and Sidney Bidulph is married to Mr. Arnold, before they can finally be wedded, however briefly, to one another. In a similar manner, both works include the narrative of a character who returns from the West Indies. The attitude of both works towards the value systems advocated in the female conduct books of the period, however, is even more striking. As Jean Coates Cleary has observed of Sheridan's novel,

> *Sidney Bidulph* has a haunting layer of implication, at times a rebellious authorial anger, which is [not] . . . present in the conduct books proper. Sheridan's novel engages our interest by calling its own ethical system into question – even as it supports it, honours its heroine's fidelity to it, and passes it along in urgently dramatized form to the coming age of conservative reaction to Enlightenment challenge. This complex doubleness – an insistent promotion of conduct doctrine coupled with an aggressive exposure of its unfortunate effects – operates with particular forcefulness in the matter of female delicacy, but it is a sabotaging presence as well in Sidney's subservience to higher, parental-spousal will and in her devotion to the religious principles which make such self-abnegating deference a virtue.[36]

In his Introduction to a recent authoritative edition of Charke's *Narrative*, Robert Rehder observed that throughout Charke's autobiography, her failures seem to be 'fore-ordained'. 'Her comments', he noted, 'show that often she is aware as she is doing things that she is going about them in the wrong way'.[37] Rehder further speculated that 'the major purpose, conscious or unconscious of the autobiography, is to unify and connect all her impulsive, disparate, contradicting behaviours and to show that she has a stable identity'.[38] If such, indeed, was her fundamental purpose, Charke in many ways rather obviously and even spectacularly failed to achieve it. The *Narrative* is populated not by one Charlotte Charke, but by a multitude of Charkes, all of whom seek to be pardoned and reconciled with her father. The *History of Henry Dumont, Esq., and Charlotte Evelyn* – explicitly connected as it is by Charke herself to the story of her life – indicates that the author readily acknowledged the failure of her strategy of supposedly transparent and open confession in the autobiography, and sought to restrict the 'morality' of her penitence or atonement within the form of what she felt to be an even more artfully crafted fiction. In doing so, she made a rather remarkable contribution to the debates that would continue throughout the early eighteenth and nineteenth centuries regarding the role of women's writing in the development of an enlightened self and, more particularly, the ways in which the possibilities of genre related to the era's definitions of power, representation, and truth; at the very least, in both her novel and her autobiography, Charke anticipates the changing relationship and interchange between sexuality and forms of representation that would become so strong a focus of the coming generations of 'romantic' writers. The world of Charke's writing – though shaped by a complex influence of social, economic, and political factors – displays with often dazzling power the potentially disruptive energy of female sexual desire – a desire that will resist all attempts to codify and confine its energies, and insists on its right to express the freedom of the self.

Conclusion

When I first began to look into the structures of parody throughout an extended period of seventeenth- and eighteenth-century literature, those structures appeared to be relatively clearly defined. Beginning to flourish for the first time in the English tradition in the earliest years of the seventeenth century – and developing in an era of unprecedented religious, political, and rhetorical crises – parody was at one and the same time emphatically both a personal and an inescapably public or political act. Poets such as John Dryden, certainly, seemed to demonstrate the consistent use of parody and of literary appropriation to attack the political opposition and, likewise, the consistent use of self-deprecating, self-parodic techniques to deflect subsequent parodists of one's own poetry. The techniques of text-specific parodic appropriation were shaped by – and found their initial expression in – an era that saw poetry being used as one of the most persuasive, effective, and indeed *dangerous* tools of party-political debate.

As the specific political and religious issues that had galvanized the final decades of the seventeenth century were in turn obscured (if not entirely resolved) in the general prosperity and expansion that characterized much of the eighteenth century, however, parody seemed arguably to lose something of its political or polemical edge. Whilst the parodic activity of the early eighteenth century (the activity of writers such as Swift and Pope, at least) often attempted to preserve the goal of political action and efficacy that had characterized the inter-textual dialogues of the Restoration and late seventeenth century, mid-century parodists frequently seemed to be less interested than their forerunners in engaging in any specifically public or political debates. They seemed, in fact, to be moving inexorably and logically in the direction of their nineteenth-century successors, who appeared in turn to be interested in the possibilities of parody almost exclusively as a means of mere stylistic critique. The progress of parody, in other words, appeared precisely to be the progress of both public and personal depoliticization. I had initially been prepared to argue that the eighteenth century itself witnessed the decline of parody as a politically effective tool – that the period saw parody become less political, and more private; less publicly engaged, and more self-involved or at least self-concerned.

My subsequent readings and research on parody have convinced me that such a representation of the literary history of the parodic mode would be far from entirely truthful. Although it is demonstrably true that the parodists of the mid and late eighteenth century (and, indeed, the parodies of the nineteenth century as well) come to concern themselves less with the overtly political – less, that is, with the specific issues and actualities of public debate – it is nevertheless clear that the use of the parodic mode in the period can hardly be described as apolitical or politically unconcerned. Even seemingly anecdotal or personal parodies such as Richard Owen Cambridge's rewriting of Pope's *Eloisa to Abelard*, or Charlotte Charke's own parodic, fictional re-crafting of the *Narrative* of her own life, if not in some respects overtly 'political', prove on closer examination to be intimately connected with the structures of power and gender that effectively construct the primary forum for political action. Indeed, writers such as Charke seem often to be very much alive to the power of the parodic mode to connect and to expose the personal and the political. What I have referred to early in these pages as the 'anxieties' of parody (which we saw so powerfully manifested in the desire on the part of poets such as Ben Jonson to impose the figurative language of disease on the mode, and to exclude it from the proper taxonomies of literary endeavour), rather than being calmed or assuaged in the course of the eighteenth century, are in fact augmented. The parodists of the late eighteenth century, certainly, would continue to encode their critiques of individuals and of entire political structures in a literary mode that had developed to accommodate a wide range of public action and that remained at all times conscious of its own pedigree and heritage as a superbly effective weapon of public debate. The personal and the political do not disappear from parody; they simply become more deeply inscribed.

Any further examination of the many parodists of the writers of the late eighteenth century will no doubt work to support such admittedly broad generalizations. The many parodies in the period of poets including Thomas Gray, Oliver Goldsmith, William Collins, and William Cowper continue to be informed by an often explicit 'political' agenda, in the widest sense of that term. It now seems naïve to suppose that a century in England that was eventually to manifest an understandable anxiety regarding the possibilities of revolution (and indeed, witnessed the cataclysmic upheaval of the revolution in France) could somehow have remained insensible to the political efficacy and the public voice of the parodic mode. There must remain some connection, too, between the rise of the highly political graphic satire of artists such as Hogarth, Rowlandson, and Gillray (whose caricature so often seems to form the graphic counterpart to the exaggerated tactics of formal literary parody) and the mode of parody in print. Perhaps we will find that the subsequent representation by the critics of the late nineteenth and twentieth centuries of literary parody as a 'polite art' and the simultaneous dismissal of the parodies of the seventeenth and eighteenth centuries as the responses borne precisely of the recognition of just how powerful and destabilizing the parodic mode could actually be. Linda Hutcheon once observed that 'there has been a close historical connection between political censorship and the denigration of parody. . . . Parody is often officially trivialised to muzzle satire's subversive criticism'.[1] Further studies of literary parody will need to take into account the possibility that the parodies of the late nineteenth and twentieth centuries were themselves more highly encoded and 'politically' volatile than we have commonly acknowledged – that, in fact, the standard representation of such works as simple *vers de société* may itself be yet another instance of the self-protective tactics so typical of the parodic mode.

Most importantly, however, I hope here at least to have begun to demonstrate the extent to which parody is at once more pervasive and simply more important to 'serious' literary endeavour than critics have commonly acknowledged. It has been my central concern to stress the fact that parody is not an isolated literary mode that stands apart from and comments on what might safely be styled the 'mainstream' of literary practice. Rather, parody – in the more expansive sense in which I have been using the term – is an imitative mode that remains alive to the possibilities of creative inter-textuality, and forms a part of almost all literary practice. Parody implies dialogue, and from the literary dialogues that ensue from parodic practice we invariably witness greater creative development, and a greater understanding of the varieties of interpretation of existing literary documents. Although I have certainly stressed the propensity of text-specific parody to provoke anxiety on the part of the 'targeted' author, I have nevertheless been equally concerned, I trust, to demonstrate the manner in which parody always remains available to that same artist as part of his or her own literary technique. As our recognition and understanding of the creative – and far from parasitic – possibilities of inter-textuality continue, we will undoubtedly be turning our attention more frequently to parody as one of the literary modes that most forcefully engages in dialogues with both past and contemporary literary texts.

Notes

1 Introduction

1. Edward Young, *Conjectures on Original Composition. In a Letter to the Author of Sir Charles Grandison* (London: A. Millar and R. and J. Dodsley, 1759): 42.
2. 'Aye, There's the Rub'. Interview with Phillip Pullman, *The Observer*, Review (27 November 2005).
3. Malcolm Bowie, 'Jacques Lacan', in John Sturrock, ed., *Structuralism and Since: From Lévi-Strauss to Derrida* (Oxford: Oxford University Press, 1979): 116.
4. Malcolm Bowie, 'Jacques Lacan': 116.
5. On the notion of the possible 'monumentality' or independence of works of literature see M.M. Bakhtin, *Speech Genres and Other Late Essays*, trans. V.W. McGee, eds Caryl Emerson and Michael Holquist (Austin, Texas: University of Texas Press, 1986): 95. Cited in Graham Allen, *Inter-textuality*. The New Critical Idiom Series (New York and London: Routledge, 2000): 19.
6. See David Boucher's discussion in his 'In Defence of Collingwood: Perspectives from Philosophy and the History of Ideas', in R.G. Collingwood, *The Philosophy of Enchantment: Studies in Folktale, Cultural Criticism, and Anthropology*, eds David Boucher, Wendy James, and Philip Smallwood (Oxford: Clarendon Press, 2005): xcvi–xcvii. Note also Joyce Appleby, 'One Good Turn Deserves Another: Moving beyond the Linguistic: A Response to David Harlan' in *American Historical Review*, 94 (1989): 1327.
7. The English translation of Roland Barthes's original, influential essay was reprinted as 'The Death of the Author' in the Barthes essay collection *Image-Music-Text: Essays Selected and Translated by Stephen Heath* (London: Fontana-Collins, 1983): 142–48. For a succinct account of the manner in which Foucault shortly thereafter elaborated on and extended Barthes's fundamental ideas and the ways in which the autonomy of the individual author was systematically reduced in much subsequent theory, see Donald E. Pease's contribution s.v. 'Author' in Frank Lentricchia and Thomas McLaughlin's *Critical Terms for Literary Study* (Chicago and London: University of Chicago Press, 1987): 105–17.
8. This notion of the 'positive ethos' of post-modern parody was most fully explored in works such as Linda Hutcheon's *A Theory of Parody: The Teaching of Twentieth-Century Art Forms* (New York and London: Methuen, 1985). See the discussion pertaining to Hutcheon and her work in Chapter 2. For other, wide-ranging and general revaluations of the parodic mode, see Catherine Bernard, 'The Cultural Agenda of Parody in Some Contemporary English Novels' in *European Journal of English Studies*, 3, no. 2 (1999): 167–89; Christine Brooke-Rose, 'Illusions of Parody' in *American Studies* 30, no. 2 (1985): 225–33; Seymour Chatman, 'Parody and Style' in *Poetics Today*, 22, no. 1 (Spring 2001): 25–39; Vincent Crapanzano, 'The Postmodern Crisis: Discourse, Parody, Memory' in Amy Mandelker, ed., *Bakhtin in Contexts: Across the Disciplines* (Evanston, Illinois: Northwestern University Press,

1995): 119–36; Michele, Hannoosh, 'The Reflexive Function of Parody' in *Comparative Literature*, 41, no. 2 (Spring 1989): 113–27; Jean-Jacques Lecercle, 'Parody as Cultural Memory' in *REAL: The Yearbook of Research in English and American Literature*, 21 (2005): 31–44; Robert Phiddian, 'Are Parody and Deconstruction Secretly the Same Thing?' in *New Literary History: A Journal of Theory and Interpretation* 28, no. 4 (Autumn 1997): 673–96; M.N. Scott, 'On the Nature of Parody' in *Northwest Review* 30, no. 3 (1992): 6–11.

9. *The Dialogic Imagination: Four Essays* by M.M. Bakhtin, ed. Michael Holquist, trans. Caryl Emerson and Michael Holquist (Austin, Texas: University of Texas Press, 1981): 71.
10. Fredric Jameson, *Postmodernism, or, the Cultural Logic of Late Capitalism* (London and New York: Verso, 1991): 17.
11. Fredric Jameson, *Postmodernism*: 17–18.
12. See, for example, Dan Harries, *Film Parody* (London: British Film Institute, 2000): note the subsequent discussion of Harries's ideas in Chapter 2.
13. Colin Falck, *Myth, Truth, and Literature*. 2nd edn (1989; Cambridge: Cambridge University Press, 1994): 96–7.
14. Colin Falck, *Myth, Truth, and Literature*: 90.
15. The notion of a 'culture of repudiation' as 'the systematic examination of the high culture of bourgeois society, with a view to exposing and rejecting its assumptions' is clearly if polemically addressed in some detail in Roger Scruton's *Modern Culture* (London and New York: Continuum, 2000): 123–34; esp. 132–3.
16. R.G. Collingwood, *The Principles of Art* (Oxford: Clarendon Press, 1938): 318–19.
17. Colin Falck, *Myth, Truth, and Literature*: 138.
18. John Beale was the London printer who, in 1631, printed for bookseller Robert Allott several of Jonson's later plays, including *Bartholomew Fair* (1614). On their professional relationship, see Anne Barton, *Ben Jonson: Dramatist* (Cambridge: Cambridge University Press, 1984): 253–5.
19. On the *Poetomachia* or 'War of the Theatres' involving Jonson, John Marston, Thomas Dekker, and George Chapman, generally, see R.A. Small, *The Stage Quarrel between Ben Jonson and the So-Called Poetasters* (Breslau: 1899).

2 'We Cannot Think of What Hath Not Been Thought': Or, How Critics Learned to Stop Worrying and Love Literary Parody

1. Robertson Davies, *World of Wonders* [1975] in *The Deptford Trilogy* (Harmondsworth, Middlesex: Penguin, 1983): 633.
2. Leavis's remarks on parody were reprinted in *The New Oxford Book of Light Verse*, ed. Kingsley Amis (Oxford: Oxford University Press, 1978), xiv–xv. They originally appeared in 1962 in the British weekly, *The Spectator*, on which occasion they had been prompted by a review, by Julian Jebb, of a recent parody anthology. Jebb had praised the perceptive and critical powers of parody, noting that 'the most satisfying parody presupposes an intensity and acuteness of reading from which sympathy cannot be wholly

absent, and to sustain the perverse creativity necessary, the parodist must identify himself with his subject ... '. To this generous assessment of the creative possibilities of parody and recognition of the necessary empathy of an effective parodist, Leavis had replied: 'There is only one thing that could be learnt by the attempt to parody a writer whose distinction makes him worthy of close study; that is, how inaccessible to any but the most superficial, and falsifying, the truly characteristic effects of such writers are. ... The cult of parody, in fact, belongs to that literary culture ... which, in its obtuse and smug complacency, is always the worst enemy of creative genius and vital originality'. See *The Spectator* (2 January 1962): 13. On Leavis's specific proposal that the parody 'was to be deplored because it demeaned the integrity of [its] subject', see also D.J. Taylor, 'Too Funny for Words', review of Craig Brown's *This is Craig Brown*, in *The Spectator* (8 February 2003). Leavis's own criticism and style attributed to one 'Simon Lacerous' and included in Frederick C. Crews's extraordinarily clever collection of academic parodies, *The Pooh Perplex: A Student Casebook* (London: Robin Clark, 1984), inspired his well-known parody, 'Another Book to Cross Off Your List'.

3. William Hazlitt's frequently repeated observation that 'Rules and models destroy genius and art' was first included in his essay 'On Taste' in his *Sketches and Essays* (1839).

4. J.B. Price, 'Parody and Humour', in *Contemporary Review*, no. 180 (1951): 243.

5. See Dwight Macdonald, ed. *Parodies: An Anthology from Chaucer to Beerbohm and After* (New York: Random House, 1960): 563–4.

6. Simon Brett's successful *Faber Book of Parodies* (London: Faber & Faber, 1984) includes a mere handful of parodies of the works of Restoration and eighteenth-century authors, and cites only three very short examples of parodic material actually written in the Augustan period. Walter Hamilton's impressive *Parodies of the Works of English and American Authors*, 5 volumes (London: Reeves and Turner, 1884–89) had of course favoured the work of nineteenth-century authors over that of their predecessors. The trend continued in collections such as Carolyn Wells's *A Nonsense Anthology* (1902; rpt. New York: Blue Ribbon Books, 1930), and belle-lettres efforts such as Ralph Lyon's *The Mocking Bards: A Collection of Parodies, Burlesques, and Imitations* (Evanston, Illinois: Ridgeville Press, 1905). A notable exception to the rule was William Zaranka's *Brand X Anthology of Poetry* (Cambridge, Massachusetts: Apple-wood Books, 1981), which at least included a healthy collection of parodies of seventeenth- and eighteenth-century authors ranging from John Dryden and the Earl of Rochester to Samuel Johnson. Kenneth Baker's *Unauthorized Versions: Poems and Their Parodies* (London: Faber & Faber, 1990) likewise included a reasonably wide chronological range of parodies from the mainstream English literary tradition. The authors of several influential surveys of eighteenth century verse have likewise tended to devalue literary parody. A generation of critics were taught by critics such as James Sutherland (*A Preface to Eighteenth-Century Poetry* [Oxford: Oxford University Press, 1948]) that the optimistic and rule-bound poets of the period valued 'order', 'beauty', and a polite 'dignity' at the expense of innovative and iconoclastic forms of satire and parody, and that parodic activity in the period tended to be restrained and polite and – above

all – conservative. Even those literary historians who initially worked to revise this reductive and monolithic conception of eighteenth-century verse tended to be dismissive of literary parody as a creative mode. Eric Rothstein's otherwise enormously salutary volume *Restoration and Eighteenth-Century Poetry, 1660–1780* (London: Routledge & Kegan Paul, 1981), for example, dismissed most eighteenth-century parodies as wasteful, 'malicious', 'playful', and 'abusive', and argued that they were consequently less interesting uses of the past than were, say, classical borrowings (98). Other supposedly 'revisionist' histories of eighteenth-century literature (e.g., Leopold Damrosch's *Modern Essays on Eighteenth-Century Literature* [Oxford: Oxford University Press, 1988]) conspicuously failed to include any explicit or extended discussion of parody and burlesque.

7. Frances Stillman, *The Poet's Manual and Rhyming Dictionary* (London: Thames and Hudson, 1966; 1991): xiv–xv. The necessary element of the 'ridiculous' is similarly stressed in the definitions s.v. 'parody' in, for example, M.H. Abrams, *A Glossary of Literary Terms*, 4th edn (New York: Holt, Rinehart and Winston, 1981); J.A. Cuddon, *A Dictionary of Literary Terms* (London: Penguin Books, 1977, 1992); William Harmon and C. Hugh Colman, *A Handbook to Literature*, 7th edn (Upper Saddle River, New Jersey: Prentice Hall, 1990).

8. George Kitchin, *A Survey of Parody and Burlesque in English* (London: Oliver and Boyd, 1931).

9. Kitchin, *A Survey of Parody and Burlesque in English*: xiii.

10. See Gilbert Highet, *The Anatomy of Satire* (Princeton: Princeton University Press, 1962): 67–147; Richmond P. Bond, *English Burlesque Poetry, 1700–50* (Cambridge, Massachusetts: Harvard University Press, 1932): *passim*. Some early critical recognition of the possibly 'positive' and 'constructive' aspects of parody were, however, noted by several critics in the latter half of the century. See, for example, Rosemary Freeman's 'Parody as Literary Form: George Herbert and Wilfred Owen' in *Essays in Criticism*, XII (1963): 307–22.

11. See Walter Jackson Bate, *The Burden of the Past and the English Poet* (New York and London: W.W. Norton, 1970) and Harold Bloom, *The Anxiety of Influence: A Theory of Poetry* (Oxford: Oxford University Press, 1973).

12. Joseph Dane, *Parody: Critical Concepts versus Literary Practice: Aristophanes to Sterne* (Norman, Oklahoma: University of Oklahoma Press, 1988): 4.

13. Mary Orr, in her *Inter-textuality: Debates and Contexts* (Cambridge: Polity Press, 2003) includes an appendix entitled 'Directory of Alternative Terms for "Intertext", "Inter-textuality"', which, whilst including in its listings (as one might expect) 'parody', 'pastiche', 'burlesque', 'travesty', etc., comprehends close to 1200 alternative forms 'which inter-textuality has embraced' (238–46).

14. See George Steiner, *After Babel: Aspects of Language and Translation* (Oxford: Oxford University Press, 1974): 1–48.

15. In Samuel Butler, *The Note-books*, selected, arranged, and edited by Henry Festing Jones (London: Fifield, 1918).

16. On such terminology, see Roland Barthes, *Fragments d'un discours amoureaux* (Paris: Editions de Seuil, 1977); English translation, *A Lover's Discourse: Fragments* (New York: Hill and Wang, 1978); see also John Sturrock's excellent discussion of the vocabulary of Barthes's later essays in his 'Roland Barthes',

is included in his edited collection *Structuralism and Since: From Lévi-Strauss to Derrida* (Oxford: Oxford University Press, 1979): 52–80.

17. See Liddell and Scott's *Greek–English Lexicon* (Oxford: Clarendon Press, 1871), s.v. 'παρα'; ἀείδω'.

18. See Liddell and Scott, *Greek–English Lexicon*, s.v. 'παροδός'. For the original context of Aristotle's use of the term 'parody' in his *Poetics*, see M.E. Hubbard's translation of that work in *Classical Literary Criticism*, eds D.A. Russell and M. Winterbottom (Oxford: Oxford University Press, 1989): 53.

19. Edward Said, 'On Originality' in *The World, the Text, and the Critic* (London: Faber & Faber, 1984): 135.

20. Margaret Rose makes use of the term 'refunctioning' – a translation of Brecht's *Umfunktionierung* – to refer to the 'new functions' generated by any text when presented within the new context of a parody. See Margaret Rose, *Parody/Metafiction: An Analysis of Parody as a Critical Mirror to the Writing and Reception of Fiction* (London: Croom Helm, 1979): 36, n.12.

21. Samuel Taylor Coleridge, *Biographia Literaria, or, Biographical Sketches of My Literary Life and Opinions*, eds James Engell and Walter Jackson Bate, 2 vols (Princeton: Princeton University Press, 1983): ii.151.

22. Said, *The World, the Text, and the Critic*: 138.

23. Baldassare [Baldesar] Castiglione, *The Book of the Courtier*, translated by Sir Thomas Hoby (1561), reprinted in *Three Renaissance Classics* (New York: Charles Scribner's Sons, 1953), 286; see also *The Book of the Courtier*, trans. Charles S. Singleton (New York: Doubleday & Company, 1959): 43.

24. Pierre de Ronsard, *Ode à Michel de L'Hospital* (1552), l.810; quoted in David Quint, *Origin and Originality in Renaissance Literature* (New Haven and London: Yale University Press, 1983): 30.

25. Said, *The World, the Text, and the Critic*: 135.

26. For a reasonably comprehensive discussion of literary imitation in English prior to the late seventeenth century, see Harold Ogden White, *Plagiarism and Imitation during the English Renaissance: A Study in Critical Distinctions* (Cambridge, Massachusetts: Harvard University Press, 1935). On originality, imitation, and indebtedness, see 'The Originality Paradox' in Thomas McFarland's *Originality and Imitation* (Baltimore, Maryland: Johns Hopkins University Press, 1985): 1–30. Rolf P. Lessenich's *Aspects of English Preromanticism* (Cologne: Bohlua-Verlag, 1989): 37–57, discusses the revaluation of originality – 'a shift in emphasis from the final end-product to the generic origin' – in the late eighteenth century. On the origin of the concept of plagiarism in the sixteenth and seventeenth centuries, see Thomas Mallon's *Stolen Words: Forays into the Origins and Ravages of Plagiarism* (New York: Ticknor and Fields, 1989). On attitudes towards imitation, allusion, and poetic borrowing, see Roger Lonsdale's 'Gray and Allusion: The Poet as Debtor' in *Studies in the Eighteenth Century*, IV, eds R.F. Brissenden and J.C. Eade (Canberra: Australian National University Press, 1979): 31–55.

27. See Sir Philip Sidney, *A Defence of Poetry*, edited with an introduction and notes by Jan Van Dorsten (Oxford: Oxford University Press, 1966): 19.

28. Edmund Spenser, 'Two Cantos of *Mutabilitie*' (VII.vi.5, ll.1–4), in Edmund Spenser, *The Faerie Queene*, ed. A.C. Hamilton (London and New York: Longman, 1977): 715.

29. As in, for example, Quintilian's *Institutio Oratorio*, trans. H.E. Butler, in the Loeb Classical Library (Cambridge, Massachusetts: Harvard University Press, 1922): X.ii.1–7, or Lucian's *Rhetoron Didaskalos*, trans. A.M. Harmon, in the Loeb Classical Library (Cambridge, Massachusetts: Harvard University Press, 1925): viii. Note also H.O. White's discussion of classical imitation in his *Plagiarism and Imitation*: 3–19.
30. David Nokes, *Jonathan Swift* (Oxford: Oxford University Press, 1985): 44.
31. On parody as an exemplary form of 'double-voiced words', see Gary Saul Morson and Caryl Emerson, *Mikhail Bakhtin: Creation of a Prosaics* (Stanford: Stanford University Press, 1990): 152–3; Mary Orr, *Inter-textuality*: 107–8.
32. Mikhail Bakhtin, *Problems of Dostoevsky's* Poetics, ed. and trans. Caryl Emerson (Minneapolis: University of Minneapolis, 1984): 193.
33. An English translation of Victor Shklovsky's article on 'Sterne's *Tristram Shandy* and the Theory of the Novel', first printed in Russian in 1921, was reprinted in *Russian Formalist Criticism: Four Essays*, eds Lee T. Lemon and Marion J. Reis (Lincoln, Nebraska: University of Nebraska Press, 1965): 25–57. On Tynanov and parody, see Peter Steiner's *Russian Formalism: A Metapoetics* (Ithaca: Cornell University Press, 1984): 119–22.
34. See Cleanth Brooks, 'The Case of Miss Arabella Fermor' in *The Well-Wrought Urn* (New York: Harcourt Brace, 1947): 80–104; William Empson, *Some Versions of Pastoral* (London: Chatto and Windus, 1935): *passim*.
35. 'Parody is what art must do when it had become critique; . . . parody comes about because art can no longer be pious to either the journey or the pity in the old forms, and has not yet found a means to settle on new forms'. R.P. Blackmur, *Selected Essays*, ed. Denis Donoghue (New York: Ecco Press, 1986): 333–57.
36. See, for example, Hans Robert Jauss, *Aesthetic Experience and Literary Hermeneutics*, trans. Michael Shaw (Minneapolis: University of Minnesota Press, 1982): 182; 189–220.
37. M.M. Bakhtin, *The Dialogic Imagination*, trans. Caryl Emerson and Michael Holquist; ed. Michael Holquist (Austin, Texas: University of Texas Press, 1981): 41–83. See also Bakhtin's essay 'Discourse Typology in Prose' in *Readings in Russian Poetics: Formalist and Structuralist Views*, eds Ladislav Matejka and Krystyna Pomorska (Cambridge, Massachusetts: M.I.T. University Press, 1971): 176–96.
38. Michel Foucault, *The Order of Things* (New York: Random House, 1970): 46–50.
39. Michel Foucault, *The Order of Things*: 49.
40. Vladimir Nabokov, *Lectures on Don Quixote*, edited by Fredson Bowers with an introduction by Guy Davenport (London: Weidenfeld and Nicolson, 1983).
41. See Elaine Showalter, *A Literature of Their Own: British Women Novelists from Brontë to Lessing* (Princeton: Princeton University Press, 1977): 282–97. Note also Toril Moi's critique of Showalter in her *Sexual/Textual Politics: Feminist Literary Theory* (London: Methuen, 1985): 2–8.
42. See, for example: Patricia A. Sullivan, 'Female Writing beside the Rhetorical Tradition: Seventeenth-Century British Biography and a Female Tradition in Rhetoric' in *International Journal of Women's Studies*, 3 (1980): 143–60; Marilyn Manners and R.L. Rutsky, 'Post-Human Romance: Parody and Pastiche in *Making Mr. Right* and *Tank Girl*' in *Discourse: Journal for Theoretical Studies in Media and Culture*, 21, no. 2 (Spring 1999): 115–38; Andrea

Austin, 'Shooting Blanks: Potency, Parody, and Eliza Haywood's *The History of Miss Betsy Thoughtless*' in *The Passionate Fictions of Eliza Haywood: Essays on Her Life and Works*, eds Kirsten T. Saxton and Rebecca P. Bocchicchio (Lexington, Kentucky: University of Kentucky Press, 2000); Marilyn Brooks and Nicola Watson, 'Northanger Abbey: Contexts' in *The Nineteenth-Century Novel: Realisms*, ed. Delia da Sousa Correa (London: Routledge, 2000); Janet Beer and Avril Horner, ' "This Isn't Exactly a Ghost Story": Edith Wharton and Parodic Gothic' in *Journal of American Studies*, 37, no. 2 (August 2003), 269–85; Esther Sánchez-Pardo González, ' "What Phantasmogoria the Mind Is": Reading Virginia Woolf's Parody of Gender' in *Atlantis: Revista de la Asociación Española de Estudios Anglo-Norteamericanos*, 26, no. 2 (December 2004): 75–86.

43. Luce Irigaray, 'The Power of Discourse and the Subordination of the Feminine', in *This Sex which Is Not One*, trans. Catherine Porter with Carolyn Burke (Ithaca: Cornell University Press, 1985): 76. On the necessity of revising a male-oriented language parodically see 'The Thieves of Language: Women Poets and Revisionist Mythmaking' in *The New Feminist Criticism*, ed. Elaine Showalter (New York: Pantheon, 1985): 314–38; see also Toril Moi, *Sexual/Textual Politics*: 140.

44. Ella Shohat, 'Ethnicities-in-Relation: Toward a Multicultural Reading of American Cinema' in Lester D. Friedman, ed., *Unspeakable Images: Ethnicity and the American Cinema* (Urbana, Illinois: University of Illinois Press, 1991): 238.

45. See Henry Louis Gates, Jr., *The Signifying Monkey: A Theory of African-American Literary Criticism* (Oxford: Oxford University Press, 1988): 103–13.

46. Geoffrey Galt Harpham, *On the Grotesque: Strategies of Contradiction in Art and Literature* (Princeton: Princeton University Press, 1982): xv–xviii. Harpham likewise characterizes parody itself as one of the 'tributary ideas' funnelling into the concept of the grotesque. A similar relationship between parody and nonsense verse has been postulated by Wim Tiggs in his *Anatomy of Literary Nonsense* (Amsterdam: Rodopi, 1988), although, strikingly, the protean capacities of the parodic mode in fact lead Tiggs to omit parody from the specific taxonomies he devises for nonsense verse.

47. Tuvia Shlonsky, 'Literary Parody: Remarks on Its Method and Function' in *Proceedings of the Fourth Congress of the International Comparative Literature Association*, ed. F. Jost, 2 vols (The Hague: Mouton, 1966): II.797–98.

48. Shlonsky, 'Literary Parody': 799.

49. Leon Guilhamet, *Satire and the Transformation of Genre* (Philadelphia: University of Pennsylvania Press, 1987): 14.

50. Edward A. Bloom and Lillian D. Bloom, *Satire's Persuasive Voice* (Ithaca: Cornell University Press, 1979): 175–9.

51. Paula R. Backscheider, 'Daniel Defoe' in *The First English Novelists: Essays in Understanding*, ed. J.M. Armistead, Tennessee Studies in Literature, Vol. 29 (Knoxville: University of Tennessee Press, 1985): 41–66.

52. Claudia L. Johnson, *Jane Austen: Women, Politics and the Novel* (Chicago: University of Chicago Press, 1988): 30–6. Johnson argues that the 'polyvalent irony' of Austen's early parodies pokes fun not only at novelistic formulas, but at the political realities concealed by literary conventions. For example, the Radcliffean gothic fiction parodied in *Northanger Abbey*, Johnson

contends, conceals a political agenda that includes a Burkean rationale for patriarchal repression. 'Austen may dismiss "alarms" concerning stock gothic *machinery* – storms, cabinets, curtains, manuscripts – with blithe amusement, but alarms concerning the central gothic *figure*, the tyrannical father, she concludes, are commensurate with the threat they actually pose' (35). On Austen's parodies note also Edward M. White, *Jane Austen and the Art of Parody*. Diss. Harvard, 1960; Lloyd W. Bean, *Bits of Ivory: Narrative Techniques in Jane Austen's Fiction* (Baton Rouge, Louisiana: Louisiana State University Press, 1973): 199–235.

53. Paul Lehmann, *Die Parodie im Mittelalter* (Stuttgart: Hiersemann, 1963): *passim*.
54. Ulrich Weisstein, 'Parody, Travesty, and Burlesque: Imitation with a Vengeance', in *Proceedings of the IVth Congress of the International Comparative Literature Association*: II.802–11.
55. G. D. Kiremidjian, 'The Aesthetics of Parody', in *Journal of Aesthetics and Art Criticism*, 28 (1969): 232.
56. Joseph Dane, *Parody: Critical Concepts versus Literary Practice*: 4.
57. Joseph Dane, *Parody*: 6.
58. Gérard Genette, *Palimpsestes: La Littérature au Second Degré* (Paris: Éditions du Seuil, 1982).
59. See Gérard Genette, 'Boundaries of Narrative', in *New Literary History*, Vol. 8, no. 1 (1976): 231.
60. See, for example, Orr, *Inter-textuality*: 108–9.
61. Genette, *Palimpsestes*: 91.
62. Rose, *Parody/Metafiction*: 59.
63. Rose, *Parody/Metafiction*: 59; see also, on the significance and some of the practical, interpretative consequences of Rose's definition, Deborah Knight, 'Popular Parody: *The Simpsons* Meet the Crime Film', in *The Simpsons and Philosophy*, eds William Irwin, Mark Conard, and Leon J. Skoble (London: Curtis Publishing, 2001): 103.
64. Jacques Derrida, *Of Grammatology*, trans. Gayatri Spivack (Baltimore, Maryland: Johns Hopkins University Press, 1976): 158.
65. Phiddian, *Swift's Parody*: 13–14. This same passage is quoted at slightly greater length by Simon Dentith in his *Parody* (see note 67, below).
66. Robert Phiddian, 'Are Parody and Deconstruction Secretly the Same Thing' in *New Literary History: A Journal of Theory and Interpretation* 28, no. 4 (Autumn, 1997): 673.
67. Phiddian, 'Are Parody and Deconstruction Secretly the Same Thing': 690.
68. Linda Hutcheon, *A Theory of Parody: The Teachings of Twentieth-Century Art Forms* (London: Methuen, 1985).
69. Linda Hutcheon, *A Poetics of Postmodernism: History, Theory, Fiction* (New York: Routledge, 1988); *The Politics of Postmodernism,* 2nd edn (London: Routledge, 2002 [1989]).
70. Note Michael J. Conlon's discussion of the *para* prefix in his 'Singing Beside-Against: Parody and the Example of Swift's *A Description of a City Shower*' in *GENRE*, 16 (1983): 219–32.
71. Hutcheon, *A Theory of Parody*: 30–49.
72. Hutcheon, *The Politics of Postmodernism*: 94.
73. Hutcheon, *The Politics of Postmodernism*: 93.

74. Hutcheon, *The Politics of Postmodernism*: 101.
75. On the work of Robert Burden, see note 84, below.
76. Clive Thomson, 'Parody/Genre/Ideology' in *Le singe à la porte: Vers une théorie de la parodie* (New York: Peter Lang, 1984): 95–103.
77. On ancient definitions of parody see F.J. Lelièvre, 'The Basis of Ancient Parody' in *Greece and Rome*, 2nd ser., 1 (1954): 66–91.
78. On the related form of the cento see Scott McGill's excellent *Virgil Recomposed: The Mythological and Secular Centos of Antiquity* (Oxford: Oxford University Press, 2006).
79. Lelièvre, 'The Basis of Ancient Parody': 71. For the definitions of parody cited here, see, for example, John Entrick's *The New Spelling Dictionary Teaching to Write and Pronounce the ENGLISH Tongue with Ease and Propriety* (London, 1766), s.v. 'parody'.
80. 'On the Burlesque Style', in *Gray's Inn Journal*, 50 (6 Sept. 1754): 297–8; reprinted in Richmond P. Bond's *English Burlesque Poetry, 1700–50*: 55.
81. See H.D. Weinbrot, 'Parody as Imitation in the Eighteenth Century' in *American Notes and Queries*, 9 (May, 1964): 31–4. Note also Weinbrot's discussion of the relationship between imitation and parody in *The Formal Strain: Studies in Augustan Imitation and Satire* (Chicago: University of Chicago Press, 1969), esp. 23–30.
82. Warburton, *The Works of Alexander Pope*, 9 vols (London: Lintot, Tonson, and Draper, 1751): IV.51.
83. Thomas Warton, *History of English Poetry*, ed., W. Carew Hazlitt 4 vols (London: Reeves and Turner, 1871): IV.367–8.
84. Robert Burden, 'The Novel Interrogates Itself: Parody as Self-Consciousness in Contemporary English Fiction', *Stratford-upon-Avon Studies*, no. 18 (1979): 136.
85. Simon Dentith, *Parody*, in 'The New Critical Idiom', series editor, John Drakakis (London and New York: Routledge, 2000): ix. Two of the other volumes in founder editor John Jump's original 'Critical Idiom' series that were of relevance to the study of parody included Jessica Milner Davis's title on *Farce* and, even more pertinently, Arthur Pollard's excellent *Satire* (London and New York: Methuen, 1970).
86. Dentith, *Parody*: 5.
87. Dentith, *Parody*: 5–6.
88. Gary Saul Morson, 'Parody, History, and Metaparody', in *Rethinking Bakhtin, Extensions and Challenges*, eds Gary Saul Morson and Caryl Emerson (Evanston, Illinois: Northwestern University Press, 1989): 63–4.
89. Dentith, *Parody*: 8–9; specific emphasis in this quotation, however, is my own.
90. Dentith, *Parody*: 9
91. Dentith, *Parody*: 190–5.
92. Dan Harries, *Film Parody* (London: British Film Institute Publishing, 2000): 3.
93. Harries, *Film Parody*: 3.
94. One noteworthy exception to this rule is the work of Jonathan Bate. Bate stressed the many complimentary parodies of Shakespeare's dramas in the eighteenth and early nineteenth centuries, and suggested that throughout the period Shakespeare's canonical status enables him 'to be the means rather than the end of parody'. See Jonathan Bate, *Shakespearean Constitutions: Politics, Theory, Criticism, 1730–1830* (Oxford: Clarendon Press, 1989): 108.

3 Parody as Plague: Ben Jonson and the Early Anxieties of Parodic Destabilization

1. Thomas Dekker, 'Newes from Graves-end: Sent to Nobody', reprinted in *The Plague Pamphlets of Thomas Dekker*, ed., F.P. Wilson (Oxford: Clarendon Press, 1925): 84.
2. The *OED* (2nd edn) mistakenly dates Jonson's usage of the word parody or 'parodie' in *Every Man in His Humour* as the earliest illustrative quotation for its definition of parody as 'a composition . . . in which the characteristic turns of thought and phrase in an author . . . are imitated . . . in such a way as to make the author appear ridiculous'. The entry is dated 1598. Kno'well's interjected definition of parody in Jonson's comedy, however, is not included in the original Quarto version of the play (first performed in 1598, entered in the Stationers' Register in 1600, but not published until 1601). The lines were inserted by Jonson in the substantially revised version of the play that appeared in the 1616 Folio. *See OED* 2nd edn, s.v. 'parody'. On Jonson's revision of the play see Gabriele Bernhard Jackson, ed., *Every Man in His Humour*, by Ben Jonson (New Haven: Yale University Press, 1969), Appendix I: 215–19.
3. Ben Jonson, *Works*, eds, C.H. Herford and Percy and Evelyn Simpson, xi vols (Oxford: Oxford University Press, 1925–52), F EMI, Dramatis Personae, 12–3. Quotations, unless otherwise indicated, refer to this edition; those from *Every Man in His Humour* and *Sejanus* will be cited in the text, although for the convenience of the reader I have made use when referring to extended passages of G.A. Wilkes's modernized edition of Herford and Simpson's text. See *The Complete Plays of Ben Jonson*, 4 vols, ed. G.A. Wilkes (Oxford: Oxford University Press, 1981–2).
4. Kyd's *Spanish Tragedy* was probably written around 1589, and was published anonymously in 1592. Although the play enjoyed a tremendous popularity, running through ten editions by 1633, its bombast and language were soon targets of ridicule. Jonson, who may in fact have contributed several hundred additional lines to Kyd's original when the drama was 'modernized' at Henslowe's request in 1601–02, nevertheless, refers both to *The Spanish Tragedy* and to Shakespeare's *Titus Andronicus* (1594) in the Induction to *Bartholomew Fair* (1614) as old-fashioned and outdated dramatic favourites ('Hee that will sweare, *Ieronimo*, or *Andronicus* as the best playes, yet, shall pass unexcepted at, here, as a man whose judgement shewes it is constant, and hath stood still, these five and twentie, or thirtie years' [*BF* Induction, 106–9]). The 'doleful' and 'horrible fierce' rhetoric of the play comes in for a more extended parodic treatment in the 1616 Folio version of *Poetaster* (cf. *P.* III.iv.187–274).
5. See F *EMI* V.v.19. Note also Jackson's gloss on 'writ o' rebellion' in his edition of *Everyman in His Humour*: 179. See also Wilkes, *Complete Plays*, i.17–18.
6. Essex is mentioned in the Scriptorum Catalogus of Jonson's *Timber: or, Discoveries*: 368–70; 580–4. Essex may also be represented as Acteon – the victim of Cynthia-Elizabeth's 'divine injustice' – in *Cynthia's Revels* (1601).
7. For Jonson's possible 'involvement' in the Gunpowder Plot and the ensuing investigations, see David Riggs, *Ben Jonson: A Life* (Cambridge: Harvard University Press, 1989): 127.

8. On Jonson's reference to the Vinegar House, see Jackson, *Every Man in His Humour*: 238.

9. For an excellent discussion of the 'kingdom of poets' as an imitation of the political state, see Alan Roper, *Dryden's Poetic Kingdoms* (London: Routledge & Kegan Paul, 1965): 137. See also Jonson's own *Discoveries* in Herford & Simpson: 1031–38: 'I could never thinke the study of *Wisdome* confin'd only to the *Philosopher*: or of *Piety* to the *Divine*: or of *State* to the *Politicke*. But that he which can faine a *Common-wealth* (which is the *Poet*) can governe it with *Counsels*, strengthen it with *Lawes*, correct it with *Judgements*, informe it with *Religion* and *Morals*: is all these'.

10. For a concise account of the book-burnings and censorship of 1599, see John Peter, *Complaint and Satire in Early English Literature* (Oxford: Clarendon Press, 1956): 148–52.

11. Peter, *Complaint and Satire in Early English Literature*: 148–52. Anne Barton argued that the book-burnings were an act of literary criticism supported in some measure by Jonson himself. 'Jonson's attitude towards [Marlowe] and, through him, to what he regarded as literary bad practices of the day', Barton notes, 'is entirely condemnatory'. See Anne Barton, *Ben Jonson: Dramatist* (Cambridge: Cambridge University Press, 1984): 55.

12. Julia Briggs, *This Stage-Play World: English Literature and Its Background 1580–1625* (Oxford: Oxford University Press, 1982): 105–6.

13. See Thomas Nashe, *Works*, ed. R.B. McKerrow (Oxford: Basil Blackwell, 1958): 195–9.

14. Briggs, *This Stage-Play World*: 106.

15. See Jonson's translation of the *Art of Poetry* in Herford & Simpson: 483, 487.

16. From 'Vittorino de Feltre' in William Harrison Woodward, *Vittorino de Feltre and Other Humanist Educators* (Cambridge: Cambridge University Press, 1897); reprinted as Classics in Education no. 18, with a Foreword by Eugene F. Rice, Jr. (New York: Columbia University–Teacher's College Press, 1963): 28.

17. See, for example, Tom Lockwood, *Ben Jonson in the Romantic Age* (Oxford: Oxford University Press, 2005).

18. For the effects of the 1603–04 plague see Charles F. Mullett, *The Bubonic Plague and England* (Lexington, Kentucky: University of Kentucky Press, 1956): 105–42; see also F.P. Wilson, *The Plague in Shakespeare's London* (Oxford: Clarendon Press, 1927): 114–29; J. Leeds Barrol, 'Shakespeare and the Plague', in *Shakespeare's Art from a Comparative Perspective*, ed. Wendell M. Aycock (Lubbock, Texas: Texas Tech. Press, 1981): 13–29; William H. McNeill, *Plagues and People* (New York: Doubleday, 1976): 164–72; for a general account of responses to the plague in England, see Walter George Bell, *The Great Plague of London* (1924; London: Bracken Books, 1994).

19. Frances Herring, *Certain Rules, Directions, or Advertisements for This Time of Pestilential Contagion* . . . (London: William Jones, 1603; rpt. Amsterdam: De Capo Press, 1973). sig. A4r. See also Wilson, *The Plague in Shakespeare's London*: 81.

20. Herring, *Certain Rules* . . . , sig. A3v.

21. Terry Castle, *Masquerade and Civilization: The Carnivalesque in Eighteenth-Century English Culture and Fiction* (Stanford, California: Stanford University Press, 1986): 87–8.

22. See Jonson, *Timb.* 575–6 in Herford & Simpson. On parody as 'parasitic' see, for example, Israel Davidson, *Parody in Jewish Literature* (New York: AMS Press, 1966 [1907]): xvii. Terry Castle points out that the 'imagery of contagion' is similarly applied to the ritualized disorder of the eighteenth-century masquerade. See Castle, *Masquerade and Civilization*: 85.

23. Susan Sontag, *AIDS and Its Metaphors* (New York: Farrar, Strauss, & Giroux, 1989): 45.

24. *Middle English Dictionary*, s.v. 'parody'.

25. see Walter W. Skeat, *An Etymological Dictionary of the English Language*. 1st edn, 1879–82 (Oxford: Clarendon Press, 1978), s.v. 'parody'.

26. Daniel Defoe, *A Journal of the Plague Year* (New York: Penguin, 1966): 23: 'It was about the beginning of September, 1664, that I, among the rest of my neighbours, heard in ordinary discourse that the plague was returned from Holland . . .'.

27. The remarks of F.R. Leavis are reprinted in *The New Oxford Book of Light Verse*, ed. Kingsley Amis (Oxford: Oxford University Press, 1978): xiv–xv.

28. Roger Henkle, *Comedy and Culture: England 1820–1900* (Princeton: Princeton University Press, 1980): 13.

29. 'Thackeray and Dickens', Henkle notes, 'conspicuously· begin their careers with parodies of writing styles that have become stultified or moribund'. See Henkle, *Comedy and Culture*: 13. Charles Newman, writing in 1985 of the counter-genre in post-modern fiction noted (with an apparent disregard for literary practitioners prior to the late twentieth century) that 'even beginning writers now start with parody rather than imitation'. Newman at least observes that such parodies succeed not by destroying their prede-cessors but by constructively building on the formulaic success of already-existing models. See Charles Newman, 'The Anxiety of Non-Influence' in *The Post-Modern Aura: Acts of Fiction in an Age of Inflation* (Evanston, Illinois: Northwestern University Press, 1985): 86–9.

30. Beerbohm's remarks on parody, which originally appeared in *A Christmas Garland, Woven by Max Beerbohm* (London: William Heinemann, 1912), are reprinted in Lawrence Danson's *Max Beerbohm and the Act of Writing* (Oxford: Oxford University Press, 1989): 27.

31. Danson, *Max Beerbohm and the Act of Writing*: 27.

32. For his discussion of the generality theory of value see Michael McKeon, *Politics and Poetry in Restoration England: The Case of Dryden's Annus Mirabilis* (Cambridge, Massachusetts: Harvard University Press, 1975): 2–3.

33. Samuel Johnson remarked to James Boswell that 'Nothing odd will do long. *Tristram Shandy* did not last'. See James Boswell, *Life of Johnson*, ed. R.W. Chapman (1904; rpt Oxford: Oxford University Press, 1980): 696.

34. See F.J. Lelièvre, 'The Basis of Ancient Parody' in *Greece and Rome*, 2nd series, I (1954): 78–9.

35. Ernst Cassirer, *Language and Myth*. trans. Susanne K. Langer (New York: Harper & Brothers, 1946): 36.

36. See David Riggs, *Ben Jonson: A Life* (Cambridge, Massachusetts: Harvard University Press, 1989): 9; see also Marchette Chute, *Ben Jonson of Westminster* (New York: Dutton, 1953): 14–16.

37. For some of the practicalities of brick making and brick building in the period, see Liza Picard, *Elizabeth's London: Everyday Life in Elizabethan London* (London: Weidenfeld & Nicolson, 2003): 42–4.
38. Riggs, *Ben Jonson: A Life*: 9.
39. Riggs, *Ben Jonson: A Life*: 53.
40. Chute, *Ben Jonson of Westminster*: 26–7.
41. See discussion by J.W. Lever, ed. in his Introduction to Ben Jonson, *Every Man in His Humour: A Parallel Text Edition of the 1601 Quarto and the 1616 Folio*. Regents Renaissance Drama Series (Lincoln, Nebraska: University of Nebraska Press, 1971): xi–xxiii.
42. Thomas Campbell, *Specimens of the British Poets* (London: 1819).
43. It is significant, too, that the first recorded use of the word 'plagiary' – in Joseph Hall's *Virgidemiarum* – also dates from 1598. See H.O. White, *Plagiarism and Imitation in the Renaissance: A Study in Critical Distinctions* (Cambridge, Massachusetts: Harvard University Press, 1935): 120–1.
44. Peter, *Complaint and Satire*: 133.
45. See Thomas P. Roche, Jr. *Petrarch and the English Sonnet Sequences* (New York: AMS, 1989): 114.
46. Chaucer's 'Thopas', L.H. Loomis went so far as to observe, is 'in no wise a parody of any one school of romance' though Chaucer may have taken 'hints and phrases' from any number of Middle English sources. J.A. Burrow, asserting that since Chaucer's poem is itself a burlesque it can therefore be compared to other medieval burlesques, traces indebtedness to the thirteenth-century French text *La Prise de Nuevile*. See J.H. Loomis in *Sources and Analogues of Chaucer's Canterbury Tales*, ed. W.F. Bryan and Germaine Dempster (Chicago: University of Chicago Press, 1941): 486–559; J.A. Burrow, 'Chaucer's *Sir Thopas* and *La Prise de Neuvile*' in *English Satire and the Satiric Tradition*, ed. Claude Rawson (Oxford: Basil Blackwell, 1984): 44–55. On Chaucerian parody, see also Joseph Dane, *Parody: Critical Concepts versus Literary Practice* (Norman, Oklahoma: University of Oklahoma Press, 1988): 185–203. For Skelton's parodies of the service of the dead, see John Skelton, *Complete English Poems*, ed. John Scattergood (New York: Penguin, 1983): 405–6.
47. On the *Gesta Romanorum* and the typical medieval practice of Christianizing secular lyrics such as 'The Nut-Brown Maid', see Peter, *Complaint and Satire in Early English Literature*: 52.
48. See Barbara Lewalski, *Protestant Poetics and the Seventeenth-Century Religious Lyric* (Princeton: Princeton University Press, 1979): 486, n.31; see also Rosamund Tuve, 'Sacred Parody of Love Poetry, and Herbert' in *Studies in the Renaissance*, 8 (1961): 249–90.
49. For a sample of the many answering poems in the sixteenth century see *Tottel's Miscellany 1557–1587*, ed. Hyder E. Rollins, 2 vols (Cambridge, Massachusetts: Harvard University Press, 1965), rev. edn of 1928, I: 201–2.
50. Peter, *Complaint and Satire in Early English Literature*: 39. See also Raman Selden, *English Verse Satire, 1590–1765* (London: Allen & Unwin, 1978): *passim*.
51. *The Works of Sir Thomas Browne*, ed. Geoffrey Keynes, 4 vols (Chicago: University of Chicago Press, 1964), iii: 245–6.
52. George de Forest Lord, gen. ed., *Poems on Affairs of State: Augustan Verse Satire, 1660–1714*, I (New Haven: Yale University Press, 1963): xxvii.

53. For Jonson's relationship to classical texts and the idea of authorship, see Howard Erskine-Hill, *The Augustan Idea in English Literature* (London: Edward Arnold, 1983): 169–74; Leo Braudy, *The Frenzy of Renown: Fame and Its History* (Oxford: Oxford University Press, 1986): 322–26.
54. Peter Stallybrass and Allon White, *The Politics and Poetics of Transgression* (Ithaca, New York: Cornell University Press, 1986): 66–79.
55. Stallybrass and White, *The Politics and Poetics of Transgression*: 76.
56. Richard Helgerson, *Self-Crowned Laureates: Spenser, Jonson, Milton, and the Literary System* (Berkeley: University of California Press, 1983): 103.
57. For Dryden's references to Jonson's poetic 'borrowings', see John Dryden, *Selected Criticism*, eds, James Kingsley and George Parfitt (Oxford: Clarendon Press, 1970): 55–66; 94–104; 120–30.
58. Stephen Orgel, 'The Renaissance Artist as Plagiary', in *ELH,* 48 (1981): 476–94.
59. See *Epig.* LVI: 8 and Q *EMI*: 322.
60. See *Conv.*: 34–7.
61. See *Poetaster* 'To the Reader', l.102 (*H & S*: 320).
62. See *Poetaster* 'To the Reader', l.112 (*H & S*: 320).
63. '[T]he War of the Theatres', Katherine Maus noted, 'renders Jonson acutely conscious of the vulnerability of [his] moral ideals to dramatic travesty'. See Katherine Maus, *Ben Jonson and the Roman Frame of Mind* (Princeton: Princeton University Press, 1984): 36. Robert Watson notes that while Jonson was not the only playwright to employ a complex parodic strategy (Shakespeare, Beaumont and Fletcher, Marston, Chapman, and Webster all 'made occasional gestures to show that they were sardonically alert to the traditions in which they worked'), Jonson 'deployed parodic strategy far more systematically and effectively than any of his rivals'. See Watson, *Jonson's Parodic Strategy*: 8–9.
64. For an excellent discussion of the parodic impulse in the seventeenth century as a form of literary 'ventriloquism' see Margaret Anne Doody, *The Daring Muse: Augustan Poetry Reconsidered* (Cambridge: Cambridge University Press, 1985): *passim.*
65. See *Timb.*: 2515–19. See Parfitt's edition of Jonson's prose (note 92, below).
66. See *Timb.*: 422–27.
67. See *Timb.*: 2387–89.
68. See *Timb.*: 914–16.
69. Harold Bloom, *The Anxiety of Influence: A Theory of Poetry* (Oxford: Oxford University Press, 1973): 26.
70. On the subject of parody generally, see Simon Dentith, *Parody*. The New Critical Idiom Series (London: Routledge, 2000): 1–38.
71. See Harold Love, *English Clandestine Satire, 1660–1704* (Oxford: Oxford University Press, 2004).
72. Mark Knights, *Representation and Misrepresentation in Later Stuart Britain: Partisanship and Political Culture* (Oxford: Oxford University Press, 2005).
73. See John G. Sweeney, '*Sejanus* and the People's Beastly Rage', in *ELH*, 48 (1981): 61–82.
74. Jonson, in *Works*, eds, Herford and Simpson, 'Prologue' l.25 (iv.206).
75. Jonson, in *Works*, eds, Herford and Simpson, iv: 323–4: *Poetaster, 'Apologetical Dialogue, To the Reader'* (ll.209–22). See also Wilkes, *Complete Plays*, ii.228.

76. Jonson, in *Works*, eds Herford and Simpson, iv.324: *Poetaster*, *'Apologetical Dialogue, To the Reader'* (ll.237–39. See also Wilkes, *Complete Plays*, ii.228).

77. Philip J. Ayres, ed., 'Introduction' to Ben Jonson, *Sejanus, His Fall*. The Revels Plays. (Manchester and New York: Manchester University Press, 1990): 9.

78. Ayres, 'Introduction', *Sejanus*: 10.

79. Ayres, 'Introduction', *Sejanus*: 11.

80. Katherine Duncan-Jones, 'Just a Jiglot', review of Ben Jonson's *Sejanus* (Swan Theatre, Stratford-upon-Avon) in the *Times Literary Supplement*, no. 5340 (5 August 2005): 18.

81. Note Oscar G. Brockett, 7th edn, 'European Theatre and Drama in the Middle Ages' in his *History of the Theatre* (London: Allyn and Bacon: 1995): 124–5.

82. See *The Treatise of Aeneas Sylvius Piccolomini*, in *De Liberorum Educatione* in *Vittorino da Feltre and Other Humanist Educators*, William Harrison Woodward, ed. (New York: Columbia University – Teachers College Press, 1897): 1963, 134–58; esp. 151.

83. See *The Revels History of Drama in English*, Gen. eds Clifford Leech and T.W. Craik. Volume III, eds J. Leeds Barroll, Alexander Legatt, Richard Hosley, Alvin Kernan (London: Methuen, 1975): 337.

84. For a succinct summation of the situation under Tiberius in general, and of the ambitions of Sejanus, see Marcel Le Glay, Jean-Louis Voisin and Yann Le Bohec, trans. Antonia Nevill, *A History of Rome* (Oxford: Blackwell Publishers, 1996): 231–5; note also Chris Scarre, *Chronicle of the Roman Emperors: the Reign-by-Reign Record of the Rulers of Imperial Rome* (London: Thames & Hudson, 1995): 31–5.

85. Jonson, in *Works*, eds, Herford and Simpson, iv (*Poetaster* I.36–7).

86. Ayres, 'Introduction', *Sejanus*: 16–17.

87. Ayres, 'Introduction', *Sejanus*: 19.

88. Ayres, 'Introduction', *Sejanus*: 8.

89. Katherine Duncan-Jones, 'Just a Jiglot': 18.

90. Stephen Booth, *King Lear, Macbeth, Indefinition and Tragedy* (New Haven: Yale University Press, 1982).

91. From Juvenal, Satire X. 365–6. See Peter Green, trans. Juvenal, *Sixteen Satires* (Harmondsworth: Penguin, 1967): 217, 225.

92. See Ben Jonson, *The Complete Poems*, ed. George Parfitt (New Haven and London: Yale University Press, 1975) from the *Underwoods: Consisting of Diverse Poems*, 'An Execration Upon Vulcan' ll. 204–8: 187.

4 Minding True Things by Mock'ries: The *Henry V* Chorus and The Question of Shakespearean Parody

1. Jonson, in *Works*, eds. Herford and Simpson.

2. *Dictionary of the English Language*, Samuel Johnson, ed. (London: 1755), s.v. 'chorus'.

3. Johnson's *Dictionary* cites only ll.31–2. See *Henry V*, Prologue. 28–34, in William Shakespeare, *Complete Works*, ed. Alfred Harbage (New York: The Viking Press, 1977). All quotations to Shakespeare's work refer to this edition and will be cited in the text.

4. On the nature of the Chorus in classical drama see Graham Ley, *A Short Introduction to the Ancient Greek Theatre* (Chicago and London: University of Chicago Press, 1991): 22–5.

5. *Dictionary of the English Language*, 2nd edn, s.v. 'Chorus'.

6. Samuel Johnson, *Johnson on Shakespeare*, 2 vols (New Haven: Yale University Press, 1968), II: 528.

7. Johnson, II: 535.

8. Johnson, I: 97–8. It is now generally agreed that the last two lines of the Chorus ('But, till the king come forth, and not till then/Unto Southampton do we shift our scene') were added to the original speech to explain the comic episode involving Bardolph, Nym, and Pistol, still set in London, which follows at II.i.

9. Johnson, II: 566.

10. See Johnson, I: 73.

11. Samuel Taylor Coleridge, *Shakespeare Criticism*, 2 vols (London: J.M. Dent, 1960), II: 57.

12. William Hazlitt, *Complete Works*, ed. P.P. Howe (London: J.M. Dent 1930), IV: 287–9.

13. See, for example, Alfred Harbage, ed., *William Shakespeare: The Complete Works* (New York: The Viking Press, 1977): 741–4.

14. Ivo Kamps, 'Materialist Shakespeare: An Introduction', in *Materialist Shakespeare: A History*, ed. Ivo Kamps (London: Verso, 1995): 15.

15. Warren D. Smith, 'The *Henry V* Choruses in the First Folio', in *Journal of English and Germanic Philology*, LIII, no. 1 (1954): 38–57.

16. G.P. Jones, '*Henry V*: The Chorus and the Audience', in *Shakespeare Survey*, 31 (1978): 93–104.

17. Lawrence Danson, '*Henry V*: King, Chorus, and Critics', in *Shakespeare Quarterly*, 34, no. 1 (1983): 27–43.

18. Cited by Moody E. Prior in *The Dream of Power: Studies in Shakespeare's History Plays* (Evanston, Illinois: Northwestern University Press, 1973): 312.

19. Dean Frye, 'The Question of Shakespearean Parody' in *Essays in Criticism*, xv (1965): 23.

20. Lamb, writing in a letter to Thomas Manning in 1803, joked 'You are Frenchified. Both your tastes and morals are corrupt and perverted. By and by you will come to assert that Bonaparte is as great a general as the old Duke of Cumberland, and deny that one Englishman can beat three Frenchmen. Read *Henry the Fifth* to restore your orthodoxy'. Charles Lamb, *Complete Works and Letters* (New York: Modern Library, 1935): 734.

21. See William Babula, *Shakespeare in Production, 1935–1978* (London: Garland Publishing, 1981): 100–108.

22. Adrian Noble, dir., *Henry V* by William Shakespeare, with Kenneth Branagh, Royal Shakespeare Theatre, Stratford-upon-Avon, March–September, 1984.

23. Kenneth Branagh, dir. *Henry V* (M.G.M., 1989). Starring Derek Jacobi, Kenneth Branagh, and Simon Shepherd.

24. See Pauline Kael, 'Second Takes,' in *The New Yorker*, 27 November 1989: 105.

25. See Nicholas Shrimpton, 'Shakespeare performance in Stratford-upon-Avon and London, 1983–4,' in *Shakespeare Survey*, 38 (1985): 204–7.

26. Anne Righter, *Shakespeare and the Idea of the Play* (New York: Penguin Books, 1967); Francis Fergusson, *The Idea of a Theatre* (Princeton: Princeton University Press, 1949): 12.

27. Thomas Tomkis, *Lingua*. 1607; rpt Tudor Facsimile Texts, 1912.
28. *Jack Juggler*, 1553; rpt Tudor Facsimile Texts, 1912.
29. *The Triall of Treasure*, 1567; rpt Tudor Facsimile Texts, 1908.
30. *Tom Tyler*, 1661[c.1540]; rpt Tudor Facsimile Texts, 1912.
31. George Wapull, *The Tide Tarrieth No Man*, 1576; rpt Tudor Facsimile Texts, 1910.
32. *The History of the Two Valiant Knights Sir Clyomon and Clamydes*, 1599; rpt Tudor Facsimile Texts, 1913. Prologue 15–16.
33. *Wily Beguiled*, 1660; rpt Tudor Facsimile Texts, 1912. Prologue 1–46.
34. *David and Bethsabe*, Prologue, 16–20, in *Pre-Shakespearean Drama*, A.H. Thorndike, ed. (London: J.M. Dent & Sons, 1910).
35. My reading here of *Henry V* as a drama that focuses on the transformed role of the king – and, indeed, on a transformed notion of what 'kingship' is all about – through its attitudes towards ritual and ceremony, of course owes much to Alvin B. Kernan's masterful discussion of the play in his 'The Henriad: Shakespeare's Major History Plays' in *Modern Essays in Shakespearean Criticism: Essays in Style, Dramaturgy, and the Major Plays*, Alvin B. Kernan, ed. (New York: Harcourt Brace Jovanovich, 1970): 245–75.

5   John Dryden and Homeopathic Parody in the Early Augustan Battleground

1. *The Poems and Letters of Andrew Marvell*, ed. H.M. Margoliouth, 2 vols (Oxford: Clarendon Press, 1927): I, 3.
2. On this 'protective' aspect of late-seventeenth-century parody and the concept of literary 'ventriloquism', see Margaret Anne Doody, *The Daring Muse*: 30–56.
3. See *The Poems of John Cleveland*, ed. Brian Morris and Eleanor Withington (Oxford: Clarendon Press, 1967): 27.
4. The text of the first edition of Robert Wild's *Iter Boreale* is reprinted in the first volume of George DeF. Lord's 1963 collection of *Poems on Affairs of State* (New Haven: Yale University Press, 1963): 2–19.
5. See A.C. Hamilton's gloss on Spenser's lines in his edition of *The Faerie Queene* (London: Longman, 1977): 27.
6. See *The Poems of John Wilmot, Earl of Rochester*, ed. Keith Walker (Oxford: Basil Blackwell, 1984), 'A Letter from Artemiza in the Towne to Chloe in the Countrey': 83.
7. See Edmund Waller, *Poems, &c. Written upon several occasions and to several persons . . .* (London: H. Herringman, 1664).
8. See Terry Belanger, 'Publishers and Writers in Eighteenth-Century England', in *Books and Their Readers in Eighteenth-Century England*, ed. Isabel Rivers (London: St. Martin's Press, 1982): 5–25; Natalie Davis, 'Printing and the People', in *Society and Culture in Early Modern France* (Stanford: Stanford University Press, 1975): 189–226; Elizabeth Eisenstein, 'Some Conjecture about the Impact of Printing on Western Society and Thought', in *The Journal of Modern History*, 40 (1968): 1–56; David Foxon in *Pope and the Early Eighteenth-Century Book Trade*, rev. and ed. James McLaverty (Oxford: Oxford University Press, 1991): 237–51; John Guillory, *Cultural Capital: The Problem*

of Literary Canon Formation (Chicago: University of Chicago Press, 1991); Alvin Kernan, *Printing Technology, Letters, and Samuel Johnson* (Princeton: Princeton University Press, 1987); Jonathan Brody Kramnick, *Making the English Canon: Print Capitalism and the Cultural Past, 1700–1770* (Cambridge: Cambridge University Press, 1998).

9. See Walter Benjamin, 'The Work of Art in the Age of Mechanical Reproduction', in *Illuminations*, Hannah Arendt, ed., H. Zohn, trans. (London: New Left Books, 1977). See also Samuel Johnson, *The Rambler*, no. 23 (5 June 1750), in *Samuel Johnson*, Donald Greene, ed. (Oxford: Oxford University Press, 1984): 184.

10. see Jürgen Habermas, *The Structural Transformation of the Public Sphere*. trans. Thomas Burger (Cambridge, Massachusetts: Harvard University Press, 1989). Habermas's volume had originally appeared in 1962. One of the most succinct and helpful discussions of the manner in which the notion of the public sphere can be seen to play an important role in the new print culture of the era can be found in David Fairer's *English Poetry of the Eighteenth Century 1700–1789* (London: Pearson Education, 2003): 3–5.

11. Kernan, *Printing Technology, Letters, and Samuel Johnson*: 6. See also James Boswell, *Life of Johnson*, R.W. Chapman, ed. (Oxford: Oxford University Press, 1980): 379–84.

12. Stallybrass and White, *The Politics and Poetics of Transgression*: 61.

13. See *The Poems and Letters of Andrew Marvell*, ed. H.M. Margoliouth: I, 3.

14. On this 'underclass' see, for example, James M. Levine, *The Battle of the Books: History and Literature in the Augustan Age* (Ithaca and London: Cornell University Press, 1991): *passim*.

15. My thoughts on this contrived separation of 'high' and 'low' culture, and the persistent attempts of authors in the eighteenth century to keep these barriers firmly in place, were stimulated by – and no doubt owe something of their current expression to – a lecture given by Dr. Brean Hammond, of the University of Liverpool, at Princeton University on 4 Oct. 1989, entitled 'Guarding the Barrier: Pope and the Partitioning of Culture.' see B.S. Hammond, *Professional Imaginative Writing in England: 1670–1740: 'Hackney for Bread'.* Oxford: Clarendon Press, 1997, *passim*.

16. *The Works of John Dryden*, ed. Edward Niles Hooker, H.T. Swedenberg Jr., *et al.* (20 vols, in progress, Berkeley and Los Angeles: University of California Press, 1956–): I.17. Quotations from Dryden's poetry will follow this edition, and will be cited in the text. Quotations from Dryden's critical prose have been taken from *John Dryden: Selected Criticism*, eds James Kinsley and George Parfitt (Oxford: Clarendon Press, 1970), and will be cited in the text by page number.

17. McKeon uses the phrase 'pattern of reversal' to describe the process of critique and counter-critique, which leads to the formulation of new genres (such as the novel) and new ideologies. See Michael McKeon, 'Generic Transformation and Social Change: Rethinking the Rise of the Novel', in *Modern Essays in Eighteenth-Century Literature*, ed. Leopold Damrosch, Jr. (Oxford: Oxford University Press, 1988): 159–80. McKeon's article originally appeared in *Cultural Critique*, 1 (1985): 159–81.

18. H.T. Swedenberg, *et. al.*, eds. *The Works of John Dryden*: II, 250.

19. Jack's comments originally appeared in his *Augustan Satire, 1660–1750* (Oxford: Clarendon Press, 1962), p. 68n. They are reprinted in *The Works of John Dryden*: 250.

20. Tomkis's *Albumazar* – first performed before James I at Cambridge in 1615 – was revived on 22 February 1668, at Lincoln's Inn Fields. The revival – Dryden's new prologue notwithstanding – was not a success. Pepys commented of Tomkis's play: 'I do not see anything extraordinary in it, but was indeed weary of it before it was done.' Tomkis's play would be revived more successfully in 1747 (with Dryden's Prologue spoken by David Garrick). See *The London Stage 1660–1700*, ed. William Van Lennep (Carbondale: Southern Illinois University Press, 1965): 130.

21. See Hugh Ormsby-Lennon, 'Poetic Standards in the Early Augustan Battle-ground' in *Studies in Eighteenth-Century Culture*, 5 (1976), ed. Ronald C. Rosbottom (Madison, Wisconsin: University of Wisconsin Press, 1976): 253–80.

22. George McFadden, *Dryden, the Public Writer, 1660–1685* (Princeton: Princeton University Press, 1978), 72–9.

23. James Anderson Winn, *John Dryden and His World* (New Haven: Yale University Press, 1987): 189–91. See also Dennis D. Arundell, *Dryden and Howard: 1664–1668* (Cambridge: Cambridge University Press, 1929).

24. Note George Williamson, 'The Occasion of an *Essay of Dramatic Poesy*' in *Essential Articles for the Study of John Dryden*, ed. H.T. Swedenberg (London: Frank Cass., 1966), 65–82. While tracing one of the particular occasions of the 'Essay of Dramatic Poesy' through a previously unidentified allusion in the piece, Williamson notes that Dryden's 'dual motivation' renders the criticism 'like most of his essays, both occasional *and* general in nature', and keeps its special place in his criticism by virtue of its 'ambitious program, disciplined form, and basic principles'.

25. Note James Anderson Winn's remarks in the preface to his *John Dryden and His World*, xvi: 'To say "we" as Dryden habitually does is to make a gesture of inclusion. If the group included by the "we" varies from the nation as a whole to some smaller particular group to the poet himself in the role as the monarch of one of his literary kingdoms, it is virtually never the intimate couple of Donne's love poems.... Nor is it normally an exclusive club of those who already agree; Dryden's inclusive "we" invites us to join him in the consideration of religious truth, political propriety, and literary excellence'.

26. George Steiner, *After Babel*: 23.

27. For some accounts of the Rose Alley Ambuscade see George DeF. Lord's *Poems on Affairs of State*: I, 396–9; James Winn, *John Dryden and His World*: 325–30.

28. The *Essay upon Satire* of John Sheffield, Earl of Mulgrave, is reprinted in *Poems on Affairs of State*: I, 396–413.

29. George Villiers, Duke of Buckingham, *The Rehearsal*, I.i.110–12. Buckingham's play is reprinted in *Burlesque Plays of the Eighteenth Century*, ed. Simon Tressler (Oxford: Oxford University Press, 1969): 1–54.

30. A postscript signed J.D. added to a 1681 reprinting of Dryden's 1659 poem on Cromwell (*Heroic Stanzas to the Glorious Memory of Cromwell*) made similar use of the same lines from *The Conquest of Granada* ('Then I'll go, for libels

I declare/Best friends no more than worst of foes I'll spare/And all this I can do because I dare'). The postscript is reprinted in *Poems on Affairs of State*, ed. Elias F. Mengel, Jr., II, 500.

31. For a recent discussion of Dryden's 'theory of satire' in the 'Discourse Concerning the Original and Progress of Satire' see William Frost, *John Dryden: Dramatist, Satirist, Translator* (New York: AMS Press, 1988): 41–70.
32. Shadwell's parody is reprinted in *Poems on Affairs of State*: III, 75–95.
33. See 'Dryden and Langbaine,' in James M. Osborn's *John Dryden: Some Biographical Facts and Problems* (Gainesville: University of Florida Press, 1905), 234–40.
34. Louis Bredvold, *The Intellectual Milieu of John Dryden* (Ann Arbor: University of Michigan Press, 1934): 20.
35. Note Winn, *John Dryden and His World*: 428. 'Dryden's friend Frances Lockier remembered him weeping over [*The Hind and the Panther Transvers'd*...] exclaiming at the cruelty of "two young fellows that I have always been very civil to" and calling himself "an old man in misfortunes" '.
36. See Michael McKeon, *Politics and Poetry in Restoration England: The Case of Dryden's Annus Mirabilis* (Cambridge: Harvard University Press, 1975): 250.
37. These include the anonymous *Absalom's Conspiracy; or, The Tragedy of Treason* (1680), and John Caryll's 1679 *Naboth's Vineyard, or the Innocent Traytor*. See Miner, *Dryden's Poetry*: 107; note also R.F. Jones, 'The Originality of *Absalom and Achitophel*,' *MLN*, XLVI (1931): 211–18.
38. Samuel Johnson *Lives of the English Poets*, 2 vols (London: J.M. Dent, 1925): I, 190; 256–7.
39. T.S. Eliot, 'John Dryden' in *Selected Essays* (London: Faber & Faber, 1932): 307.
40. Ian Jack, *Augustine Satire: Intention and Idiom in English Poetry 1660–1750* (Oxford: Clarendon Press, 1952): 51.
41. Hugh Macdonald, 'The Attacks on Dryden,' in *Essential Articles for the Study of John Dryden*: 32.
42. David Hopkins, *John Dryden* (Cambridge: Cambridge University Press, 1986): 42.
43. *Twentieth-Century Literature in Retrospect*, ed. Reuben A. Brower (Cambridge, Mass.: Harvard University Press, 1971): 47.
44. See James M. Osborn, *John Dryden: Some Biographical Facts and Problems* (New York: Columbia University Press, 1940): 155.
45. Luttrell's remarks are reprinted in the California Dryden. See Dryden, *Works*, II, 209.
46. The *Declaration to All His Loving Subjects, Touching the Causes & Reasons that Moved Him to Dissolve the Two Last Parliaments* was published on 8 April. See Winn, *John Dryden*: 342–50 and 596n.
47. On the basis for this attribution see Winn, *John Dryden*: 343.
48. [Henry Care] *Towser the Second, A Bull-Dog. Or a Short Reply to Absalom and Achitophel* (London: 1681).
49. Earl Miner, *Dryden's Poetry* (Bloomington: Indiana University Press, 1967): 112.
50. 'Poetical Reflections on a Late Poem Entitled *Absalom and Achitophel*' (London: Richard Janeway, 1681).
51. 'A Panegyrick on the Author of *Absalom and Achitophel*' (London: Charles Leigh, 1681).

52. See *Poems on Affairs of State*: II, 500.
53. See *Poems on Affairs of State*: II, 500.
54. [Christopher Nesse] 'A Whip for the Fools Back, Who Styles Honourable Marriage a Curs'd Confinement' (London: T. Dawks, 1681; 'A Key (With the Whip) To Open the Mystery and Iniquity of the Poem Called, *Absalom and Achitophel*' (London: T. Snowden, 1681).
55. 'Absalom's IX Worthies: Or a Key to the late Book or Poem, Entitled A. B. & A. C.' (London: 1682).
56. Samuel Pordage, *Azariah and Hushai* (London: 1682). Reprinted in *Anti-Achitophel* (1682), ed. Harold Whitmore Jones (Gainesville: Scholar's Facsimiles and Reprints, 1961): 73.
57. Hopkins, *John Dryden*: 3.
58. Hopkins, *John Dryden*: 88.

6 Parodying Pope's *Eloisa to Abelard:* Richard Owen Cambridge's *An Elegy Written in an Empty Assembly Room*

1. Richard Owen Cambridge, *The Scribleriad: An Heroic Poem. In Six Books* (London: 1751): Preface, vii; v–vi.
2. See, for example, the amount of attention devoted to *Eloisa to Abelard* and to the poetic form of the verse letter more generally in David Fairer's superb survey, *English Poetry of the Eighteenth Century, 1700–1789*. Longman Literature in English Series (London: Pearson Education Ltd., 2003), 60–78.
3. Charles Kerby-Miller, ed. *The Memoirs of the Extraordinary Life, Works, and Discourses of Martinus Scriblerus* (Oxford: Oxford University Press, 1950; rpt 1988); Steven Shankman, ed. *The Iliad of Homer, Translated by Alexander Pope* (London: Penguin, 1996).
4. See Cleanth Brooks, 'The Case of Miss Arabelle Fermor' in *The Well-Wrought Urn* (New York: Harcourt, Brace, 1947): 80–104; J.S. Cunningham, *The Rape of the Lock* (London: Arnold, 1961).
5. On this designation and its significance to Pope's later career, see Miriam Leranbaum, *Alexander Pope's 'Opus Magnum' 1729–1744* (Oxford: Clarendon Press, 1977).
6. Johnson's comment is recorded in his critical observations on Pope in *Prefaces, Biographical and Critical, to the Work of the English Poets*. See *Samuel Johnson*, ed. Donald Greene (Oxford: Oxford University Press, 1984): 744.
7. The volume edited by G.S. Rousseau and Pat Rogers for the tercentenary in 1988, for example – *The Enduring Legacy: Alexander Pope Tercentenary Essays* (Cambridge: Cambridge University Press, 1988) – while devoting separate subsections on the *Essay on Man*, 'Pope translations', and even 'Pope and Women', contained only a passing reference to *Eloisa and Abelard*. A typical earlier selection of essays, *The Art of Alexander Pope*, edited by Howard Erskine-Hill and Anne Smith (London: Vision Press, 1979), had contained only one essay that devoted itself (at least partially) to Pope's 1717 poem.
8. See David Fairer, *Pope's Imagination* (Manchester: Manchester University Press, 1984): 25.

9. See David B. Morris, 'The Visionary Maid: Tragic Poetics and Redemptive Sympathy in *Eloisa to Abelard*' in *Modern Critical Views: Alexander Pope*, ed. Harold Bloom (New York: Chelsea House, 1982): 62–66.
10. Morris, 'The Visionary Maid': 68.
11. Maynard Mack, *Alexander Pope: A Life* (New Haven and London: Yale University Press, 1985): 323.
12. Mack, *Alexander Pope: A Life*: 329; on the conjectured date of the composition of Pope's poem see Geoffrey Tillotson, ed. *The Rape of the Lock and Other Poems* (London: Methuen, 1940): 311–12. See also Pope, *Correspondence*, I.338.
13. For a convenient summary of the eighteenth-century parodies and imitations of Pope's *Eloisa to Abelard* (a summary from which, however, Richard Owen Cambridge's parody, discussed below, is omitted), see Lawrence Wright, 'Eighteenth-Century Replies to Pope's *Eloisa to Abelard*' in *Studies in Philology*, XXXI (1934), 519–33.
14. All quotations from the poetry of Alexander Pope in this chapter are taken from *The Poems of Alexander Pope*, ed. John Butt (London: Methuen, 1963).
15. Pope, in a conversation with Joseph Spence in February 1744: [Spence]: 'After my reading a canto of Spenser two or three days ago to an old lady between seventy and eighty, she said that I had been showing her a collection of pictures'. [Pope.]: 'She was very right, and I don't know how it is but there's something in Spenser that pleases me as strongly in one's old age as it did in one's youth. I read the *Faerie Queene* when I was about twelve with a vast deal of delight, and I think it gave me as much when I read it a year or two ago'. The anecdote is reprinted in Edmund Spenser: *A Critical Anthology*, ed. Paul J. Alpers (New York: Penguin, 1969): 96.
16. Mack, *Alexander Pope: A Life*: 132.
17. Horace Walpole, *The Letters of Horace Walpole*, ed. Paget Toynbee (Oxford: Clarendon Press, 1903–25): iii. 318.
18. Gibbon's characterization is included within James Sambrook's entry on Cambridge in the revised *DNB*. See James Sambrook, 'Cambridge, Richard Owen (1717–1802)', *Oxford Dictionary of National Biography*, Oxford: Oxford University Press, 2004 [accessed online 15 June 2005]: http://www/oxforddnb.com/view/article/4430]
19. Richard D. Altick, *Richard Owen Cambridge: Belated Augustan* (Philadelphia: University of Pennsylvania Press, 1941): 108.
20. Eric Rothstein, *Restoration and Eighteenth-Century Poetry* (London: Routledge and Kegan Paul, 1981): 131; 215.
21. See Margaret Anne Doody, *Frances Burney: The Life in the Works* (New Brunswick, New Jersey: Rutgers University Press, 1989): 151.
22. See Michael F. Suarez, S.J., ed., Robert Dodsley's *A Collection of Poems by Several Hands,* VI vols (New York: Routledge, 2001), i.131.
23. See James Sambrook, 'Cambridge, Richard Owen (1717–1802)' in *Oxford Dictionary of National Biography* (2004); note also Eric Rothstein, *Restoration and Eighteenth-Century Poetry*: 131; 215. See also Allen G. Debus, ' *The Scribleriad*: Alchemy in the Eighteenth-Century Mock-Heroic Poem' in *Clauda Pavonis: Studies in Hermiticism* 20, no. 2 (Fall 2001): 19–24.

24. Robert Paltock's novel received a well-deserved reprinting when it was included as part of Oxford's World's Classics series in 1990 edited by Christopher Bentley, with an Introduction by James Grantham Turner.

25. The *Elegy* first appeared on 11 April 1756. Two subsequent editions were published on 2 May and 5 May that same year. See Altick, *Richard Owen Cambridge*: 149 and Ralph Straus, *Robert Dodsley, Poet, Publisher and Playwright* (London: John Lane, 1910): 359.

26. Horace Walpole, *The Letters of Horace Walpole*, ed. Paget Toynbee (Oxford: Oxford University Press, 1903–25): iii.114.

27. John Martin, 'Townshend, Etheldreda, Viscountess Townshend' (*c.* 1708–1788) in *Oxford Dictionary of National Biography*. Oxford: Oxford University Press, 2004 [accessed online 7 December 2004: http://www/oxforddnb.com/view/article/4430.]

28. Martin, 'Townshend, Etheldreda' in *DNB*.

29. Erroll Sherson, *The Lively Lady Townshend and Her Friends* (London: William Heinemann, 1924): 1.

30. See Altick, *Richard Owen Cambridge*: 125. The identification was first made by W.P. Courtney in *Dodsley's Collection of Poems: Its Contents and Contributors* (London: Printed for private circulation, 1910).

31. Walpole, *Letters*: iii.396.

32. Rosemary Baird, *Mistress of the House: Great Ladies and Grand Houses, 1670–1830* (London: Weidenfeld and Nicholson, 2003): 145.

33. Walpole, *Letters*: iii.396.

34. Christopher Simon Sykes, *Private Palaces: Life in the Great London Houses* (London: Viking, 1986): 129.

35. Sykes, *Private Palaces*: 129.

36. The contemporary description of the exterior of Norfolk House is included in Desmond Fitzgerald, *The Norfolk Music Room* (London, 1973): 49; it is reprinted in Christopher Sykes, *Private Palaces*: 130.

37. David Fairer, *English Poetry of the Eighteenth Century, 1700–1789* (London: Pearson Education Limited, 2003): 60.

38. *The Art of Poetry on a New Plan: Illustrated with a Great Variety of Excerpts from the English Poets; and of translations from the Ancients* 2 vols (London: Newberry, 1762): i.116–17.

39. Fairer, *English Poetry of the Eighteenth Century*: 60.

40. On the development of a specific terminology to describe the potential range of parodic functions in literary texts, see Simon Dentith, *Parody*: esp. 9–38; 190–5. Note also Linda Hutcheon's *A Theory of Parody* (London: Methuen, 1985): 1–29.

41. Alexander Pope, 'Eloisa to Abelard' in *The Poems of Alexander Pope*, ed. John Butt (London: Methuen., 1963). All references to Pope's original poem are to this edition.

42. Jacob H. Adler, *The Reach of Art: A Study of the Prosody of Pope* (Gainesville, Florida: University of Florida Press, 1964): 51.

43. R.D.S. Jack, 'Pope's Medieval Heroine: Eloisa to Abelard' in *Alexander Pope: Essays for the Tercentenary*, ed. Colin Nicholson (Aberdeen: University of Aberdeen Press, 1988): 206–7.

44. Jack, 'Pope's Medieval Heroine': 207.

45. Tillotson, in his edition of *Eloisa to Abelard*, notes many of the phrases borrowed by Pope's Eloisa from the Hughes retelling of Abelard's letters. See Tillotson, *The Rape of the Lock and Other Poems*: 334–49. Note also D.W. Robertson's account of the history of the texts of the medieval romance and its imitations in his thorough *Abelard and Heloise* (New York: Dial Press, 1972). A more recent account of the romance (James Burge's *Heloise & Abelard: A Twelfth-Century Love Story* [London: Profile Books, 2003.]) makes no mention of Pope's poem or its imitations.
46. See James E. Wellington, ed., *Eloisa to Abelard, by Alexander Pope, with the Hughes Letters* (Miami: University of Miami Press, 1965): 114n.
47. David Morris, 'The Visionary Maid: Tragic Poetics and Redemptive Sympathy in *Eloisa to Abelard*' in *Modern Critical Views: Alexander Pope*, ed. Harold Bloom (New York: Chelsea House, 1982): 72–3.
48. David Hume, 'Of Personal Identity' in his *Treatise of Human Nature*, 2 vols (London: J.M. Dent, 1968): i.238–49. See also Morris, 'The Visionary Maid': 72–3.
49. Thomas Hobbes, *Leviathan* (New York: Penguin, 1968): 217.
50. John Locke, *An Essay concerning Human Understanding*, ed. Peter H. Nidditch (Oxford: Clarendon Press, 1975): 113; 335. E.T. Higgins (1987), 'Self-Discrepancy: A Theory Relating Self and Affect' in *Psychological Review* 94: 319–40; cited in Richard P. Bentall, *Madness Explained: Psychosis and Human Nature* (London: Allan Lane, 2003): 250–1.
51. Morris, 'The Visionary Maid': 72–3.

7   Parody, Autobiography, and the Novel: *A Narrative of the Life of Mrs Charlotte Charke* and *The History of Henry Dumont, Esq., and Miss Charlotte Evelyn*

1. J.P. Donleavy, as quoted by David Lodge, 'Happiness and the Novel', The Happiness Lectures, BBC Radio 4 Features Archive. See www.bbc.co.uk/radio4/discover/archives_features.
2. All references to Whyte's account are to 'Account of a Visit to Mrs. Charlotte Charke, by Samuel Whyte of Dublin', in David Erskine Baker, *Biographia Dramatica* (London: 1782): 106–7. Baker's original 1764 work, edited by Stephen Jones, was updated by Isaac Reed in 1782, and is generally credited with giving wider currency to Whyte's account of Charke's circumstances towards the end of her life. Whyte's description was also published under the heading 'Anecdote of Mrs Charke' in the *Monthly Mirror* (June 1794, from British Library unprinted scrapbook 939.b.1).
3. Arnold Bennett, *Riceyman Steps* (Chicago: Academy Chicago Publishers, 1984): 11.
4. On the historical industries of Clerkenwell, see *Greater London*, eds J.T. Coppock and Hugh C. Prince (London: Faber & Faber, 1964): 231–4.
5. Peter Ackroyd, *London: The Biography* (London: Vintage, 2001): 469.
6. Ackroyd, *London*: 471.
7. On Whyte's relationship with the Sheridan family, see Percy Fitzgerald, *The Lives of the Sheridans* (Dublin: 1886): I.25. Whyte reprinted some of the correspondence that passed between himself and Frances Sheridan and her

husband, and which includes mention of her work for the stage as well as her enormously popular 1761 novel, *Memoirs of Sidney Bidulph* in his *Miscellanea Nova 1800* (New York and London: Garland, 1974). See also Fintan O'Toole, *A Traitor's Kiss: The Life of Richard Brinsley Sheridan* (London: Granta Books, 1997): 22–3; Linda Kelly, *Richard Brinsley Sheridan: A Life* (London: Sinclair-Stevenson, 1997): 15–16.

8. See Samuel Whyte, 'The Theatre' in *A Collection of Poems on Various Subjects*... (Dublin: 1792): 1–44.

9. Charlotte Charke, *A Narrative of the Life of Mrs Charlotte Charke*. Edited with an Introduction and Notes by Robert Rehder (London: Pickering and Chatto, 1999): 139. All references to Charke's *Narrative* are to this edition. Charke's autobiography had originally appeared as *A Narrative of the Life of Mrs Charlotte Charke, Youngest Daughter of Colley Cibber, Esq.* (London: A. Dodd, W. Reeve, and E. Cooke, 1755). On the Cibber Family generally, see Leonard Ashley, 'Colley Cibber: A Bibliography' in *Restoration and Eighteenth-Century Theatre Research*, vol. 6: 14–27; 51–75. Also: Richard Hindry Barker, *Mr. Cibber of Drury Lane* New York: 1939; William Burling, 'Theophilus Cibber and the Experimental Theatre Season of 1723 at Drury Lane' in *Theatre History Studies* vol. 7: 3–11; Helen Coone, *Colley Cibber: A Biography* (1986). Cibber's controversial 1740 autobiography, *An Apology for the Life of Colley Cibber*, was reprinted in an annotated edition by B.R.S Fone (Ann Arbor, Michigan: University of Michigan Press, 1974), and again as *A Critical Edition of 'The Life of Mr. Colley Cibber, Comedian*, ed. John Maurice Evans (New York: Garland, 1987). Noteworthy studies relating specifically to Charke in addition to those specifically referred to below include the several essays brought together in Philip E. Baruth, ed., *Introducing Charlotte Charke: Actress, Author, Enigma* (Urbana, Illinois: University of Illinois Press, 1999); Charles D. Peavey, 'The Chimerical Career of Charlotte Charke' in *Restoration and Eighteenth-Century Theatre Research* 8.1 (1969): 1–12.

10. Edmund Burke, in 'The Reformer' no. 7, 10.3.47/48, quoted in A.P. Samuels, *The Early Life of Edmund Burke* (Cambridge: Cambridge University Press, 1923).

11. See Whyte, 'Account of a Visit to Mrs Charlotte Charke...': 106–7.

12. See J.P. Hardy, 'Introduction' to Samuel Johnson, *The History of Rasselas Prince of Abissinia* (Oxford: Oxford University Press, 1968): ix.

13. The notice appeared in the *Gentleman's Magazine* (February, 1756): 95. 'The copy [of the novel] in the British library', as Robert Rehder has observed, 'has no indication of the price'. Even so, Rehder notes, 'the *Narrative* sold for two shillings and sixpence. At that price, Charke's fifty copies of her novel are worth six pounds five shillings, and the sale of 100 copies would allow the publishers to gross 25 per cent more than their investment'. See Rehder, ed. *Narrative*: li.

14. All references to Charke's novel will be cited parenthetically in the text and are taken from *The History of Henry Dumont, Esq., and Miss Charlotte Evelyn* (London, 1756).

15. On the possible connections between cross-dressing and same-sex involvements in the Hanoverian era in general, and in addition to those concerned exclusively with Charke (noted below), see G.S. Rousseau, *Perilous Enlightenment* (Manchester: Manchester University Press, 1991); also Kristina Straub, *Sexual Suspects: Eighteenth-Century Players and Sexual Ideology* (Princeton: Princeton University Press, 1992).

16. On Charke's transvestism, see Terry Castle, 'The Culture of Travesty: Sexuality and Masquerade in Eighteenth-Century England' in G.S. Rousseau and Roy Porter, eds, *Sexual Underworlds of the Enlightenment* (Chapel Hill, North Carolina: University of North Carolina Press, 1988): 156–80; note as well Castle's more comprehensive discussion of sexuality, travesty, and disguise in her *Masquerade and Civilization: The Carnivalesque in Eighteenth-Century English Culture and Fiction* (Stanford, California: Stanford University Press, 1986). Note also Pat Rogers, 'The Breeches Part' in *Sexuality in Eighteenth-Century Britain*, ed. Paul-Gabriel Boucé (Manchester: Manchester University Press, 1982): 244–58; Sallie Mintner Strange, 'Charlotte Charke: Transvestite or Conjurer' in *Restoration and Eighteenth-Century Theatre Research*, 15, no. 2 (1976), 54–9; Annie Woodhouse, *Fantastic Women: Sex, Gender, and Transvestism* (New Brunswick, New Jersey: Rutgers University Press, 1989); also, in Baruth, *Introducing Charlotte Charke*, cited above, see specifically the following: Joseph Chaney, 'Turning to Men: Genres of Cross-Dressing in Charke's *Narrative* and Shakespeare's *The Merchant of Venice*', and Kristina Straub, 'The Guilty Pleasures of Female Theatrical Cross-Dressing and the Autobiography of Charlotte Charke'; and, finally, Fraser Easton, 'Bad Habits: Cross-Dressing and the Regulation of Gender in Eighteenth-Century British Literature and Society', Dissertation Abstracts International 51, no. 3 (August 1993): 861A.
17. Fidelis Morgan, *The Well-Known Troublemaker: A Life of Charlotte Charke* (London: Faber, 1988): 199–200.
18. On this issue see, especially, Polly Stevens Fields, 'High Drama in the Little Theatre, 1730–37: Henry Fielding, Eliza Haywood, Charlotte Charke and Company' in Dissertation Abstracts International 54, no. 2 (August 1993), 530A-531A. To a certain extent, Charke's own departure was simply the result of the unusually volatile and unstable nature of the London theatre world at that particular moment in time. Sir Walpole's Stage Licensing Act of 1737 – a bill that had been created largely in response to Henry Fielding's political satire *The Historical Register for 1736* (in which Charke has herself played a part) – exercised a profound effect on the emerging West End. And that, of course, was precisely what it had been intended to do. Performances were subsequently restricted to the two patent houses only – the Theatre Royal, Drury Lane, and the Theatre Royal, Covent Garden – and all new plays were required to be submitted for licensing (and censorship) to the Lord Chancellor. Henry Fielding's dangerously innovative company at the Haymarket, where Charke had been working at the time, was completely disbanded.
19. See Janet Malcolm, *The Silent Woman: Sylvia Plath and Ted Hughes* (New York: Vintage, 1994): 7–10.
20. David Magarshack, 'Stanislavski' in *The Theory of the Modern Stage*, ed. Eric Bentley (Harmondsworth, Middlesex: Penguin, 1968): 227.
21. B.R.S. Fone, 'Introduction' to *An Apology for the Life of Colley Cibber*, xxii.
22. For the most significant feminist criticism of Charke's work, in addition to those noted above, see: Lynne Friedli, ' "Passing Women" – A Study of Gender Boundaries in the Eighteenth Century" in Rousseau and Porter, eds, *Sexual Underworlds of the Enlightenment*; Felicity Nussbaum, *The Autobiographical Subject: Gender and Ideology in Eighteenth-Century England* (Baltimore, Maryland: Johns Hopkins University Press, 1989); Sidonie Smith, '*A Narrative of the Life*

of Mrs Charlotte Charke: The Transgressive Daughter and the Narrative of Self-Representation' in *A Poetics of Women's Autobiography: Marginality and the Fictions of Self-Representation* (Bloomington, Indiana: Indiana University Press, 1987); Patricia Meyer Spacks, *Imagining a Self: Autobiography and Novel in Eighteenth-Century England* (Cambridge, Massachusetts: Harvard University Press, 1976); Cheryl Wanko, 'The Eighteenth-Century Actress and the Construction of Gender: Lavinia Fenton and Charlotte Charke' in *Eighteenth-Century Life* 18 (May 1994): 75–90.

23. Sue Churchill, ' "I Then Was What I Had Made Myself": Representation and Charlotte Charke' in *Biography* 20:1 (Winter 1997): 76.

24. Erin Mackie, 'Desperate Measures: The Narrative of the Life of Mrs Charlotte Charke' in *ELH* 58 (1991): 841–65.

25. Mackie: 841–2.

26. Mackie: 850.

27. Mackie: 843.

28. Mackie: 844.

29. See, for example, Henry Fielding, *Jonathan Wild*, ed. David Nokes (Harmondsworth: Penguin, 1982): 73.

30. Joseph Addison, *Cato*, I.iv.147–55; in *British Dramatists from Dryden to Sheridan*, eds George Nettleton and Arthur Case, and revised by George Winchester Stone, Jr., 2nd edn (New York: Houghton Mifflin, 1969): 482.

31. Norma Clarke, *The Rise and Fall of the Woman of Letters* (London: Pimlico, 2004): 265.

32. See Randolph Trumbach, 'Sodomitical Subcultures: Sodomitical Roles and the Gender Revolution of the Eighteenth Century: The Recent Historiography' in *'Tis Nature's Fault: Unauthorised Sexuality during the Enlightenment*. ed. Robert Maccubbin (Cambridge: Cambridge University Press, 1987): 109–21.

33. *Lexicon Balatrocinium: A Dictionary of Buckish Slang, University Wit, and Pickpocket Eloquence* (London: 1861): s.v. 'Bill at Sight'.

34. Ben Jonson, *Bartholomew Fair* (II.ii.48–50), in *Three Comedies*, ed. Michael Jamieson (Harmondsworth, Middlesex: Penguin, 1966): 361. Mackie (855) draws attention to the connections between Jonson's stage character and Charke's subsequent creation, noting that important characteristics of the type had been outlined in Patricia Parker, *Literary Fat Ladies: Rhetoric, Gender, Property* (New York: Methuen, 1987).

35. Elizabeth Inchbald, *A Simple Story* (Oxford: Oxford University Press, 1967;1988): 1.

36. Jean Coates Cleary, 'Introduction' to Frances Sheridan, *Memoirs of Miss Sidney Bidulph* (Oxford: Oxford University Press, 1995): xix.

37. 'Introduction' to Rheder, ed. *Narrative*: xi.

38. 'Introduction' to Rheder, ed. *Narrative*: xii.

Conclusion

1. Linda Hutcheon, 'Authorized Transgression: The Paradox of Parody' in *Le Singe à la Porte: Vers une Théorie de la Parodie* (New York: Peter Lang, 1981): 17.

Selected Bibliography

Absalom's IX Worthies: Or a Key to the Late Book or Poem. [Entitled] A.B. & A.C. London: 1682.

Ackroyd, Peter. *London: The Biography*. London: Vintage, 2001.

Adler, Jacob H. *The Reach of Art: A Study of the Prosody of Pope*. Gainesville, Florida: University of Florida Press, 1964.

Allen, Graham. *Intertextuality*. The New Critical Idiom Series. London and New York: Routledge, 2000.

Alpers, Paul J. ed. *Edmund Spenser: A Critical Anthology*. New York: Penguin, 1969.

Altick, Richard D. *Richard Owen Cambridge: Belated Augustan*. Philadelphia: University of Pennsylvania Press, 1941.

—— *The Shows of London*. Cambridge, Massachusetts: Harvard University Press, 1978.

Amis, Kingsley, ed. *The New Oxford Book of Light Verse*. Oxford: Oxford University Press, 1978.

Arundell, Dennis D. *Dryden and Howard: 1664–1668*. Cambridge: Cambridge University Press, 1929.

Atkins, J.W.H. *English Literary Criticism: 17th & 18th Centuries*. London: Methuen, 1951.

Auerbach, Erich. *Mimesis: The Representation of Reality in Western Literature*, trans. Willard R. Trask. Princeton: Princeton University Press, 1953.

Ayres, Philip J., ed. 'Introduction' to Ben Jonson, *Sejanus, His Fall*. The Revels Plays. Manchester and New York: Manchester University Press, 1990.

Babula, William. *Shakespeare in Production, 1935–78*. London: Garland, 1981.

Backscheider, Paula R. 'Daniel Defoe' in *The First English Novelists: Essays in Understanding*, ed. J.M. Armistead. Knoxville, Tennessee: University of Tennessee Press, 1985:41–66.

Baird, Rosemary. *Mistress of the House: Great Ladies and Grand Houses, 1670–1830*. London: Weidenfeld and Nicholson, 2003.

Bakhtin, M.M. *The Dialogic Imagination*, trans. Caryl Emerson and Michael Holquist; ed. Michael Holquist. Austin, Texas: University of Texas Press, 1981.

—— 'Discourse Typology in Prose' in *Readings in Russian Poetics: Formalist and Structuralist Views*, eds Ladislav Matejka and Kyrstyna Pomorska. Cambridge, Massachusetts: M.I.T. University Press, 1971, 176–96.

—— *Rabelais and His World*, trans. Hélène Iswolsky. Bloomington, Indiana: Indiana University Press, 1984.

Barrol, J. Leeds. 'Shakespeare and the Plague' in *Shakespeare's Art from a Comparative Perspective*, ed. Wendell M. Aycock. Lubock: Texas Tech Press, 1981, 13–29.

Barth, John. 'The Literature of Exhaustion' in *Surfiction: Fiction Now . . . and Tomorrow*, ed. Raymond Federman. Chicago: Swallow Press, 1975.

Barton, Anne. *Ben Jonson, Dramatist*. Cambridge: Cambridge University Press, 1984.

Baruth, Philip E., ed., *Introducing Charlotte Charke: Actress, Author, Enigma*. Urbana, Illinois: University of Illinois Press, 1999.

261

Bate, Jonathan. *Shakespearean Constitutions: Politics, Theory, Criticism, 1730–1830*. Oxford: Clarendon Press, 1989.

Bean, Lloyd W. *Bits of Ivory: Narrative Techniques in Jane Austen's Fiction*. Baton Rouge, Louisiana: Louisiana State University Press, 1973.

Beerbohm, Max. *A Christmas Garland, Woven by Max Beerbohm*. London: William Heinemann, 1912.

Belanger, Terry. 'Publishers and Writers in Eighteenth-Century England' in *Books and Their Readers in Eighteenth-Century England*, ed. Isabel Rivers. London: St. Martin's Press, 1982, 5–25.

Bell, Walter George. *The Great Plague of London*. London: Bodley Head, 1924; repr. London: Bracken Books, 1994.

Benjamin, Walter. *Illuminations*. trans. H. Zohn, ed. Hannah Arendt. London: New Left Books, 1977.

Black, Jeremy. *The English Press in the Eighteenth Century*. Aldershot: Scolar Press, 1991.

Blackmur, R.P. *Selected Essays*, ed. Denis Donoghue. New York: Ecco Press, 1986.

Bloom, Edward A. and Lillian D. Bloom. *Satire's Persuasive Voice*. Ithaca, New York: Cornell University Press, 1979.

Bloom, Harold. *The Anxiety of Influence: A Theory of Poetry*. Oxford: Oxford University Press, 1973.

Bond, Richmond P. *English Burlesque Poetry, 1700–1750*. Cambridge Massachusetts: Harvard University Press, 1932.

Booth, Stephen. *King Lear, Macbeth, Indefinition and Tragedy*. New Haven: Yale University Press, 1982.

Boswell, James. *Life of Johnson*, ed. R.W. Chapman. Oxford, 1904; repr. Oxford: Oxford University Press, 1980.

Braudy, Leo. *The Frenzy of Renown: Fame and Its History*. Oxford: Oxford University Press, 1986.

Bredvold, Louis. *The Intellectual Milieu of John Dryden*. Ann Arbor, Michigan: University of Michigan Press, 1934.

Brett, Simon, ed. *The Faber Book of Parodies*. London: Faber & Faber, 1984.

Briggs, Julia. *This Stage-Play World: English Literature and Its Background 1580–1625*. Oxford: Oxford University Press, 1983.

Brockett, Oscar G. *History of the Theatre*. 7th edn. London: Allyn and Bacon, 1995.

Browne, Thomas. *The Works of Sir Thomas Browne*, ed. Geoffrey Keynes. 4 vols. Chicago: University of Chicago Press, 1964.

Burden, Robert. 'The Novel Interrogates Itself: Parody and Self-Consciousness in Contemporary English Fiction' in *Stratford-upon-Avon Studies*, no. 18 (1979): 133–56.

Burge, James. *Heloise & Abelard: A Twelfth-Century Love Story*. London: Profile Books, 2003.

Burney, Fanny. *Evelina*. ed. Edward A. Bloom. Oxford: Oxford University Press, 1968.

Burrow, J.A. 'Chaucer's *Sir Thopas* and *La Prise de Neuville*' in *English Satire and the Satiric Tradition*, ed. Claude Rawson. Oxford: Basil Blackwell, 1984.

Cassirer, Ernst. *Language and Myth*, trans. Susanne K. Langer. New York: Harper and Brothers, 1946.

Castle, Terry. 'The Culture of Travesty: Sexuality and Masquerade in Eighteenth-Century England' in *Sexual Underworlds of the Enlightenment*, eds G.S. Rousseau and Roy Porter. Chapel Hill, North Carolina: University of North Carolina Press, 1988, 156–80.

—— *Masquerade and Civilization: The Carnivalesque in Eighteenth-Century English Culture and Fiction*. Stanford, California: Stanford University Press, 1986.

Charke, Charlotte. *The History of Henry Dumont, Esq., and Miss Charlotte Evelyn*. London: 1756.

—— *A Narrative of the Life of Mrs Charlotte Charke*, ed. with an Introduction and Notes by Robert Rehder. London: Pickering and Chatto, 1999.

Chatman, Seymour. 'Parody and Style' in *Poetics Today* 22, no. 1 (2001): 25–39.

Churchill, Sue. ' "I Then Was What I Had Made Myself": Representation and Charlotte Charke' in *Biography* 20:1 (Winter, 1997): 72–94.

Chute, Marchette, *Ben Jonson of Westminster*. New York: Dutton, 1953.

Cibber, Colley. *An Apology for the Life of Colley Cibber*. repr. in an annotated edition by B.R.S Fone. Ann Arbor, Michigan: University of Michigan Press, 1974.

—— *A Critical Edition of the Life of Mr. Colley Cibber, Comedian*, ed. John Maurice Evans. New York: Garland, 1987.

Clarke, Norma. *The Rise and Fall of the Woman of Letters*. London: Pimlico, 2004.

Cleary, Jean Coates. 'Introduction' to Frances Sheridan, *Memoirs of Miss Sidney Bidulph*. Oxford: Oxford University Press, 1995.

Cleveland, John. *The Poems of John Cleveland*, eds Brian Morris and Eleanor Withington. Oxford: Clarendon Press, 1967.

Clifford, James L. ed. *Eighteenth-Century English Literature: Modern Essays in Criticism*. Oxford: Oxford University Press, 1959.

Coleridge, Samuel Taylor. *Biographia Literaria, or Biographical Sketches on My Literary Life and Opinions*, eds James Engall and Walter Jackson Bate. 2 vols. Princeton: Princeton University Press, 1983.

—— *Shakespeare Criticism*. 2 vols. London: J.M. Dent, 1960.

—— *Specimens of Table Talk*, ed. Henry H. Coleridge. 2 vols. London: John Murray, 1835.

Collingwood, R.G. *The Principles of Art*. Oxford: Clarendon Press, 1932.

—— *The Philosophy of Enchantment: Studies in Folklore, Cultural Criticism, and Anthropology*, eds David Boucher, Wendy James, and Philip Smallwood. Oxford: Clarendon Press, 2005.

Conlon, Michael J. 'Singing Beside-Against: Parody and the Example of Swift's *A Description of a City Shower*' in *GENRE*, 16 (1983): 219–32.

Coppock, J.T. and Hugh C. Prince, eds. *Greater London*. London: Faber & Faber, 1964.

Cradock, Joseph. *Literary and Miscellaneous Memoirs*. London: J. Nichols, 1846.

Cunningham, Peter. *A Handbook for London: Past and Present*. 2 vols. London: John Murray, 1849.

Damrosch, Leopold. *Modern Essays on Eighteenth-Century Literature*. Oxford: Oxford University Press, 1988.

Dane, Joseph. *Parody: Critical Concepts versus Literary Practice: Aristophanes to Sterne*. Norman, Oklahoma: University of Oklahoma Press, 1988.

Danson, Lawrence. '*Henry V*: King, Chorus, and Critics' in *Shakespeare Quarterly*, 34, no. 1 (1983): 27–43.

—— *Max Beerbohm and the Act of Writing*. Oxford: Oxford University Press, 1989.

Davidson, Israel. *Parody in Jewish Literature*. New York, 1907; repr. New York: AMS Press, 1966.

Davies, John. *The Complete Works of John Davies of Hertfordshire*, ed. A.B. Grosart. 2 vols. Edinburgh: Edinburgh University Press, 1878.

Davis, Natalie Zemon. 'Printing and the People' in *Society and Culture in Early Modern France*. Stanford, California: Stanford University Press, 1975.

Debus, Allen G. '*The Scribleriad*: Alchemy in the Eighteenth-Century Mock-Heroic Poem' in *Clauda Pavonis: Studies in Hermiticism* 20, no. 2 (Fall 2001): 19–24.

Defoe, Daniel. *A Journal of the Plague Year*. New York: Penguin, 1966.

Dekker, Thomas. *The Plague Pamphlets of Thomas Decker*, ed. F.P. Wilson. Oxford: Clarendon Press, 1925.

Dentith, Simon. *Bakhtinian Thought: An Introductory Reader*. London: Routledge, 1995.

—— *Parody*. The New Critical Idiom Series. London: Routledge, 2000.

Dickens, Charles. *Sketches by Boz: Illustrations of Every-Day Life and Every-Day People*. London: Chapman and Hall, 1836–7.

Donoghue, Frank. *The Fame Machine: Book Reviewing and Eighteenth-Century Literary Careers*. Stanford: Stanford University Press, 1996.

Donne, John. *The Complete English Poems*, ed. A.J. Smith. New York: Penguin, 1971.

Doody, Margaret Anne. *The Daring Muse: Augustan Poetry Reconsidered*. Cambridge: Cambridge University Press, 1985.

—— 'The Future of Pope Criticism' in *Scriblerian* 21 (1988): 8–12.

Dryden, John. *The Works of John Dryden*, eds Edward Niles Hooker, H.T. Swedenberg, Jr., *et al.*, 20 vols. Berkeley and Los Angeles, California: University of California Press, 1956–.

—— *John Dryden: Selected Criticism*, eds James Kinsley and George Parfitt. Oxford: Clarendon Press, 1970.

Duncan-Jones, Katherine. 'Just a Jiglot', rev. of Ben Jonson's *Sejanus* (Swan Theatre, Stratford-upon-Avon) in *Times Literary Supplement*, no. 5340 (5 August 2005): 18.

Eisenstein, Elizabeth. *The Printing Revolution in Early Modern Europe*. Cambridge: Cambridge University Press, 1983.

—— 'Some Conjectures about the Impact of Printing on Western Society and Thought' in *The Journal of Modern History* Volume 40, no. 1 (1968): 1–56.

Eliot, T.S. *Selected Essays*. London: Faber & Faber, 1932.

Elliot, Robert C. *The Power of Satire: Magic, Ritual, Art*. Princeton: Princeton University Press, 1960.

Empson, William. *Some Versions of Pastoral*. London: Chatto and Windus, 1935.

Erskine-Hill, Howard. *The Augustan Idea in English Literature*. London: Edward Arnold, 1983.

Fairer, David. *English Poetry of the Eighteenth Century, 1700–1789*. London: Pearson Education Limited, 2003.

—— *Pope's Imagination*. Manchester: Manchester University Press, 1984.

Falck, Colin. *Myth, Truth, and Literature: Towards a True Post-Modernism*, 2nd edn Cambridge: Cambridge University Press, 1994.

Fergusson, Francis. *The Idea of a Theatre*. Princeton: Princeton University Press, 1949.

Fielding, Henry. *Jonathan Wild*, ed. David Nokes. Harmondsworth: Penguin, 1982.

Fitzgerald, Percy. *The Lives of the Sheridans*. Dublin: 1886.

Foucault, Michel. *The Order of Things*. New York: Random House, 1970.

Freeman, Rosemary. 'Parody as Literary Form: George Herbert and Wilfred Owen' in *Essays in Criticism* XII (1963): 307–22.

Frost, William. *John Dryden: Dramatist, Satirist, Translator*. New York: AMS Press, 1988.

Frye, Dean. 'The Question of Shakespearean Parody' in *Essays in Criticism*, XV (1965): 22–36.

Gates, Henry Louis, Jr. *The Signifying Monkey: A Theory of African-American Literary Criticism*. Oxford: Oxford University Press, 1988.

Greene, Donald. *The Art of Exuberance: Backgrounds to Eighteenth-Century English Literature*. New York: Random House, 1970.

—— ed. *Samuel Johnson*. Oxford: Oxford University Press, 1984.

Guerinot, J.V. ed. *Pamphlet Attacks on Alexander Pope, 1711–1744*. London: Methuen, 1969.

Guilhamet, Leon. *Satire and the Transformation of Genre*. Philadelphia, Pennsylvania: University of Pennsylvania Press, 1987.

Guillory, John. *Cultural Capital: The Problem of Literary Canon Formation*. Chicago: University of Chicago Press, 1991.

Hamilton, Walter. *Parodies of the Works of English and American Authors*. 5 vols. London: Reeves & Turner, 1884–89.

Hammond, B.S. *Professional Imaginative Writing in England: 1670–1740: 'Hackney for Bread'*. Oxford: Clarendon Press, 1997.

Hannoosh, Michele. 'The Reflexive Function of Parody' in *Comparative Literature* 41, no. 2 (1989): 113–27.

Hardy, J.P. 'Introduction' to Samuel Johnson, *The History of Rasselas Prince of Abissinia*. Oxford: Oxford University Press, 1968.

Harpham, Geoffrey Galt. *On the Grotesque: Strategies of Contradiction in Art and Literature*. Princeton: Princeton University Press, 1982.

Hazlitt, William. *Complete Works*, ed. P.P. Howe. London: J.M. Dent, 1930.

Helgerson, Richard. *Self-Crowned Laureates: Spenser, Jonson, Milton, and the Literary System*. Berkeley: University of California Press, 1983.

Henkle, Roger. *Comedy and Culture: England 1820–1900*. Princeton: Princeton University Press, 1980.

Herring, Frances. *Certain Rules, Directions, or Advertisements for This Time of Pestilential Contagion . . . .* London: 1603; repr. Amsterdam: De Capo Press, 1973.

Higgins, E.T. 'Self-Discrepancy: A Theory Relating Self and Affect' in *Psychological Review* 94 (1997): 319–40.

Highet, Gilbert. *The Anatomy of Satire*. Princeton: Princeton University Press, 1962.

The History of Two Valiant Knights Sir Clyomen and Clamydes. 1599; repr. Tudor Facsimile Society, 1913.

Hobbes, Thomas. *Leviathan*, ed. C.B. Macpherson. London: Penguin, 1968.

Hodgart, Matthew. *Satire*. London: Weidenfeld and Nicolson, 1969.

Hopkins, David. *John Dryden*. Cambridge: Cambridge University Press, 1986.

Hume, David. *Treatise of Human Nature*. 2 vols. London: J.M. Dent & Sons, 1968.

Hutcheon, Linda. *A Theory of Parody*. London: Methuen, 1985.

Inchbald, Elizabeth. *A Simple* Story, with a new introduction by Jane Spencer. Oxford: Oxford University Press, 1988.

Irigaray, Luce. 'The Power of Discourse and the Subordination of the Feminine' in *This Sex which Is Not One*, trans. Catherine Porter with Carolyn Burke. Ithaca: Cornell University Press, 1985.

Iser, Wolfgang. *The Implied Reader: Patterns of Communication in Prose Fiction from Bunyan to Beckett*. Baltimore: Johns Hopkins University Press, 1974.

Jack, Ian. *Augustan Satire: Intention and Idiom in English Poetry, 1660–1750*. Oxford: Clarendon Press, 1962.

Jack Juggler. 1553; repr. Tudor Facsimile Texts, 1912.

Jameson, Fredric. *Postmodernism, or, the Cultural Logic of Late Capitalism*. London and New York: Verso, 1991.

Jauss, Hans Robert. *Aesthetic Experience and Literary Hermeneutics*, trans. Michael Shaw. Minneapolis: University of Minnesota Press, 1982.

Jensen, James. H. *A Glossary of John Dryden's Critical Terms*. Minneapolis: University of Minnesota Press, 1969.

Johnson, Claudia. *Jane Austen: Women, Politics, and the Novel*. Chicago: University of Chicago Press, 1988.

Johnson, Samuel. *Dictionary of the English Language*. London, 1755.

—— *Johnson on Shakespeare*. 2 vols. New Haven: Yale University Press, 1968.

—— *Lives of the English Poets*. 2 vols. London: J.M. Dent, 1925.

Jones, G.P. '*Henry V*: The Chorus and the Audience' in *Shakespeare Survey*, 31 (1978): 93–104.

Jones, Harold Whitmore, ed. *Anti-Achitophel [1682]*. Gainesville, Florida: Scholar's Facsimiles and Reprints, 1961.

Jones, R.F. 'The Originality of *Absalom and Achitophel*' in *Modern Language Notes*, XLVI (1931): 211–18.

Jonson, Ben. *Every Man in His Humour*, ed. Gabriele Bernhard Jackson. New Haven: Yale University Press, 1969.

—— *The Complete Poems*, ed. George Parfitt. New Haven and London: Yale University Press, 1975.

—— *Three Comedies*, ed. Michael Jamieson (Harmondsworth, Middlesex: Penguin, 1966.

—— *Works*. C.H. Herford and Percy and Evelyn Simpson. XI vols. Oxford: Oxford University Press, 1925–52.

Kael, Pauline. 'Second Takes' in *The New Yorker* (27 November 1989): 104–5.

Kelly, Linda. *Richard Brinsley Sheridan: A Life*. London: Sinclair-Stevenson, 1997.

Kerby-Miller, Charles, ed. *The Memoirs of the Extraordinary Life, Works, and Discourses of Martinus Scriblerus*. Oxford: Oxford University Press, 1950.

Kernan, Alvin B. *The Cankered Muse: Satire of the English Renaissance*. New Haven, Yale University Press 1959; repr. Hamden, Connecticut: Archon, 1976.

—— 'The Henriad: Shakespeare's Major History Plays' in *Modern Shakespearen Criticism: Essays on Style, Dramaturgy, and the Major Plays*, ed. Alvin B. Kernan. New York: Harcourt Brace, 1970, 245–75.

—— *Printing Technology, Letters, and Samuel Johnson*. Princeton: Princeton University Press, 1987.

Keymer, Thomas, and Jon Mee. *The Cambridge Companion to English Literature 1740–1830*. Cambridge: Cambridge University Press, 2004.

Kinsley, James, ed. *Dryden: The Critical Heritage*. London: Routledge & Kegan Paul, 1971.

—— and George Parfitt, eds. *John Dryden: Selected Criticism*. Oxford: Clarendon Press, 1970.

Kiremidjian, G.D. 'The Aesthetics of Parody' in *Journal of Aesthetics and Art Criticism*, 28 (1969): 231–42.

Kitchin, George. *A Survey of Parody and Burlesque in English*. London: Oliver and Boyd, 1931.

Knights, Mark. *Representation and Misrepresentation in Later Stuart Britain: Partisanship and Political Culture*. Oxford: Oxford University Press, 2005.

Kramnick, Jonathan Brody. *Making the English Canon: Print Capitalism and the Cultural Past, 1700–1770*. Cambridge: Cambridge University Press, 1998.

Kuhn, Thomas S. *The Structure of Scientific Revolutions*, 2nd ed Chicago: University of Chicago Press, 1970.

Lamb, Charles. *Complete Works and Letters*. New York: Modern Library, 1935.

Lecercle, Jean Jacques. 'Parody as Cultural Memory' in *REAL: The Yearbook of Research in English and American Literature* 21 (2005), 31–44.

Lehmann, Paul. *Die Parodie im Mittelalter*. Stuttgart: Hiersemann, 1963.

Lelièvre, F.J. 'The Basis of Ancient Parody' in *Greece and Rome*, 2nd ser. 1 (1954): 66–91.

Lennep, William van, ed. *The London Stage 1660–1700*. Carbondale, Illinois: Southern Illinois University Press, 1965.

Leranbaum, Miriam. *Alexander Pope's 'Opus Magnum' 1729–1744*. Oxford: Clarendon Press, 1988.

Lewalksi, Barbara. *Protestant Poetics and the Seventeenth-Century Religious Lyric*. Princeton: Princeton University Press, 1979.

Lexicon Balatrocinium: A Dictionary of Buckish Slang, University Wit, and Pickpocket Eloquence. London: 1861.

Locke, John. *An Essay concerning Human Understanding*, ed. Peter H. Nidditch. Oxford: Clarendon Press, 1975.

Lockwood, Tom. *Ben Jonson in the Romantic Age*. Oxford: Oxford University Press, 2005.

Lonsdale, Roger. *The New Oxford Book of Eighteenth-Century Verse*. Oxford: Oxford University Press, 1984.

Loomis, L.H. *Sources and Analogies in Chaucer's Canterbury Tales*, eds W.F. Bryan and Germaine Dempster. Chicago: University of Chicago Press, 1941.

Lord, George deF., gen. ed., *Poems on Affairs of State: Augustan Verse Satire, 1660–1714*. New Haven: Yale University Press, 1963.

Love, Harold. *English Clandestine Satire, 1660–1704*. Oxford: Oxford University Press, 2004.

Lucian [Lucianus of Samosata]. *Rhetoron Didaskalos*, trans. A.M. Harmon. Cambridge, Massachusetts: Harvard University Press, 1925.

Lyon, Ralph, ed. *The Mocking Bards: A Collection of Parodies, Burlesques, and Imitations*. Evanston, Illinois: Ridgeville Press, 1905.

Macdonald, Dwight, ed. *Parodies: An Anthology from Chaucer to Beerbohm and After*. New York: Random House, 1960.

Macdonald, Hugh. 'The Attacks on Dryden' in *Essential Articles for the Study of John Dryden*, ed. H.T. Swedenberg, Jr. London: Frank Cass, 1966.

—— *John Dryden: A Bibliography of Early Editions and Drydeniana*. Oxford: Clarendon Press, 1936.

McFadden, George. *Dryden, the Public Writer, 1660–1685*. Princeton: Princeton University Press, 1978.

McFarland, Thomas. *Originality and Imitation*. Baltimore, Maryland: Johns Hopkins University Press, 1985.

McGill, Scott. *Virgil Recomposed: The Mythological and Secular Centos of Antiquity*. Oxford: Oxford University Press, 2006.

268   Selected Bibliography

5

McHenry, Robert W., Jr., ed. *Contexts 3: Absalom and Achitophel*. Hamden, Connecticut: Archon, 1986.
—— and David Lougee, eds. *Critics on Dryden*. Readings in Literary Criticism, no.15. London: George Allen & Unwin, 1973.
Mack, Maynard. *Alexander Pope: A Life*. New Haven: Yale University Press, 1985.
McKeon, Michael. 'Generic Transformation and Social Change: Rethinking the Rise of the Novel' in *Modern Essays in Eighteenth-Century Literature*, ed. Leopold Damrosch, Jr. Oxford: Oxford University Press, 1988.
—— *Politics and Poetry in Restoration England: The Case of Dryden's Annus Mirabilis*. Cambridge, Massachusetts: Harvard University Press, 1975.
Mackie, Erin. 'Desperate Measures: The Narrative of the Life of Mrs. Charlotte Charke' in *ELH* 58 (1991): 841–65.
McLaverty, James, ed. *Pope and the Early Eighteenth-Century Book Trade*. Oxford: Oxford University Press, 1991, 237–51.
McNeill, William H. *Plagues and Peoples*. New York: Doubleday, 1976.
Magarshack, David. 'Stanislavski' in *The Theory of the Modern Stage*, ed. Eric Bentley. Harmondsworth, Middlesex: Penguin, 1968, 219–74.
Malcolm, Janet. *The Silent Woman: Sylvia Plath and Ted Hughes*. New York: Vintage, 1994.
Mallon, Thomas. *Stolen Words: Forays into the Origins and Ravages of Plagiarism*. New York: Ticknor & Fields, 1989.
Martin, John. 'Townshend, Etheldreda, Viscountess Townsend (*c*.1708–1788) in *Oxford Dictionary of National Biography*. Oxford: Oxford University Press, 2004.
Marvell, Andrew. *The Poems and Letters of Andrew Marvell*, ed. H.M. Margoliouth. 2 vols. Oxford: Clarendon Press, 1927.
Maus, Katherine. *Ben Jonson and the Roman Frame of Mind*. Princeton: Princeton University Press, 1984.
Millis, J. Hillis. 'The Critic as Host' in *Deconstruction and Criticism*, ed. Harold Bloom. New York: The Seaburg Press, 1979, 217–53.
Miner, Earl. *Dryden's Poetry*. Bloomington, Indiana: University of Indiana Press, 1967.
Moi, Torel. *Sexual/Textual Politics: Feminist Literary Theory*. London: Methuen, 1985.
Morgan, Fidelis. *The Well-Known Troublemaker: A Life of Charlotte Charke*. London: Faber, 1988.
Morris, David B. 'The Visionary Maid: Tragic Poetics and Redemptive Sympathy in *Eloisa to Abelard*' in *Modern Critical Views: Alexander Pope*, ed. Harold Bloom. New York: Chelsea House, 1982.
Mullet, Charles F. *The Bubonic Plague and England*. Lexington, Kentucky: University of Kentucky, 1956.
Nashe, Thomas. *Works*, ed. R.B. Kerrow. Oxford: Basil Blackwell, 1958.
[Nesse, Christopher] *A Key (With the Whip) to Open the Mystery and Iniquity of a Poem Called Absalom and Achitophel*. London: T. Snowden, 1681.
[——] *A Whip for the Fool's Back, Who Styles Honourable Marriage a Curs'd Confinement*. London: T. Dawks, 1681.
Nettleton, George, and Arthur Case, eds. *British Dramatists from Dryden to Sheridan*, 2nd edn. New York: Houghton Mifflin, 1969.
Nevill, Antonia. *A History of Rome*, trans. Marcel Le Glay, Jean-Louis Voisin and Yann Le Bohec. Oxford: Blackwell Publishers, 1996.

Newman, Charles. 'The Anxiety of Non-Influence' in *The Post-Modern Aura: Acts of Fiction in the Age of Inflation*. Evanston, Illinois: Northwestern University Press, 1985.

Nichols, John. *Illustrations of the Literary History of the Eighteenth Century*. London: J.B. Nichols, 1828.

Nicholson, Colin, ed. *Alexander Pope: Essays for the Tercentenary*. Aberdeen: Aberdeen University Press, 1988.

Noble, Adrian, dir. *Henry V*. By William Shakespeare. With Kenneth Branagh, Royal Shakespeare Theatre, Stratford-upon-Avon, March–September, 1984.

Nussbaum, Felicity. *The Autobiographical Subject: Gender and Ideology in Eighteenth-Century England*. Baltimore, Maryland: Johns Hopkins University Press, 1989.

O'Hara, D.T., *Radical Parody: American Culture and Critical Agency After Foucault*. New York: Columbia University Press, 1992.

Orgel, Steven. 'The Renaissance Artist as Plagiary' in *English Literary History*, 48 (1981): 476–94.

Ormsby-Lennon, Hugh. 'Poetic Standards in the Early Augustan Battleground' in *Studies in Eighteenth-Century Culture 5*, ed. Ronald C. Rosbottom. Madison, Wisconsin: University of Wisconsin Press, 1976, 253–80.

Osborn, James M. *John Dryden: Some Biographical Facts and Problems*. New York: Columbia University Press, 1940.

Ostriker, Alicia. 'The Thieves of Language: Women Poets and Revisionist Mythmaking' in *The New Feminist Criticism*, ed. Elaine Showalter. New York: Pantheon, 1985, 314–38.

O'Toole, Fintan. *A Traitor's Kiss: The Life of Richard Brinsley Sheridan*. London: Granta Books, 1997.

'A Panegyrick on the Author of *Absalom and Achitophel*'. London: Charles Leigh, 1681.

Parker, Patricia. *Literary Fat Ladies: Rhetoric, Gender, Property*. New York: Methuen, 1987.

Patai, Daphne, and Will H. Corral, eds. *Theory's Empire: An Anthology Of Dissent*. New York: Columbia University Press, 2005.

Peavey, Charles D. 'The Chimerical Career of Charlotte Charke' in *Restoration and Eighteenth-Century Theatre Research* 8.1 (1969): 1–12.

Peter, John. *Complaint and Satire in Early English Literature*. Oxford: Clarendon Press, 1956.

Phiddian, Robert. 'Are Parody and Deconstruction Secretly the Same Thing?' in *New Literary History: A Journal of Theory and Interpretation* 28, no. 4 (1997): 673–96.

—— *Swift's Parody*. Cambridge: Cambridge University Press, 1995.

Picard, Liza. *Elizabeth's London: Everyday Life in Elizabethan London*. London: Weidenfeld & Nicolson, 2003.

'Poetical Reflections on a Late Poem [Entitled] *Absalom and Achitophel*'. London: Richard Janeway, 1681.

Pope, Alexander. *The Correspondence of Alexander Pope*, ed. George Sherburn. 5 vols. Oxford: Clarendon Press, 1956.

—— *The Poems of Alexander Pope*, ed. John Butt. London: Methuen, 1963.

Prior, Moody. *The Dream of Power: Studies in Shakespeare's History Plays*. Evanston, Illinois: Northwestern University Press, 1973.

Quintillian [Marcus Fabius Quintilianus]. *Institutio Oratio*, trans. H.E. Butler. Cambridge, Massachusetts: Harvard University Press, 1922.

Ricks, Christopher. 'The Poet as Heir' in *Studies in the Eighteenth-Century*. III, eds R.F. Brissenden and J.C. Eade. Canberra: Australian National University Press, 1979, 95–132.

Ridley, Aaron. *R.G. Collingwood: A Philosophy of Art*. London: Orion Publishing, 1998.

Riggs, David. *Ben Jonson: A Life*. Cambridge, Massachusetts: Harvard University Press, 1989.

Righter, Anne. *Shakespeare and the Idea of the Play*. New York: Penguin, 1967.

Roche, Thomas P., Jr. *Petrarch and the English Sonnet Sequences*. New York: AMS Press, 1989.

Rogers, Pat. *The Augustan Vision*. London: Weidenfeld Nicolson, 1974.

—— 'The Breeches Part' in *Sexuality in Eighteenth-Century Britain*. ed. Paul-Gabriel Boucé. Manchester: Manchester University Press, 1982, 244–58.

Rogers, Samuel. *Recollection of the Table Talk of Samuel Rogers*. London: Edward Moxon, 1956.

Rollins, Hyder E., ed. *Tottel's Miscellany, 1557–87*. 2 vols. Cambridge, Massachusetts: Harvard University Press, 1965.

Roper, Alan. *Dryden's Poetic Kingdoms*. London: Routledge & Kegan Paul, 1965.

Rose, Margaret. *Parody/Metafiction: An Analysis of Parody as a Critical Mirror to the Writing and Reception of Fiction*. London: Croom Helm, 1979.

—— *Parody: Ancient, Modern, and Post-Modern*. Cambridge: Cambridge University Press, 1993.

Rothstein, Eric. *Restoration and Eighteenth-Century Poetry, 1660–1780*. London: Routledge & Kegan Paul, 1981.

Rousseau, G. S. and Pat Rogers, eds. *The Enduring Legacy: Alexander Pope Tercentenary Essays*. Cambridge: Cambridge University Press, 1988.

Said, Edward. *The World, The Text, and the Critic*. London: Faber & Faber, 1984.

Sambrook, James. 'Cambridge, Richard Owen (1717–1802)' in *Oxford Dictionary of National Biography*. Oxford: Oxford University Press, 2004.

Scarre, Chris. *Chronicle of the Roman Emperors: the Reign-by-Reign Record of the Rulers of Imperial Rome*. London: Thames & Hudson, 1995.

Scott, M.N. 'On the Nature of Parody' in *Northwest Review* 30, no. 3 (1992): 6–11.

Scott, Walter. *The Life of John Dryden*. London: 1834, repr. Lincoln, Nebraska: University of Nebraska Press, 1963.

Scruton, Roger. *Modern Culture*. London and New York: Continuum, 2000.

Selden, Raman. *English Verse Satire, 1590–1765*. London: Allen & Unwin, 1978.

Shakespeare, William. *Complete Works*, ed. Alfred Harbage. New York: Viking Press, 1977.

Shankman, Steven, ed. *The Iliad of Homer, Translated by Alexander Pope*. London: Penguin, 1996.

—— *Pope's Iliad: Homer in the Age of Passion*. Princeton: Princeton University Press, 1983.

Sherson, Erroll. *The Lively Lady Townshend and Her Friends*. London: William Heinemann, 1924.

Shrimpton, Nicholas. 'Shakespeare Performance in Stratford-upon-Avon and London, 1983–84' in *Shakespeare Survey* 38 (1985): 204–7.

Shlonsky, Tuvia. 'Literary Parody: Remarks on Its Method and Function' in *Proceedings of the Fourth Congress of the International Comparative Literature Association*, ed F. Jost. 2 vols. The Hague: Mouton, 1966, 797–801.

Shklovsky, Victor. 'Sterne's *Tristram Shandy* and the Theory of the Novel' in *Russian Formalist Criticism: Four Essays*, eds Lee T. Lemon and Marion J. Reis. Lincoln, Nebraska: University of Nebraska Press, 1965, 25–57.

Showalter, Elaine. *A Literature of Their Own: British Women Novelists from Brontë to Lessing*. Princeton: Princeton University Press, 1977.

Skeat, Walter W. *An Etymological Dictionary of the English Language*, 1st edn, 1879–82. Oxford: Clarendon Press, 1978.

Skelton, John. *The Complete English Poems*, ed. John Scattergood. New York: Penguin, 1983.

Small, R.A. *The Stage Quarrel between Ben Jonson and the So-Called Poetasters*. Breslau, 1899.

Smith, Sidonie. *A Poetics of Women's Autobiography: Marginality and the Fictions of Self-Representation*. Bloomington, Indiana: Indiana University Press, 1987.

Smith, Warren D. 'The *Henry V* Choruses in the First Folio' in *Journal Of English and German Philology*, LIII, no. 1 (1954): 38–57.

Smollett, Tobias. *The Expedition of Humphrey Clinker*, ed. Lewis M. Knapp. Oxford: Oxford University Press, 1984.

Sontag, Susan. *AIDS and Its Metaphors*. New York: Farrar, Strauss, & Giroux, 1989.

Spacks, Patricia M. *Imagining a Self: Autobiography and Novel in Eighteenth-Century England*. Cambridge, Massachusetts: Harvard University Press, 1976.

Spenser, Edmund. *The Faerie Queene*, ed. A.C. Hamilton. London: Longman, 1977.

Stallybrass, Peter, and Allon White. *The Politics and Poetics of Transgression*. Ithaca, New York: Cornell University Press, 1986.

Steiner, George. *After Babel: Aspects of Language and Translation*. Oxford: Oxford University Press, 1974.

Steiner, Peter. *Russian Formalism: A Metapoetics*. Ithaca: Cornell University Press, 1984.

Strange, Sallie Mintner. 'Charlotte Charke: Transvestite or Conjurer' in *Restoration and Eighteenth-Century Theatre Research*, 15, no. 2 (1976): 54–9.

Sturrock, John, ed. *Structuralism and Since: From Lévi-Strauss to Derrida*. Oxford: Oxford University Press, 1979.

Suarez, Michael F., S.J., ed. *Robert Dodsley's A Collection of Poems by Several Hands*. VI vols. New York: Routledge, 2001.

Sutherland, James. *A Preface to Eighteenth-Century Poetry*. Oxford: Oxford University Press, 1948.

Sweeney, John G. '*Sejanus* and the People's Beastly Rage' in *English Literary History*, 48 (1981): 61–82.

Swift, Jonathan. *The Complete Poems*, ed. Pat Rogers. New Haven: Yale University Press, 1983.

—— *The Prose Works of Jonathan Swift*, ed. Herbert Davis. 14 vols. Oxford: Basil Blackwell, 1939.

Sykes, Christopher Simon. *Private Palaces: Life in the Great London Houses*. London: Viking, 1986.

Thomas, W.K. *The Crafting of Absalom and Achitophel: Dryden's Pen for a Party*. Waterloo, Ontario: Wilfri Laurier University Press, 1978.

Thomson, Clive. 'Parody/Genre/Ideology' in *La signe à la porte: Vers une théorie de parodie*. New York: Peter Lang, 1984, 95–102.

Thorndike, A.H., ed. *Pre-Shakespearean Drama*. London: J.M. Dent, 1910.

Tiggs, Wim. *Anatomy of Literary Nonsense*. Amsterdam: Rodopi, 1988.

Tillotson, Geoffrey, ed. *The Rape of the Lock and Other Poems*. London: Methuen, 1940.

Tomkis, Thomas. *Lingua*. 1667; repr. Tudor Facsimile Texts, 1912.

Tom Tyler. 1661; repr. Tudor Facsimile Texts, 1912.

The Triall of Treasure. 1567; repr. Tudor Facsimile Texts, 1908.

Towser the Second, a Bull-Dog. London: 1681.

Tressler, Simon, ed. *Burlesque Plays of the Eighteenth Century*. Oxford: Oxford University Press, 1969.

Trumbach, Randolph. 'Sodomitical Subcultures: Sodomitical Roles and the Gender Revolution of the Eighteenth Century: The Recent Historiography' in *'Tis Nature's Fault: Unauthorised Sexuality during the Enlightenment*, ed. Robert Maccubbin. Cambridge: Cambridge University Press, 1987, 109–21.

Turberville, A.S., ed. *Johnson's England: An Account of the Life and Manners of His Age*. 2 vols. Oxford: Clarendon Press, 1933.

Tuve, Rosamund. 'Sacred Parody of Love Poetry, and Herbert' in *Studies in the Renaissance*, 8 (1961): 249–90.

Van Doren, Mark. *John Dryden: A Study of His Poetry*. Bloomington, Indiana: University of Indiana Press, 1920.

Van Ghent, Dorothy. *The English Novel: Form and Function*. New York: Harper and Row, 1961.

Waller, Edmund. *Poems, &c. Written upon Several Occasions and to Several Persons. . . .* London: H. Herringman, 1664.

Wanko, Cheryl. 'The Eighteenth-Century Actress and the Construction of Gender: Lavinia Fenton and Charlotte Charke' in *Eighteenth-Century Life*, 18 (May 1994): 75–90.

Wapull, George. *The Tide Tarrieth No Man*, 1576; repr. Tudor Facsimile Texts, 1910.

Warburton, William. *The Works of Alexander Pope*. 9 vols. London: Lintot, Tonson, and Draper, 1751.

Wasserman, Earl. 'The Limits of Allusion in *The Rape of the Lock*' in *The Journal of English and Germanic Philology*, 65 (1966): 433–44.

Watson, Robert N. *Ben Jonson's Parodic Strategy: Literary Imperialism in the Comedies*. Cambridge, Massachusetts: Harvard University Press, 1987.

Weinbrot, Howard D. *Eighteenth-Century Satire*. Cambridge: Cambridge University Press, 1988.

—— 'Parody as Imitation in the Eighteenth Century' in *American Notes & Queries*, 2 (May 1964): 31–41.

Weisstein, Ulrich. 'Parody, Travesty, and Burlesque: Imitation with a Vengeance' in *Proceedings of the Fourth Congress of the International Comparative Literature Association*, ed. F. Jost. 2 vols. The Hague: Mouton, 1966, 802–11.

Wellington, James E., ed. *Eloisa to Abelard, by Alexander Pope, with the Hughes Letters*. Miami: University of Miami Press, 1965.

Wells, Carolyn, ed. *A Nonsense Anthology*. New York, 1902; repr. New York: Blue Ribbon Books, 1930.

Warton, Thomas. *History of English Poetry*, ed. W. Carew Hazlitt. 4 vols. London: Reeves and Turner, 1871.

White, Edward. *Jane Austen and the Art of Parody*. Diss. Harvard, 1960.

White, Harold Ogden. *Plagiarism and Imitation during the English Renaissance: A Study in Critical Distinctions*. Cambridge, Massachusetts: Harvard University Press, 1935.

Whyte, Samuel. 'Account of a Visit to Mrs. Charlotte Charke, by Samuel Whyte of Dublin', in David Erskine Baker, *Biographia Dramatica*. London: 1782, 106–7.

Williamson, George. 'The Occasion of *An Essay of Dramatic Poesy*' in *Essential Essays for the Study of John Dryden*, ed. H.T. Swedenberg, Jr. London: Frank Cabs, 1966.

Wilson, F.P. *The Plague in Shakespeare's London*. Oxford: Clarendon Press, 1927.

Wily Beguiled. 1660; repr. Tudor Facsimile Texts, 1912.

Winn, James Anderson. *John Dryden and His World*. New Haven and London: Yale University Press, 1987.

Woodhouse, Annie. *Fantastic Women: Sex, Gender, and Transvestism*. New Brunswick, New Jersey: Rutgers University Press, 1989.

Woodward, William Harrison, ed. *Vittorino da Feltre and Other Humanist Educators*. Cambridge: Cambridge University Press, 1897; repr. as *Classics in Education* no. 18, with a Forward by Eugene F. Rice, Jr. New York: Columbia University-Teacher's College Press, 1963.

Wordsworth, William. *Lyrical Ballads, With Other Poems*, 2nd edn. London: T.N. Longman and O. Rees, 1800.

Woty, William. *The Shrubs of Parnassus*. London, 1760.

Wright, Lawrence S. 'Eighteenth-Century Replies to Pope's *Eloisa to Abelard*' in *Studies in Philology*, XXXI (1934): 519–33.

Wroth, Warwick. *The London Pleasure Gardens in the Eighteenth Century*. London: Macmillan, 1896.

Zamonski, John A. *An Annotated Bibliography of John Dryden: Texts and Studies, 1949–73*. New York: Garland Publishing, 1975.

Zaranka, William, ed. *Brand X Anthology of Poetry*. Cambridge, Massachusetts: Apple-wood Books, 1981.

Zwicker, Stephen. *Dryden's Political Poetry: The Typology of King and Nation*. Providence, Rhode Island: Brown University Press, 1972.

Index

Pardoner and the Frere, The, 114
Parliament
  House, 55
  Oxford Parliament, 146
parody
  age of, 1
  'celebration', 3
  disease of, 8, 9
  parodoi, 67
  parodos/parodia, 63
  parody(e)/paradoie, 63
  post-modern, 7
  rhapsodes, 67
pastiche, 4, 27
Peele, George, 118
  David and Bethsabe, 118
Pelham, Henry, 204
Pembroke, Earl of, 69
Persius, 45, 76, 139, 141
Peter, John, 56, 73, 75–6
Petrarch, 28, 73–4
Phiddian, Robert, 41–2
  Swift's Parody, 41
Pitt, William, 168
Pius II (Aeneas Sylvius Piccolomini),
    91
  De Liberorum Educatione, 91
plague (1603–1604), 60
  bubonic, 64
  'Great Visitation' of 1665, 64
Plautus, 49
Plutarch, 139
'Poetical Reflections, on a late poem
    Entitled *Absalom and Achitophel*',
    146, 149–51
  Amiel/Finch, Lord Chancellor, 151
  Bathsheba/Queen Catherine, 151
Pomfret, John, 217
  'The Choice', 217
Pope, Alexander, 11, 12, 29, 33, 39,
    44, 106, 126, 158, 160–170, 173,
    177–8, 231, 232
  Abelard, 162–3, 178–85
  The Dunciad, 11, 158, 163, 166, 167,
    168, 169
  *Elegy on the Death of an Unfortunate
    Lady*, 163
  Eloisa, 162–3, 178–87

Eloisa to Abelard, 11, 12, 158, 161–4,
    167, 169, 177–80, 183, 184,
    188, 232
Epilogue to the Satires, 161
'Epistle to Augustus', 161
Essay on Criticism, 161
Essay on Man, 163
Iliad, 161, 166
Moral Essays, 161
The Rape of the Lock, 11, 33, 39, 161,
    166, 167
  Belinda, 166
  Cave of Spleen, 166
  Clarissa, 166
'Spenser: The Alley', 165
Pordage, Samuel, 147, 153–6
'Azariah and Hushai', 146–7, 153–4
  Amaziah/Charles II, 154–6
  Azariah/Monmouth, 154–6
  Azrid/Sir Edmund Bury Godfrey,
    154
  Baal, 154, 156
  Canaanites/Roman Catholics, 154
  Chemerarins/Jesuits, 154
  Eliakim/James, Duke of York, 154
  Elshima/Macclesfield, 155
  Hushai/Shaftesbury, 154–5
  Jews, 154, 156
  Judea/England, 154
  Libni/Titus Oates, 154
  Nashai/Essex, 155
  Shimei/Dryden, 155
Post-structuralists, 5
Preston, Thomas, 114
  Cambises, 114
Price, J.B., 18
Privy Council, 55, 60
Propp, Vladmir, 33
Provok'd Husband, The, 198, 204
Pullman, Phillip, 1
Pythagoras, 28

Quinn, Michael, 109
Quintilian, 70

Rabelais, François, 39
Radcliffe, Ann, 37
  The Mysteries of Udolpho, 37
Raleigh, Sir Walter, 75